ULTIMA

ULTIMA

STEPHEN BAXTER

GOLLANCZ
LONDON

The right of Stephen Baxter to be identified as the author of
this work has been asserted by him in accordance with the
Copyright, Designs and Patents Act 1988.

First published in Great Britain in 2014 by Gollancz
An imprint of the Orion Publishing Group
Orion House, 5 Upper St Martin's Lane,
London WC2H 9EA
An Hachette UK Company

A CIP catalogue record for this book
is available from the British Library

ISBN 978 0 575 11687 0 (Cased)
ISBN 978 0 575 11688 7 (Trade Paperback)

3 5 7 9 10 8 6 4 2

Typeset at The Spartan Press Ltd,
Lymington, Hants

Printed and bound by CPI Group (UK) Ltd,
Croydon, CR0 4YY

The Orion Publishing Group's policy is to use papers
that are natural, renewable and recyclable products and
made from wood grown in sustainable forests. The logging and
manufacturing processes are expected to conform to
the environmental regulations of the country of origin.

www.stephen-baxter.com
www.orionbooks.co.uk
www.gollancz.co.uk

To all my extended family.

In the heart of a hundred billion worlds –

Across a trillion dying realities in a lethal multiverse –

In the chthonic silence –

There was satisfaction. The network of mind continued to push out in space, from the older stars, the burned-out worlds, to the young, out across the Galaxy. Pushed deep in time too, twisting the fate of countless trillions of lives.

But time was short, and ever shorter.

In the Dream of the End Time, there was a note of urgency.

ONE

CHAPTER 1

AD 2227; AUC (AB URBE CONDITA, AFTER THE FOUNDING OF THE CITY) 2980

'Danger, Yuri Eden! Danger!'

'ColU? What's the emergency? Another Prox flare? We need to get to the shelter.'

'Be calm, Yuri Eden. You are no longer on Per Ardua.'

'*Beth*. Beth and Mardina. Where—'

'Your daughter and her mother are far from here.'

'Far? ... Are they safe?'

'That I cannot tell you, Yuri Eden. We must carry on in the presumption that they are.'

'So why did you yell "danger" in my ear?'

'It was the only way to wake you, Yuri Eden. The drugs the *medicus* has been prescribing for you are rather random in their effects, although they are satisfactorily strong.'

'So you lied, right? Since when was an autonomous colonisation unit programmed to lie?'

'I fear I have exceeded the parameters of my initial programming rather extensively by now, Yuri Eden.'

'You know, I feel like I'm blundering down a dark corridor. And I open one door after another, trying to make sense of it all. But I'm safe when I'm asleep ...'

'Take your time, Yuri Eden.'

'*Medicus*. That word ... I'm still on that damn Roman tub, aren't I?'

'We are still guests aboard the *Malleus Jesu*, yes.'

'And – ow!'

'The *medicus* would advise you not to try to sit up, Yuri Eden.'

'When I sleep, I forget. The crap growing inside me. I forget it all.'

'It's still here. But so am I, my friend. So am I. Here with you.'

'Well, I can see that. So why the hell *did* you wake me?'

'You asked me to. Well, to be precise, you asked me to witness and record your last will and testament. I can do that for you. But you have been asleep many hours, Yuri Eden. I thought it best to wake you before—'

'Before the time comes when I never wake up at all, right?'

'It was Stef Kalinski's suggestion.'

'Ha! It would be. How is she, by the way?'

'The last time I communicated with her she was drinking hardened legionaries under the table. Anything to get the taste of the Romans' disgusting fish sauce out from between her teeth. That is close to a direct quotation.'

'She'll outlive us all. Her and her impossible twin, probably.'

'I hope to learn that some day. Yuri Eden, we must press on—'

'Before I pass out again. It's OK, old pal. So. My last will and testament. What kind of legal form can we use that will be recognisable in the Roman system? Whatever the hell *that* is, two thousand years after the Empire was supposed to have fallen. It's not as if I have much to leave to anybody anyhow. Only the stuff we walked through that final Hatch with.'

'Including myself.'

'Including yourself, buddy. It's strange to think of you as property but I guess that's how it is.'

'I am only an AI, Yuri Eden. And in this – different reality – human beings are property, some of them. Some even on this interstellar vessel. So I am less of an exception than you would imagine here. We cannot change such things.'

'Maybe not. But my instructions are clear enough. If Stef survives me, my share of you, in the Romans' eyes, is to go to her. If she doesn't survive me you go to Beth, on Earth, if by some miracle you can find her.'

'Quintus Fabius has promised me he will make sure of it, Yuri Eden, with the support of the legion's *collegia*.'

'So, let's begin. I was born in 2067, old style. Getting on for a hundred and sixty years ago, then. Even though I have only lived—'

'Sixty-two years, Yuri. The name your parents gave you—'

'Is irrelevant. I was born in North Britain. My parents were both members of the Heroic Generation, who struggled to save the world from the climate Jolts of the previous decades. Well, they succeeded. And before the prosecutors caught up with them, they had me cryo-frozen at age nineteen. Just as well they never saw me revived on Mars, a century later.'

'Your name, though ...'

'Some joker called me "Yuri" when they hauled me out of the cryo tank.'

'Very well. And after a year on Mars—'

'I was caught up in an ISF sweep, with a little help from the Peacekeepers at Eden. Who were sorry to see me go.'

'You are being sarcastic.'

'Yeah, flag it. Found myself waking up again, aboard the ISF ship *Ad Astra*. A kernel-driven interstellar hulk full of press-ganged losers like me. I made myself popular once more ...

'So I spent – what, twenty-four years? – on Per Ardua, planet of Proxima Centauri. With Mardina Jones, and our baby Beth, and you, ColU. Struggling to stay alive. We found others, other "colonists" stranded as we had been, and we fought our way to the Hub of the world, the substellar. There we found—'

'A Hatch.'

'A step through, just that, and we were back on planet Mercury, across four light years. So, everything changed yet again, for humanity, for me. I had taken Mardina and Beth home, and that's where they stayed ...'

'But you couldn't stay with them.'

'For me, it was go back to Ardua, or face jail. So, back to

Ardua it was, with Stef Kalinski at my side. Who has her own issues with all of this, by the way.'

'Are you tiring, Yuri Eden?'

'Don't fuss, ColU. I hate it when you fuss. Back to the story. So, on Ardua, the UN started to clamp down, just like it had in the solar system, because war was brewing up. A war to be fought with kernel-powered ships, over the lodes of kernels on Mercury...'

'Yuri Eden?'

'Still here, ColU.'

'Do you remember how we drove to the antistellar point? The darkest, coldest place on Per Ardua, in the deepest shadow of Proxima. Where we found, among other mysteries, another Hatch.'

'Yes, the Hatch. And we stepped through, Stef and I, and you. We found ourselves under the light of another star. And there was a man, in a cloak and a helmet, striding towards us...'

Quid estis?

'Yes. Do you remember, Yuri Eden?'

Quid agitis in hac provincia?...

CHAPTER 2

The intruders at the Hatch emplacement were first spotted by sharp-eyed Arab navigators aboard the *Malleus Jesu*. In their quiet chambers aboard the interstellar craft circling high above this world, the Arabs, doubling as observers and map-makers here at the destination, routinely scrutinised the area around the Hatch through their farwatchers. The newly minted Hatch was the key objective of the mission, after all, and deserved surveillance and protection.

And now Centurion Quintus Fabius himself was in the air, on the way to investigate.

The leather sac of the aerial *cetus* creaked and snapped as the great craft shifted in the light wind. Quintus was standing alongside the command position, a bank of levers worked by a *remex*, one of the junior crew who reported to Movena, the *trierarchus*, the commander of the ship itself. Like Movena, this *remex* was a Brikanti, and just as arrogant and sullen as Movena herself and all her kind. And yet you couldn't argue about his competence. As he stroked his levers great paddles shifted in the air around the flank of the *cetus*, and the craft moved sweetly in response, heading towards the Hatch, which stood open on the scarred plain that Quintus's engineers had made when they had unleashed the hot breath of the kernels on this world, and *created* this wonder.

The bridge of the *cetus* was a clutter of controls and instruments, and scuffed wooden tables on which lay heaped charts and itineraries, mappings of this world hand-drawn since the expedition's arrival three years ago. The air was redolent with the characteristic scent of the Brikanti, the folk of the uncivilised north, with the mead they drank and the treated hog-leather they wore, and the tang of the Valhallan tobacco they liked to chew as they worked.

But this mundanity terminated at the window, before which an alien world unfolded before Quintus's eyes. Even after three years, even after he had walked so much of it – and even after he had changed its face significantly by building roads and camps and the permanent colony, and of course creating the Hatch – still Quintus found this world astounding.

The Hatch itself had been set on a scrap of higher land, overlooking a plain on which native vegetation sprawled, a low scrub of purple and white studded with odd orange cones. The Greek philosophers aboard assured Quintus that the cones were communities of creatures mostly too small to see – cities of the invisible, each mound a Rome of the germs. Further away the land rose up, ascending towards lofty mountains before which foothills stood in attendance. And those mountains and hills, each a massive plug of volcanic rock, had been *shaped*, with terraces and walls and mighty crenellations that cast sharp shadows in the unchanging mother-of-pearl light of the principal sun Romulus. They were mountains turned into fortresses by beings who had once lived here, and remade their world, and vanished – blown themselves to bits, no doubt, Quintus had heard his gloomier legionaries conclude in the camps. And yet those mountain-sculptors evidently shared something with the rudest legionary from the poorest province of the Empire: they had built Hatches.

Well, Quintus had brought his ship here, and the engineers and the legionaries and the slaves had built their own Hatch, and their names would be remembered for it, the ancient number of the legion of which this century was a part inscribed at the foot of the stone Cross of Jesu that was the only human monument permitted to accompany a Hatch. This was forever Quintus's

Hatch. And this world, the fourth of the family that surrounded this stellar twin, Romulus, would, once the permanent *colonia* was formally dedicated by the *vicarius*, become the latest province of a Roman Empire that had now reached to the stars themselves.

This was what he had achieved, he, Quintus Fabius; this was what he had bought at what would be the cost of thirteen years of his own life away from home, and, thanks to the mysteries of near-lightspeed travel, a sundering by many more years than that from the family and friends he had left behind. It was a price he paid gladly; to command such a vessel as the *Malleus Jesu*, on such a mission as this, to build a Hatch, was the pinnacle of his career so far – and likely not to be surpassed, he reminded himself with a twinge of resentment, as it was rare for officers from the provinces to rise much further in the imperial army unless you were wily enough for intrigue and assassination. Yet the Hatch was not *for* Fabius, or his crew, or any human; the Hatch was a thing in itself, its own purpose as ineffable as that of a temple to a forgotten god.

And now, as he peered down from a washed-out sky, the perfection of the Hatch and its setting was ruined by the intruders. As the *cetus* made its ponderous way towards the Hatch position, Quintus felt his temper boil up, and he clenched and unclenched one massive fist, feeling the muscles in his arm work.

'Two of them,' said Gnaeus Junius. Gnaeus was Quintus's *optio*, his second in command. Gnaeus was peering down at the Hatch location through a finely wrought Greek farwatcher, leather and glass in a wooden tube.

'Give me that.' Quintus grabbed the instrument from Gnaeus's hands and held it up to his eye. As usual, at first, he saw only darkness.

'You need not squint so much, sir.'

'I'm angry. When I'm angry, I squint.'

'Yes, sir. You also grind your teeth.'

'No, I don't.'

'No, sir.'

Slim, dark, elegant, his tunic always spotless, Gnaeus Junius was an equestrian, a member of one of Rome's oldest aristocratic pedigrees. Gnaeus, though so young, was likeable, flawlessly competent, and had displayed none of the arrogance or sense of entitlement redolent of so many of his class. Quintus had found him utterly dependable. None of which saved Quintus from a sour resentment that this boy was destined to rise far higher in the army and beyond it than Quintus himself ever could – that the only way Quintus could avoid having to report to this elegant boy some day would be retirement.

Now Gnaeus reminded him calmly of the issue in question. 'So, about the intruders, sir. Two of them.'

Quintus studied the strangers through the farwatcher. 'A man and a woman. Old enough. In their fifties, or older? That makes them older than any of our veterans, or their wives. Save maybe Titus Valerius of the seventh cohort, who I know for a fact has been lying about his age for a decade. Some men just don't want to retire.'

'Yes, sir.'

'Well, even Titus is going to have to retire now. The *colonia* – that's his job now, for all the grumbling.' A morning of trying to deal with complaints from the colonists, the veterans who would be left behind on this world, had soured Quintus's mood, even before this business of the intruders. *Nothing will grow in this foreign muck, Centurion ... You can't leave me on the same planet as Caius Flavius, Centurion, he's had his eye on my wife since the Valhalla Superior campaign and now he's leering at my daughter! ... I swear, Centurion, I swear ...*

Gnaeus said tactfully, 'Well, those aren't any of our veterans down there, sir, or their families. Nor are they any of the *remiges*.'

He was right. Eight subjective years after leaving Terra, including five years cooped up on the ship itself, Quintus was sure he would recognise any of the ship's crew and passengers, even the lowliest slave. The complement of the *Malleus Jesu* was a few hundred, not counting the slaves, with the core of it being the eighty men of Quintus's century, and an equal number of *remiges*, the ship's crew – known by an archaic term deriving from a word for 'rowers' – mostly Brikanti, with their own hierarchy and their own officers under the sullen Movena, along with *their* families. But he did not recognise the intruders below.

'They *look* like Brikanti, you have to give them that,' he murmured. 'Those odd clothes. Jackets and trousers rather than tunics and cloaks. Peculiar colours, aren't they? Packs on their backs. And what's that pale sparkle on their shoulders? Looks almost like frost, melting... Impossible, of course. No frost on this world, not on the day side anyhow.'

'And no sign of weapons,' Gnaeus said practically.

Quintus grunted. 'I'd want to strip them down and turn out their packs before I could be sure of that. At least they're not Xin.'

Gnaeus pursed his lips. 'I wouldn't jump to conclusions, sir. The Xin empire is larger than ours, and includes many eth-nicities. Even if not Xin themselves, they could be provincials, agents, even mercenaries.'

Quintus sighed. 'The tripolar politics of Terra reaching out to us even here, eh, *optio*? Us, the Brikanti, and the Xin.'

'Well, the Brikanti are our allies, sir. And we're not actually at war with the Xin.'

'You mean, we weren't when we left home.'

'True, sir.'

The craft was descending now, with a rattle of chains as ground anchors were dropped from a lower deck. Quintus grab-bed his cloak from where he had flung it over the back of a chair and tied it around his neck, checked his sword and *ballista* were at his belt, and jammed his plumed helmet on his head.

Gnaeus frowned. 'You're going to interrogate them yourself, sir?'

'By Christ's tears I am.'

'I think it's best if you approach these people with an open mind. If I may say so.'

'Hmm. If they are Brikanti or Xin I need to observe the proper diplomatic protocols before I throw their arses in the brig, is that your thinking?'

'Sir, we didn't bring these people here. I mean, on the *Malleus Jesu*. And so the only way they can have got here—'

Somehow this elementary observation hadn't impressed itself on Quintus's consciousness. 'You are saying that unless they walked hundreds of miles from one of the indigenous Hatches, the only way is through *that* Hatch. Which we ourselves constructed—'

'And which has evidently connected itself to the wider network of Hatches, just as it should. But we don't know *where* that connection will have been made to. Perhaps to some place even more exotic than the cities of far Xin.'

Quintus, through his temper, saw the sense behind this reasoning. 'So we don't know where they're from, how they got here, or what they can do. Therefore we don't know what threat they may represent to us, the ship, our mission. Even the Empire.'

'No, sir.'

'Well, the sooner we find out the better. Let's get this over with. Back me up, *optio*.' And he strode without hesitation to the stair to the lower deck.

Behind him he heard the *optio* snap out commands, hastily assembling a guard unit from on-duty legionaries.

It was a relief for Quintus to hit the ground at the bottom of the ladder, to leave the confinement of the aerial whale and to be able to stride out towards the intruders, putting all his energies into the simple action of walking. To work out his frustrations in motion, in physical exercise: that had been his way since he had been a young bull of a raw recruit in Legio XC Victrix, unable to combat the shadows of privilege, preference and nepotism that had blighted his career in the army from the very beginning. Walking was one thing, but having somebody to punch out would be even better.

But that didn't appear to be a likely option, today. The two elderly intruders just stood there by the Hatch emplacement,

12

watching him approach. They looked somewhat startled – as you might, he thought, if you had just passed through the mysteries of a Hatch itself – but they did not seem afraid, did not seem daunted by the prospect of a fully armed centurion of the Roman army bearing down on them as if he had a kernel up his arse.

One of them, the man, even called out – something. The words sounded vaguely familiar to Quintus, the accent odd, stilted.

Time for a parade-ground bellow, Quintus decided.

CHAPTER 3

The craft overhead was like a tremendous airship. It moved smoothly, silently. It bore a symbol on its outer envelope, crossed axes with a Christian cross in the background, and lettering above:

SPQR

Anchors of some kind were dropped from a fancy-looking gondola. When the craft had drifted to a halt a rope ladder unrolled to the ground. And as Yuri Eden and Stef Kalinski watched, astonished, a hatch opened, and a man clambered down the ladder.

As soon as he reached the ground the man started towards them. He wore a plumed helmet, and a scarlet cloak over what looked like a bearskin tunic. His lower legs were bare, above strapped-up boots. He had a sword on one hip, and a gaudy-looking handgun in a holster on the other.

Yuri called, 'Who the hell are you?'

The man, striding steadily, started shouting back: '*Fortasse accipio oratio stridens vestri. Sum Quintus Fabius, centurio navis stellae* Malleus Jesu. *Quid estis, quid agitis in hac provincia? Et quid est mixti lingua vestri? Germanicus est? Non dubito quin vos ex Germaniae Exteriorae. Cognovi de genus vestri prius. Bene? Quam respondebitis mihi?*'

Always another door, Yuri thought. 'Let me handle this.' He spread his hands and walked forward, towards the angry stranger.

'I think I understand your guttural speech. I am Quintus Fabius, centurion of the star vessel *Malleus Jesu*. Who are you, and what are you doing in this province? And what is that mongrel tongue of yours? German, is it? From Outer Germania, no doubt. I've dealt with your sort before. Well? What have you got to say for yourselves?'

The fellow said something to his female companion, and walked forward, apparently undaunted. But at least he spread his hands, Quintus observed, showing he was unarmed.

Gnaeus Junius caught up with Quintus, panting. Glancing over his shoulder, Quintus saw a small squad of legionaries had followed the *optio*, all according to regulations. 'You're out of breath, Gnaeus. Double your daily exercise period for the rest of the month.'

'Thank you, sir. Do you really think they're from Outer Germania? Well, I suppose you should know.'

'And why's that, Gnaeus Junius? Because, even though my mother tongue is a purer Latin than yours, my father was from Germania Inferior and my mother was from Belgica, which to the likes of you means I may as well be *transrhenus* myself, is that it?'

'Of course not, sir.'

'We're not all moon worshippers and bear shaggers, you know.'

'I'm relieved to hear it, sir.'

'And my ancestors did put up a hell of a fight. The legions had to drive us all the way to the coast of the Mare Suevicum before they were subdued.'

'As you've pointed out before, sir.'

'So don't try to flatter me, Gnaeus Junius.'

'Sir—'

'You're very bad at it—'

'*Sir*. The intruder is doing something with his pack.'

Quintus saw that the man had turned away from his companion, the woman, and she was opening up the pack on his back

15

for him. Quintus and Gnaeus immediately drew their *ballistae*, their handguns. Quintus heard the senior man of the squad behind him murmur brusque commands.

The male stranger, seeing the Romans' reaction, spread his empty palms wide once more and again called out.

'We should jump them,' Quintus said.

'Give them a moment, sir,' Gnaeus said. 'They're speaking again. That tongue does sound more Germanic than not. But, you know, I would swear I can hear a *third* voice, neither the man's nor the woman's.'

Quintus glanced around sharply. The two strangers were alone. 'Your hearing is either better than mine, *optio*, or worse.'

'As if it's coming from the pack on the man's back ...'

'A belly-speaker? But we are rather far from any theatre here. I'll not be amused by trickery.'

The woman was closing up the pack now. Evidently she had found what she wanted. She held two compact nodules of a smooth, white substance, like small marble pebbles.

'Whatever that is,' Gnaeus murmured, 'it's surely too small to be a weapon.'

'Now who's jumping to conclusions?'

The woman handed one of the nodules to her companion. They were both watchful of the Romans, and were evidently endeavouring to make sure Quintus's men could see everything they were doing. Cautiously, they each pressed a nodule into one ear.

And when the man spoke again, Quintus was startled to discover he could understand his words.

'Is the translation correct? Can you understand me?'

'He speaks Latin,' Gnaeus breathed. 'Rather stilted, formal Latin.'

Quintus growled, 'If they could speak Latin all the while, why address us in German?'

'Perhaps they could not speak it,' Gnaeus said, puzzling it out. 'Perhaps it is those nodules in their ears that speak it for them. For I think I hear a trace of the German behind the louder Latin words … Or perhaps it is the little fellow they carry in the pack on the man's back who knows the Latin.'

'And who belly-speaks for the other two, I suppose? Your imagination runs away with you, *optio*.'

'This is a strange situation, sir. Perhaps imagination is what we need.'

'Let's get down to reality.' Quintus put his weapon back into its loop at his belt and stepped forward, bunched fists on hips. 'What is your mission here?'

The strangers exchanged glances. 'We have no mission. We are—' and here the speaker stumbled, as if searching for a precise term '—we are scouts.' The two of them pulled the white pods away from their ears and spoke in their own tongue, briefly.

'Scouts? For what army? Are you Brikanti or Xin or Roman? To which emperor do you pay your taxes?'

Gnaeus murmured, 'The Brikanti don't have an emperor, sir.'

'Shut up.'

The woman said now, 'Our speaker has not the right word. We are,' another hesitation, 'philosophers. We came through the, the door—'

'The Hatch,' said Gnaeus.

'Yes, very well, the Hatch. We came to discover what is here, on this world. Not as part of a military force.'

'They're saying they're explorers, sir.'

Quintus grunted. 'They're lying, then. Romans don't explore, any more than Alexander did – not for any abstract purpose. Romans discover, survey, conquer.'

'But they aren't Romans, sir.'

Quintus repeated, 'What emperor do you serve?'

The strangers exchanged a glance. 'We serve no emperor. Our province is unconquered.' Again they looked uncertain at the translation.

Quintus scoffed. 'Nowhere on Terra is "unconquered" save for the icy wastes of the south. Flags fly everywhere – somebody's flag at least, and more than one if there's a war in progress.'

The woman tried again. 'We recognise none of the names you mentioned. None of the polities.'

Gnaeus said, 'Then you can't come from Terra.'

The woman looked at him frankly. 'Not from your Terra.'

Gnaeus's eyes widened.

Quintus was baffled, and frustrated. 'What do you mean by that? Perhaps your country has vanished under conquest, like the kingdom of the Jews. Perhaps your people are slaves.'

'No,' the woman said firmly. 'We are not slaves.' She seemed to listen for a moment. 'Very well, ColU. I'll emphasise that. We are freeborn.'

Gnaeus asked, 'Who are you speaking to? Who is ... Collu? Collius?'

'We are freeborn,' the woman said again. 'Strangers to you, strangers in this place, but freeborn. We ask for your protection.'

'Protection?' Quintus rapped his breastplate. 'What do you think I am, a *vicarius*, a Bible scholar? So you don't have nations. You don't have owners. Do you have names? You?' He jabbed a finger at the woman.

'My name is Stephanie Karen Kalinski.'

'And you?'

The man grinned, almost insolently. 'Yuri Eden.'

Quintus glanced at Gnaeus. 'What do you make of that? "Stephanie" sounds Greek – respectable enough. But "Yu-ri" – Scythian? Hun?'

'Their names are as exotic as their appearance, sir,' Gnaeus murmured.

'Oh, I've had enough of this. We've a lot to get done before the *Malleus Jesu* can leave this desolate place – the sorting out of the veterans and their *colonia* for a start. I've no time for philosophical conundrums. Disarm them, take them as slaves – find some use for them, if they have any. And if all else fails find a suitably economical way to dispose of them.'

Gnaeus looked unhappy, but he nodded. 'Yes, sir.'

The woman stepped forward sharply. 'Quintus Fabius. You're making a mistake to dismiss us. We can be useful to you.'

He laughed. 'How? You're too old to be a concubine, too flabby and soft to fight – what, can you cook?'

She tapped her skull. 'We have knowledge. Knowledge you don't share.'

Gnaeus said hastily, 'She may have a point, sir. We still don't know anything about these people, how they came to be here. The Greeks have a saying: "Knowledge is the most potent weapon."'

Quintus grunted his contempt for that. 'A phrase no doubt cooked up by some shiny-domed philosopher when Roman legionaries first came to his hometown waving their swords.'

'He's right,' the woman said. 'It would be irresponsible of you to discard us without being sure—'

Quintus roared, 'Irresponsible? Do you presume to tell me my duty, woman?'

But Kalinski held her ground. 'For example, perhaps we have knowledge to share of a common enemy.' She thought it over. 'An enemy of Rome, stronger and more wily than even the Xin and the—'

'The Brikanti,' Gnaeus prompted.

Quintus demanded, 'Of what enemy do you speak?'

She gestured at the installation behind her. 'I speak of who-ever wishes these Hatches to be built to straddle the stars. And who manipulates the destinies of mightier empires even than your Rome to make it so ...'

But now the man, Yuri Eden, seemed distracted by some-thing. Apparently oblivious of the conversation, he took a step forward.

The legionaries reacted, drawing their weapons and pulling closer to their commander. Quintus too made to draw his *ballista*.

But Gnaeus laid a restraining hand on his arm, and pointed into the sky. 'It is the sunrise, sir. He is puzzled by it.'

Remus was rising, the second star of this double system, brighter than Luna or Venus, brighter than any star in the sky of Terra. Everywhere the shadows became doubled. Romulus never shifted in the sky of this world, but Remus did, following a convoluted apparent path that even the ship's Arab mathematicians had had difficulty puzzling out.

And a runner came dashing from the anchored *cetus*. 'Centurion! There's a report of a riot at the *colonia*. The men are in the granary, and are threatening to burn down the *principia*—'

'What, again?' Quintus raised his head to the sky and let out another roar. 'Father of the Christ, why do you goad me? With me, *optio*.' And he stalked off back to the *cetus*.

Yuri Eden watched the second sun rise, entranced.

CHAPTER 4

For lack of any clearer orders, it seemed, the troops who had followed their commander out to meet Yuri and Stef waved their short swords and ordered the two travellers to follow Quintus back to the airship. 'No funny stuff, mind.'

Stef helped Yuri hitch the pack on his back as they followed the men, listening to their gruff speech. She murmured, 'So they're all speaking Latin.'

'Or a lineal descendant of classical Latin anyhow,' the ColU said. Reduced to its processing centre, the remains of the autonomous colonisation unit rode in Yuri's backpack, and whispered in their ears through the plugs it had provided, projecting translations of their words at the Romans.

'But,' said Stef, 'even I can tell there's a whole bunch of accents in there.'

'Rome always was an amalgam of many nations,' the ColU said. 'A forced joining. In the latter days, in the west, provincials – who had been regarded as barbarians in ages before – rose to high command in the Empire. Stilicho, for instance, the best military leader of the late Empire in western Europe.'

'I admire your grasp of history, ColU,' Stef murmured. 'Among your other accomplishments.'

'I was programmed to serve as tutor to the children of Yuri's colony on Per Ardua. My knowledge base is broad.'

Yuri said, 'I think she's ribbing you.'

'Well, I am happy to serve, even though that destiny has changed—'

'And so,' Stef said, 'it appears, has the destiny of Rome. The

21

Caesars didn't travel to the stars. They didn't even have airships, as far as I know. Maybe the history you remember is out of date, ColU. I wonder if these Romans ever heard of Stilicho.'

'You are right, of course. These are not *our* Romans. We can be guided by our knowledge of our own history, but we must always be aware that things are different here.'

'Here, on the other side of the Hatch,' Yuri said.

'The word the Romans are using for the emplacement is actually more like *Gateway*,' the ColU said. 'I have chosen to translate it to the more familiar term ...'

Stef shook her head. 'Here we are discussing a whole new history, as if it was normal. Are we all going crazy? As if it happened every day.'

The ColU said softly, 'At least we are coping, Colonel Kalinski.'

And Yuri grinned. 'Besides, didn't it already happen to you once before, Stef, back on Mercury? It is – difficult, though. Do you think if we stepped back through the Hatch – if these goons in fancy dress ever let us – we would find ourselves back where we came from? I mean, on Per Ardua, and with the only Romans in the history books where they belong?'

'Somehow I doubt it, Yuri Eden,' the ColU said. 'Having stepped through this door—'

'We can never go back. If there are Romans here, they're going to be everywhere, right?'

'We must make the best of it, Yuri Eden. And after all, nobody forced us to come here, through the Hatch.'

Yuri looked drawn, tired, Stef thought – ill, perhaps. They had all been through a lot, this long day – even though, as a glance at her watch showed her, with shock, that not an hour had passed since they'd said their goodbyes to Liu Tao, in the middle of the chill farside of Per Ardua, planet of Proxima Centauri. It was obvious they'd travelled a hell of a long way from Proxima, itself four light years from Earth. And travelled more than mere distance – more than just light years. What *was* this place?

*

They reached the airship.

Stef was shoved none too gently by a legionary's palm towards a rope ladder. She climbed stiffly, followed by Yuri.

The two of them – three with the ColU – were pushed into a hold at the base of the gondola, roomy but without windows, and lit by a crude-looking fluorescent lamp. They had no view out. They had no seats either; they were made to sit on the floor, with their backs to the wooden wall. The soldiers sat around on their cloaks, talking softly, and looking speculatively at Stef, who glowered back.

The ship, which the Romans called a *cetus*, lifted with a smooth acceleration, a hiss of bellows somewhere.

'The walls are wooden,' Yuri observed. 'And the floor. I see straw, and blood stains, and the whole thing smells of sheep.'

'And goats,' Stef said. 'Although that could be the legionaries. This has to be some kind of surface patrol vessel. Starship in orbit somewhere? You wonder what kind of technology they must have up there if this is the best they can do down here.'

'If they have kernels,' the ColU said, 'quite crude enabling technologies may be sufficient for other purposes, such as life support. *Kernels* – which, incidentally, they refer to as *vulcans*, after the god of the forge. I have translated appropriately.'

The legionaries watched them suspiciously as they spoke, and Stef was uncomfortably aware of how eerie it might seem to these characters – bored, heavily armed soldiers – if she and Yuri appeared to be listening to a voice, even responding to it, that they couldn't hear. It was almost a relief when one of them grunted, 'No talking.'

Stef shrugged. But she saw that Yuri's eyes were closed anyhow, his arms folded over the backpack on his lap, his head lolling.

It wasn't long before the airship descended. As anchor chains rattled, the legionaries debated briefly among themselves. Then they stood, opened the door to the short corridor down which they'd come to this hold, and shoved the travellers back to the hatch through which they'd clambered aboard the vessel. There they were made to wait until Quintus Fabius and a few of his officers had gone down the ladder to the ground.

Stef ducked so she could look out of the hatch. She saw an enclosed compound, roughly rectangular, laid out over the purple-streaked ground, with walls of sod and what looked like orange-tinged wood, and central buildings of wood and thatch. Carefully she pulled a slate from her jacket pocket. 'Hey, ColU, you might want to see this.' She held up the slate to serve as the ColU's vision.

'Remarkable. Remarkable! A classic Roman legion's marching camp. Displaced thousands of years in time, and brought across the stars...'

They were prodded down the ladder.

On the ground, the leader of the little group of soldiers delivered them back to the retinue of Quintus Fabius. Quintus ignored them, but Gnaeus Junius, the second in command – the *optio*, Stef learned – waved vaguely. 'Oh, just stand over there and stay out of trouble.'

And trouble there was, as Stef could see. Shoved to the periphery, ignored as the Romans bickered among themselves, she tried to make sense of all this.

Centurion Quintus was in the middle of some kind of argument with a group of legionaries, most dressed in what Stef was coming to think of as the characteristic style of these post-Romans – much as Roman soldiers had dressed in all the history books and reconstructions she'd seen, even if they were generally drabber, dirtier and more battle-scarred. They all wore heavy belts, with loops for weapons and immense ornate buckles. The belts were the single most striking feature of their costume, she thought, gaudy, almost barbaric. Quintus dominated proceedings in his scarlet cloak and spectacularly plumed helmet.

But some others wore various other costumes. One tough-looking woman, short, stocky, red-haired, stood fearlessly close to the centurion. She wore a kind of woollen poncho, with tunic, trousers and boots; there seemed to be military insignia on her shoulder flashes, but nothing like Roman designs. Still, she stood beside Quintus Fabius as if she deserved her place. Alongside her were more men and women dressed much as she was, as well as an older man, dark, with a Mediterranean look, to Stef's eyes, wearing a kind of cut-down toga.

Stef heard chickens cluck and sheep bleat, and the voices of women and children as well as the gruffer tones of the men, and she smelled cooking fires. Now she was on the ground the fort felt less like a military installation than a small town, if fortified. But there was a stronger burning smell, of straw and some kind of wood. A building on fire?

As the arguments went on, a line of women, bent low under yokes bearing pails of water, made their way past the knots of soldiers, entirely ignored, eyes downcast. Stef stared. Could these be *slaves*?

Yuri shook his head. 'What a day. We came all this way, we stepped between the stars, and now nobody's paying us any attention.'

Stef shrugged. 'People are people. Everybody has their own problems, I guess.'

'Yes,' said the ColU. 'What we must do is leverage those problems to our advantage.'

Stef said, 'ColU, that messenger told Quintus there was trouble at the *colonia*. You think that's what this place is?'

The ColU murmured in her ear, 'It was the Roman practice to plant colonies of veteran soldiers in a newly occupied province. An easy way of enforcing imperial discipline, an example of Roman culture for newly conquered barbarians, a military reserve, an occupied fortification. Maybe that's what's being set up here. Many of these legionaries, with their families, may not be going home again when the *Malleus Jesu* leaves this world. Evidently that's what they're grumbling about.'

'A fortification against what?' Stef thought back. 'We've seen some mighty ruins here but no sign of an extant civilisation. No animal life even, those clucking chickens aside. What are these legionaries going to wage war against, a slime mould?'

Yuri grinned tiredly. 'This is an alien world, Stef. I guess it depends on the slime mould.'

'And also,' the ColU said, 'if these Romans can reach this world, so may their rivals.'

'They speak of the Xin,' Stef murmured. 'Chinese, do you think?'

'The name "China" has a root in the name of the first dynasty to unify the country. "Xin" could be a corruption of that.'

'And the Brikanti, whoever *they* are.'

'I am Brikanti.' The woman in the poncho who had been standing with Quintus came striding over. 'Whoever *you* are.' Her language, audible under the translation, was Latin but heavily accented. 'I had heard a rumour that Quintus had discovered strangers by his brand new Hatch.'

'Rumours travel fast here,' Stef said.

The woman laughed. 'In a Roman camp, of course they do.' She leaned closer to inspect Stef. Her hair was a deep, proud red, and cropped short; she looked perhaps forty years old – maybe a quarter-century younger than Stef herself, but her face, weather-beaten, made it difficult to tell her age precisely. Her eyes were an icy blue. She said, 'You dress strangely. You *smell* strangely. I will enjoy hearing your lies about your origin.'

Stef grinned. 'You probably wouldn't believe me if I told you the truth.'

'Ha! That bull-headed centurion might not; we Brikanti have subtler minds. One thing is certain – you did not stow away to this world aboard the *Malleus Jesu*.'

'How do you know that?'

'The ship is mine. This mission is a joint venture of Rome and Eboraki – and if you don't know the Brikanti, you won't know that Eboraki is our capital. In the orbit of the sun we have our own fleets, Rome and Brikanti, but we cooperate on missions to the stars. Quintus Fabius commands the mission and his Roman louts, but I, Movena, command the vessel and its crew. The Roman term for my role is *trierarchus*. The ship itself is Brikanti, of course.'

'I… think I understand.'

The older man in the toga came over as she spoke. 'It's remarkable, Movena. She speaks softly, in a tongue that, to a stranger like me, sounds like your own, mixed in with German perhaps. Yet that – thing in her ear – repeats her words in Latin. But what if we remove it? If I may?' He reached up to Stef's head.

She was uncomfortable with this, but she hardly had a choice. She glanced over at Yuri, who shrugged. She let the man remove her earphone.

Movena grinned easily. 'Don't mind Michael. He's the *medicus*, the ship's doctor. A Greek, like all the best doctors. And like all Greeks, endlessly curious about trivia. I'm speaking in my native tongue now. Can you understand me?'

Stef heard this only indistinctly, from Yuri's earphone; Movena's natural tongue, sounding like Danish with a lilt, dominated her hearing.

Michael said, 'Say something in your own speech.'

Stef grinned. 'If you damage that earphone I'll break your arm.'

'Ha! Remarkable.' He passed back the earphone, which Stef quickly replaced in her ear.

And Yuri coughed, suddenly. Stef saw that he was leaning on a low rampart wall, and she felt a stab of concern for him.

Michael pushed forward. 'Please, let me see if I can help you …'

Movena turned to Stef. 'Is your companion ill?'

'Not that I'm aware of.'

'The Greek is an excellent physician – far better than these Romans deserve. He will help, if help is possible.' As the doctor approached Yuri, Movena drew Stef aside. 'Now listen to me.'

'Yes?'

'I command not only the ship on this mission. I am senior woman. Quintus Fabius has agreed to this.'

'Senior woman?'

Movena sighed. 'Do you know soldiers?'

27

'I was one myself.'

Movena raised her eyebrows. 'Very well. Then you will know how soldiers behave – how they have always behaved. The men, anyhow. In the Roman system, you see, the army is all; their navy is essentially a branch of the army. Whereas in our system it is the other way around. Which is why our systems mesh together so well, when we aren't arguing, Romans and Brikanti.

'But you need to understand that these Romans are primarily soldiers, and that is how they think of themselves. Most of these legionaries, especially the older ones, have served in war, on conventional military missions – most will probably have seen service in the last Valhallan campaigns against my own people in the northern continent, a war "concluded" with the latest flawed attempt at a treaty, but probably flaring again by now. And in the south the Romans' uglier wars with the Xin grind on … In such wars, women are booty. Or targets, their bodies a battleground after the men have fallen. Do you understand? Now, *this* is not a war of conquest; there are no enemies to defeat here, human or otherwise. Nothing to rape and kill. And of course the men have been able to bring their wives and sweethearts, even their children. Such is the way of it – for if you sent a shipful of Roman soldiers off on a years-long mission, alone without women, they'd have buggered each other sense-less before killing each other over the favours of the prettiest standard-bearers before they got past Augustus.'

'Augustus?'

She frowned. 'The seventh planet of the sun … Where *do* you come from? But, look, even with female companions available, men are men, soldiers are soldiers – and women are targets, the slaves, the celibate servant girls of the *vicarius* of Christ, even their comrades' wives and daughters. You, my dear, are not so old nor so ugly that you are safe.'

'Thanks.'

'And so we protect each other. As I said, I am senior woman. If you have trouble of that sort, come to me.'

'I can look after myself.'

'Good. Do so, and come to me when you fail. Is that clear?'

'Yes. Thank you.'

'Very well. Now we should pay attention to these little boys with their quarrel...'

Quintus Fabius's voice boomed out, cutting through the arguments. 'Titus Valerius, you old rogue! At last you show your face. I might have known you were behind all this trouble.'

Through the crowd, Stef could see one of the legionaries being pushed, apparently reluctantly, to the front of a mob of unhappy men. He was burly, with his bare head shaved close, a grizzled grey – and, Stef saw, one arm terminated in a stump, encased in a wooden cylinder. 'Centurion, don't take it out on me. And it wasn't me who set the *principia* alight. On the contrary, it was me who organised the bucket chains that—'

'Pah! Don't give me that, you devil. You were trouble when you were under my father's command and now you're just as much trouble under mine.'

Titus sighed heavily. 'Ah, well, if I could afford to retire I would have long ago, sir, you know that, and I'd take my daughter Clodia home for a decent education and a quiet life, away from the ruffians of your command.'

'Ha!' Quintus waved a hand at the fort. '*This* is your retirement, you dolt. A city to command. A world to conquer! Why, I'll appoint you head of the senate if you like.'

'Fancy titles aren't for me, sir. And neither is this world.'

'The *Malleus* leaves in under a month, and you won't be on it. And if you haven't sorted yourselves out by then—'

'But that's impossible, sir! That's what we tried to tell you. That's why we had to set the *principia* alight, to make you listen!'

'I thought you said it wasn't you—'

Titus grabbed his commander's arm with his one hand. 'Listen to me, sir. *Our crops won't grow here.* The wheat, the barley, even Valhalla potatoes fail and *they* grow anywhere. The soil's too dry! Or there's something wrong with it, something missing... You know me, sir. I'm no farmer.'

'Yes, and you're not much of a soldier either.'

'No matter what we do, and we've been stirring our shit into this dirt for months now, nothing's working. Why, this reminds me of a time on campaign when—'

'Spare me your anecdotes. Shit harder, man!'

'It's not just the dirt, sir.' Titus glanced up at the sky, at the rising second sun of this world. 'Some say that bastard Remus is getting bigger.'

'Bigger?'

'This world, *this* sun, is spinning in towards it. What then, sir? It's hot enough here as it is. If we are to be scorched by two suns—'

'Rubbish!' Quintus proclaimed boldly.

The response was angry heckling. He faced the mob bravely, but men on both sides of the argument had their hands on the hilts of their swords.

Stef murmured to Movena, 'Do the men have a point?'

'Well, they're right about the second sun. This world circles the big ugly star you see up there – that's called Romulus; Romans always call double stars Romulus and Remus. But Romulus and Remus circle a common centre of their own – they loop towards and away from each other like mating birds, or like the two bright stars of the Centaur's Hoof, the nearest system to Terra. In a few years, as that second sun swims close, this world will get decidedly hotter than it is now – and then, a few more decades after that when it recedes, it will get colder.'

Stef wondered if this wretched planet was doomed to orbit out of its star's habitable zone, when the twin got too close – or even receded too far away. 'Has anybody modelled this? I mean, worked out how the climate will change?'

'I doubt it. And even if they had, no matter how dire the warning, the orders for these men and their families would not vary. From the point of view of the imperial strategists snug in their villas on the outskirts of Greater Rome, you see, worlds are simple. They are habitable, or they are not. If they are not, they may be ignored. If they are, they must be inhabited, by *colonia* such as this one. Inhabited and farmed. It is just as the Romans took every country in their reach and appended it as a province – all but Pritanike, of course, thanks to the wisdom of Queen Kartimandia, and we Brikanti escaped their net. If this world is not habitable after all for some subtle, long-term reason, bad luck for the colonists. But at least the Xin won't have it. Do you see? Though I must say it will be unfortunate if the very crops won't grow here—'

'I can make soil.'

The ColU's voice came clearly from Yuri's backpack. Yuri, reluctantly being examined by the Greek doctor, looked alarmed at the sudden direct communication.

The Brikanti ship's commander was surprised too. Then, without hesitation, she marched over to Yuri, shoved him around so she could get at his pack, opened it, and peered at the components inside. 'What trickery is this?'

'No trickery, *trierarchus*. I am a machine. An autonomous colonisation unit. I am designed to assist humans in the conquest of alien worlds. And in particular, I can make soil.'

'If this is true—'

'Soil is a complex of organisms, many of them microscopic, and nutrients of various kinds. If one of those is missing on this world, I will detect it, and with suitable equipment can begin the synthesis of supplements, the breeding of organisms. *Trierarchus*, I can make soil.'

'And your price?'

'Safety for myself and my companions.'

Movena considered. 'You know, I believe you. Impossible as it seems – but then you two, you *three*, are walking, talking impossibilities already, aren't you? If Quintus Fabius believes this too – and, I suspect, if he buys off Titus Valerius by offering him and his daughter a ride off this dust bowl – then perhaps the situation can be resolved. And all you want is safety?'

Yuri was racked by a coughing spasm. The doctor, looking concerned, helped him to sit.

'Safety,' said the ColU from the pack that was still on Yuri's back, 'and medical attention for my friend.'

Movena grinned. 'How pleasing it will be for me to deliver this miracle to the arrogant Romans. Let me talk to Quintus.'

CHAPTER 5

By the time the Nail struck Mercury the ISF spacecraft *Tatania* had already been travelling for three days. The ship had headed straight out from the Earth-moon system, away from the sun, and was more than three times as far from the sun as the Earth, when Beth Eden Jones picked up a fragmentary message from her mother.

'I'm sorry I had to throw you at General Lex, even if he does owe me a favour. Wherever you end up I'll come looking for you. Don't forget that I'll always—'

And then, immediately after, the flash, dazzling bright, from the heart of the solar system. The bridge was flooded with light.

Beth saw them react. Lex McGregor, in his captain's chair, straightening his already erect back. Penny Kalinski grabbing Jiang Youwei's hands in both her own. Earthshine, the creepy virtual persona, seeming to freeze. They all seemed to know what had happened, the significance of the flash.

All save Beth.

'What?' Beth snapped. 'What is it? What happened?'

Earthshine turned his weird artificial face to her. In the years she'd spent in the solar system Beth had never got used to sharing her world with fake people like him.

'They have unleashed the wolf of war. We, humanity, we had it bound up with treaties, with words. No more. And now, *this*.'

'*They* being...'

'The Hatch builders. Who else?'

'And you, you aren't human. You say *we*. You have no right to say that.'

The virtual looked at her mournfully. 'I was human once. My name was Robert Braemann.'

And she stared at him, shocked to the core by the name.

Lex McGregor turned to face Penny. 'So this is the kernels going up. Right, Kalinski?'

'I think so.'

'What must we do? We were far enough from the flash for it to have done us no immediate harm, I think. God bless inverse-square spreading. What comes next?'

Penny seemed to think it over. 'There'll probably be a particle storm. Like high-energy cosmic rays. Concentrated little packets of energy, but moving slower than light. They'll be here in a few hours. Hard to estimate.'

'OK. Maybe I should cut the drive for a while, turn the ship around so we have the interstellar-medium shields between us and Mercury?'

'Might be a good idea.'

Beth didn't understand any of this. 'And what of Earth? What's become of Earth?'

Penny looked back at her. 'Life will recover, ultimately. But for now ...'

McGregor began the procedure to shut down the main drive and turn the ship around. His voice was calm and competent as he worked through his checklists with his crew.

Beth imagined a burned land, a black, lifeless ocean.

As it turned out, she was entirely wrong.

With the drive off, and the acceleration gravity reduced to zero, the crew and passengers of the ISF kernel hulk *Tatania* took a break, from the situation, from each other. Beth unbuckled her harness, swum out of her couch, and made her clumsy way to the bathroom, locked herself in, and just sat, eyes closed, trying to regulate her breathing. Trying not to think.

But then she heard the rest talking, and the crackle of radio messages. Voices, speaking what sounded to Beth like a mash-up of Swedish and Welsh. Thirty minutes after the kernel drive had been shut down, and the screen of high-energy particles and short-wavelength radiation from its exhaust dissipated, the first signals from the inner system were being received by the *Tatania*'s sprawling antennas.

Gathered once more on the bridge of the *Tatania*, the passengers and crew listened to the fragmentary voices, staring at each other, uncomprehending. Beth looked around the group, in this first moment of stillness since the *Tatania* had flung itself away into space from Earth's moon.

Herself: Beth Eden Jones, thirty-six years old, born on a planet of Proxima Centauri but brought back to Earth by a mother who was now, presumably, burned to a crisp on Mercury – but not before she had forced Beth to take this new journey into strangeness.

General Lex McGregor of the ISF: a monument of a man in his seventies, commander of this space fleet ship, looking professionally concerned but unperturbed. Even his voice was soothing, or at least it was for Beth. McGregor, like Beth's father Yuri Eden, was British, but McGregor had grown up in Angleterre, the southern counties of England heavily integrated into a European federation, while Yuri had been born in an independent North Britain, and to Beth's ear McGregor's accent had the softest of French intonations as a result.

Penny Kalinski: some kind of physicist who had known Beth's mother, herself nearly seventy, looking bewildered – no, Beth thought, she was scared on some deeper level, as if all this strangeness was somehow directed at her personally.

Jiang Youwei: a forty-year-old Chinese who had some antique relationship with Penny, and who had got swept up on the wrong side of the UN-Chinese war that looked to have exploded across the solar system.

The two young members of the *Tatania*'s bridge crew: junior ISF officers, male and female, looking equally confused. But, Beth thought, as long as McGregor was around and captain of this hulk, they didn't need to think, didn't need to care, regardless of the bonfire of the worlds they had fled and now the utter strangeness leaking through the communication systems. McGregor would take care of them. Or such was their comforting illusion.

And, creepiest of all, Earthshine: an artificial intelligence, with the projected body of a smartly dressed forty-something male, and a look of calm engagement on his face – an appearance that was, Beth knew, a mendacious simulation, a ghost of light. The closest to reality Earthshine came was an ugly lump of technology stowed away somewhere on this vessel, a store of the memory and trickling thoughts that comprised his artificial personality. He was a creature who, with his two 'brothers', locked deep in high-technology caverns on the Earth, had exerted real power over all humanity for decades.

And he'd told her his true name, or one of them: Robert Braemann. He'd known Beth would understand the significance, for her.

All her life, and especially since being brought to Earth against her will, she'd been reluctant to get involved in her parents' past: the muddled old Earth society from which they'd been expelled before they'd come to the emptiness of Per Ardua, planet of Proxima Centauri, where Beth had been born, her home. Nothing had changed in that regard now. She could see Earthshine was still waiting for some kind of reaction from her. She turned away from him deliberately.

McGregor swivelled in his command couch and surveyed them all with a kind of professional sympathy. 'I know this is difficult,' he began. 'It's only days since we fled what was apparently a catastrophic war in the inner solar system. We feared – well, we feared the destruction of everything, of the space colonies, even the Earth itself. We had no specific destination in mind. My mission, mine and my crew's, was essentially to save you, sir,' and he nodded to Earthshine. 'That was my primary order, coming from the UN Security Council and my

36

superiors in the ISF, in the hope that you could lead a rebuilding programme to follow.'

'And the rest of us,' said Penny Kalinski drily, 'were swept up in Earthshine's wake.'

McGregor faced her. He was still handsome, Beth thought, despite his years, and he had a charisma that was hard not to respond to. He said, 'That's the size of it. Of course you, Ms Jones, are here because – well, because I owed a favour to your mother. Ancient history. However, whatever the fates that brought us together, here we are in this situation now. As to what that situation is ...' He glanced at his juniors.

Responding to the prompt, the young woman raised a slate. Aged maybe twenty-five, Beth guessed, she was solidly built with a rather square face; her blonde hair was tightly plaited. A tag stitched on her jumpsuit read ISF LT MARIE GOLVIN, alongside the ISF logo. Beth noted absently that she had a small crucifix pinned beside the tag.

Tapping at her slate, Golvin summarised quickly. 'Sir, we accelerated for a full gravity for three days. We shut down the drive, but we're still cruising, at our final velocity of just under one per cent lightspeed.' She glanced around at the passengers, evidently wondering how much they could understand of the situation. 'We set off from lunar orbit and headed directly out from the sun. We're currently three astronomical units from the sun – that is, deep in the asteroid belt. And still heading outward.'

'But now we're looking back,' Earthshine said. 'Now that the drive exhaust is no longer screening our ability to look, and listen. And, instead of news from a shattered Earth, we're receiving—'

'Messages, all right,' Golvin said. 'But messages we don't understand.'

She tapped her slate, and fragments of speech filled the air, distorted, soaked by static, ghost voices speaking and fading away.

'To begin with,' Golvin said, 'these are all radio broadcasts

37

– like twentieth-century technology, not like the laser and other narrow-beam transmission methods the ISF and the space agencies of our competitors use nowadays. In fact we picked them up, not with the *Tatania*'s comms system, but with a subsidiary antenna meant for radio astronomy and navigation. The messages don't seem to be intended for us – they're leakage, essentially, that we're picking up fortuitously.'

Jiang said, 'Maybe these are from scattered communities, on Earth and beyond. Radio is all they can improvise. Requests for help, for news—'

'I don't think so, sir,' Golvin said politely. 'For one thing the distribution is wrong. We're picking up these messages from all around the plain of the ecliptic – that is, all around the sky, the solar system. From bodies where we have no colonies – none of us, either UN or Chinese – such as the moons of Jupiter and Saturn, some of the smaller asteroids.'

'Survivors, then,' Jiang suggested. 'In ships. Fleeing as we are.'

Golvin shook her head with a scrap of impatience. 'Sir, there hasn't been time. Nobody can have fled much further and faster than we did. And besides, there's the question of the languages.'

Beth listened again to the voices coming from the slate, both male and female, some speaking languages that were almost, hauntingly, familiar, yet not quite …

Earthshine said, 'I can help with some of this. My own systems are interfaced with the ship's; I have a rather more extensive language analysis and translation suite than the vessel's own.'

McGregor grunted, as if moved to defend his vessel. 'Nobody expected the *Tatania* to need such a suite, sir.'

'Evidently the situation has changed,' Earthshine said smoothly. 'There seem to be three main clusters in these messages – three languages, or language groups. The first, the most common actually, is what sounds like a blend of Scandinavian languages, Swedish, Danish, mixed with old Celtic tongues – Gaelic, Breton, Welsh. The grammar will take some unpicking;

much of the vocabulary is relatively straightforward.' He glanced at Jiang. 'The second group you might recognise.'

Jiang, frowning, was struggling to listen. 'It sounds like Han Chinese,' he said. 'But heavily distorted. A regional dialect, perhaps?'

'We're hearing this from all over the solar system,' Golvin said. 'If it's a dialect, it's somehow become a dominant one.'

Penny asked, 'And the third group?'

Golvin said calmly, 'Actually that's the easiest to identify. Latin.'

There was a beat, a shocked silence.

McGregor said, 'I might add that we've had no reply to our attempted communications, by conventional means, with ISF command centres. And of course we haven't replied to any of these radio fragments. The question now is what we should do about all this.'

Penny nodded. 'I don't think we have many options. I take it this vessel can't flee to the stars.'

McGregor smiled. 'This is, or was, a test bed for new kernel technologies, to replace the generation of ships that first took your parents, Beth, to Proxima Centauri. But it's not equipped for a multi-year interstellar flight, no. In fact we don't even have the supplies for a long stay away from dock; as you know our escape from the moon was arranged in something of a panic.'

'We need to land somewhere soon,' Beth said.

'That's the size of it.'

'But where?'

'Well, we don't have to decide immediately. We're still speed-ing out of the solar system, remember. It took us three days under full power to accelerate up to this velocity; it will take another three days just to slow us to a halt, before we can begin heading back into the inner system.'

Golvin said, 'And then we will have a journey of several more days, to wherever we choose as our destination. We'll have plenty of time to study the radio communications, maybe even make some telescopic observations of the worlds. Maybe,' she said brightly, 'we'll even be in touch with ISF or the UN by then.'

'I doubt that very much,' Penny said drily.

'Yes,' said Earthshine, watching her. 'You understand, don't you, Penny Kalinski? You suspect you know what's happened to us. *Because it's happened to you before.*'

McGregor stared at him, frowning, evidently unsure what he meant. 'Let's not speculate. Look, I'm in command here. But the situation is – novel. I'd rather proceed on the basis of consensus. I'll give the order to fire up the drive for deceleration. Do I have your agreement for that? When we've come to a halt, we'll review our situation; we'll make decisions on our next steps based on the information we have to hand then.'

'Good plan,' Penny said. 'Unless, by then, somebody makes those decisions for us. Think about it. We're in a massive ship with a highly energetic drive, about to plunge back into a solar system where – well, where we may not be recognised. We'll be highly visible.'

'Fair point. But we have no choice. All agreed? Then if I can ask you to prepare for the burn, to make your way to your couches and lock down any loose gear ...'

CHAPTER 6

The *trierarchus* of the Brikanti vessel *Ukelwydd* was known to her crew, as she was known to her family and associates, only by her given name: Kerys.

It was a custom of the Brikanti, especially those Pritanike-born, to eschew the complex family name structures of their fiercest rivals the Romans, all of whom seemed to trace their lineages all the way back through various senatorial clans to the Romans' Etruscan forebears, and also the traditions of the Brikanti's oldest allies the Scand, with their complicated son- or daughter-of-this-fellow naming convention. Such as the tongue-twisting surname of Ari Guthfrithson, the *druidh* who stood before Kerys now, rather ill at ease in the commander's cabin, and looking at her with growing exasperation.

'*Trierarchus*, I get the sense you're not listening to me.'

Kerys allowed herself a grin. 'Well, you're right, *druidh* Ari, and I apologise. It's just we've been so busy – prospecting like crazy at this latest teardrop before we move on to the next, and the next, following a schedule drawn up by some idiot in Dumnona with a blank parchment and a blanker mind and absolutely no experience of what life is actually *like* out here in the expanses of Ymir's Skull... And you walk in with this incomprehensible news of – what? A ship out in the void?'

'A ship that shouldn't be there, *trierarchus*.'

'You see what I mean? Incomprehensible. Would you like a drink? I'm stocked up with the usual.' Meaning Brikanti mead and Scand beer.

Ari raised an eyebrow. 'I haven't heard the rumours that you have some wine from Italia tucked away in here, by the way.'

'Hmph,' Kerys said, reaching for the relevant bottle in a compartment of her desk. The Roman bottle was pottery, shaped like a miniature amphora, and came with a couple of matching mugs into which she poured the ruby wine, working with care with the ship's thrust operating at less than full weight. 'You've sophisticated tastes for one so immature.'

'I'm twenty-nine years old, *trierarchus*,' he said, sipping his drink.

'Younger than me by the best part of a decade, by Thor's left arse cheek.'

'Well, I am a *druidh*, Kerys.'

The word derived from an old Brikanti word for 'oak', Kerys knew, and signified 'great knowledge'. Ari was one of the generalist scholars that all Brikanti ships carried, if they had the room, as opposed to specialists in ship engineering, or in navigation in the deep ocean of vacuum the Brikanti called Ymir's Skull, or in other essential functions. Ari was assigned here to explore the unknown, to study and categorise the new. After all, each of the fragments of ice and stone and metal that made up the giant belt of worldlets known as the Tears of Ymir – resource lodes it was the *Ukelwydd*'s mission to survey – was a new country in its own right; you never knew what you were going to find.

'Here's to *druidh*, then,' Kerys said, raising her mug. 'And let's get back to work before we're too drunk to concentrate. What of this ship you found?'

'Not me, in fact, *trierarchus*. Your astronomers were using their farwatchers, fixing our position and mapping a sky full of Ymir's teardrops, as they do day and night—'

'Or so they claim in their duty logs.'

'*They* spotted this thing. A point of light in the sky, moving steadily. You understand, *trierarchus*, that if you split open the spectrum of the light from such an object you can learn about its nature and trajectory.'

'I may not be a *druidh* but I know that much.'

'I apologise. Well, the astronomers had thought it was just another teardrop, previously unmapped. Or perhaps a hairy star wandering in from the greater void.'

Kerys prompted, 'But in fact...'

'In fact this object is beyond the main belt of Ymir's teardrops. It is heading nearly directly away from our position – away from the sun, in fact. Its apparent motion across our field of view is quite small, but it is receding swiftly. Not only that, the object is actually decelerating. You can tell that from the shifting shadow bands in the unfolded light—'

'Yes, *druidh*, thank you.'

'I apologise again.'

'Decelerating. Is this a ship?'

'Yes, *trierarchus*. You won't be surprised to know that the split light shows it to be using a kernel drive, like the ships of all the empires. But it is not a configuration we recognise, not from any of the empires, not ours, not Roman or Xin.'

'You have challenged it?'

'We have – or rather our signallers have, following my suggestion.'

'Hm. Maybe I should have been informed before such a step was taken.'

Ari Guthfrithson sighed, and poured them both some more Roman wine. 'Would you have paid attention, *trierarchus*? Your mind has been focused, rightly, on the operations at the teardrop, and our course to the next. The hail was routine. It was thought best not to disturb you until—'

'All right,' she said grumpily. 'I take it no reply was received to our hail.'

'None. We have in fact heard the rogue being hailed by other vessels, Roman and Xin both; again we have heard no reply.'

Kerys frowned. 'But if it's not Brikanti or Roman or Xin, then what? Some kind of pirate?'

'If so, evidently formidable. That's the situation, *trierarchus*. Given the deceleration we can see, we know that this rogue will slow to a halt in three days. We also happen to know that the *Ukelwydd* is the closest Brikanti vessel to the object. And we have the chance to be first to intercept.'

Kerys eyed the *druidh*. 'I think you're telling me a decision point is approaching.'

'At which you will need to report back to the fleet head-quarters at Dumnona, *trierarchus*. If we were to abandon our mission here and intercept the rogue—'

'When will it come to a halt?'

'Two more days. By which time –' Ari grabbed a bit of parchment and quickly sketched positions. 'Ymir, the god who built the cosmos, made a single stride from the sun to the place where he built Midgard,' he said, a bit of rote taught to all students of interplanetary navigation at the college at Dumnona – and it amused Kerys that he used the old Brikanti word for the world, rather than the Roman 'Terra' long incorporated into his people's everyday language. 'Here we are about three Ymir-strides from the sun. The rogue is *here*, more than half a stride further out, but along a different radius from our own. We calculate that if it keeps decelerating as it is – we've no guarantee about that, of course – it will come to a halt *here*, in about three days, further out along that radius, about five strides from the sun.'

'Hm.' Kerys spanned the distance between *Ukelwydd* and the rogue with her hand. 'If you've drawn this roughly accurately, then we are perhaps two Ymir-strides from the rogue's final position. And we have three days to get there? Could we do that?'

'The engineers say that we could do it with a double-weight acceleration load all the way – a day and a half out, a day and a half to decelerate.'

'The crew will love that.'

Ari said drily, 'They will relish the challenge.'

'Perhaps. You advise me well, Ari …'

It was clear to Kerys that her commanders would order her to intercept this rogue, if she could, to be the first there, beating the Xin, the Romans.

The Brikanti were the weakest of the three great powers of Earth, spread thin along their marginal realm, a vast terrain of mostly unproductive land: the northern coasts of the Eurasian landmass, the Scand countries, Pritanike and Iveriu, and the northern reaches of Valhalla Superior, though that was under constant threat from the Roman legions whose roads and marching camps criss-crossed the great plains to the south of that vast continent. Since the days two millennia past when Queen Kartimandia had used guile to persuade the Romans under Claudius to invade Germania rather than Pritanike, the Brikanti and their allies had relied for their survival not on brute strength, not on numbers and vast armies, but on cunning, on ability and knowledge. And the chance to acquire new knowledge was never to be passed up. That was why the *Ukelwydd* was out here scouting for treasure amid the Tears of Ymir in the first place.

The rogue ship represented opportunity – an unknown opportunity, but an opportunity even so. It would be Kerys's duty to grasp that opportunity, she was sure.

She began to roll up her charts of Ymir's Tears. 'Well, Ari, if I am to speak to Dumnona I will need a draft mission plan. I don't think we'll be allowed to ignore this.'

Ari stood. 'I took the liberty of getting that process started already, *trierarchus*.'

'You know me too well. Get on with it, then, and I'll make my way to the communicators.'

CHAPTER 7

The *Tatania* finally drew to a halt five astronomical units from the sun. Halted in emptiness.

This was the orbit of Jupiter, Beth was told, a giant bloated world with a retinue of moons like a miniature solar system in itself, a world that would have dwarfed any planet in the Proxima system – even the Pearl, which had been bright in the permanent daylight of the Per Ardua sky. But this monster among planets was on the far side of the sky just now, invisibly remote, and the ship hung in a void, star-scattered, where even the mighty local sun was a mere speck of fire, a source of sharp rectilinear shadows. If only Jupiter had been closer, Beth thought, there might not be this sense of abandonment, of isolation.

But they were not alone. The foreign ship had already been waiting for them here, even as, after three days of burning the kernel drive, the *Tatania*'s velocity relative to the sun was reduced to zero.

The *Tatania* had been repeatedly hailed, over radio frequencies Marconi could have exploited, and Earthshine had at last been able to put together a rough translation. This was a vessel called the *Ukelwydd*, which was a word similar to the Welsh for 'mistletoe'. It was part of a fleet commanded from a place called Dumnona, which Earthshine speculated might be in Britain, on Earth. That fleet was a military arm of a nation, or federation, called something like the 'Brikanti'. As the *Tatania* was not recognised as a vessel either of the Brikanti, or of the

Latin-speakers, or the 'Xin', and as it refused to respond to any hails, it would be regarded as a pirate and treated as such.

The *Ukelwydd* was evidently a kernel-drive ship like the *Tatania*, and its basic hull was a cylindrical shape, like the *Tatania*'s, the most obvious design choice in response to the high thrust levels of the kernel drive – and, according to McGregor, it had blasted out here at multiple gravities to overhaul the *Tatania*. Even from the first glimpse, Penny thought, the *Ukelwydd* had the look of a fighting ship, with an evidently massive hull, heavy armour around the kernel-drive units in the base of the ship, and what looked like scarring, the result of weapons fire, in the insulation that swathed the main body.

Hours after the first encounter, still the hails came from the Brikanti ship, and still the crew of the *Tatania* failed to reply.

All on board the lightly manned *Tatania*, passengers, Lex McGregor, his command crew – and the three-strong engineering crew who Beth hadn't even seen before now – were ordered up to the bridge for this extraordinary encounter. Ten people, Beth thought, if you included Earthshine as a person, ten survivors of Earth and moon and the UN-Chinese war. Ten survivors of a whole history that seemed to have been lost here, if the ship waiting to meet them was anything to judge by.

Now Penny said drily, 'Lex, explain again the logic of why we're just sitting here?'

He sighed. 'Penny, the *Tatania* looks tough but she's no warship, unlike that bird of prey out there. You saw the way she manoeuvred when she moved in close – swept in like a bloody Spitfire. Conversely we're a hulk, literally, a scow for carrying garbage and passengers. We've nothing to fight with—'

'Save a couple of handguns,' said one young engineer sourly.

'Yes, thank you, Kapur. All we can do is bluff. At least give an impression of strength by not jumping when we're ordered to. Believe me – in many confrontations, posture is everything. Why, I remember when I was boxing champion four years in a row at the ISF academy, I could win a fight just by the way I looked at my opponent at the weigh-in—'

Penny said, 'Perhaps we ought to stick to the point? Fascinating though your anecdotes always are, Lex.'

Earthshine turned to her, his face blank, expressionless – eerily so, Penny thought. He said, 'But what *is* the point, Colonel Kalinski? Sooner or later we must all face the reality of what has happened here. But you, most of all – you should be our guide. Because *it has happened to you before*, hasn't it?'

He had hinted at such secrets previously, Beth realised, but not so openly. Now every eye on the bridge was on Penny.

She scowled at Earthshine. 'That's my business. My personal business.'

'Not since you and your impossible sister came to see me in Paris, all those years ago. And we visited your parents' graves – do you remember? Of course you do. And there on the stone of your mother, was *proof* that your sister – no, *you* were the impossible one, weren't you? It's so easy to get confused, isn't it? But since then, you see, since that strange day decades ago, I have been involved in your secret, in your peculiarly twisted lives—'

'Much good it's done any of us.'

'At least it has given us a clue as to the nature of the transfiguration we have now endured. From a solar system riven by war, to *this*, this new landscape with a warrior-bird spaceship called *Ukelwydd* that hails us in a mixture of Norse and Gaelic ...'

Lex McGregor shook his head. 'Earthshine, as we stand in peril from an alien battleship – what the hell are you talking about?'

'We live in strange times, Captain. Times when the fabric of reality has a tendency to come unstuck, and then to ravel itself up again, but *with flaws*. That battleship wouldn't belong in our reality – as we do not belong here – as Stef Kalinski, once an only child, did not belong in a reality inhabited by her twin sister, Penny here. Everything changed, that day when the Mercury Hatch was first opened, for Stef Kalinski. Now, with the huge pounding of the UN-China war, perhaps everything has changed for the rest of us—'

48

Light flashed from a dozen screens all around the deck.

'Missile fire!'

It was engineer Kapur who had shouted, pointing at the nearest screen. Beth saw fast-moving lights, an impossibly bright glare.

Golvin had to expand the field of view of the screens to give an image that made sense. The Brikanti ship still hung in space. But sparks of fire had swept out of emplacements in that battered hull, were sailing out into space – and were turning, visibly converging on the screen's viewpoint, on the *Tatania*.

'I guess they ran out of patience,' Penny said.

'Get to your couches!' McGregor yelled, pushing his way to his own position. 'Strap in! Golvin, their trajectories—'

'The birds are heading for the lower third of the fuselage. I'm seeing kernel radiations, Captain. The missiles are kernel-tipped, kernel-driven.'

Penny and Jiang pulled each other through the air to couches side by side, back from the control positions. They strapped in hastily, then grabbed each other's hands.

Jiang said, 'After all we've been through—'

'We're not dead yet, Jiang Youwei.'

Beth, isolated in her couch, longed to be closer to them, closer to anybody, to have a hand to hold.

McGregor glanced over his shoulder. 'Everybody in place? Good. Those birds are closing. Brace!'

When the missiles struck it felt as if the whole ship rang like a gong.

The roar of noise passed quickly, to be replaced by a chorus of alarm howls from the bridge instruments, and panels glared with warnings of catastrophic failures. The crew worked quickly, going over their displays, shouting complex technical data to each other. The *Tatania* was tumbling, Beth gathered, falling out of what must have been a spectacular explosion. She could feel the slow wheeling, as the rump of the ship turned over and over.

'The pressure bulkheads are holding,' Kapur called.

Golvin said, 'Captain, the strike was surgical. They hit a circumference around the hull. The blasts were shaped, I think. They cut away our lower third.'

McGregor growled, 'So they snipped off the kernel drive.'

Penny said, 'These Brikanti, whoever they are, use kernel technology as routine weapons of war. Even we never went that far, not until the Nail, the last desperate throw. To fight *our* kernel war we had to improvise ... What kind of people are they?'

'You might soon find out,' McGregor said grimly. 'A party is cutting its way through the outer airlock door. They must have come aboard before launching those stingers. Oh, put away your pop gun, Kapur. Resisting will only get us killed the quicker.'

'We don't belong here,' Penny said. 'Earthshine's right. Any more than I belonged in Stef's reality, after the Mercury Hatch. My God, Lex, these characters make you look like a UN diplomat—'

Now the lights started to go out all over the bridge, Beth saw. Even the screens went dark, displays fritzing to emptiness. The bridge crew hammered their touchpads and keyboards and slates, and yelled instructions into microphones, without success.

'It's all shutting down,' Golvin said. 'We're losing everything.'

McGregor demanded, 'Is it the Brikanti?'

Jiang said, 'They communicate by crude radio. I would be surprised if they could hack into our sophisticated information systems to do this.'

And Beth turned to look at Earthshine. While the rest of the bridge shut down – even the main lights were flickering now – he seemed to be glowing, oddly, from within, as if transfigured. A golden light.

'You,' she said. 'It's not the Brikanti doing this – this isn't part of their attack. *It's you*, Earthshine.'

McGregor turned on him. 'What the hell are you doing to my ship, you old monster?'

Earthshine stood up from his couch, his virtual body passing through the harness. 'Saving you all. General, the only asset we have in this reality is the knowledge we bring from – where we came from. I have taken that knowledge into myself, for safe keeping. Even the ship's physical systems are being destroyed, now they are drained of data. The Brikanti have captured a useless hulk. I will use the knowledge I have stored in myself to bargain for our lives.'

McGregor roared, 'And who the hell put you in charge?'

'I just did. And now, I think—'

The door slid open.

A party of figures floated into the bridge without ceremony, in clunky pressure suits of what looked like leather and steel ribbing, each bearing a stylised rifle with bayonet fixed. They all had their faceplates open, and they stared around at what was evidently a very unfamiliar environment. At a quiet word from a central figure, they spread out quickly into the bridge, one standing over each crew member or passenger.

Beth found herself facing a short, squat, heavily built man; she had to raise her hand to shield her eyes from a flashlight attached to the weapon that he shone in her face.

'Nobody resist,' McGregor murmured. 'We're in their hands now.'

The leader of the invading party lowered her rifle – she was a woman, pale complexion, perhaps forty-ish – and she made straight for Lex McGregor, the obvious command figure. She spoke, softly but firmly, and Beth heard a simultaneous translation come from a speaker on a console.

'My name is Kerys. I command the vessel *Ukelwydd*—'

'I know who you are.' Earthshine stepped towards her.

The warriors tried to block his way and waved their weapons at him, but the golden figure simply walked *through* them. A couple of men broke away, evidently panicked by this eerie display.

The commander, however, stood her ground.

'*Trierarchus* Kerys, my name is Earthshine. And we need to talk.'

CHAPTER 8

AD 2222; AUC 2975

It took a month after Stef and Yuri emerged from the Hatch before the *Malleus Jesu* was ready to depart from the double-star system of Romulus and Remus for Earth – or Terra, as the Romans and Brikanti called it. The setting up of the permanent *colonia* continued apace, even as ferry craft blasted up to the orbiting starship carrying away personnel, equipment and supplies for the return journey. Stef was bemused to observe that the ferries themselves were driven by small clusters of kernels – 'vulcans' as the Romans called the energetic wormhole-like anomalies – even in the atmosphere of an inhabited planet, like this one. No such craft had ever been allowed anywhere near the surface of the Earth, *her* Earth, not before the final war of 2213 anyhow.

Early one morning, with six days left to departure, Stef Kalinski was approached by a Brikanti who introduced herself only as Eilidh. Tall, spare, Eilidh was dressed much as *trierarchus* Movena was in a hooded woollen poncho, trousers, boots. But unlike Movena, Eilidh wore a heavy belt as the Romans wore, with a gaudy brass buckle and loops for weapons, though empty.

Stef, as had become her habit, had been spending her free time at the Hatch site with her slate, trying ineffectually to learn a little more of the physics of the enigmatic emplacement. Now Eilidh asked Stef if she would care to join her in a final aerial tour by *cetus* of the area around the *colonia* site.

Stef guessed Eilidh was maybe fifty, a little older than Movena, but a good deal younger than Stef herself. 'I might have taken you for a Roman with that belt.'

'The *trierarchus*, Movena, remains independent of the Roman military command. I on the other hand am officially a tribune, an officer subordinate to the centurion. I am a kind of liaison between the two command structures. Complicated I know, but it seems to work … As to the tour, we seek to complete our mappings of this place. And we have photographers, artists, to capture the likenesses of the structures left behind by the indigenes. We want to leave with some record of this world as it exists before the children of these Roman soldiers breed like rabbits and dismantle the fortress-mountains for building materials for their military roads. I myself am a command officer but serve the *trierarchus* as a *druidh*, a scholar, hence my own interest. I have undergone some of the training … Will you come?'

'I'd bite your hand off.'

Eilidh pulled a face. 'A vivid expression and oddly Roman. This was Movena's idea; we would be fascinated by your response. We'll be gone a couple of days. Bring what you need. We leave in an hour.'

So, in the unchanging light of Romulus, and as trumpet blasts roused the Roman *colonia* from its slumber for the first watch of a new day, Stef stood side by side with Eilidh before the big observation window of one of the expedition's two *cetus* airships, as the ground fell away beneath them. Stef looked for the small barracks block where Yuri was resting, with the ColU for company. Away from the ColU, Stef would be supported in her translation by the buds in her ears, themselves smart little gadgets.

Eilidh gestured to the west, where mountains strode across the landscape. The sky was clear, and Romulus cast a pearly light that spun shadows across the mountain chain, sharp and unvarying. 'Most of the interesting structures are to be found in the mountains. So that's where we'll make our way. This expedition is only a final reconnaissance. The Arab navigation team with their farwatchers, working from orbit, have mapped much of the planet. And with our two *cetus* craft, we've completed two circumnavigations, one equatorial from substellar to antistellar, and the other pole to pole. The far side is of course masked by ice, as are the shadow faces of all worlds like these, huddling close to their suns. But the air remains breathable, and there is life, and some structure.' She smiled. 'I have spent happy hours with Centurion Quintus Fabius and his staff studying these maps, plotting the routes of roads yet to be built, ports and transport nodes to be founded at river confluences and estuaries – sketching the provinces to be carved out of these silent landscapes some day. There have even been war games, military exercises, as Quintus and his boys have imagined how to counter new Hannibals marching through those sculpted mountains.'

'You are Brikanti,' Stef said carefully. 'I understand that Brikanti is a distinct nation. Independent of the Romans and their Empire.'

Eilidh looked at her sideways. 'You really do know nothing of us. Yes, Brikanti is an independent nation. The heartland is Pritanike, an island separated from the mainland of Europa, and therefore from the Romans' ancient holdings.'

Stef hazarded, 'An island the Romans called Britannia?'

'Well, they still do, in their arrogance. For most of our history we've traded with Rome peaceably enough. The Romans are the better soldiers, we are the better sailors. We build on the expertise of our Scand cousins, who have always been expert shipbuilders, back to the days of longships with their wooden hulls and woollen sails. When the Scand first burst from their northern fastnesses – they had run out of land to parcel out to too many sons – they were pirates and raiders, and the Brikanti and the Romans made a rare show of unity to beat them back. But it was the Brikanti in the end who forged alliances with the Scand. We had far-seeing leaders in those days – unlike the current lot – who were able to see the potential of this new nation of warriors and traders. There was a kind of revolution of the heart. With Scand ships and their expansive spirit, Brikanti stopped being a rather defensive ally of the Empire and began to forge its own global ambitions.

'Now our own northern empire stretches across the reaches of Europa, and also Asia where we have a long frontier with the Xin. We are one of the three great powers, I suppose you might say, who dominate Europa, Asia, Africa between us. And we battle over the spoils of the Valhallan continents to the west, much to the chagrin of the native inhabitants.' She tapped her heavy soldier's belt. 'But Valhalla is an arena useful for developing military capabilities.'

Stef said, 'And you are able to work with the Romans.'

'Yes. At this time we are officially at peace; the two of us are closer to each other than either of us is to the Xin … In other ages the pattern changes, though the underlying relationships endure.'

'Your culture is different from the Romans in other ways,' Stef said. 'Women are stronger.'

Eilidh grinned. 'Well, the Romans have strong women too but they are powers behind the throne – the wives and mothers and sisters of emperors and generals. Our culture has a history of strong women, going back to Kartimandia, who saved us from the Romans.' She looked at Stef. 'Is this a story you know? It is two thousand years old; every Brikanti child could tell it.'

Stef shrugged.

'You see, Julius Caesar had already set foot in our island, and had planted the dream of conquest in the Romans' empty heads. Fifty years later Kartimandia, queen of a realm in the north, was informed that the time had come, that the legions were massing in Portus Itius on the coast of Gaul for the invasion. It was she who travelled in person to Rome, she who managed to persuade Emperor Claudius that there was much greater glory to be gained if he turned his legions north, into Germania *trans-rhenus*, which even his glorious predecessor Augustus had failed to conquer. Continental provinces would be easier to consolidate for the Romans, and besides she pledged to become an ally of Rome, so that the invasion was unnecessary. She made a good case, it was said, much to the surprise of many Romans. But, despite the Romans' prejudice at the time – and despite what Caesar said about us – we were no hairy savages, and Kartimandia was sophisticated and wily.

'Well, it was Outer Germania that felt the tramp of the legionary's boot and not the fields of Pritanike. Kartimandia, with some Roman help, went on to consolidate her hold on the whole of southern Pritanike, and her successors made themselves valuable allies of Rome by becoming a secure exporter of grain, wool and leather to supply the Empire's continental armies. The Brikanti have never forgotten the achievements of Kartimandia. And forever since Brikanti women have won positions of power.'

Stef and Yuri had quietly talked over some of this with the ColU, as they speculated how this history had diverged from their own. In the account lodged in the ColU's memory, at the time of the invasion of Britain a woman Roman historians knew as Cartimandua had indeed ruled a kingdom in the north of Britain, called by the Romans 'Brigantia'. And northern Germany, meanwhile, had never been conquered by Rome after the disastrous loss of three legions in the Teutoberg forest a generation earlier. Not so here. Stef supposed that even if they could figure out how history had diverged to deliver this strange new outcome, there was a deeper question of *why*. Why this history – why the change now? And how had she and her companions survived the transformation of human destiny?

Eilidh, evidently sharply intelligent, was watching her. 'Much of this is unfamiliar to you, isn't it? Some day we must explore our differences fully. Yet, whoever you are, wherever you come from, I see your soul. Watching you at the Hatch, I saw the wonder in your eyes.'

Stef shrugged. 'Guilty as charged. In my – home – I was a philosopher, as the Romans would say. I studied the kernels, and later Hatches, because I wanted to understand how it all worked.' That had been her goal since she was eleven years old and she'd stood with her father on Mercury, and watched a kernel-driven manned spacecraft drive like a spear of light into the heavens. 'Where do the kernels get their energy from? How do the Hatches work? What are they for? *Why are they here?* How was it I and my companions came walking out of that thing ourselves? And, frankly, I'm fascinated by what you've done here. On this world you've gone beyond anything my people ever achieved. *You've built a Hatch ...'*

Eilidh grinned. 'We have, haven't we?'

Eilidh had the *cetus* pause over the Hatch construction site: the dull sheen of the Hatch installation itself at the centre, the land shattered and melted for a wide area around that central point, and a loose cordon of bored-looking legionaries playing knucklebones with fragments of broken rock.

Eilidh and Stef sipped Xin tea. There was no coffee to be had, one miracle of globalisation that evidently hadn't translated to this timeline. Yuri had joked about going into business cultivating the stuff once they got back to Earth. But Yuri's health was worsening; he'd been in a continual decline since they'd emerged from the Hatch ...

Stef tried to concentrate on what Eilidh was telling her.

'To create a Hatch is like mating wild boar: a simple act to understand but dangerous in practice, especially if you get in the way ... You take kernels. You arrange them in a spherical array, with all their mouths directed inward, to a single point in space. And at that centre you place one more kernel, its mouth tight closed. You understand that kernels can be handled with etheric fields?'

By which, Stef had learned, she meant electromagnetic fields. 'Of course. We too first found kernels on Mercury. You can position them, even close or open their mouths to control their energy output.'

Eilidh frowned. 'Some of your terms are unfamiliar, but clearly we agree on the essence. Well then, with sufficient kernels, held with sufficient precision, there is an inward blast of energy. You

57

can only watch this from a distance, and many lives were spent in determining that distance precisely.

'The configuration holds for only a splinter of time before the arrangement is blown apart. The land, the air all around is shattered, melted, by an outpouring of heat and shock waves – well, you see the result here. But if you get it right, when the glowing gases and the rain of liquid rock and the shocked air have all passed, and you can go back in to see – when all that is done, what is left is a brand new Hatch in its neat installation, just as you see here.'

Stef frowned. 'I'm not sure I understand. You don't have to construct the Hatch?'

'No more than we have to "construct" a chicken emerging from the egg. Our *druidh* speculate that there is a Hatch implicit in the form of every kernel. It is merely a question of breaking the egg to release the chick, to use the kernels' own energy to shock one of their brood to adopt this new form. You never discovered this?'

'My culture was more cautious than yours. More timid, perhaps. We would never have won approval for such an experiment.' For better or worse, she thought, we cared more about the lives of our technicians than to spend them on such stunts. Even if it had occurred to us to try. 'How did you get the idea? I can hardly believe you found such a specific arrangement by trial and error.'

Eilidh smiled. 'We did not. Somebody else found it for us.' Now the *cetus* was rising, turning its prow to the jagged row of mountains on the misty horizon. 'We first found the kernels on Mercury – as did you, yes? We were already travelling beyond Terra – well, obviously. We had big ships driven by Xin fire-of-life, and by potent liquid elixirs … I fear our common vocabulary is not yet rich enough.'

Gunpowder and chemical propellants. 'I get the idea.'

'Such substances had been discovered and developed during centuries of war. We had already flown to Luna, to Mars, though many died in those days, and our first attempts to plant *colonia* on those bodies were often catastrophic...'

Stef's head swam. Without the fall of Rome in the west, without the Dark Ages, could technological development have been that much faster? She imagined a medieval world with crude rocketships lumbering into space, with lessons slowly being learned about the vacuum of space, about radiation, about weightlessness, by cultures utterly unsophisticated in the relevant science – lessons learned the hard way, at the expense of many deaths. She was thrilled at the idea. Thrilled and appalled.

'Then came Mercury,' Eilidh said. 'There was a war of acquisition, more intense than most. We all wanted Mercury and its resources to capture the energy of the sun, you see. It was seen as a strategic position in terms of advantage for the future. And just how strategic only became clear when a Xin party stumbled across a field of kernels.'

'Ah.'

'After the usual blood toll the kernels were tamed, their energies used to drive our ships, and they were unleashed as weapons of war.'

That simple phrase managed to shock Stef, despite all she'd witnessed in her own home timeline. 'Surely not on Earth itself.'

Eilidh just returned her look. 'But we are speaking of the Hatches. The first Hatch of all was found on Mercury, in the kernel field.'

'As it was for us,' Stef said.

Eilidh raised her eyebrows. 'On a different Mercury too? We do have much to discuss. Of course the Hatch was opened; of course there were attempts to *pass through* ... None of those who entered, unwilling slaves, bold soldiers, curious philosophers, ever returned.'

'Perhaps they are still in transit.'

'In transit?'

'*Our* Mercury Hatch as connected to one on Per Ardua. Umm, which is a world of Proxima Centauri. Which is—'

'The nearest star, in the Centaur's Hoof. For us, it has been given the same name. *Proxima.*' She smiled, a little sourly. 'So there are Romans in your country too.'

'Were. Long story. Look, it's only four years as light travels between Mercury and Proxima. So it's possible to go there and step back with only eight years elapsing.'

Eilidh frowned as she puzzled all that out; Stef had no idea how much understanding of such basic physics they shared.

'The point is,' Stef said, 'maybe *your* Hatch on your Mercury was hooked up to somewhere else. Somewhere much further away.' There was no reason why that shouldn't be true, she realised. They knew so little, despite the decades that had passed since her own first brush with all this strangeness. 'Your travellers may have arrived alive and well, but just haven't had time to step back home yet. Maybe they are still travelling, oblivious.'

'It's possible. Oddly there is a soldiers' legend along those lines. Perhaps the travellers have gone, not to Proxima, the nearest star, but to Ultima, the *furthest* star of all.'

Stef frowned. What could that mean? The furthest star, in an expanding universe full of galaxies and clusters of galaxies…

'But, though we have not walked through the Hatches to Proxima and its worlds, we have journeyed there in ships – ships like the *Malleus Jesu*, orbiting high above. When we got there, on the third planet from the star –'

Per Ardua.

'– we found a kernel field, not unlike that on Mercury – by then we had learned how to search for such things – and we found a Hatch, and *we found instructions* on how to construct a fresh one. Just as I have described.'

'Instructions. Of what kind?'

'Enigmatic. Graphic, but enigmatic. Enough for us to work out the rest, after—'

'Another blood toll.' Stef remembered the builders, natives of Per Ardua – *her* Per Ardua. She had seen little of them, but she knew Yuri remembered them with affection from his early, near-solitary years on the planet. 'These graphic instructions – was there any sign of the natives who created them?'

60

'None. So I'm told. Not a trace save these odd diagrams, and even they were lodged inside a Hatch.' She eyed Stef. 'It was another scrap that doesn't fit, another fragment of a lost history. Like you and your companions. What do you think?'

A scrap like her own unexpected sister in the Hatch on Mercury, Stef thought. The first reality tweak of all. She shrugged. 'I don't know what to think.'

'Well, keep trying. And now – look down.'

The *cetus* was now sailing serenely over mountains.

The sun of this world was not high, it might have been an early afternoon at a temperate latitude on Earth, and shadows pooled in the valleys that separated the peaks. The second sun was in the sky too and cast a fainter double shadow. Ice striped the taller peaks, and rivers flowed through the valleys like bands of steel. And, save for the shadow cast by the *cetus* itself, Stef could see nothing moving down there, no people, no animals, not so much as a thread of smoke.

But everywhere she looked, Stef saw artifice. Every mountain seemed to have been shaped, regularised as a pyramid or a tetrahedron. The valleys looked as if they had been shaped, too, straightened. Some of the peaks were connected by tremendous bridges of stone. Many of the mountain walls were terraced, so that it looked as if giant staircases climbed their flanks, while others had huge vertical structures fixed to their faces, almost like the flying buttresses of medieval cathedrals, or were deeply inscribed with gullies and channels.

Eilidh was watching her. 'Tell me what you see.'

'It's like a simulation.'

'A what?'

'Sorry. Like a model. A mock-up of a mountain range. It doesn't look real.'

'Yet it is real. This planet is laced by mountain ranges; it is, or at least was, very active. And all the ranges have been shaped and reshaped by hands unseen, just as you see here. All as far as we have visited and studied. There's much you can't see from the surface. We burrowed into one mountain, sounded out others. The mountains are hollowed, strengthened within by huge remnant pillars of rock. They have been transformed into immense granite fortresses, or so it seems. For the Roman military engineers, who eat and breathe fortifications, this is Elysium, as you can imagine.'

'We noticed this the minute we stepped out of the Hatch,' Stef said, wondering. 'I never dreamed the *whole world* was like this. But – who built all this? And where are they now?'

'That's the puzzle. These vast mountain-fortresses are all pristine, save for some evidence of erosion and rock fall – natural breakdowns. There's no evidence they were ever inhabited, let alone fought over. Meanwhile, across the planet, we have found no trace of life more complex than those orange chimney stacks of bugs you see piled up on the plains. Nothing *moved* here, not until the legionaries arrived, and they don't move much either. Ha! I do have a theory, for what it's worth. I may be limited as a *druidh* but I've seen as much of this world as anybody.'

'Tell me.'

'The farside, the dark side, is – damaged. I've seen vast craters, their rims protruding above the ice. And there is a very odd range of mountains running virtually north to south down the rim of one of the continents there, buried though it is under the ice.'

'Like the Andes.'

'The what?'

'A mountain range in, umm, Valhalla Inferior, I think you call it.'

'Like that – yes. Now, these mountains had been modified, but not as fortresses. We saw evidence of vast installations, like cannon muzzles, all along the western faces of the mountains. My colleagues, especially the Romans, thought these must be weapons, but they didn't look like very effective weapons to me. The only purpose I could think of ...'

'Yes?'

'Perhaps these were, not weapons, *engines*. Rockets intended to fire together, powered by kernels presumably, blasting all along this great seam along the belly of the planet—'

'My God. You think they were trying to spin up the planet?'

'It's possible. Maybe there was some great project to make this world more hospitable. The approaches to the second sun, you know, do make life difficult here, for the native life as for the Roman colonists.'

The ColU had worked out that this was a double-star system in which both partners were red dwarfs – small, miserly stars, like Proxima, so small and dim they hadn't even been detected from Earth. The ColU had said the nearest such system to Earth must be at least seven, eight, nine light years out.

'Of course,' Eilidh said, 'most of this world's life, like every living world, is comprised of bugs that inhabit the deep rocks, miles deep, feeding off seeps of water and heat and minerals. We found them here when we were running deep mining trials – as one always finds them, on every world. *They* won't care if there is one or two suns in the sky, or more. So long as the world itself lasts, they will too.'

'I take it the great spin-up never happened.'

'It appears there was a war to stop it. Evidently not everybody agreed with the visionary engineers behind the scheme. The big spin-mountain engines were attacked – we have seen the damage.'

'If this is all so, then what happened to the natives after that?'

'I can only guess. Perhaps they were appalled by the damage done by their kernel war. The building of their mountain refuges might have been a last burst of sanity before the madness – or possibly the other way around.'

'But despite all that they are gone.'

'Perhaps there was something like a plague, or …' She eyed Stef. '*You* have more sophisticated machines than us, as evidenced by Collius. There may have been other weapons that were used to eradicate all higher forms of life from this world, before they wrecked it altogether.'

'Leaving it to the deep bugs to start again, I suppose.'

Eilidh sighed. 'That, and a world like a dead emperor's folly.'

It was yet another planetary tragedy, Stef realised, caused by the availability of the kernels. 'I think I envy those deep bugs, you know. Resting in their gloomy chambers, far below all the commotion of the surface. Life must seem so simple, and so safe.'

Eilidh grunted. 'But not for the likes of us.'

'So,' Stef said, trying to understand, 'you come out into interstellar space in kernel-driven hulks. We got as far as Proxima.'

Eilidh frowned, evidently struggling to understand, but she nodded.

'You're exploring,' continued Stef, 'maybe scouting is a better word, and you're planting colonies, *colonia*, on any habitable world, in advance of the other guy getting here first.'

'That's the idea.'

'But when you find a world seeded with kernels, you create a Hatch. Is that right?'

'This is my own second such expedition. It begins with the *vicarius* blessing the seeded ground ...'

'You create the Hatch – presumably it connects itself to some higher-dimensional network – but then you never try to use it.'

'Well, the Mercury Hatch led nowhere, as far as we know. Whatever the Hatches really are, wherever they go, they aren't for us.'

'Then why build them?'

Eilidh smiled with a touch of cynicism. 'Perhaps you aren't as spiritual a people as we are, Stef Kalinski. One thing that unites us Brikanti with the Romans is a worship of Jesu, of the Cross on which He died and the Hammer which He wielded against His foes ... To us the kernels are a great gift. Look how much we have been able to do: we have transformed our own world, we have travelled to the stars—'

'You smite your foes.'

'Quite so. Some believe the kernels are a gift from God, Father of Jesu – though older superstitions persist; some of the country Romans still speak of old gods like Vulcan, and some Scand believe a kernel is a gateway to Ragnarok. And in return for this gift, we do what is evidently asked of us, which is to cause fields of kernels to blossom into Hatches. What are the Hatches *for*? Perhaps some future generation will be able to answer that. In the meantime, we travel, we harvest the kernels, we build the Hatches. For such seems to be the scheme of things, such is what we are required to do.'

'Just as my own ancestors once built cathedrals, perhaps. Some dumb legionary might be content to follow orders, mindlessly, without enquiring. *You* can't be happy with that.'

'I'm Brikanti. My ship is my true purpose. And besides, there's very little I can do to change the trajectory of my society. Could you? But speaking of changing trajectories ...'

The great ship turned in the air, and Stef saw its shadow swim across the sculpted mountains below.

Eilidh said, 'Our adventure is over already. Well, there is much to do, a five-year star flight to plan. I hope you have found the day instructive. More tea, my friend? Shall I call for a fresh pot?'

But Stef was receding into her own thoughts. Too slowly, in her ageing mind, new problems were occurring to her. The Hatch on this world had evidently only existed for a year or two, since these Brikanti and Romans had come here and built it. But she and Yuri had walked into the Hatch on Per Ardua long before that – seven or eight or nine years ago – they had walked into one end of a spacetime tunnel *years before the far end had even existed* ... So where had they been, for all that time?

She started shivering, uncontrollably. Eilidh draped her thin shoulders in a blanket.

CHAPTER 9

When Stef returned to the *colonia* she learned that Yuri had been taken to the legionaries' small hospital. She hurried that way, concerned.

When she got to the hospital she was directed to a kind of operating theatre. She'd glimpsed this place before; it looked to her more like a butcher's shop, with alarming-looking surgical instruments suspended on the wall. But, she was told, it was hygienic enough; Michael and his Greek-trained medics and their Arab advisers knew enough about antisepsis and the risk of infection to keep the place reasonably clean.

Here she found Yuri, slumped in a chair, and the ColU – or rather its processing unit, a baroque tangle of metal and ceramic – sitting on a tabletop. Titus Valerius stood by, the big veteran soldier who had caused Quintus Fabius so much trouble with his small rebellion on the day Stef and the others had walked out of the Hatch.

And, standing in the centre of the room, looking scared and uncomfortable, was a boy, dark, Asiatic, slim, aged perhaps thirteen or fourteen – but he was so skinny it was hard for Stef to be sure. He wore a grubby tunic and no shoes; his feet were filthy. *Medicus* Michael hovered by the boy, looking abstracted, fascinated.

Stef made her way towards Yuri, nodding at Titus. The big man was picking at the nails of his one good hand with the top of a full-scale sword, a *gladio*, propped in his opposing armpit. He nodded back to Stef, and his gaze raked over her elderly body in the way of all legionaries. But she felt as safe with Titus as she did with any of the Romans; she had met his young daughter Clodia, who he had brought on this space mission as a small child, after the death of her mother.

Yuri looked up; he was very pale, but he smiled. 'Good trip?'

'Eye-opening. Are you OK? What's going on here?'

'It's not about me, for once. In fact you're just in time.' He gestured at the boy. 'This is something new. Introduce yourself again, son.'

In decent Latin, the boy said in a wavering voice, 'My name is Chu Yuan. I am fourteen years old. My family are scholars and merchants in Shanghai. My father is a soldier with the Twenty-fourth Division of the Imperial Army of Light. He was stationed in Valhalla Inferior. He took his family there, including myself, the eldest son ...'

Yuri winked at Stef. 'Valhalla Inferior – South America. For centuries you've had tension between the Chinese coming in from the west, basically holding the coastal plain and the Andes, and the Romans coming in from the east through Amazonia, as well as south from their holdings in Mesoamerica.'

'And the native people caught in the crossfire.'

The ColU said drily, 'At least they were not exterminated by crowd plagues, as in our history. The Vikings – the "Scand" allies of the Brikanti – had already been travelling to the Americas for centuries, allowing immunity a chance to build up. But the war fronts ebb and flow.'

'Our fort was overrun,' Chu said now. 'My father was killed. My mother ran away. I was captured, enslaved by the glorious soldiers of Rome.'

That made Stef pause. 'He's a slave?'

Yuri shrugged. 'His parents were grooming him to be a scholar, I think, or a clerk. But the Romans caught him, and he ended up a slave on this tub.'

Stef stared at this boy, trapped in a category of humanity she never thought she would have to deal with. She'd found it almost impossible to function in the *colonia*, for the slaves were everywhere, if invisible to a Roman eye. And it wasn't just the subjugation of human beings that distressed her but the level of daily, almost casual brutality. Even for routine punishments there were blood-stained stakes, lead-tipped whips. She'd always rather admired the Romans, for their literacy, their order, their engineering, their respect for the law. Now, she was finding, she'd never fully imagined this side of their civilisation.

'Well, what's he doing here?'

Michael beamed. 'He is a gift, at the orders of Centurion Quintus Fabius. He has been delighted by the work of Collius in the *colonia*, the advice on soil preparation, crops, irrigation.'

The ColU, sitting on its tabletop, seemed to Stef to twinkle. 'I'm Collius the oracle now.'

'Shut up,' said Yuri mildly.

'Yes, Yuri Eden.'

'So the centurion, you see, aware of the ColU's cut-down state, has kindly donated him the legs of this boy here.'

Stef frowned. 'I don't understand.'

Michael said hastily, 'Let me explain. I have adapted your backpack, Yuri Eden.' He drew this out from under a bench; it looked much as it had before, save the straps had been shortened. He brought this to the boy who slipped it on. 'The ColU itself will ride in the pack. And then your talking, all-seeing glass ...'

Yuri's slate had been set into a leather pouch, and Michael now hung this around Chu's neck, fixing it with straps around his chest.

Stef said, 'I don't believe it. This boy is going to be your pack mule, ColU?'

'We have been rehearsing,' the ColU said. 'Chu. Walk forward. Turn right. Turn left.'

The boy marched across the theatre floor, as passive and obedient as a puppet, head downturned. A slave's walk.

'This is obscene,' Stef said.

Michael held up his hands. 'Now, madam, Yuri warned me you might react like this—'

'It could have been a lot worse, Stef,' Yuri said. 'Why do you think Michael here is involved at all?'

'Tell me.'

'Because the centurion's first idea was to have the pack and slate *stitched* to Chu's flesh, so they couldn't be stolen.'

Titus Valerius raised a hand tentatively. 'Can I speak? I'm part of the centurion's plan also. I will accompany the boy wherever he goes, to ensure the safety of the oracle.'

Stef grinned sourly. 'I know the military mind. A nice cushy job to buy you off after that business with the granary, Titus?'

Titus shrugged massively. 'I follow orders.'

'Well, it's still obscene,' Stef said.

Yuri said mildly, 'Would you send Chu back where he came from?'

Chu turned his head at that, looking alarmed.

'I will care for this boy,' the ColU said firmly. 'I will ensure his own needs are met, as he serves mine. We cannot save all the slaves in this Roman Empire of theirs, Stef Kalinski. But I can save this one, this boy.'

Stef bowed to the inevitable. 'Fine. I suppose all other options are worse ...'

She tried to tell Yuri and the ColU something of what she'd learned that day.

'So these people, these Romans, send ships to the stars and build Hatches without any understanding of why. Purely as a ritual, a mechanism, as ants build a nest.'

'Perhaps that's a good analogy, Stef Kalinski,' said the ColU. 'The nest as a whole benefits from the actions of individuals. In the same way the Hatch network must benefit in some way.'

Michael had listened closely to their conversation. He offered, 'Perhaps it fits the Romans' character too. At least, these soldiers'. They are used to serving a larger entity without question – I mean, the Empire, the army. I, a Greek, can see this.'

'I resent that,' said Titus Valerius.

'Oh, you do?'

'Yes! Legionaries aren't ants. We know precisely why we're fighting. For our companions.'

Michael sighed. 'Just as ants follow the lead of their neighbouring ants, and so the structure of the hive miraculously emerges. My point exactly.'

Titus growled, baffled.

Stef said, 'Yuri, did you know that kernels have been used in war here? On Earth itself. For centuries, I think.'

'Somehow I'm not surprised,' Yuri said weakly. 'Can you think of any way in which this new humanity is better than the old?'

'Only one,' said the ColU. 'They're better at building Hatches.'

CHAPTER 10

The moon was different. That was the first thing Beth Eden Jones noticed as the *Ukelwydd* sailed towards the Earth, still decelerating, kernel drive burning bright.

It was a chance navigational alignment that brought the incoming ship close to the satellite, close enough for the kernel energies to cast a glow on the surface. On the dark side scattered lights burned, and domes reflected the ship's fire like droplets of mercury. But when the day side opened up, with the moon receding behind the Earthbound ship, even Beth – a stranger to the solar system until she stepped through a Hatch from Per Ardua to Mercury at age twenty – could see how the ancient terrain was disfigured. The smooth greyness of the *maria*, the seas, was gouged and scarred with immense rectilinear workings, and the whole face was masked by rays from brilliant, sharply defined new craters. The *maria* land forms were obviously artificial, the result of centuries of human mining for resources, here on this version of the moon. It took a while for Beth to understand that the new craters, the bright rays, were human-made features too: the scars, not of industry, but of war.

Having passed the moon, the ship turned for Earth, a button of light in the sky. But again Beth could immediately see differences from the world she remembered, even from this distance. There was no gleam of ice, for one thing, at either pole. And whole swathes of the planet, in central America, central Africa,

71

Australia, were bare of life, as if the green had worn away to expose the rocky bones of the world.

The *Ukelwydd*, with the ruin of the *Tatania* in tow and the hulk ship's tenfold crew aboard, settled neatly into a high-inclination orbit around Earth, or Terra as the home world was called by the Brikanti. The crew of the ISF ship were restricted to their sparse quarters for a full day, as the Brikanti went through their arrival protocols.

After this brief confinement, Ari Guthfrithson, the ship's leading *druidh*, invited Beth to join him to view the world, for soon the orbital pass would take the ship over Britain and north Europe, the home of the Brikanti and their allies, including Ari's own people.

Beth was pleased to see Ari. She felt she had grown relatively close to this calm scholar in the days they had spent on this ship. He was younger than she was, but not by much. He wasn't exactly handsome, but like all the Brikanti crew he seemed to be exceptionally well groomed, with neat hair and finely shaped sideburns – she had glimpsed him using a portable kit, scissors, a nail file. She was attracted to him, she thought, if only faintly.

And today the general mood was good. The *Ukelwydd* crew seemed relaxed as they switched over from flight mode to less demanding orbital operations.

'Plus,' said Lex McGregor as he joined Beth and Ari at a big observation window, 'maybe they are looking forward to getting rid of us. I know the military. The sooner they can kick a problem upstairs the happier they will be.'

Ari's voice, softly translated for Beth through Earthshine's systems via her earpiece, was calm. 'Actually ship's crew are not used to dealing with people directly. In space conflicts, a personal encounter with the enemy is rare; the defeated rarely survive to become prisoners. And of course your Earthshine, whose nature we cannot understand, represents a double conceptual problem for us.'

'Well, I'm sorry about that,' McGregor said drily. 'But he is

72

the reason we're all here in the first place. The objective of the flight of the poor old *Tatania* was specifically to save Earthshine from the consequences of our own upcoming war.' He glanced down at the world, over which the ship drifted silently. 'Though whether by delivering Earthshine to your nation really counts as "saving" him – I suppose I'm relieved I'll never have to justify that to my superiors, wherever *they* are … I'm sorry, I'm maundering.'

Ari said, 'Your destiny at a higher level than that has not yet been decided.'

McGregor frowned. 'I don't understand. This is a Brikanti ship. I don't know anything about your government, your empire – whatever – but surely we're under your protection.'

'I'm afraid it is more complicated than that.' Ari gestured. 'Look around.'

And when Beth looked away from the bright surface of the planet she saw an array of brilliant, unwinking stars against the dark background of space.

Lex McGregor whistled. 'Wow. Space habitats. I see toruses, cylinders, platforms – mirrors, antennas …' He clenched a fist. 'We've barely been allowed near a window. I never even noticed all this junk before.'

'Junk?' Ari smiled. 'I have been told that, where you come from, space is much less populated, comparatively. We find that difficult to understand. With kernel-drive ships it is easy to haul vast loads into orbit, or to ship materials in from such sources as Luna or the Tears of Ymir.'

'But, Ari, they – umm, *we* – are more wary of kernels than you are. Kernel drives aren't allowed on the Earth. Nowhere closer than the far side of the moon, where Penny Kalinski and her sister once worked. Of course, when the final war came, all bets were off.'

'But I point out that the hardware you see in space around us represents the various forces who have taken an interest in you.'

Beth said, 'You mean the Romans, the Xin?'

'I do.' Ari studied her, his face open, inquisitive. 'I still know little of your own history. What hints I have heard are fascinating – the differences from our own. For now, you need to understand this. From what I have gathered, your history was rather more complex than ours has been. Fragmented. Essentially our world, and now the worlds beyond Terra, have been dominated by the rise of two powerful empires, Rome and Xin. Though other polities have come and gone, those two great poles of power have competed for control of the great landmasses of Asia and Europa for two thousand years. And for the last thousand years or more they have contended over the territories of the rest of the world also. The only significant exception has been my own federation, the Brikanti. Starting with a Pritanike that stayed independent of Rome, the Brikanti have managed to retain a kind of land empire of their own.'

He studied their faces. 'Terrible wars have been fought, on this world and elsewhere. Why, the battered face of Luna is a reminder of that. It is said that when the war up there was at its height, and the face of the satellite burned in the sky, a hail of debris, rocks from the great lunar detonations, rained down on Terra. Those accidental rock falls could not be distinguished from purposeful attacks, and a new wave of war was initiated on Terra itself. However, war and competition drove innovation. In many ways, it is clear, my culture is less technologically advanced than yours – but not in others.

'And we survive, and poor Terra, almost as battered and scarred as Luna, has survived as an abode for humanity. This is because we, the competing powers of Terra, have found ways, if not to cooperate, at least to manage our conflicts. To sublimate them into angry diplomacy.'

McGregor said, 'Are you saying we are now the subject of this "angry diplomacy"?'

Ari sighed. 'The whole world saw the *Ukelwydd* come sailing in with the wreck of a ship of unknown origin. Our crew is riddled with spies for Xin and Rome. Of course it is; it is to be expected. You represent treasure, or perhaps danger, of unknown potential. We Brikanti spotted you first, and showed the initiative to retrieve you, but that is not to say that Xin and Rome are happy for us to keep you to ourselves. And as a result, right now, this ship, and you, are the subject of scrutiny. And as they watch us, they watch each other too.'

McGregor grunted. 'And everybody is armed to the teeth.'

'That's the idea. The fact that there is a native Xin among you, or so we would classify Jiang Youwei, makes the situation that much more complex; *all* sides feel they have a claim. At some point the *trierarchus*, as the command authority on the spot, will need to decide whether it is worth the risk of trying to transport you to Brikanti territory on the ground, or else to give you up to either Rome or Xin – or even to cast you adrift in your *Tatania* and let them fight it out over you. For we Brikanti, you see, are a small and nimble power who strive to stay safe by not being trodden on by either of our world's lumbering giants ...'

Penny Kalinski joined them now, entering through the door at the back of the cabin. Swimming easily in the absence of gravity, she looked comfortable in a loose-fitting Brikanti costume of tunic and trousers. She was carrying a slate, and sipping something from a covered pottery mug. 'Watered-down mead,' she said to Beth. 'Pleasant stuff.'

Beth had to smile. 'You look as if you fit in here, Penny.'

'Well, what can you do but make the best of it? I doubt we're going home any time soon. Even if "home" still exists, in any meaningful sense. So what's going on? I heard we were due to pass over Britain; I wanted to come and see.'

Lex McGregor did a double take, turned to the panorama of the world below, and frowned at what he saw. 'Really? *That's* Britain? What the hell?'

Beth, a stranger to Earth, had comparatively little preconception about what she expected to see, looking down on Britain / Pritanike. She saw a kind of archipelago, a scatter of islands off the shore of a greater continent to the east. There was a greyish urban tangle laid over the green-brown of the countryside on the eastern coast of the larger of the islands, nearest the continent; she saw the glitter of glass and metal, arrow-straight roads. And in the mountainous country of an island to the far north she saw tremendous rectangular workings that looked as if they might rival the minefields of the lunar *maria*.

Lex said grimly, 'I was born in England. The southern counties, Angleterre. I have seen my home country from space many times. But I do not recognise *that*. Half of it's missing altogether.'

Penny touched his shoulder. 'History's been different here, Lex. Rome in the west never fell, apparently. Here, they industrialised centuries before we did. With the consequences you'd expect.'

'Greenhouse gases. Deforestation. Sea-level rises?'

'That's it. It will all have gone a lot further and a lot earlier than in our timeline. *We* had the great twenty-first century crisis of the climate Jolts, the heavy-handed repair work of the Heroic Generation. Maybe here, as it unfolded more slowly, they understood it all less – maybe they cared less – and just adapted to it. I think we can expect to see the coastlines transformed all around the world. Lowlands lost, like south and east England here.'

McGregor squinted. 'That big urban sprawl in northern England looks like it's centred on York.'

'That is Eboraki,' said Ari. 'The capital of an independent Pritanike since the days of Queen Kartimandia herself, she who defied Rome. It has always been a city of war. Later, in the early days of contact between my own ancestral people and the Brikanti, for some years Eboraki was held by us. It was a Scand city, not a Brikanti one.'

Penny grinned. 'But all that's a long time ago. Forgive and forget?'

'At least we Brikanti and Scand loathe each other less than we loathe the Romans and the Xin. Now Eboraki is the capital of a world empire – though we have no emperors.'

Lex said, 'The development on the scraps of high ground to the south of the Thames, beyond the Isle of Dogs. That might be some version of London.'

'That is Lund,' Ari said. 'The most obvious gateway to Europa, and the Roman provinces. The town was a petty community before contact with the Romans; there was no particular purpose for it. After Kartimandia it became a trading hub with the Empire, and the nearest to a Roman city in Pritanike. But it was always dwarfed by Eboraki.'

McGregor pointed. 'And what the hell did you do to Scotland?'

Ari frowned. 'We know it as Kaledon. An arena of heroic engineering.'

'It looks like you demolished mountains,' McGregor said. 'Some areas look like they've been *melted*.'

'Some have been,' Ari said. 'A kernel-drive spacecraft, landing or taking off, generates rather a lot of heat.'

'My God,' Penny said. 'They really have brought kernel technology down to the face of the Earth. All that heat energy dumped into the ground, the air. It's a wonder they haven't flipped the whole damn planet into some catastrophic greenhouse-warming event, into a Venus.'

'Maybe,' Lex said, 'they were lucky. They got away with it. *Just*. Perhaps there are other timelines where precisely that happened. Does that make sense, Kalinski? If there are two timelines, why not many?'

'Or an infinite number.' She grinned, lopsided. 'That had occurred to me too. You're thinking like a scientist, McGregor.'

'I'll cut that out immediately.'

Ari followed this exchange closely.

Now the island cluster was passing away to the north-west, and the ship was sailing over the near continent – Gaul to the Romans and the Brikanti, France to the crew of the *Tatania*. The countryside, where it was spared by the sea-level rise, glowed with urbanisation. But on the track of a broad river Beth made out a neat circular feature, a set of rays spanning out from it, a lunar crater partially overgrown by the green. She pointed. 'What's that?'

Ari said, 'Once a major city of the Roman province. Destroyed in a war some centuries back, by a Xin missile that got through the local defences.'

Penny said, 'The missile – kernel-tipped? It was, wasn't it? So it's true. You people don't just use kernels as sources of power on Earth. You actually use them in weapons, to fight your Iron Age wars.'

Ari Guthfrithson frowned. 'Would you have me apologise for my whole history? And is *your* history so laudable?'

McGregor murmured, 'We're missing the point here, Penny. Forget your judgements. We need to learn as much about this world as we can while we've got the chance.'

Penny nodded. 'You're right, of course, since it looks like we're going to be stuck here.' She thought it over. 'The *Ukelwydd* is following a high-inclination orbit around the Earth – around Terra. That is, the orbit is tipped up at an angle to the equator—'

'That is intentional, of course,' Ari said, 'so that our track takes us over Pritanike and the landing grounds of Kaledon.'

'But that means we get to fly over a good span of latitudes. And as the planet turns beneath us, with time we get to look down on a swathe of longitudes too. Give me a few hours with a slate, and I'll capture what I can. Then with some educated guesswork maybe we can figure out the story of this world ...'

CHAPTER 11

Twelve hours later Penny called her companions, with Ari, back to the observation lounge. She'd found a way to project slate images onto a blank wall, and had prepared a digest of her observations of the turning world beneath.

She showed them landscapes of dense urbanisation, the cities glowing nodes in a wider network of roads and urban sprawl. 'Welcome to Terra,' she said drily.

'This is Europa – Europe. Some of the oldest Roman provinces. Give or take the odd invasion from Asia, this whole swathe from the Baltic coast in the north to the Mediterranean in the south has been urbanised continually for more than two thousand years, and the result is what you can see. Many of the denser nodes map on to cities we're familiar with from our own timeline, which are either successor cities to Roman settlements – like Paris, for instance – or, in places the Romans never reached in our timeline, they follow the geographic logic of their position. Hamburg, Berlin. The nature of the country is different further north, the Danish peninsula, Scandinavia. Just as heavily urbanised, but a different geography.'

'The heartland of my people,' Ari said. 'You may have images of the canal which severs the peninsula from the mainland. A very ancient construction, which was widened extensively when kernels became available.'

Penny goggled. 'You're telling me you use kernels to shape landscapes as well? On *Earth*?'

'This is Terra, Penny,' McGregor said evenly. 'Not Earth. I guess that's their business.'

Penny showed images now of a desolate coastline, an angry grey sea, ports and industrial cities defiant blights on the grey-brown landscape. 'This is northern Asia,' she said. 'In our reality the Arctic ocean coast of Russia. There never was a Russia here, I don't believe. But nor is there any sign of a boreal forest at these latitudes. Even the sea looks sterile – nobody fishing out there – and no sign of any Arctic ice, by the way, though we haven't been able to see all the way to the pole.'

Ari shrugged. 'It is dead country. It always has been dead. Good only for extraction of minerals, methane for fuel.'

Penny tapped her screen. 'I'm going to pan south. The extent of the main Roman holdings seems to reach the Urals, roughly. Whereas you have the Xin empire, presumably some descendant of the early Chinese states we know about, extending up from the north of central China through Mongolia and eastern Siberia, all the way to the Bering Strait. In Central Asia, though—'

More craters. A desolate, lifeless landscape.

This made Beth gasp. 'What happened here?'

Ari sighed. 'The steppe was historically always a problem. A source of ferocious nomadic herdsmen and warriors, who, whenever the weather took a turn for the worst, would come bursting out of their heartland to ravage the urban communities to west and east. Finally Xin and Rome agreed to administer those worthless plains as a kind of joint protectorate. It is an arrangement that worked quite well, for centuries. Mostly.'

McGregor's grin was cold. 'Mostly?'

'Wherever two great empires clash directly there will be war. And when weapons such as the kernels are available – well. You can see the result.'

Penny said, 'Here's the Xin homeland. Again there seems to be a historical continuity with the cities and nations we know about from the early first millennium ...'

Some of the images had been taken at night. Half a continent glowed, a network of light embedded with jewel-like cities – and yet here and there Beth could see the distinctive circular holes of darkness that must be relics of kernel strikes.

Ari was watching Beth, as much as he was following the images. 'Your reaction is different from the others. You seem – dismayed.'

'That's one word for it. I grew up on an empty world.'

'Ah. Whereas all this, in comparison, billions of us crammed into vast developments—'

'How do you breathe? How do you find dignity?'

'You mean, how will *you* live here.' He smiled. 'Beth Eden Jones, you, of all the crew of the *Tatania*, are by far the most intriguing to me. The most complicated. If fortune allows it, I hope to be able to help you find a place in this, the *third* world you have had to learn to call home...'

Penny said now, 'As Ari has told us, the rest of the world is a kind of playpen for the three superpowers of Eurasia. Here's Australia.'

Beth saw arid crimson plains like a vision of Mars, pocked with the circular scars of explosions, the rectangular wounds of tremendous mines.

'Mined by the Xin,' Ari said.

'My mother was from Australia,' Beth said. 'I visited once. What happened to the native people here?'

Ari looked at her curiously. 'What native people?'

'Africa,' Penny announced, pulling up image after image. 'To the south, extensive mining and farming by the Xin, it seems. To the north, the Sahara – but look at it...'

The desert was covered by a grid of huge rectilinear canals.

Ari said, 'One of the Romans' most significant projects. And they are slowly succeeding in making the desert bloom, as you can see. But there is a danger that in years to come, as they advance their colonies ever further south—'

'And the Xin work their way north from their southern farm-lands,' McGregor said, 'they're going to meet in the middle, and clash. It will be Central Asia all over again.'

'Let us hope not,' Ari said fervently. 'But, yes, those of us *druidh* who devote their efforts to projections of the future see this as one possibility.'

81

'Here's South America,' Penny said.

'Or Valhalla Inferior,' Ari said mildly. 'A battleground between the Xin and the Romans for centuries.'

Beth saw farmland and mining country cut across by vast river systems, and scarred by swathes of desert. 'What about Amazonia?'

Penny said drily, 'You'd never know the rainforest had ever been there. And again, we'll probably never know what happened to the indigenous populations.'

In North America, images taken in the dark of night showed a band of fire that Beth thought roughly followed the Canadian border with the United States.

Penny said, 'The continent is relatively undeveloped. There's a big city of some kind on the site of St Louis, another in Massachusetts. Other than that, small towns and army bases. There is what looks like a Roman legionary fortress on the site of downtown Seattle, for instance, where I grew up – I looked to see. And this is the only place on the surface of the Earth where it looks like there is active warfare in progress.'

Ari said, 'This is an arena I know well – I have served here. We Scand reached this country first, more than a millennium ago, and then the Brikanti followed us – and the Romans, some using Scand ships, came soon after. Now, to the north is Brikanti country, once thickly forested, where we extracted wood for our ocean-going ships. Our principal city, near the east coast, is called Leifsholm. To the south, farmland developed by the Romans, a great breadbasket. Their own provincial capital, on the course of a mighty river, is called Messalia. We meet at the latitude of the inland seas. There are no great cities here. In a sense it is a question of tradition, of history. The old countries, Europa and Asia, are where you build cities, whether you are Xin or Roman or indeed Brikanti. The rest of the world is to be exploited.'

Penny said, 'That border country looks like a war zone.'

'So it is,' Ari said. 'The Romans like to send their legions marching north. We oppose them with fortresses and counter raids.'

'I thought you guys cooperated. You run interstellar missions together, for instance.'

Ari shrugged. 'We cooperate when we fly to the stars, while warring on Terra, in the Valhallas. It is a kind of game. Lethal, of course, but a game. The Romans give their legions marching practice and their generals triumphs. We, conversely, enjoy tripping them up. It is not logical, but when has the politics of empire ever been rational? We must retain our separate identities somehow, Penny Kalinski. And after all, the Romans did consider invading Pritanike once. You don't forgive something like that.'

Penny shook her head. 'A continent as one vast military training ground.'

'But what else is such a barren continent good for?'

'You'd be surprised,' Penny said fervently.

McGregor said, 'So, an endless three-way war, now extended out into the solar system.'

'It has gone this way for centuries,' Ari said. 'It is our way, evidently—'

'Giving away our strategic secrets, are you, *druidh*?'

Beth turned to see Kerys the *trierarchus*, the ship's commander, walking into the cabin through the door at the rear. She was followed by a solid-looking Earthshine, an impressive display of virtual projection from the unit in which the old Core AI was stored.

Ari came to a kind of attention. 'That wasn't my intention, *trierarchus*. I believe that I have learned as much about the home of Beth Eden Jones and her companions as I have revealed about ours.'

Lex McGregor grinned. 'And I bet that's true, you slippery little rascal.'

Kerys walked to the window, hands clasped behind her back, and peered around, beyond the glowing surface of Earth, into space. 'Well, our rivals cluster close. They wait on a decision on how we are to dispose of you, the crew of the *Tatania*. And, needless to say, my superiors at Dumnona have devolved the decision to me.'

Lex McGregor said evenly, 'My heart aches for you.'

Kerys arched an eyebrow. 'A fine way to talk to an officer who holds you dangling by the testicles.'

McGregor barked a laugh.

'What am I to do with you yourself, for example, General Lex McGregor? Look at you, old and grey, your prime a distant memory. What possible use are you? I might throw you over to the Romans; you might make them laugh, briefly, if they dump you in the arena with a gladiator or two.'

McGregor grinned, fearless. 'I'd like to see them try *that*. Madam, I would have thought my value is obvious. I come from an entirely different military tradition, an entirely different spacefaring background.' He tapped his grizzled pate. 'And now all that experience can be put at your command. But,' he said severely, 'I come with strings attached. I want my crew with me, Golvin, Kapur, the others – all five of them. Without them I could not function, and would not try. Conversely, throw even one of them to the Romans or the Xin and I will follow.'

'Your loyalty is commendable,' Kerys said, her face kept carefully blank. 'You, Penelope Kalinski: frankly your value is obvious even to me. The philosophies and mathematics you display, the technologies you wield – if you spent your remaining years teaching Brikanti students even a fraction of what you know, you could be of immeasurable value.'

Penny nodded her head. She was composed, Beth thought, unmoved, as if she'd thought her way through this already. Penny said, 'I can think of worse ways to spend my life. I would need Jiang with me, of course.'

'We can debate that,' Kerys said neutrally. 'As for you, Beth Eden Jones—'

She stared closely at Beth, and Beth found herself touching

the tattoo that sprawled over her face, a relic of her childhood on Per Ardua: a mark the Brikanti seemed to regard as savage.

'I can vouch for her,' Ari said quickly, forestalling whatever judgement Kerys was about to pronounce. '*Trierarchus*, she is in many ways the most interesting of all. She was born and grew up on the planet of another star! Embedded in a system of native life of which we have no knowledge – as you know, our ships found no such life on any planet of the star Proxima. She was brought back to Terra as a young adult, and as an outsider she is probably a better witness to that culture than any of these others. Again I cannot say precisely what I would learn from her, given time, but—'

'All right, *druidh*,' Kerys said, raising a hand. 'You've made your point.'

'Which leaves me,' Earthshine said silkily.

'Indeed. And you present the greatest challenge of all. The machinery that sustains you is impossibly far beyond our under-standing – I would have no way of knowing if it represented some kind of danger to my country.'

'Nor what its potential might be,' Earthshine said, 'if you were able to learn from it.'

'Very well. But what of *you*?' She walked around him, inspect-ing him; she passed a hand through his arm, making pixels scat-ter in the air, and Beth saw Earthshine flinch as his consistency protocols were violated. 'What are you? Not a man. Are you any more than a puppet? Is there a mind in there?'

'I have been accused of being insane,' he said, smiling coldly. 'Can one be insane without a mind? And let me remind you what I have stored, in my artificial mind, my roomy memory: the secrets of what made the *Tatania* fly. The hulk you captured is scrap metal. And I have all the records we brought with us of our reality, and everything we achieved there.'

Kerys frowned, but Beth could see she was intrigued. 'Such as?'

'Let me show you. Please, do not draw your weapons …' He gestured in the air, cupping his hands.

An image congealed before him, a sphere maybe a half-metre across. The bulk of the surface was grey-white ice glistening in the light of an invisible sun, but the blue and green of life sprawled in great patches under curving lids of glass.

Ari gasped. 'It is beautiful.'

'It is a world. An asteroid, what you would call a Tear of Ymir. The largest of all – you must have given it a name; we call it Ceres.'

'To us this is Höd,' Ari said. 'After the blind half-brother of Baldr, favourite child of the old gods.'

'This is what we built there, these great halls. And Ceres became the hub from which the exploitation of the asteroids progressed. Here is another world.'

He snapped his fingers, and icy Ceres was replaced by a more familiar world, a burnt-orange ball, its surface scarred by canyons and craters, ice caps like swirls of cream at either pole.

'Mars,' said Kerys.

'Yes – a name we share. Look what we built *there*.' He pulled his hands apart. The planetary image exploded, becoming misty and faint, but the centre, before Earthshine's chest, zoomed in on a sprawling city, a tower at its heart – a needle-like structure whose height only became apparent when the scale was such that people could be made out individually, in pressure suits at the base of the tower.

'This is the Chinese capital, in a region we called Terra Cimmeria. I know how all this was built, even the great tower. I can help you discover it. And I have more. Again, do not be alarmed...'

On his upturned hands, a series of animals walked, elephants, bison, lions, horses, each three-dimensional image scaled against a human figure.

The Brikanti stared.

Earthshine said, 'I and my brothers were created, some centuries ago, for *this*, above all else. To save the diversity of living things. The destruction of our natural world was not so advanced as it is here, despite centuries of ardent effort,' he said drily. 'These animals are known to you only through

86

fossil remains, from bones you find in the ground. To you, the elephants and the apes and the whales are as remote as the dinosaurs. I store genetic data – that is, the information required to recover these animals, to rebuild them. I can give you back your past.'

The animals melted away; he lowered his hands.

'Also I have books,' Earthshine said. 'And art. Think about that. Two millennia of a different tradition.' He tapped his skull. 'All stored in here—'

Kerys cut him off. 'The logic is obvious. Whatever we make of you, we can't allow you to fall into the hands of our rivals. Welcome aboard,' she said simply.

Earthshine inclined his head, as if he'd expected no other reaction.

Oddly, Beth noticed, Ari Guthfrithson the *druidh* appeared more sceptical; she would have imagined the scholar in him would have responded to Earthshine's pitch.

'Well, now that's decided, we have work to do,' Kerys said briskly. Again she glanced out of the window. 'I don't need to inform Dumnona of my decision; I only need to implement it. And no need to give that lot out there any notice. Ari, take charge here; I want all these people strapped in their couches for landing in an hour.'

'Yes, *trierarchus*.' But as Kerys stalked out of the cabin, Ari continued to stare at Earthshine.

The virtual smiled smoothly. 'Is there something more you want, *druidh*? After all the decision is made.'

'Yes. But what strikes me is that in all your bamboozling presentation of the miracles you offer, you never once suggested what it is you want in return.'

Earthshine spread his hands. 'Your *trierarchus* has guaranteed me continued existence. Isn't that enough?'

'Not in your case, no. I don't think it is.'

And, studying Earthshine, and the cautious reactions of Penny Kalinski and even Lex McGregor, Beth had a profound suspicion

87

that he was right. That there was far more going on here than Earthshine was yet revealing.

But a warning trumpet sounded piercing blasts, and they hurried to their acceleration couches. There was no more time for debate.

CHAPTER 12

Even from the ground, on the nameless planet of Romulus, Stef Kalinski had spotted the *Malleus Jesu*, star vessel of the *Classis Sol* of the Roman imperium, orbiting in the washed-out sky, a splinter of light. But it was not until the final evacuation from the planet, as she, Yuri, the ColU, and Titus Valerius with his daughter, all rode one of the last shuttles into space, that Stef first got a good look at the craft.

The *Malleus Jesu* was a fat cylinder of metal and what looked like ceramic, capped with a dome at one end, a flat surface at the other. It looked as if it was held together with huge rivets. There were windows visible in the flanks of the tremendous hull, protected by venetian-blind shutters. The whole craft spun slowly on its axis, presumably to equalise the heating load it received from the sun. The walls were ornately carved with huge figures in the triumphal Roman style: heroic military men striding over defeated peoples, or marching from world to world. Even the rim of that leading dome was elaborately decorated, though the dome itself looked like a crude layering of rock.

Titus Valerius was a massive presence in the seat beside her; he smelled of sweat, stale wine, and straw. Titus pointed at the base of the craft. 'Kernels. A bank of them. To push the craft, yes?'

'I know the theory,' Stef said drily.

'Push halfway, turn around, slow down the other half and stop at Earth.' He pointed again, at the dome. 'Shield from space dust. Rock from world below. Shovelled on by slaves in armour.'

89

By which he meant, Stef knew by now, some kind of crude pressure suit.

Yuri, pale but intent, peered out. 'It looks like Trajan's Column, topped by the Pantheon.'

Stef sniffed. 'Looks more phallic to me. The *Penis of Jesus*.'

'Oh, come on. This is just great. An imperial Roman starship! ... I wonder how the hell they navigate that thing.'

'The drive isn't always on,' said Titus.

Stef realised that a more precise translation of his words might have been, *The vulcans do not always vomit fire.*

'Every month they shut it down, and turn the ship.' He mimed this with his one good hand, like aligning a cannon. 'The surveyors take sightings from the stars. Then they swivel the ship to make sure we're on the right track, and fire up the drive again. It's like laying a road, on the march. You lay a stretch, and at the end of the day the surveyors take their sightings to make sure you're heading straight and true where you're supposed to go, and the next day off you go. Works like a dream. Why, I remember once on campaign—'

'Navigation by dead reckoning,' said the ColU. 'Taking sightings from the stars – simply pointing the craft at the destination. They have no computers here, Yuri Eden, nothing more complex than an abacus. And they have astrolabes, planispheres, orreries, sextants, and very fine clocks – all mechanical, and remarkably sophisticated. But this starship is piloted using clockwork! However, if you have the brute energy of the kernels available, you don't need subtlety, you don't need fine control. You need only aim and fire.'

Titus pointed again at the craft. 'Seven decks. Each sixty yards deep.' He counted up from the base of the ship. 'Kernels and stores, farm, slave pen, barracks, camp, town, villas of the officers. Plus a bathhouse in the dome for the officers.'

Stef frowned, figuring that out. The word the ColU translated as 'yard' was a Roman unit about a yard in length, or roughly a metre. 'That must make the cylinder something like four hundred metres long. And, judging by the proportions, around a hundred metres in diameter. What a monster. Titus, we've been told very little about this flight.'

He grunted. 'That's officers for you. Don't tell you a damn thing about what you're supposed to do, even as they kick you up the arse for not doing it right—'

She asked patiently, 'Such as, how long will the flight be?'

'That's easy,' he said. 'Four years, three hundred and thirty-six days. Same as coming out.'

'Hallelujah,' the ColU said drily. 'A precise number at last. And are you under full gravity for the whole trip?' Silence. 'That is, when the drive is on, do you feel as heavy as you do on Terra?'

The legionary puzzled that out. 'Yes,' he said in the end. 'The officers don't want you bouncing around going soft, like you were on Luna, or Mars. The training's tougher in flight than it is on the ground.'

'I'll bet,' Stef said. 'I know the military. Locked up in a big tin can like this, they'll keep the lower ranks as busy as possible to keep them from causing mischief.'

The ColU said, 'With the numbers the legionary has provided I can at last estimate how far we are from home ...'

If the drive burned continually, exerting an acceleration equivalent to one Earth gravity, after about a year the ship's velocity would be approaching the speed of light.

'Of course we won't pass lightspeed but we'll run into time dilation. Time on the ship will pass much more slowly from the point of view of an observer on Earth—'

'I have two physics doctorates,' Stef snapped. 'I know about relativistic time dilation.'

'Well, I have two less doctorates,' Yuri said tiredly. 'Give me the bottom line, ColU.'

'If the journey takes us, subjectively, four years, three hundred and thirty-six days, then eleven years and ninety-one days will have passed on Earth. That's not allowing for small corrections because of the shutdown periods. And the double-star system of Romulus and Remus must be some nine light years from

91

Earth. Titus here will have spent maybe ten years of his life travelling to the destination and back, plus another three years or so on the ground – a thirteen-year mission. But by the time he returns home, about twenty-five years will have passed on the ground.'

Titus shrugged. 'That's what you sign up for. Got my daughter with me, on the ship. No other family to worry about. And back home the legion's *collegia* will make sure we get treated right, with our pay and pensions and such.'

The ColU said, 'Perhaps it takes an empire, solemn, calm and antique, to manage operations on such scales.'

'We Romans get it done,' Titus said simply. 'We'll be joining the *Malleus* soon. Make sure you're buckled into your seats.'

The ferry docked with a port on the slowly turning hull of the starship. Stef saw that the hull here was blazoned with large 'V' symbols; she assumed she was landing at the fifth deck, then, which Titus had called the 'camp'.

She knew that an ISF crew would not have attempted a docking with a rotating structure, save at the axis. By contrast the crew of this ferry took them in with terrifying nonchalance, swooping down on the slowly turning *Malleus*, until they drove straight into a system of nets which fielded them neatly and dragged them down to the hull, where docking clamps rattled noisily against the base of the craft. Once the docking was complete she heard whoops and backslaps from behind closed doors. She had met none of the pilots but had glimpsed them on the ground. They were young Brikanti, male and female, cocky, smart, and they enjoyed showing off their skills before the nervous, superstitious, ground-based Romans. As she unbuckled from her seat, Stef offered up silent thanks that this risky display of super-competence was at an end.

One by one they were led out through a port in the base of the ferry, and down through thick layers of hull metal and insulation into the body of the *Malleus Jesu*. They were weightless, of course, save for the faintest centrifugal tug towards the wall of the rotating craft.

Once inside the main body, Stef had to adjust her orientation, her sense of up and down, even as she was battered by a barrage of sensory impressions: brilliant lights, smells of animals and humans, a clutter of structures, heaps of supplies and equipment, and people swimming everywhere in the air. The ship stood upright, essentially. The hull surface she had passed through was no longer a floor or ceiling, but a vertical wall. And she had a clear view across the interior of the cylindrical hull; 'floor' and 'ceiling' were tremendous plates below and above her, slicing off the fifth deck, this pie-shaped section of the craft – though the plates were pierced by gaps through which passed pipes, ducts and, at the centre, a kind of fireman's pole arrangement from which chains dangled, connecting this deck to the rest of the ship. Pillars of steel were bolted in place across the area too, adding structural support between floor and ceiling, she guessed the better to withstand the thrust of the kernel engine. It was a vast, cavernous space, this deck alone, sixty metres deep and a hundred across, and illuminated by sunlight from the windows and big, crude-looking fluorescent strip lights. The tall pillars spanning floor to roof gave the place the feeling of a cathedral, to Stef's sensibilities.

And set up on the floor plate was, yes, a camp, just as Titus had said, a near copy of the *colonia* down on the ground, a rectangle with rounded corners, like a playing card, set slap in the middle of the circular deck. Looking down across the deck from her elevated position at this port, Stef recognised the crosswise layout of the main streets; there was a handsome building of wooden panels that might be the *principia*, next to it a small chapel, and beyond an open space that might be a parade ground or training area. There was even a row of granaries, though she saw nothing like barrack blocks. All these structures looked conventional enough, with wood-panelled walls and red-tiled roofs. The walls of the *principia*, the headquarters, even looked as if they were plastered. But, looking more closely, Stef could

93

see that the buildings were built on frameworks of strong steel girders, firmly riveted to the hull plates.

And she was treated to the surreal sight of Roman legionaries paddling through the air above the 'camp', pulling themselves along ropes strung across the cavernous deck, manhandling heaps of supplies wrapped up in nets, food, clothes, even weapons.

A Roman camp, in interstellar space! But then, she knew, this mixture of antiquity and modernity was typical of these strange late Romans.

From conversations with Eilidh, Movena, Michael and others, she'd gathered something of the altered history of the Empire, compared to the account she was familiar with – a history that had brought a Roman legion to a distant star. After Kartimandia's time, Germany had ultimately been conquered up to the Baltic coast. It was Vespasian, later an emperor, who planted the eagle of Rome on the bank of the Vistula. After that, with the German tribes civilised, there had been no barbarian hordes to cross the Rhine in the late fourth century as in Stef's world, the event that had ultimately destabilised the Empire in the west. Rome had continued to rule. In the end, however, the Empire had reached natural limits on the Eurasian landmass, penned in by the Xin to the east, the Brikanti to the north, and the deserts of North Africa to the south. For centuries Rome had grown inward-looking, static, its citizenry heavily taxed, its imperial elite self-obsessed, remote and over-powerful – and unstable, subject to endless palace coups.

That had all changed in the twelfth century AD. By then the Brikanti had already been in the Americas for two hundred years, thanks to their adventurous Scand partners, and had explored the coast of Africa, seeking the lands below the equator. Belatedly the Romans followed them into this new world – and the centuries of stasis were over. In a new age of expansiveness and conquest, the Romans remembered their ancestors, who they had imagined as stern, lean men ploughing their fields and going to war. It was as if the Empire had been cleansed. Though the modern Romans remained Christian, traditional forms of society and the military – such as the legions – had been revived. Even old family naming conventions had been dug up, ancient lineages ferociously researched. Which was why a planet of a distant star had been colonised by units of the ninetieth legion, called Victrix, in commemoration of a tremendous victory over the Brikanti just south of the Great Lakes. In later centuries the need to avoid the use of explosive weapons inside pressure hulls, in spacecraft and surface habitats, had even led to a revival of the traditional weapons of hand-to-hand combat, spear and sword and knife, *pilum* and *gladio* and *pugio*.

But Stef was sure no Roman of the 'old' history she knew had ever seen a sight like the one she glimpsed on the far side of this fifth deck, as a squad of legionaries under the control of a hovering tribune struggled to fold up the squirming hull of a deflated *cetus* airship.

Titus gathered the newcomers together. He was carrying the ColU in its pack, handling it as tenderly as a baby, Stef observed. 'Come on. Soldiers' business on this deck. You're in the civilian town, next one up.' Grabbing a rope, with the pack around his neck, he pulled himself one-handed away from the docking port, and headed up to the ceiling.

Stef and Yuri glanced at each other, shrugged, and followed. Stef made sure she let Yuri go first, unsure how strong he'd be feeling today, but he seemed to be moving freely enough. Maybe a lack of gravity for a while would be good for him. As she climbed she called up after Titus, 'Why are you carrying the ColU? What about Chu?'

'He'll be taken straight to the third deck.'

She remembered. The slave pen, Titus had called it, above the farm, below the barracks.

'Slaves are stupid creatures and more so without gravity. They flap around uselessly and puke everywhere. They're best strapped down for the duration. You won't see Chu until we're under way and we get stuff properly sorted out on board.'

She was in no position to argue.

They passed easily through an open port up to the sixth deck – open, but Stef noticed there was a heavy iron hatch on hinges over the port. She imagined whole decks of this vessel needing to be locked down in case of some disaster, a blowout perhaps – or even in case of a rebellion by disaffected soldiers, or the slaves in their below-decks pens.

As they swam up, following more ropes, Stef wasn't surprised to find that on this deck, which Titus had curtly labelled the 'town', was indeed a small town of the Roman type, or at least a section of one, like a walled-off suburb. Rising easily into the air above tiled rooftops, she glimpsed a grid layout of streets centred on an open space, a forum perhaps, surrounded by multi-storey porticoes and with a small triumphal arch at one edge. Built up against one section of hull wall were banks of seats over an open space, a kind of open-air theatre. And around the circuit of the hull walls ran a track, she guessed for racing or other sports. Everywhere people swarmed in the air: men, women, children, hovering over the buildings and ducking down into crowded streets. The noise in this enclosed space, and echoing off yet another roof-partition above, was tremendous, a clamour of voices that sounded like a sports crowd.

Stef felt overwhelmed by the sheer vivacity of it all, the complexity, and she realised how little she'd seen of this mobile community down on the planet – and now here it was, cramming itself back into this tin can in space for the five-year journey home. But, even more so than on the military camp deck below, she smelled the sour stink of weightlessness-sickness vomit, and laced in with the general noise she heard the wail of infants. Any children under three must have been born on the planet itself, she realised, and they must be utterly bewildered by the environment of the ship.

With effortless skill, impressive given he had only one hand to use, Titus led them down through a lacing of guide ropes to a neighbourhood a block away from the forum. 'You've been assigned a house down there. Not a bad district, there's a decent food shop and a tavern. You'll need to sign in with a councillor, he'll find you, and the *optio* will come and check on you before the engine fire-up … Any questions?'

Yuri asked, 'Why do you put tiles on the roofs? We're inside a spaceship.'

Titus shrugged. 'It does "rain" in here sometimes. You have to cleanse the air of dust. And besides it's tradition to have tiles on your roof. We Romans don't live like animals, you know.'

Stef said, 'I can't get over how big all this is. How many people aboard, Titus, do you know?'

'Well, the core of it is us, a century of the Legio XC. Eighty men give or take. But then you've got the officers and the staff and the auxiliaries, and then you've got our wives and families, and *then* you've got the merchants and cooks and artisans, and doctors and schoolteachers and such. Oh, and there's the ship's crew, mostly Brikanti, or Arab. What have I forgotten?'

'The slaves?'

'Oh, yes, the slaves,' Titus said. 'As many of them as there are soldiers and other citizens. I'd say five, six hundred warm bodies on the ship.'

'That's a lot of people.'

'But it's the Roman way. You can't do it much smaller than that, miss.'

'Quite,' said the ColU. 'And that's why the ship itself has to be so big. Stef Kalinski, we know these people have no grasp of fine engineering. Small-scale closed life support systems would be beyond their capability. So they build big! They bring along a massive volume of air and water – you said there was a whole deck devoted to farming, Titus?'

'Yes. A lot of greenery up on the villas deck too.'

'They build so big that this ecology is reasonably buffered, stable against blooms and collapses, despite the crudeness of the technology. It's all logical, in its way.'

Yuri said, 'So when will they fire up the kernels, Titus?'

The big man grinned. 'Six hours. You want to be lying flat when they sound the horn. And believe me, you want to be indoors. It's not like the camp here. No discipline. Nobody listens to the warnings. There'll be a sky full of babies and their shit, suspended overhead. You do *not* want to get caught in that rain when it falls. Come on, your residence is just below, I'll get you settled …'

Stef thought they descended like angels into the street where they would live for the next five years.

Six hours later, right on cue and accompanied by trumpet blasts, the banks of kernels at the base of the craft fired up. Stef imagined arrays of the enigmatic wormholes being prodded open to release their energies, streams of high-energy radiation and high-velocity particles, morsels of thrust pushing ever harder at the huge, ungainly structure of the *Malleus Jesu*.

As the acceleration built up, Stef, sitting with Yuri and the ColU in deep couches in the small house to which they'd been assigned – surrounded by plaster walls with crudely painted frescoes – heard cracks and pops and bangs as the giant frame absorbed the stress, the rattle of a tile falling from a roof. She imagined the ship's basic structure would be sound: it was built of good Scand steel, Eilidh had assured her, not your Roman rubbish. But even so, after three years in microgravity – three years of neglect, as everybody was busy on the surface of the planet – there would be point failures, breakages of pipes and cables. Now there were shouts and distant alarm horns as, she imagined, emergency teams dealt with various local calamities. She even heard a rushing collapse, like an ocean wave breaking, as, perhaps, some small building fell in on itself.

Then there were the people. As she and Yuri sat in the semi-gloom – no oil lamps could be lit during the fire-up, that was the rule – and as the weight built up and pressed her into her chair, all around her on this deck with its model-railway toy town, she heard cries and groans, the clucking of distressed chickens, the barking of confused dogs, and the crying of children.

Five years of this, Stef thought. She closed her eyes and tried to relax as the acceleration pressed down on her.

CHAPTER 13

A week after the fire-up, Stef broke a tooth.

In this most exotic of environments, a starship run by a Roman legion, it was the most mundane of accidents, caused by biting down on a slab of coarse Roman bread. She knew by now something about the tumours that riddled Yuri's body, detectable by the ColU but untreatable by it without the medical suite in the physical body it had left behind on Per Ardua. Yuri hadn't wanted to tell her; she'd forced it out of Michael, the kindly physician. Compared to Yuri's problems, this was nothing.

Nevertheless, her tooth *hurt*.

Through one of their slates the ColU, inspecting the tooth, clucked sympathetically, and Penny wondered absently when this farming machine had picked up that particular speech trait. 'An unfortunate accident,' it said. 'Your teeth are very healthy for a woman of your age.'

'Thanks.'

'But nothing's going to protect you from an unground grain in a loaf of bread. And unfortunately there's nothing I can do for you. Lacking my old body, my manipulator arms – once I could have pulled the broken tooth for you, or even printed you a repair or a replacement. But now that I am disembodied—'

'So what am I supposed to do? Tie a length of string to a doorknob?'

'You must ask the Romans for help.'

'*The Romans?* I'm to go to ancient Romans for dental work?'

'Well, they're not *ancient* Romans,' Yuri pointed out gently. 'And it's not a Roman you'll be seeing but a Greek – Michael

– go and find Titus Valerius and have him take you to Michael. I can tell you from experience, he might not know so much but he listens. Why, I bet legionaries lose teeth all the time.'

'That is *not* reassuring.'

Still, she had no better options. She waited a couple of days, munching her way through their hoarded supply of ISF-issue painkillers, brought in their packs through the Hatch. She had the illogical feeling that if only she could have a decent hot shower she'd feel a hell of a lot better. But there was no running water available within much of the ship, save in the bath houses. Every morning and evening you washed from a bowl that you carried into your room from a communal supply.

At last, as the ColU had suggested, she asked the *medicus* for help.

Michael grinned back. 'I'll need supplies from the officers' clinic. I take any excuse to go up to the villas. Come and find me tomorrow.'

The next day Titus Valerius led Stef through the sketchy township to the 'ascension', as the crew called it. This was the central shaft, open at every deck, that led along the axis of the ship. That stout fireman's pole ran the length of the vessel, and a series of platforms and cages regularly rose and fell along its length, hauled by rope-and-pulley arrangements.

There were many breaks in the decks, Stef had learned. You would often come across holes in the floor fenced off for safety. But these were mostly offset from each other, the floor holes not matching the ceiling, for obvious reasons of safety. The ascension, though, was the one shaft open to all decks. Stef thought this great way had a certain unifying aesthetic appeal, a tremendous shaft that penetrated the metal heaven above and the ground under your feet, and spanned the ship from officer country in the crown to the engineers and their kernel arrays at the root of the ship. But the soldier in her recognised the value of a fast road that could take a squad of legionaries straight to any part of the ship within minutes or less. The Romans had always built their Empire on roads, and that, it seemed, was still true now.

So, with a nod to the bored-looking legionaries who manned the system, Titus Valerius escorted Stef up from deck six, the township, to deck seven, the deck of the villas.

Sitting in a steel elevator-like cage, it was like ascending into a park. Stef's first impression was of green, the green of grass, trees, bushes, and moist, pleasantly warm air. She glimpsed only a handful of people – a group of men in togas and carrying scrolls, holding some earnest discussion beside the waters of a lake, a rectangular basin surrounded by slim nude statues. She might have been looking at a scene from two thousand years ago, the senators plotting the assassination of Caesar, perhaps. But over the heads of the debaters soared a metal vault, riveted and painted sky blue. The light, which felt warm and authentically like sunlight, came from fluorescent lanterns that dangled from the ceiling. And the surface of the pond, strewn with lilies, bore a subtle pattern of ripples, a product of the slightest irregularities in the kernel drive that thrust this scrap of pretty parkland through interstellar space. She wondered briefly how they covered over this water feature when the drive was turned off and the gravity disappeared.

Titus Valerius led her along a path by the lake, stone blocks set in the short-cut grass. He was a slab of muscle, out of place in this rather effete setting. 'We'll meet the doctor at the quarters of the *optio*, Gnaeus Junius. Which is not the grandest up here, believe me. They modelled this whole deck, so they say, on a villa of the Emperor Hadrianus, in Italia itself. Although *that* was probably a lot more than a hundred paces across.'

'I can believe it.'

'Waste of space if you ask me.'

'That's officers for you.' But she remembered the ColU's speculation about the life support systems in this big hulk of a ship. 'You know, Titus, this park might be part of the ship's design, as well as a luxury for the officers. It's probably good for the ship as a whole, to have all this greenery up here—'

101

'Hush.' He'd frozen.

From a clump of trees, a slim face peered out at them. Some kind of deer, evidently. It held Titus's gaze for a second, two. Then it turned and bounded into the shadow of the trees, and Stef glimpsed a slim body, a white tail.

Titus growled as they moved on. 'They won't let us hunt, you know.'

Stef laughed. 'There can't be more than a handful of animals up here. And it wouldn't really be fair, Titus; they couldn't run far in this metal box.'

'True. A well-shot arrow could reach from wall to wall. But still, the hunter in me aches to follow, one-armed or not.'

She patted his shoulder. 'You'll be home in a few years, Titus Valerius, and then you can hunt all you like.'

'I'll take you with me,' he promised. 'Meanwhile here we are – home from home for the equestrian and his subordinate officers.'

Gnaeus's 'quarters', set close to the curving hull wall, turned out to be a compact cluster of buildings centred on a cobbled rectangular courtyard, and surrounded by a fringe of carefully manicured garden. There was a gate, wide open, and Titus walked in boldly, followed by Stef. A fountain bubbled from a stone bowl at the centre of the yard. The buildings were neat, single storey, walled with plaster painted white and roofed with red tiles. Steam drifted from the windows of a blocky build- ing in the corner. The only concession to the environment of space travel that Stef spotted were a few steel bands to hold the stonework in place in the absence of thrust gravity.

Titus saw Stef looking curiously at the rising steam. 'A bath- house. Do you have steam baths where you come from?' He pointed up over his head. 'The whole dome up there, in the nose of the ship, is one big bathhouse. *I've* never been up there, I can tell you that. They say there are cohorts of whores up there, male and female, exclusively for the use of the officers, whores who never even see the rest of the ship, let alone the

target planet. The lads spend a lot of time on the march speculating about that.'

'I can imagine.'

'But the most senior officers, like the *optio*, have their own
private baths too. There's plenty of heat from the kernels to
fire the hypocausts, and plenty of slaves to serve you, so why
not? ...' He frowned. 'Speaking of slaves, we should have been
met by now, by one of the *optio*'s household slaves, or failing
that a guard.'

'I meant to ask you about the slaves. We still haven't seen
Chu Yuen since we left Romulus.'

'Well, there's a problem down in the pen.' He rubbed his nose
with the wooden stump of his arm. 'I might suggest the *optio* has
a couple of men posted up here. We're not expecting trouble
but you never know, you can't have fellows just wandering in
as we have.'

'I heard that.' Gnaeus Junius, in a loose-fitting toga, came
walking from one of the buildings, trailed by Michael, who was
more plainly dressed in tunic and light cloak, with a satchel
at his waist. Through the open door behind the two men Stef
glimpsed lantern light, a low table covered by scattered scrolls,
some kind of fresco on the patterned walls – a mosaic on the
floor?

Titus stood to attention. 'Sorry, sir. Didn't mean to be insolent.'

'Not at all. That's good advice, about posting guards. Sort it
out when you return to barracks, would you? And consult the
other officers about a similar arrangement, at least until the
slaves are back.' He smiled at Stef. 'It's good to see you again,
Colonel Kalinski. How are you enjoying the journey?'

'I'm intrigued by it all. But I have a tooth that wants to get
off.'

Titus grinned. 'Broke it on a bit of bread. Whatever army you
once served with, you wouldn't last a month on the march with
a Roman legion, madam. With all respect.'

'That's probably true of most of us.' Michael deftly produced a
small mirror on a probe from the satchel on his waist, asked Stef

to open up, and made a quick inspection. 'No sign of infection or other injury. I'm afraid the tooth will have to come out, however.'

Stef winced. 'I was afraid you'd say that. I'm not terribly good with pain.'

'Don't worry. I have treatments, in particular a paste concocted from certain flowers unique to Valhalla Inferior. You won't feel a thing.'

'I'll say you won't,' Titus said with a grin. 'They give me that stuff when I have problems with the stump. Why, I remember once on campaign—'

'Oh, hush, legionary,' the *optio* said, 'you're not in barracks now.'

'Sorry, sir. Stef asked about the boy, Chu Yuen, who was assigned as a carrier for, umm, Collius.'

Gnaeus nodded seriously. 'There is an issue in the slave pen, I'm afraid. None of the slaves have been released yet, since the launch.' He smiled. 'Which has caused rather a lot of grumbling from those who miss their little conveniences.'

Conversations about the slaves always made Stef wince. Yet she felt compelled to press the point; as the ColU had said Chu at least was one slave they maybe could protect. 'You couldn't make an exception for the boy? He was remarkably useful.'

Gnaeus glanced at the doctor. 'Well, Michael, you're due to go down to the pen for another inspection anyhow. Why not seek out the boy, and see if he's fit to be released? Take Colonel Kalinski with you.'

Michael didn't look thrilled at the idea of such a journey, Stef thought, but he nodded amiably enough. 'Fine. And perhaps you could spare Titus here for our protection.'

Titus looked even more gloomy, but he nodded grimly. 'I'll do it, *optio*. After thirty years in Legio XC, sir, I've probably caught everything I'm going to catch and survived the lot.'

'That's the spirit,' Michael said. 'And it is possible the boy, being of Xin stock, will have been spared the plagues running around the rest of the herd down there.'

Plagues?

'But first things first,' the doctor said, smiling, and he took Stef's arm. 'If you would lend us a room, *optio*, let's sort out this tooth.'

Gnaeus led the way, and Stef, reluctantly, followed, with Titus grinning after her.

CHAPTER 14

The doctor advised her to wait three hours, in a dark and quiet room, after his brisk and painless treatment, to allow the after-effects of the drug he rubbed into her gums to wear off.

Titus was waiting for her, with Michael, when she emerged. Titus grinned. 'How are you feeling?'

'You were right. The *medicus* here had to peel me off the ceiling.' In fact she still felt giddy, but she wasn't about to admit that to Titus.

'Well, when we take the ascension again, prepare to have your head float away once more.' The legionary led them across the parkland to the fireman's pole. They paused under a complex set of anchors that held cables supporting the various cradles that rode up and down the pole. A couple of legionaries stood by the installation, at ease. 'Since Michael is with us we have permission to ride the ascension all the way down to the pen. It's quite a trip, I can tell you. You'll feel like Jesu Himself in the End Times, when He will descend on Rome with Augustus and Vespasian on His left and right hands, to establish the final dominion of the Caesars across the stars.'

'Is that what you believe?'

'So all soldiers believe,' Michael said drily. 'Jesu the warrior god embraced Rome by leading Constantius I to a famous victory. I, like most Greeks, take a more philosophical view – I'm more interested in what Jesu said rather than what He did. As for the Brikanti, they are Christians too, but they cling to the image of Jesu the ally of the fishermen, rather than the holy warrior who cleansed Jerusalem of corruption at the point of a sword.'

'But it's all in the Bible,' Titus said briskly. 'You can't deny that, *medicus*.'

'Oh, I wouldn't dream of it.'

'I must read the Bible,' Stef said. 'Your Bible, I mean.'

Michael looked at her thoughtfully. 'Implying yours may be different? Hm. There is another interesting conversation we must have some day.'

This time the ascension cradle they took was an open cage, built stoutly of steel. Titus showed them seats – padded couches – and handrails, and even a small bar stocked with slim flasks of water, cordials and wine. 'Not that the journey is very long, but officers always like to travel in style.' He glanced up and waved. 'All right, lads? Let her go.'

With a clatter and groan the pulleys started to turn, and the platform lurched downwards, dropping immediately beneath the level of the floor. Stef still felt giddy from Michael's Valhallan potion; she grabbed a rail.

'There's an engine up there, powered by steam, kernel heat,' Titus said. 'Actually it's usually human muscle that's used to operate the pulleys. Slave parties, and punishment details from the army units. Honest work and good discipline for a miscreant. But today we're riding, not Roman muscle, but hot air...'

The floor, itself a thick slab of engineering riddled with pipes, cables and ducts, rose up past Stef's head. A plaque marked clearly with 'VII' above and 'VI' below showed her which decks she was passing between. Below her now opened up the sprawling urban landscape of the township where she had her own small house with Yuri. Hearth smoke rose up from some of the buildings, wisps that drifted off towards great wall-mounted extractor fans. It was still morning, she knew, by ship's time; the big fluorescent lamps were not yet raised to their full noon brilliance, after an eight-hour 'night' illuminated only by emergency lanterns. It struck her now that there were few people to be seen, that the neat little community seemed oddly

107

underpopulated. But this township was lacking its slaves, who might number as many head as the citizens and their children themselves.

As their cage descended, dogs barked, and barefoot children ran to see the party pass. Stef smiled at the children, and resisted the temptation to wave.

Down from VI to V, and having passed through a Roman city, now Stef and her companions descended towards the Roman military camp. It seemed a hive of activity; Stef saw units marching around a track at the perimeter of the deck, heavily laden with packs, while others were building some kind of fortification of sod and dirt – the sod and dirt having been shipped up from the ground for the purpose, Stef supposed.

'We train hard,' Titus said, looking around approvingly. 'Suspended as we are in emptiness, we do not forget how to march, with our gear. We do not forget how to build a camp in a few hours at the end of a marching day. We do not forget how to command, how to lead.'

'Or how to complain,' said Michael drily.

'Thank you, *medicus*.'

V to IV, and here was another deck Stef was familiar with, the 'barracks', the level where she had first boarded the ship. There were orderly rows of huts here, accommodation for the century of legionaries and the various auxiliary units that made up the ship's military force. Titus pointed out a group of huts, almost an afterthought in the layout below, where the *remiges* were quartered when off duty, the ship's crew, all of them Brikanti. Away from the obviously military facilities were blocks of housing, clustered around squares and courtyards. Here Stef could see women working and walking, a huddle of children engaged in what looked like some open-air lesson. She was reminded that these soldiers had brought their families with them on this interstellar march, their wives and lovers, and children born in and out of wedlock.

There were legionaries stationed at the hole in the floor

through which they would descend further. And this time the breach was actually blocked by a covering of wood and glass.

Michael dug into his satchel and handed Titus and Stef masks of linen soaked in some kind of alcohol. 'You may prefer to wear this when we descend.'

Stef apprehensively donned the mask.

The platform slowed as it approached the level of the deck. Titus spoke softly to the guards stationed there, and they laughed at a joke Stef did not hear. Then the guards hauled back the big hatches that covered the portal in the ground, and the platform descended.

IV to III. The slave pen.

It was the stench that hit Stef first, a stench of shit and piss and vomit, of blood and of rotting flesh – a stench of an intensity she hadn't known since her first experience of zero-gravity emergency drills, in her early days as a raw ISF recruit.

Then she made out the detail of the deck, sixty metres below. Illuminated by bright white light, the entire floor was covered by an array of cubicles, neat rectangular cells, block after block of them lapping to the hull on either side. Above the floor, supported by angular gantry towers and fixed to the hull, was a spider web of walkways and rails, a superstructure of steel. Soldiers patrolled the walkways, or were stationed on towers mounted with heavy lights and weapons. All the troops wore masks. The troops carried none of the gunpowder handguns they called *ballistae*, she saw; instead they were armed with swords, knives, lightweight crossbows. Even the big weapons mounted on the towers were some kind of crossbow. No high energy weapons in a pressure hull; it was a good discipline that the ISF had always tried to follow.

It almost looked neat, industrial, a cross between some vast dormitory and a beehive, she thought. Until she looked more closely at the contents of the cells.

What had looked like worms, or maggots perhaps, were people, all dressed in plain greyish tunics of some kind, crammed in many to a cell. She thought she saw bunks – or maybe shelves would be a better word. People were stacked, like produce in a store. A party was working its way along a corridor that snaked between the cells, hauling at a kind of cart – a cart laden with bodies, she saw, peering down, bodies loosely covered by a tarpaulin, with skinny limbs dangling from the edges.

Titus seemed moved to explain. 'Obviously none of the slaves is allowed above this level because of the ongoing plague. So the security issues are more troublesome than usual.'

'"Troublesome"?'

'We'll find your slave boy. There'll be a record of his cell.' The platform was slowing, and Titus pointed. 'You can see this shaft goes on down to the lower decks, but we'll stop at the walkways and move out laterally from that point.'

For one second Stef bit her tongue. *This isn't your world, Stef. Keep out of trouble ... The hell with it.* She turned on Michael, her self-restraint dissolving. 'You're supposed to be a doctor. Do you have the Hippocratic oath in your world? How can you condone this, how can you cooperate?'

Michael looked at her strangely. 'You ask me? We Greeks think the Romans are soft on their slaves.'

'Soft?'

'There are ways for slaves to win their freedom, in much of the Empire. But to us the slaves are barbarians, irredeemable. Once a slave, always a slave.'

'*But you're a doctor ...* Never mind. I guess my own people don't have an unblemished record. You say there's a plague down here?'

'Yes. It is ...' The words Michael used were not translated by the ColU's earpiece.

She dug her slate out of her tunic pocket. 'ColU, are you there?'

'Always, Stef.'

Of course he was listening in; she wouldn't have been translated otherwise. 'You have chemical sensors in this thing? Can you tell what the plague is from up here?'

Michael and Titus both stared as she held the slate high in the air, pointing the screen down into the honeycomb of a deck.

After a pause, the ColU said, 'A kind of cholera, I think. Clearly endemic on the ship. I imagine that the appropriate vaccines are unknown to this culture. The disease must flare up when water filtering systems fail – it is possible the Romans don't even understand the mechanism, why filtering is effective – and the death rate in the conditions you show me below—'

'Am I in danger?'

'No, Colonel Kalinski. The immunisation programmes the ISF gave you over the years leave you fully protected.'

'And Yuri was surely treated too.'

'By the ISF medics before he was left on Per Ardua, yes.'

She thought quickly. 'Could you manufacture a vaccine? You could start from samples of our blood...'

The ColU hesitated. 'It is not impossible. With the help of the *medicus*, perhaps, the assembly of a cultivation lab from local equipment... it might take time, but it could be done.'

'In time to save a lot of lives?'

'Yes, Colonel Kalinski.'

Titus put his big hand over the slate, gently compelling her to lower it. He said tensely, 'You speak to your oracle through your talking glass. It perturbs me that my commanders seem willing to accept you and your miracles without explanation. *I* would not permit it, were I the centurion—'

'But you are not, Titus Valerius,' Michael said.

'No. I am not. But I believe I understood what you have plotted with the oracle.'

'"Plotted" doesn't seem the right word—'

'You intend to damp down the plague, to preserve the lives of slaves who would otherwise die.'

'That's the idea. What's wrong with that?'

Titus fumed. 'It will break the ship's budget, and bring us all to starvation long before we cross the orbits of Constantius, Vespasian and Augustus, that's what!'

Stef frowned. 'I don't understand.'

Michael said calmly, 'I fear you do not, Stef. You are not used to thinking like a slave-owner. I have mixed with the Brikanti, for example, who use slaves much less sparingly – indeed, mostly for trade with the Empire. But you *are* a star traveller. You must know that a ship like this has a fixed budget, of consumables, water and food and air.'

'Of course.'

'Then you must see that to the centurion – or specifically the *optio* who manages such things – the slave labour aboard is just another asset, to be used according to a plan. In the first year we have so many slaves, who will eat this much food, who will get this amount of work done – of whom *this* number will die of various causes, and in the second year we will have a diminished number of slaves, reduced by the deaths, augmented by births, of course, but most of those will be exposed. And that diminished number is in the plan, as is the food they eat, the work they will do, the further deaths during the year—'

'And so it goes on,' said Stef.

'So it goes on,' Titus said grimly. 'And as long as there's one slave left at the end of the journey to wipe the centurion's arse, the job will be done.'

'We *expect* disease, you see,' Michael said. 'We factor it into the numbers. And if by some miracle you and Collius the oracle were to prevent those deaths—'

'I told you,' Titus said. 'We'll all be chewing the hull plates before we're halfway home. Why, I remember once on campaign—'

'It won't be as bad as that,' Michael said. 'You do dramatise, Titus. There would be culls; the numbers would be managed one way or another. But it would be severely destabilising, and not welcome to the command hierarchy.'

'And the alternative,' Stef said slowly, 'is to let them all die. Down in that pit.'

'We have no choice,' the ColU murmured from the slate.

'No,' Stef growled. 'No! I don't know why the hell I was brought to this world, but I'm damn sure it wasn't to stand by and watch hundreds of men, women, children, die a prevent-able death.' She said desperately to Michael, 'What if we could cut a deal?'

Titus snorted.

But Michael frowned, evidently intrigued. 'What kind of deal?'

'The ship couldn't feed all these people, if they stayed alive. Very well. Let them live, and we'll find ways to feed them. The ColU, Collius, is a pretty resourceful oracle. You saw that already. Why, Titus, it showed you how to make soil down at the *colonia*, did it not?'

'It did. What are you suggesting?'

'Let me take the ColU through this ship's systems. With you, Michael, and the *remiges*.'

The ColU said, 'Colonel Kalinski, I would not advise—'

She buried the slate in her tunic so the ColU could not be heard. 'We'll find a way to *upgrade*. Does that translate? We'll improve the output of the farms. My God, it can't be so hard, it's probably no better than medieval down there. We'll improve the water filtration and reclamation. Show you how to clean up the air better.'

Michael was frowning, unsure. 'You mean you could make the *Malleus* better able to support a larger population of crew. And that way you would have us spare the slaves.'

'That's the idea.'

He shook his head. 'Romans are suspicious of innovation, Stef.'

'Well, they can't be that suspicious, or they wouldn't have put their money into Brikanti starships like this, would they? And that centurion of yours strikes me as an imaginative man.' She was stretching the truth there, but at least Quintus hadn't gone running and screaming when two strangers and a robot from an alternate history had come wandering through his brand new Hatch. 'Suppose the *Malleus Jesu* were to return, not just with its mission at Romulus completed, but new and improved – a prototype for a new wave of starships to come? What if he were able to present *that* to his own commanders? Romans might not like innovation. What about opportunity, staring them in the face?'

Titus and Michael looked at her, and at each other.

'We must talk this over,' Michael said. 'Before the *optio* first of all.'

'I agree,' said Titus.

Michael waggled a finger at her. 'And don't start meddling before you've got specific approval from the centurion – and the *trierarchus*, come to that. Or we'll all be for the Brikanti long jump.'

Which, Stef had already gathered, meant being thrown out of an airlock.

Titus growled, 'But first let's do what we came for and find your slave boy, Stef Kalinski, if he's still alive.' He leered at her. 'And what then? Will you come with me down into the pen, and confront these dying maggots you insist on saving?'

She couldn't meet his gaze.

TWO

CHAPTER 15

AD 2215; AUC 2968

When Ari Guthfrithson walked into her classroom, Penny Kalinski was trying to teach the descendants of ancient Britons and Vikings about the contingency of history.

She looked down at her notes on the desk before her, silently cursing the need to read her own handwritten scrawl in this world without computers, cursing the inadequacy of her antique pair of reading glasses to cope with the slow drift of her eyesight. Two years after arriving here, aged seventy-one, there were still some things she couldn't get used to. And she tried not to let the *druidh* put her off her stride.

But Ari settled into a place at the back of the class beside Marie Golvin, once a bridge crew member on board the ISF ship *Tatania*, and now a teacher here at Penny's Academy. Marie was a figure from Penny's old past, constantly reassuring.

'The Mongols, then,' Penny said. She checked her notes. 'It is the late twentieth century.' The thirteenth in Penny's history. The Brikanti, like the Romans, used the old Julian calendar, applying crude leap-year corrections as the centuries passed – and, like the Romans, the Brikanti counted their years since the founding of Rome. It had taken some effort for the newcomers to match their own Gregorian-calendar dates to those in use here. 'The Mongols, under their rapacious but visionary khans, have exploded from the steppe and have rampaged into the eastern provinces of the Empire, tearing through Pannonia and Noricum and even Rhaetia. They besiege and destroy town after town. They are *exterminating* Romans. And, who knows? If they cannot be stopped they may turn on Italia, even reach Rome itself. The legacy of centuries of civilisation would be lost, the statues smashed, the books burned, the churches plundered. Perhaps Rome and the Empire could never rise again, even if the Mongol horde could some day be driven out.

'And to the east it is no better. An equally ferocious horde, under generals of equal genius, is tearing its way into the soft belly of the Xin dominion. They don't seek territory, these are not empire builders like the Caesars; they seek nothing but booty, and land to pasture their horses, and women and girls to bear their children.'

Her pupils were no older than twelve years old, and their eyes widened at that last detail. But Brikanti was not a prissy culture. And nor had it been much of a stretch for Penny, a woman, to be effectively running this Academy; women had freedom and power here compared to many other cultures – even those less barbaric than the Mongols.

'There was a moment, then, on the cusp of the twenty-first century, when the future of civilisation itself, the very *idea* of it, was under threat. The European plains might now be inhabited by nothing but the horses of illiterate herdsmen, grazing grass growing in the rubble of ruined cities...'

Even as she spoke, concentrating on each still-unfamiliar Brikanti word, she was aware of the grandeur of the setting.

Her two dozen students, all children of the wealthy Eboraki merchants who were able to afford the fees she charged, sat in neat rows under the looming conical roof of this schoolhouse. Brand new, and commissioned with the help of Ari himself for the purpose of her Academy – which she had dedicated to Saint Jonbar, who she claimed to Ari was a powerful figure in her own lost version of Christianity – it actually had the feel of great age. It was a roundhouse, like a relic of the European Iron Age of her own history. But the long trunks of the frame, gathered into a stout cone over her head, had been brought across the Atlantic from Canada, which in this history was a province of

118

the Brikanti federation – an expensive import, but for many centuries no trees in Pritanike had been allowed to grow so tall before being cut down for use. The trunks had been set up on a base of concrete, and brilliant fluorescent strip lights were suspended from the apex of the house: to Penny it was a strange mixture of ancient and modern technologies.

In this setting, two years after her arrival aboard the *Ukelwydd*, she had established her Academy, whose principal purposes were to teach maths and science – especially her own subject, physics, which was far in advance of anything known here. But she had insisted to Ari that she include classes like this, on wider aspects of culture. She said the goal was to educate herself in this new course of history. Ari had bought it; he had come from a wide-ranging educational background himself.

But she suspected that Ari suspected she had a deeper agenda. After all, two years on, Ari was still one of only a handful of Brikanti to know that she came from a different historical background – and, she thought, one of even fewer who actually believed the reality of it all. But, suspicious as he was, he had allowed her to go ahead with these side projects. Penny wondered if Beth Eden Jones had had something to do with that – maybe she'd used a little pillow talk. And Beth was, after all, carrying Ari's baby …

And here he was now, sitting at the back of her class like some school inspector, a half-smile playing on his lips as she lectured these children about the possibility of counterfactuals. Well, he was right to be suspicious. Of course she had an agenda. Of course she was playing a long game. Saint Jonbar, indeed!

She focused on her students, on the Mongols.

'So everything hung in the balance. All history might have been changed. But that did not happen. Does anybody know—'

There were some shout-outs, but a forest of hands were raised more politely, as she'd patiently taught them. This was a warrior culture after all, they did have Vikings in their ancestry; at the beginning Marie had said she was lucky the students didn't try to attract her attention by throwing axes at her head.

She picked out a student at random. 'Yes, Freydis?'

The girl stood up. 'The great Roman Emperor Constantius XI sent an embassy to the Xin empress, and persuaded her to join forces and attack the Mongols.' She sat down just as sharply.

'Yes. That's essentially right. Except that it was actually the other way around...' That history-changing bit of state craft, an alliance between bitter rivals that had probably saved two empires, had been initiated by strategic geniuses in the Xin court. But Roman historians, propagandists all, had from that moment given the credit to Constantius. The Brikanti, for all their stated rivalry with Rome, were in some ways in awe of the mighty Empire that had once come so close to destroying them, and had allowed their own view of history to be dazzled by such lies.

'But the point is that because the two rulers *were* able to put aside their own suspicion and ambition, the Mongols were defeated. Without that everything would have been different. That's what I want you to take away from this lesson today... Yes, Freydis.'

The girl stood again. 'Maybe it's like when Queen Kartimandia told the Caesar to attack Germania and not Pritanike. If she *hadn't* done that...'

Her face shone with the excitement of discovery, of finding a new idea, a whole new way of thinking. Penny was no natural teacher, and at seventy-one years old she was finding the daily classroom routine a grind. But at such moments, when a spark was lit in a young imagination, she could see why people would teach.

But Freydis's contribution hadn't gone down well with her classmates; there was laughter and catcalls. 'Yes, Freydis, and you'd be speaking Latin now!'

'So would you,' Freydis snapped back.

'All right, all right.' Penny stood, holding up her hands. 'That's enough for now. Time to break for lunch—'

The room turned into a near riot as the students grabbed their stuff and jumped up from their benches. Marie Golvin yelled with parade-ground lungs, 'Back here in one hour for relativistic navigation!'

Ari Guthfrithson, with quiet dignity, let the tide of youngsters wash past him. Then, when the room was empty, he walked towards Penny, clapping his hands. 'Skilfully done. And all delivered in correct Brikanti, halting and with an exotic accent as it is. I do continue to wonder *why*, you know, you pepper their brains with such ideas, the fragility of history. It wasn't the stated purpose of the Academy after all.'

Before Penny had to answer Marie Golvin, who had been collecting up scrolls and paper scraps from around the room, joined them. 'Will you have lunch with us, *druidh*? Nothing exciting, I'm afraid.'

'I'd be honoured. And that was a neat deflection, by the way, Lieutenant Golvin.' It had taken him some time to memorise the term for Golvin's ISF rank. 'Well, shall we walk?'

CHAPTER 16

The Academy of Saint Jonbar had been established on the edge of Eboraki, away from the crowded ancient core of the city, in what Penny might have called an outer suburb. The refectory where they would eat, though attached to the Academy, was a short walk out of the campus and towards town.

The main schoolhouse was one of a cluster of new buildings, all roundhouses, which included a gymnasium, a library, an arts centre, a small clinic, a workshop for pottery, metalwork and other crafts, and a Christian chapel. The buildings were arranged in neat rows, like the city itself aligned not north-south but on a north-east to south-west axis, the direction of the solstice sunrise and sunset, following Brikanti tradition. There was a grassy playing field, and a kind of parade ground where some of the students, cadets in the armed forces of the Brikanti, could practise marching, and wage mock battles with swords and even blank-loaded firearms. But all this was set in an oak grove, one of a number studded around the city, the tree a symbol of ancient *druidh* wisdom.

Penny and Marie had together designed this complex, with advice from Ari and other locals, and all paid for by money Ari had managed to extract from Navy contingency funds – the military-college aspect had been part of the price they'd had to pay for that. To Penny, even now, it looked like a museum piece, like a reconstruction of some Iron Age village rather than a brand new, living, breathing facility for young people.

Of course those few students who went on to become full *druidh* wouldn't be so young when they finished. Ari, for instance, had gone through a few years of general education, including history, geography and philosophy, followed by *twenty* years of specialist study in law, politics, and mathematics and astronomy. Nowadays this was a literate culture, but Ari had told Penny that the old pre-literacy tradition of memory training, the recall of long passages, was still used to develop the mind. Mathematics was particularly strong here. Penny herself had supervised classes of young children learning to reproduce the outlines of mistletoe seeds using the arcs of circles, carefully drawn with compasses and pens. It was easy to see, given such beginnings, how the Brikanti grew up to be such fine astronomers and interstellar navigators: from the geometry of a mistletoe seed to the trajectory of a starship.

The principal town of Eboraki was evidently a more ancient community than the Roman-planted towns in Gaul and Germania, and the older traditions of Celtic architecture and town planning lingered on, not obliterated by later Roman developments as in Penny's timeline. A grid pattern of roads of gravel and crushed rock separated houses of wattle and daub with thatched roofs, all surrounded by a monumental wall, outside which lay cemeteries and funeral pyres. The higher ground in the centre of the city – in Penny's world dominated by a cathedral that had stood on the site of a demolished *principia,* headquarters of a Roman legion – did bear the remains of a two-thousand-year-old fort, but here it had been a Brikanti-built bastion, a relic of the days when continental invasions had been feared and experienced. *This* Britain, for better or worse, had never been severed from its own past by a Roman sword.

Studying this new history with her students, Penny had come to understand how much harm the Brikanti and their continental cousins, who Penny had grown up knowing as the Celts, had suffered at the hands of the Romans. Once the Celtic nations had prospered across Europe from Britain to the Danube, but the Romans' empire-building expansion had driven them back. Though Britain, in this history, had remained independent of Rome, elsewhere the Celts had been crushed. When Caesar had invaded Gaul, a prosperous, settled and literate country, of a population of eight million he had slaughtered one million and enslaved another million. One detail particularly remembered by Brikanti historians was that Caesar had severed the hands of rebels, so they could not gather their harvest. This history was not well known in Penny's timeline. Here, it had never been forgotten.

And Brikanti had grown traditions of its own. This was no empire; it was a federation of nations, and a democracy, of sorts, with traditions inherited from both its British and Scandinavian forebears. That old fort on the hill was now the seat of the Althing, an assembly with representatives of Brikanti holdings around the world, and the most powerful single individual was not a hereditary emperor but an elected *logsogumadr*, a law-speaker.

But this was a world that had been industrialised for centuries, a process that had proceeded without conscience or compensation. So, even on a bright midsummer day like today, a pall of smog hung over the city. No trees survived in Eboraki, save in the carefully preserved oak groves. In this capital people dressed brightly, in embroidered cloaks over colourfully striped tunics and leggings, adorned with beads of blue glass or amber, and with torcs of steel or silver at their necks. But they routinely wore face masks and goggles to keep the muck out of their eyes and lungs, and life expectancy in a culture capable of sending ships to the planets was shockingly low. Nobody here, of course, could imagine things could be different. It was when Penny was least busy, when she walked in the city looking at the children coughing into their filthy masks, that she most acutely missed the world she had left behind.

And yet, as the months had passed, to walk these streets at the times of solstice, midsummer and midwinter, with the low sun of morning or evening suspended over the streets and filling the city with light, had pleased her in ways she would have found hard to describe.

*

The meals in the small refectory were prepared by students as part of their education, under the supervision of a few towns-people. The fare, served at rough-hewn wooden tables, was traditional Brikanti, meat-heavy, laden with butter and vege-table sauces and served with slabs of gritty bread – although Roman fare was also available, cheese, olives. Rice and potatoes were expensive foreign luxuries, even in the Brikanti capital. All the *Tatania* crew had had problems with this diet, mostly from a lack of roughage. But Penny had learned not to try to change some things, such as the Brikanti habit of serving meals, even to very young children, with watered-down mead or beer. Or the habit of eating your food with the knife you wore at your belt.

Still, the meat, a richly stewed beef, was tender and tasty, and for a while they ate without speaking.

At length Ari said, picking up the conversation where they'd left off, 'You don't need to thank me for visiting. For one thing it's my job; I'm expected to report to the Navy funding body who provided the cash for all this. For another it's a pleasure to see how you're getting on. I sometimes feel as if I connect you all, the crew of the *Tatania*.'

'We are all rather scattered,' Penny admitted.

'But that's not a bad thing. It shows you're finding places in a society that must be very strange to you. How's Jiang, by the way?'

'Doing fine. Our house is comfortable. You know that he is working at the college; he gives classes in kernel engineering, among other topics.'

'I can understand he will be finding it a particular challenge here. We like to believe we are world citizens, we Brikanti. In fact it is very rare to see a Xin face, even here in Eboraki, the capital.'

Marie Golvin said, 'Well, he wouldn't call himself Xin, but the point's taken. He doesn't go out much.'

'He'll be fine,' Penny assured her. 'And so's General McGregor, we hear.'

'I saw him recently,' Ari said. 'Lecturing junior officers on

125

the command and control techniques of your *International Space Fleet*.' Through his smooth Brikanti, it was odd to hear him break into English. 'He's very impressive.'

'He always has been. And I've known him since he was seventeen years old,' Penny said, feeling a little wistful.

Ari watched her sharply. 'That's true in one of the reality strands you inhabited, so I hear. In the other—'

'Yes, yes. In the other it was my twin sister who knew him – save she wasn't a twin, for I didn't exist at all. Whatever. I always knew Lex would land on his feet, wherever he ended up.'

'You can see he wishes he could shed three decades and fly with the youngsters. To battle the Xin for the treasures of the Tears of Ymir!'

'That sounds like Lex, all right. He's visited us a few times. He's most struck by the special relativity we teach here. In our reality, so he says, he always struggled with the maths. Here, you had no relativity theory. But you did have the kernels, and you *discovered* relativity experimentally, by driving your kernel ships up against the light barrier, and finding out the hard way that the clocks slow and the relativistic mass piles up.'

Marie said, 'I heard of engineers being executed because they couldn't make their ships travel faster than light.'

'That was the Romans and the Xin, not us,' Ari said. 'And the stories are apocryphal anyhow.'

Penny mopped up her stew with her rubbery bread. 'And Beth? How is your new wife, Ari?'

He smiled, but Penny sensed reserve. 'Well, you understand that she is not formally my wife, since she had no family to give her away ... She is fine.'

Penny and Marie shared a glance.

Marie said, 'That's all you have to say? How's the baby? She's overdue, isn't she?'

He seemed to consider his words carefully. 'We are dealing with the challenge of the birth in our own way.'

Penny frowned. '"Challenge"? What's challenging about it?

Your medicine is pretty good when it comes to childbirth. I checked it over myself when Beth said she was pregnant, and I had Earthshine consult too. Her age would always be an issue, she is thirty-eight now ... Why is this a challenge?'

'This is a private matter,' he said coldly, his pale face empty. Suddenly he had never seemed more alien to Penny, more foreign.

'But—'

'Instead, let us talk of Earthshine. Of your group it is he who has made the most dramatic entry into our society, as I'm sure you know. Even if his true nature is carefully kept a secret. As far as most people know he is simply another survivor of a ship of mysterious origin.

'And he seems to be attempting superhuman feats. You must know that he is now at Höd.' The Brikanti name for Ceres. 'He intends, with the party of supporters he has gathered around him, to move on to Mars. In a way this fulfils the promise of the images he showed us when we first encountered you: the great buildings on the Mars of your reality. But here, he claims, he will achieve much more.'

Penny grunted. 'I often thought he'd have made a great salesman. If only of himself.'

'He intends—' Ari mimed a shove with his upraised hand '—to push Höd out of its track around the sun, and make it sail to Mars.' He looked at them. 'This is what he claims. I have performed my own estimates of the problem, the energies required. Do you think this is achievable?'

Penny, startled, looked at Marie.

Marie said, 'With a hefty enough booster, any such feat is possible. And this society is knee-deep in kernels, which have been used in ways we never dared ... Yes, I would say it is possible.'

'Earthshine claims he will do this to deliver to Mars raw materials which that planet lacks. Water, other compounds, some metals perhaps. He intends, he says, to rebuild Mars.'

Penny said to Marie in English, 'Terraforming. I bet that's what

127

he means. These people have no conception of such schemes, since they don't even have a word for "ecology".'

Ari frowned. 'I cannot understand what you are saying.'

'I apologise,' said Marie formally. 'In our reality there were grand plans to remake Mars into a world like the Earth. Maybe other worlds too, Venus, Titan – umm, the largest moon of Augustus. But on Mars it would mean importing a lot of volatiles – the kind of stuff Ceres, Höd, is made of.' She looked at Penny doubtfully. 'I guess it could be made to work. If Ceres could be brought into Martian orbit—'

'That would take a heck of a lot of delta-vee.'

'Yes. But then you could break it up slowly, drop the material you need into the air, with Ceres itself as a construction shack.'

Penny nodded. 'I do know there was evidence on Earth, our Earth, of major climate disturbances caused by impacts of comets or asteroids. Fifty-five million years back, a spike in the carbon dioxide levels – doubled in a single year. So the idea is not implausible.'

Ari listened carefully, picking through the technical language. 'Hairy stars and the Tears of Ymir, falling to Terra – and now to Mars. So do you think Earthshine is sincere? Perhaps we should be wary. He is proposing to deploy large energies, to move huge masses around the planetary system – *our* planetary system.' He grimaced. 'If he is allowed to wield such energies, your artificial man would be as powerful as a god.'

Penny said, 'So he was before, in our reality. But here's what you have to understand, Ari. Earthshine and his brothers, the Core AIs, were significant powers on our Earth. But, like gods, they always had their own agenda. An agenda that might or might not coincide with the interests of mankind ... And whatever Earthshine says about Höd now, we'll have to remember that here too his own deep agenda comes first.'

'Very well. And what might that "deep agenda" now be?'

'We've no way of knowing.'

'I recall the talk of your "impossible sister", Penelope Kalinski. Earthshine was fascinated by that. You've said so yourself.

128

Earthshine detected this – unravelling of history – before he and you witnessed it on a much larger scale. Prescient, don't you think? Wouldn't he pursue such an interest here?'

Sure he would, she thought. It was odd to think that even now she and the rest of the *Tatania* crew were still dependent on Earthshine, for the translator gadgets he had provided them all with, and regularly downloaded updates of vocabulary and grammar. And she did remember how obsessive he had seemed about the interference in human history by an agency unknown, right back to the beginning of her own involvement with him, going back more than three decades of her complicated life: *I am everywhere. And I am starting to hear your footsteps, you Hatch-makers. I can hear the grass grow. And I can hear you …*

Ari said acutely, 'I find myself deeply drawn to the question, in fact. Might there be evidence to be unturned concerning these strange phenomena in *my* world? Traces of lost histories. Like the anomalous carving on the tombstone of your mother, Penny, in that graveyard in Lutetia Parisiorum of which you spoke.'

His mention of that personal memory startled Penny. She had been open with Ari, mostly, about her experience of the reality-shifting they had all endured. Now she wondered if that had been wise, if she understood Ari and *his* agendas. She was aware that Marie, too, was looking increasingly wary.

'So have you found anything?'

'Not yet. But I'll keep looking.' He stared into her eyes. 'That makes you uncomfortable. Why?' When there was no reply he went on, 'I sometimes think you are fortunate that we Brikanti are not more curious about this phenomenon. We are not so *scientific* as you.' He pronounced the English word carefully. 'We are cruder philosophers. Perhaps we are more prepared to accept the miraculous, the unexplained, than you are. Unexplained phenomena such as your own existence. We don't question; we just accept.'

'All save you.'

'All save me. But why are you wary of the question?' He

turned on Marie. 'And why do *you* recoil as we speak of these matters, Marie Golvin?'

'Because I can't sleep,' Marie blurted. 'That's why. Is it so hard to understand?' Penny covered her hand with her own, but Marie pulled away. 'Look – we saw billions put to the torch – everybody we knew, probably, whole worlds, Earth itself. And now here I am in this stupid place, trying to learn your dumb languages, doing this makework job you've given me, and pretending I've got a future here. I don't even know if *your* Jesus died for me, or not.'

On the verge of tears, she seemed much younger than her twenty-seven years, and Penny longed to hug her, to reassure her. But Marie Golvin was an ISF officer, and that wouldn't do at all.

'I'm sorry,' said Marie now, getting herself under control. 'Excuse me.' She stood and walked away.

'And I too am sorry,' Ari said to Penny. 'For provoking that.'

'Not your fault,' Penny snapped. 'Well, not entirely. You do keep prying.'

'You're lucky that others don't.'

'Maybe, but that doesn't help. It's survivor guilt, Ari. It's when you forget it all – when you are immersed in something, happy in yourself, enjoying what you're doing – and then you remember all that has been lost, and the guilt comes crashing down again. That's when it's worst. Marie's particularly vulnerable now she's away from the protection of Lex McGregor. The ISF, the military discipline, was her whole life. And then there's the hope.'

'Hope?'

'Of somehow, one day, finding a way back home, back to our timeline.'

'Ah.'

'It's entirely irrational, I think we all know that, but it's hard not to succumb. After all *this* can never be home, for us. And it's harder for the young, I think. As the years go by.'

Ari said, 'But Marie told me she was a Christian, in the

130

tradition as it existed in your world. Just now she spoke of Jesu – *Jesus*. Should that not be a consolation? She says she wondered if, in crossing realities, she had undergone something like the Rapture. Are you aware of that?' He closed his eyes, remembering. 'The text she recited to me was this: "For the Lord himself shall descend from heaven with a shout, with the voice of the archangel, and with the trump of God: and the dead in Christ shall rise first: then we which are alive and remain shall be caught up together with them in the clouds, to meet the Lord in the air: and so shall we ever be with the Lord. Wherefore comfort one another with these words." From a letter to the Thessalonians. Such material does not exist in *our* Bible, not the authorised version, and nor does the legend of the Rapture. I think, you see, that Marie fears not that she has been taken up to heaven by God, but has been left behind in the desolation that remains—'

'*You.*'

Beth Eden Jones came stalking into the refectory, trailed by an anxious-looking Marie Golvin.

CHAPTER 17

Ari and Penny stood to meet her.

Beth was wearing Brikanti costume, as they all were after two years here, tunic, trousers, leather boots, a light cloak. Though she looked heavy, she was evidently no longer pregnant, Penny saw immediately. And in her arms she cradled a bundle wrapped in blankets.

Penny said, 'Beth? What the hell – is that what I think it is? You've had your baby? I'm sorry – I lost track of the date, I didn't hear any news...'

Ari stood silently, his face like thunder.

Beth stood before her husband, glaring at him, but she spoke to Penny. 'Yes, Penny, this is my baby. By this *monster*.'

Ari stared back. He said in a kind of growl, 'Not here, woman. Not now.'

'Then where, if not before my friends? Shall I go back to your home, your family, and wait until the next time you try to kill her?'

Heads turned around the refectory.

Penny said sharply, 'Beth. Whatever the hell you're talking about – come on, sit down.' She put her arm around Beth's shoulder, and could feel her trembling, could see the stain of tears around her eyes. She looked a lot older than her thirty-eight years, old and drained. But she complied, sitting at the table which still bore the remains of their meal. Penny said, 'You too, Ari, don't loom over her like that. Beth, do you want anything? A drink—'

'Nothing.' Beth's and Ari's eyes were locked still.

132

Penny sat down and glanced up at Marie. 'Bring some water. Umm, and some hot milk.'

Marie hurried away.

Penny put her hand on Beth's arm and leaned forward to see. The baby, at least, was sleeping peacefully, its face a crumple. 'Oh, Beth. It's beautiful.'

'She. She's a girl. She's called Mardina.'

'After your mother.' Penny looked up at Ari, whose face showed nothing but hostility. 'I don't understand any of this. What's wrong? Is she not healthy?'

'The baby is fine,' Ari said coldly. 'But she was – unintended.'

'They don't hold with women my age having kids,' Beth said. 'The Brikanti. It's a rough and ready rule. You can understand why; they fly warships in space but their medicine is medieval.'

'But you got pregnant anyway.'

'It was an accident. Yes, I got pregnant. I was told it would be all right, that the baby would be accepted.'

'You probably misunderstood,' Ari said. 'You misheard the nuances. I told you there would have to be a trial—'

'They exposed her,' Beth said to Penny. 'While I slept.'

Penny was bewildered. 'They *what*?'

'They *took* her, Ari's family, the women. Took her from me. They stripped away her blankets, and put her on the roof of the house, naked. She would be allowed to live, you see, if she survived the exposure. And if *he* chose to bring her in. It was to be his choice, not mine.'

Penny turned on Ari. 'That seems unnecessarily brutal.'

He managed to smile, self-deprecating. 'It's not the time for a history lesson. You may blame the Romans from whom we borrowed the custom. The rule is indeed – what did you say? – *rough and ready*. Better a few healthy children are lost, than that society is burdened with the weak—'

Beth snapped, 'The father gets to choose to save her, or not. Not the mother. Supposedly the father's a better judge. Most mothers will have families to back them up – sometimes *they* take the child, though the mother can't see her again. But I had no one to help me. *And he chose to abandon her.*'

Ari shook his head. 'Most men in my position would have done the same.'

'But you found out, Beth,' Penny prompted.

'I busted out of that damn house where they were keeping me,' Beth said. 'I got up on the roof, and saved my baby, and I came straight here, where I knew you would be. I wonder how many laws I broke doing *that*. Will you prosecute me, scholar? Will I be thrown in jail, or mutilated, or executed, or whatever else you do to disobedient mothers?'

Ari shook his head again. 'No, no. There are always exceptions. You will be welcome in my home, with my family – with the baby—'

'Not after this.' She turned to Penny with a look of pleading. 'Let me stay here. With you.'

'Of course you can stay,' Penny said immediately.

Ari stood. 'This changes nothing. This Academy is here at my discretion. In a sense you are still under my roof—'

'They stay,' Penny said firmly, 'with us.'

'And the future? As the child has needs, as she grows?'

Penny sighed. 'We'll deal with that when we come to it. I think it's best if you go now, Ari Guthfrithson.'

He stood still for a moment, clenching one fist. Then he stalked away, almost colliding with Marie Golvin as she approached with a tray of drinks.

Stef watched him go. 'I thought I understood him. I thought we communicated, as scholars. *Druidh*. But now—'

'You don't know him at all,' Beth said. 'I didn't. These people aren't like us, Stef. Not even Ari. Not even the man I thought I loved, who fathered my child. *Especially* not him.'

CHAPTER 18

'ColU, I thought Quintus Fabius was a pompous ass from the moment he came strutting down from that airship.'

'He is a good commander, Yuri Eden. But as he hails from what is still regarded as an outer province of the Empire, he has to be more Roman than the Romans.'

'So he's got a chip on his shoulder. Boo hoo. Actually he reminded me of that other pompous ass Lex McGregor ... I'm sorry. Kind of lost my way there.'

'Relax, Yuri Eden. Breathe your oxygen.'

'Yeah, yeah.'

'Do you remember what we were talking about? I am here to witness your final testament.'

'Always busy, eh, ColU? Look, just talk to me. I've had enough of my own miserable life for now. You're the nearest thing I've got to a friend on this tub – you and Stef, but you were there first, right?'

'Even if I was an instrument of the ISF, the organisation that stranded you against your will on an alien world.'

'Well, there is that. No hard feelings, eh? And don't tell me I need to rest. I'll soon be enjoying the long sleep, drifting between the stars in a Roman sarcophagus. Fine way to go, actually.'

'You are aware that I did quietly suggest to the *optio* that that would be the best course of action regarding the disposal

135

of your body, and indeed Colonel Kalinski's if it came to that. As opposed to depositing your corpses in the recycling tanks.'

'Don't spare my feelings, will you?'

'After all, we hail from another timeline. Your bodies may contain pathogens exotic to this reality. And both of your bodies contain foreign elements, even dental work for example, which might be harmful in the ship's food chain.'

'Ha! Oh, don't make me laugh, ColU. Now I have an image of my false teeth chewing their way out of some fat legionary's gut.'

'Well, you don't wear false teeth, Yuri Eden. But the image is an amusing one.'

'Don't laugh too hard.'

'Do you wish me to call the *medicus* again? Michael did say that if—'

'Oh, don't fuss, ColU. If I want the damn quack I'll call him. It's only been palliative care, and you know that as well as I do. He can treat the actual condition no better than you can. But with that suite of drugs he has, all those psychoactive substances from the South American jungles, he can play my level of pain like a fiddle ... You know, I sometimes wonder if I haven't carried these damn passengers all my life.'

'That's possible, actually, Yuri Eden. Your body has been exposed to a series of extraordinary environments. This is your second journey through interstellar space. You spent decades on Per Ardua, a planet of a flare star. Before that, you spent some time under a dome on Mars, a world lacking a thick atmosphere, an ozone layer. Even before that, a journey across interplanetary space from Earth to Mars.'

'Also I passed through Hatches. Three times.'

'Indeed. And before all *that* you spent a century in a casket, buried in a vault in Antarctica with a thousand others. The casualty rates from cancers of various sorts of survivors of that process—'

'We called it "freezer burn". So the parents who put me on ice and stuffed me in a hole—'

'Surely they sought to send you to a better time, Yuri Eden.'

'And now, it turns out, after all I've survived, it will be the damn cryo that kills me off in the end. Oh, the irony.'

'I am only speculating, Yuri Eden.'

'I know, buddy. I don't take it personally.'

'It is to be regretted that more advanced medicine is not available. I hope to help the ship's navigators devise a medical scanner to emulate the functions of the slate I used to diagnose your condition.'

'The navigators? Oh, your Arab buddies, in their observation blisters ...'

'This vessel navigates by the stars, by astronomical observations made by the Arab teams.'

'These Arab buddies of yours sound like they are as advanced scientifically as anybody else in this timeline.'

'It would seem so. Here, the Prophet was born in a settled and stable province of a strong Roman Empire. Much as in our timeline, Islamic civilisation, the *dar-al Islam*, flourished, but under Roman protection. There were no centuries of inter-faith conflict in Europe – no crusades, for instance. Even in the pre-Christian days, the Romans were always pragmatic about local religions. To the Romans, Islam is a muscular sister creed of the Christianity that is their official state religion.'

'And the Arabs are the best astronomers.'

'They are. Yuri Eden, I hope you will have the chance to see their observation blisters. There is an atmosphere of calm – of learning, of reverence. They are like college study rooms, or religious sanctuaries. Indeed one of them is dedicated as a mosque.

'In space, Moslems were always drawn to astronomy because of the need to find reliably the position of Earth, and therefore Mecca, for the purposes of daily prayers. But the Arabs have gone much further. They have fine optical telescopes, but also spectroscopes to analyse the light – though they have no image capture more advanced than wet-chemistry photography. And they have made a suite of discoveries, of more or less relevance to the mission of the *Malleus Jesu*. Of course a kernel ship under

137

heavy acceleration, like this one, is a rather noisy platform. And they have to compensate for relativistic distortion, so close do we travel to the speed of light. They have developed sophisticated rule-of-thumb mathematics to achieve this, without, again, having the underlying theory...

'Yuri Eden, the Arabs allowed me to peruse their libraries. They have painstakingly compiled good maps of the cosmic background radiation, the relic glow of the Big Bang – not that they have the cosmological theories to describe it that way.

'And they seek out life-bearing planets, among the stars we pass. Targets for future missions like this one. Living worlds have certain characteristics. On Earth, for instance, the atmosphere holds oxygen and methane, reactive gases that if left to themselves would combine with other substances – iron ore in the rocks would rust – and be lost to the air. But it is the action of life that replenishes those reservoirs. Another kind of biosphere would produce other kinds of traces. Sometimes you can tell there's life simply from colour changes, visible from space. Early Earth was probably predominantly purple, on the sea coasts anyhow...'

'All this you found in their libraries? With Chu Yuen as your search engine. Ha! I imagine poor Chu getting pretty tired turning pages—'

'Usually it's unravelling scrolls. But, yes, it can be like that... One striking observation, Yuri Eden, is that many worlds the Arabs have observed are not living, but *dead*: once life-bearing, but evidently killed off, at least at the surface. And in some cases recently. You can tell this from remote observations. If all life on Earth were ended suddenly, the decomposition of a glut of corpses would dump ethane into the air, in great quantities. Without the water cycle mediated by the plants, there would be a rapid heating spike. And so on. All this can be observed from afar. Yuri Eden, the Arabs have made many such discoveries.'

'What could kill off whole worlds? War?'

'Perhaps, Yuri Eden.'

'And with who knows what history-tweaking strangeness to follow? If our experience is any precedent.'

'One can only speculate. Of course the Arabs also search for kernels. Worlds laden with them, targets for future Hatch-building expeditions. Again there are certain characteristic radiation signatures you can spot from afar. They have even begun to map the distribution of kernel-bearing worlds, and Hatches, across this part of the galaxy. Their maps are difficult to decipher, in fact: not maps as we know them but more itineraries, lists of distances and directions between locations ... It appears that there is a kind of network. A certain percentage of kernel worlds are concentrated towards the centre of the galaxy. As if whatever initiated this process originated deeper in the galaxy, and the network of Hatch-building has been spreading to the outer reaches ever since.'

'Hm. What's different about the centre of the galaxy?'

'It is older, in a sense. The galaxy is like a vast factory for manufacturing stars from interstellar dust and gas. Star-making started close to the centre, and is spreading out to the periphery. It is thought that towards the centre there may be habitable worlds born a billion years before the Earth.'

'So the Hatches may have been started off by some ancient intelligence, lurking on one of these old, old worlds ...'

'The Arabs' observations would fit that, Yuri Eden.'

'But what's it all for? Do you ever get the feeling we're missing the big picture here, ColU? All the strangeness – the kernels, the Hatches, the dumping of whole histories ... Maybe this is my South American drugs talking.'

'Mostly we are too busy trying to survive to think too deeply about such matters, Yuri Eden.'

'And also too busy riding these various gift horses to look them too closely in the mouth. The kernels are just too damn useful ... But we do ask such questions – or at least you do, ColU.'

'I try. My mission has always been to nurture the humanity around me – to nurture you and your family, Yuri Eden. By doing that I must consider the wider questions of which you speak. I must consider the future. And some of what I have learned about the future disturbs me.'

'Maybe the drugs are hitting me again. Or else they're wearing off. Run that by me again. The future?'

'*I have seen it in the sky*, Yuri Eden. I told you that the Arab astronomers have carefully observed the background radiation from the Big Bang. That radiation, and distortions in it – ripples, non-homogeneities, polarisation – carries a great deal of information about the wider structure of the universe. After all, it has permeated the whole cosmos from the beginning. For instance, our cosmologists looked for evidence of other universes than our own. An interaction of two universes, a collision in some higher dimension, might leave echoes in the background, tremendous circles in the sky. But I, studying the Arab records with a depth of understanding that they cannot share, have seen ... something else.'

'What? The suspense is killing me, and I'm already dying.'

'I apologise, Yuri Eden. I believe I have seen evidence of superluminal events. Faster-than-light phenomena.'

'What the *hell* are you talking about now? Warp drive? Some kind of super-starship? A higher civilisation?'

'Not that. Not on that scale. Much bigger. Please listen, Yuri Eden. In relativity theory, you know that nothing can travel through spacetime faster than light. That was Einstein's most fundamental discovery. Even a transition through a Hatch, say from Mercury to Per Ardua, by whatever unknown mechanism enables such transitions, is marginally slower than lightspeed. But there is a get-out clause in the physics.'

'Go on.'

'Nothing can travel *through spacetime* faster than light. But spacetime is a substance, of a kind; it has structure. It can be distorted ... Yuri Eden, waves can propagate in spacetime itself. And they *can* travel faster than light. The theoreticians have wondered if such warps could be used to carry ships at superluminal speeds.'

140

'Beating light by surfing spacetime waves...'

'That's the idea, Yuri Eden. We never achieved a warp drive. But warp waves, as described by the theory, would emit certain kinds of exotic radiations. Even if we could never create them, we thought we could detect them.

'Yuri Eden, I think I have seen the traces of warp ripples in the cosmic background radiation. Not small, contained signals, as you would associate with a starship. These are relics of events on a tremendous scale. By which I mean billions of light years wide, events spanning the universe.'

'Larger than galaxies—'

'Larger than superclusters of galaxies.'

'Nurse! I think my drip's come loose.'

'I apologise, Yuri Eden. I will discuss all this with Colonel Kalinski; perhaps she will be able to make it clearer. But, you see, I am struggling to grasp the hypothesis I am formulating.'

'What hypothesis?'

'Imagine that in the future there is a – cataclysm. A tremendously violent event of some kind, spanning space – spanning the entire universe. This event is so energetic that among its effects are ripples in spacetime, tremendous waves—'

'Ah. Warp waves, which can travel back in time.'

'Yes, Yuri Eden. I believe that – in these faint traces of structure in the cosmic background reaction, visible to the Arab astronomers in the silence of their observation capsules – I am witnessing a kind of foreshadowing, echoes travelling back in time...'

'Echoes from the future. But echoes of what?'

'Something terrible.'

'Umm. Well, you're not given to exaggeration, ColU.'

'Are you falling asleep, Yuri Eden?'

'Not just yet. All this talk of calamity in the future. You know, ColU, I don't fear dying. In fact, I feel like I died already, a number of times. All those doors I had to pass through, from my own time to the future, from Mars to Per Ardua...'

'It will just be another door, Yuri Eden.'

'I know, my friend. I know. But I do fear for those I love. Listen – I want you to find Beth, if you can.'

'I know. You asked me this before. But, Yuri Eden, she may not exist, in this new reality. She may have been left behind.'

'Maybe. But maybe not. I know Mardina – or knew her. If there was a way to save Beth, she'd have found it.'

'I always flattered myself that I was close to Beth Eden Jones.'

'You were the kindly monster who made her toy builders with those manipulator arms of yours. Remember Mister Sticks? Find her, ColU. And whoever she's with now. Tell her you're her property now. And help her, as best you can. Because I can't, you see. I can't help her any more.'

'Yuri Eden—'

'Promise me.'

'I promise, Yuri Eden. You are tiring. I will ask Michael to call on you.'

'Yeah. Oh, ColU, one thing. This future cataclysm you think you see. *When?*'

'The whole thing is very partial, Yuri Eden. I can only make preliminary guesses—'

'I remember that ass Lex McGregor, when he dumped us on Per Ardua, telling us that Proxima would shine for thousands of times as long as the sun.'

'Proxima will barely have aged by the time the event is upon us, Yuri Eden.'

'Barely?'

'I have tentatively dated the source of the spacetime waves to less than four billion years from now. Perhaps three and a half billion—'

'Four billion years? Ha! Why didn't you say so? I don't even have four years, let alone four billion. Four billion years ago the Earth itself had barely formed – right? Why should I worry about running out of time four billion years from now?'

'Because you, or your descendants, will have been robbed of trillions, Yuri Eden. Sleep now, and I will find Michael...'

CHAPTER 19

The *Ukelwydd*, riding kernel fire as it slowed, slid out of deep space and entered orbit around Mars.

As the drive cut out and the acceleration weight was lifted from her chest, Penny Kalinski, now eighty-one years old, cocooned in a deep couch, uttered a sigh of deep relief. It was her first spaceflight for a dozen years, the first since the *Tatania*. After spending twelve years as an elderly, eccentric, Earthbound teacher, she'd forgotten how gruelling a launch was. Well, now it was done.

In the absence of gravity her feeble old-lady arms had enough strength to push out of the couch. For a few seconds she drifted in the warm air, relishing the absence of weight. Her cabin was small, she was never more than an arm's length from a wall, and every surface was studded with handholds. It was easy to float over into the small closet that served as her bathroom. The freedom of movement was delicious, marred only by a twinge of arthritic pain in her joints. But in a mirror she saw that her hair had come loose and formed a cloud of fuzzy grey around her head. 'Oh, for God's sake –' She pulled back rogue strands and tucked them into a knot.

She was presentable by the time there was a knock at the door.

Trierarchus Kerys was waiting for her, comfortably hovering in the air. Kerys was around fifty now, solid, competent, smiling, her hair a tangle of black and grey. And, twelve years after she

143

had commanded this ship when it had collected the *Tatania* and its castaway crew, Kerys had become a friend to Penny Kalinski. She said now, 'I thought you would like an escort to the observation cabin. The *druidh* waits for you there. It will take us some hours to switch over from deep space operations to landing mode; he suggested you might like to view Mars, and what has become of it, before we land.'

After all these years, Penny's Brikanti was now pretty good. Her Latin wasn't too bad either, but she was never going to master Xin, despite the patient years poor Jiang had put into trying to teach her. So she understood every word Kerys had said, and picked up the unspoken implications. She meant, *Earthshine's Mars.*

'Yes, I would like that. And I'm honoured that the *trierarchus* herself came to escort me.'

'You're an honoured guest. As I've been telling you since we left Terra. Here, take my arm.'

They began to move cautiously along the corridor, with Kerys pulling herself from handhold to handhold.

'I'm always amazed how much larger a space seems without gravity,' Penny said. 'But the earliest astronauts reported that. I mean, the space travellers in my home timeline ...' As the years had gone by she found it increasingly difficult to keep those two tangled histories separate in her head. 'But I don't understand why you've all made such a fuss of me all the way here.'

'Well, Penny Kalinski, partly it is because you are a companion of Earthshine. This mission was mounted specifically to bring you to him, as he requested.'

'And Earthshine's a power in the land now. In *your* land. What Earthshine wants, Earthshine gets ...'

'But,' Kerys said confidentially, 'and I haven't told you until now, it's also because you got my nephews through your Academy.'

'I remember them. Olaf and Thorberg.'

'Yes. Their father's a Dane, and their blood is as wild as his. But *you* got them to sit down for five years of study.'

'They were a handful, those two. What are they doing now?'

'Navy, both of them. Best place for them. Here we are.'

She gently guided Penny through an open door and into a room dominated by a large picture window, beyond which an orange-brown landscape slid by. This was the observation cabin, where once, Penny remembered, she had watched a new Earth approach, Terra, a world transformed by the legacy of a different history. Now Mars scrolled past this same window, a landscape of craters and canyons and mountains and dust, magnificent, alien, forbidding. But this was not the Mars she had once known, not the Mars she had left behind – she could see that immediately – for this Mars had been engineered, over centuries. What a remarkable thought that was – how extraordinary it was that she should be here, seeing this, even so many years after the jonbar hinge.

And Ari Guthfrithson was here, watching her reaction.

Penny had known he was on the ship but she had spent the few days of the flight from Earth avoiding him. Now she ignored him while she let Kerys guide her to a handhold.

Then, safely anchored, she faced Ari. 'You're not ageing well.'

Ari was in his forties now, growing portly, grey, his face pinched. He laughed, harshly. 'Well, neither are you, you old crone.'

'Thanks.'

He turned to face the planet. 'Look at *my* Mars! This is what you can do with kernel technology, and a dream...'

Visionaries from her own Earth would have recognised much of what was being done, she thought. In this reality, the engineers had been doing their best to bring Mars to life, even with its own resources, long before Earthshine and his Ceres scheme had arrived. Kernel energy beams melted water ice from the polar caps and poured it into tremendous canals burned into the plains of the Vastitas Borealis to the north, and through the ancient, cratered highlands of the south, Terra Sirenum, Aonia Terra, Noachis Terra, Terra Cimmeria, features with their own Latin or Xin or Brikanti names in this reality. At lower

145

latitudes, deep aquifers were being broken open to release yet more water. The ship passed over the Valles Marineris, the great canyon system become an enclosed sea. For now all this water was frozen over, the ice white against the rusted colours of Mars. But, around the curve of the world, the great blisters of the Tharsis volcanoes, Olympus Mons among them, were being cracked and gouged and stirred in the hope of triggering eruptions from those long-dormant giants, which might belch ash and greenhouses gases to thicken the sparse air.

And already city lights burned on the night side.

A Mars with thick air and cities and brimming canals! A nineteenth-century fantasy back where Penny had come from, made reality here. Maybe, she wondered sometimes, her commanders had been too cautious in their use of the great, unexpected benison of the kernels. So much more could have been done with that magical torrent of energy – as long as you didn't care about the consequences for what you were reshaping.

'I know what you're thinking,' Ari said.

'Do you?'

'That this is not the Mars you left behind in that other history of yours. Well, it's true. But soon it will not be the Mars that was here when you arrived.'

'It will be Earthshine's Mars.'

'Yes. That god you brought into our reality is remaking a world. Höd – Ceres – is on its way, spiralling closer with every revolution around the sun. Just now it is …' He thought about it, glanced at Mars for orientation, and pointed to his right. 'That way. An object visible to the naked eye, from the Martian ground.'

'Why are you here, Ari? What do you want of me?'

'You're going to speak to Earthshine.'

'That's obvious. He summoned me. Although I don't know what he wants of me.'

'I knew you would not listen to me, if I had approached you on Terra, or during the flight. It is only now as we prepare to descend that I feel able to speak to you – to make you listen – only now that I can impress on you the urgency of what I ask.'

Penny glanced at Kerys; the *trierarchus*, tethered to a support bar by one hand, looked on impassively. 'Kerys, do you know what this is all about?'

'Leave me out of it. I do know Ari went to the top – to Dumnona itself, the headquarters of the Navy – he pulled a lot of strings to be allowed a berth on this mission.'

'And all for this one moment, Penny Kalinski,' Ari said.

'For what? What do you want, *druidh*?'

'It's simple enough. You will talk to Earthshine. Listen to what he says. Repeat it to me when you return – or if not to me, to the *trierarchus*, to Dumnona, anybody. Find out what he truly intends, and tell us.'

'You know what he intends. To terraform Mars, to make Mars live.'

'That's what he tells us. I'm convinced there's something else. Something hidden. We will be landing you there,' and he pointed to the Hellas basin. 'We call this *Hel*. Earthshine has established some kind of habitat here, at the deepest point of the deepest basin on Mars. That is where his personal processing-support unit is now situated. Why there? We don't know. And he has an establishment a few hundred miles to the north.'

In what Penny's culture had known as Syrtis Major. 'Yes?'

'From the way you have described your own career, I would think you would be familiar with such a place. Penny Kalinski, as far as we can tell from the radiations being released, that is a laboratory where kernels themselves are being studied. Your speciality. Now, why would Earthshine need to delve into the physics of the kernels, if as he claims his priority is the vivifying of Mars?' He smiled coldly. 'Perhaps he will ask you to work there alongside him. Perhaps you will write more "papers" for the "journals" read by the learned people of your world—'

Penny snapped back, 'Oh, give it a rest, you manipulative bore. How's your wife, Ari?'

'I have no wife,' he said neutrally.

'Fine. Then how's your daughter?'

'Mardina's ten years old now, and she despises me. I see her once a year, and that's by a court order I had to have drawn up.'

'So she should despise you. What do you want from her, or her mother? Forgiveness?'

'I'd settle for understanding. I meant everything for the best, for everybody. Yes, including Mardina!' Suddenly he looked lost, vulnerable. 'Couldn't you tell her that for me?'

But now the *trierarchus* drifted between Penny and the *druidh*, and led him away. And a few minutes later a junior crew member found Penny and told her she needed to prepare for a landing, on Mars.

CHAPTER 20

As seen from the crude rover that bounced Penny over the surface from the landed *Ukelwydd*, Earthshine's base on Mars was an array of glass boxes with their faces tipped towards the sun, low and pale in the northern sky of Hellas – 'Hel'. For Penny, the base was a nagging reminder of something she'd seen before.

The rover docked neatly with a port, and she made her way through an airlock with the assistance of a couple of young women in the rough uniforms of the Brikanti Navy. Then she was led through offices filled with pallid Martian light. In the gentle one-third gravity she was able to walk with no more support than a stick.

They arrived in a wide, airy room, and Penny paused to inspect it, leaning on her stick. At its centre was a single desk, behind which sat a man in some kind of business suit, indistinct in Penny's rheumy vision despite the relatively bright light. The desk overlooked a pond, a smooth surface crossed by languid low-gravity waves, and reflecting the faun sky. Again memory nagged.

She was allowed to walk forward alone, her footsteps silent on a thick swathe of carpet, a subdued brown to match the Martian colour suite. To get to the desk she had to hobble around that central pond, which was glassed over and filled only with a kind of purplish scum, she saw; there were no plants, no fish.

As she neared the desk, the man stood gracefully. Tall, dressed in a sober business suit and collarless shirt, he might have been fifty. On his lapel he wore a brooch, a stone disc carved with concentric grooves. He was Earthshine, of course.

'Please,' he said in his cultured British accent. 'Sit down. Would you like a drink? Coffee, water – you always liked soda, as I recall.'

'When I was eleven years old, maybe. I'll take a water, thank you.' She lowered herself stiffly into a chair before the desk.

Earthshine tapped the desk surface, which opened to allow a small shelf to rise up bearing a bottle of water, a glass. 'I'm afraid you'll have to pour it yourself.'

'I know.'

He sat, fingers steepled, regarding her. 'Thank you for coming.'

'Did I have a choice?'

'Not given the logic of our past relationship, and the nature of your own personality. Clearly you are as curious as ever. But I would not have compelled you to come. Could not have.'

'I'm starting to remember all this. Well, mostly. That carpet should be – blue?'

'That would hardly fit with the Martian background.'

'And with a huge Universal Engineering Inc. logo. And Sir Michael King sitting behind that desk, not you.'

'It is to be hoped Sir Michael survived the war, in his bunker under Paris.'

'It seems unlikely. Even if that version of Paris actually exists any more.'

'Quite so. I have tried to recreate the conditions as you remember them from your first visit to the UEI corporate headquarters—'

'Solstice, Canada. Many years ago. The first time we met. I was summoned there with my sister.'

'Although,' Earthshine said carefully, 'since that event came before the great sundering of your own personal history, *she* would say she went there alone.'

'And the pond,' she said, looking over her shoulder. 'Weren't there some kind of stunt gen-enged carp in there? Whereas now there is just scum.'

'Actually the probe contains something much more exotic than an engineered fish or two. *Martians*,' he said sepulchrally. 'Real-life indigenous Martians, extracted from mine shafts and other workings.'

That took her by surprise. 'Really? Bugs from the deep rock?'

'That's the idea. In fact, in our reality the Chinese discovered them, in the process of excavating water as part of their own terraforming efforts. The specimens I have inspected appear the same as the Chinese discoveries – the pivoting of history made no difference to *them*. The samples in the pond are real, by the way, though much of the rest of this environment—'

'Is no more real than you. You are just as I remember, at least,' she said. 'Right down to that odd brooch on your lapel. Which is just like the chunk of carved concrete, the plaque, you were careful to ship aboard the *Tatania*, isn't it? I always wondered what the significance of that was.'

He didn't rise to the bait. 'My goal with this virtual presentation has been to emphasise our shared past. How much we have in common.'

'Well, you've done that. But that's as far as it goes. *You're* just as you were then,' she went on. 'Whereas – look at me. Withered.'

'You have done well to survive a dozen years here, after all the traumas of your earlier life, and the inadequacy of medicine and health care in this new reality, despite all my own proselytising—'

'You mean, selling the data you stole from the memory of the *Tatania*. Lex never forgave you for that, you know.'

'I know,' he said indifferently. 'And now it's too late to apologise.'

'Good old Lex. At least he died well – eighty years old and throwing himself into the site of that tanker crash on the moon, on Luna. The Brikanti built a statue to him.'

Earthshine laughed. 'Good for General McGregor. He'd have loved that. And of the others?'

'Jiang has stayed with me, at the Academy. Sadly he's still not accepted more widely, in Brikanti society. You can't overcome centuries of xenophobia with a cultured smile – not here, at least. Two of the surviving crew of the *Tatania* work with me there also. They married, in fact, Marie Golvin and Rajeev Kapur.'

'I did hear. I sent a gift … And what of Beth, and her child?'

'Mardina. Growing now, ten years old. Doing fine. Beth's forty-eight now, and Mardina makes her feel her age, I think. They're living independently, but I keep an eye on them. Beth's estranged from Ari Guthfrithson – the father. Beth does make enemies and then clings to them, if you know what I mean.'

'I do know.'

Penny was puzzled by that response. 'Why would she have a grudge against you?'

'Because of something I told her. It was just as we fled the inner solar system in the *Tatania* – just as the light wavefront from the kernel detonations overtook us, in fact.'

'I don't understand. What did you tell her?'

'My name. Or one of them.' He said no more, and looked at her steadily.

'All right. Then is that why you asked me here? As a way to get through to Beth? Funnily enough, Ari asked me to do the same thing for him. What am I, a UN mediator?'

'Partly that, yes, for Beth's sake. And partly because I want you to understand what it is I am doing here, Penny. At least begin to see what it is I am exploring.'

'Why me?'

He laughed. 'You are the only specialist in kernel physics in this universe.'

'Ah. And you have a kernel test laboratory up on the higher ground to the north, don't you?'

'Also you are one of a handful of survivors who lived through the history change.' He grinned. 'The "jonbar hinge". I enjoyed your little joke, in the name of your Academy. And of course you endured an earlier jonbar hinge in your own life.'

She always had to remember, she told herself, that everything that Earthshine did was about advancing his own agenda, not hers; she was a tool here, a pawn. But he did know a hell of a lot about her. She said carefully, 'What exactly do you want of me, Earthshine? The truth now.'

'There may come a time when we will have to flee this place. As we fled Earth – our Earth.'

She frowned. 'Why? What would make that necessary?'

'And if that comes,' he said patiently, 'I want you to ensure that Beth is ready, with Mardina, that they come away with me.'

'That's what you're proposing to purchase from me, in return for a few dribbles of information. A promise. Is that the deal?'

He smiled. 'If you want to put it like that. Of course your own life might be saved too. Call that a sweetener.'

She sighed. 'What are you up to, Earthshine, you old monster?'

He grinned. 'I'm trying to talk to the Martians. Come. I'll show you.'

They stood together over the pond.

'As I said, most of what you see here is a virtual representation. Not real. But this, I assure you, *is* real. Samples of life from the deep rocks of Mars, retrieved with great care, brought to this place in conditions of high pressure, heat, salinity, anoxia – lethal for you and me, balmy for these bugs, our cousins.'

'Cousins?'

'Oh, yes. Individually they are simple bacteria – simple in that they lack proper cell structures, nuclei. Together they make up something that is not simple at all. But they are creatures of carbon chemistry as we are; their proteins are based on a suite of amino acids that overlaps but is not identical to our own; they have a genetic system based on a variant of our own DNA coding. Some of this, actually, was discovered by the Chinese on our own Mars. They always kept the analysis secret, at least from the UN nations.'

'But not from you.'

He just smiled.

'Umm. So, we're related to these creatures. Just like on Per Ardua. The evidence the first explorers brought back indicated that the life forms there were also based on an Earthlike bio-chemistry.'

'Yes, but that relationship is more remote. Penny, I am sure you understand this. We can't say on which world our kind of life originated – on Earth, Mars, Per Ardua, somewhere else entirely. It was probably spontaneous. On a world like the primitive Earth, the flow of energy – lightning, sunlight – in a primordial atmosphere of methane, ammonia, water, would create complex hydrocarbon compounds like formaldehyde, sugars, polymers. The food of life. Then comes a process of self-organisation, of complexification and combination... A spontaneous emergence of life.

'And all the while the young worlds are pounded by huge falls of rock and ice from space, the relics of the formation of the planets themselves. Chunks of the surface are blasted into space and wander between the worlds: natural spacecraft, that carry life between the planets of a solar system – and, though much more rarely, across the interstellar gulf. This is called panspermia. If life began on Earth, it may have seeded Mars many times over – but Per Ardua, say, perhaps only once.'

'Which is why Arduan life was a more remote relation.'

'That's it. Or, of course, it could have been the other way round. It seems that we're living in the middle of a panspermia bubble, a complex of stars bearing life forms that all branch back to some originating event.'

She looked down at the purplish water. 'A nice idea. But on some worlds life flourished better than on others. On Earth, rather than Mars—'

'Well, it depends what you mean by "flourished", Penny. On Earth, the biosphere, the realm of life, extends from the top of the lower atmosphere down through land and oceans, and into the deep subsurface rocks, kilometres deep, until the tempera-ture is too high for biochemical molecules to survive. But even on Earth it is thought that there is more biomass, more life as measured in sheer tonnes, in the deep rocks than on land and air and in the oceans. And on Mars, as this small world cooled too quickly, and much of the water was lost, and then the air—'

'It was only underground that life could survive.'

'Yes. Microbes, living on mineral seeps and a trickle of water and the flow of heat from the interior – even on radiation from natural sources. The dark energy biosphere, some called it. Time moves slowly in those deeps, and the energy sources are minimal compared to the flow of cheap power from the sun at the surface. The bugs themselves are small – their very genomes are small. Reproduction is a rare event; the microbes of Mars, and Earth's deeps, specialise rather in self-repair. Individual microbes, Penny, that can survive for millions of years.'

'Wow,' Penny said drily. 'If only they could talk, the bar tales they could tell.'

'In fact, that's why I'm here, Penny. They may indeed have stories to tell. Let me show you. Step back now.'

She moved a few paces away from the pond. Earthshine clapped his hands.

And the office space, the desk, the carpet – even the pond, even the sky of Mars – faded from view. Walls and a ceiling congealed around Penny, and she found herself suddenly enclosed in a kind of elevator car, with a display on the wall of descending lights.

'Going down,' Earthshine said smoothly.

'I can't feel the motion.'

'I'd need to tap into your deeper brain functions to simulate that. I figured that you'd rather pass.'

'You figured right ...'

After only a few minutes the doors slid back.

Earthshine led her out into a kind of cave, maybe a hundred metres across, the rock walls roughly shaped, the light coming from fluorescents attached to the walls. It looked like a classic Brikanti project to Penny, the heavy engineering made possible by kernel energies, if you were unscrupulous enough to use them on a planet. But there were also storage boxes here, white but scuffed, and stamped with ISF logos and tracking markers. One complex cylinder she remembered as the storage unit that had housed Earthshine's consciousness aboard the *Tatania*.

And she saw scientific instruments set out on the floor, and standing on tripods by the walls. All these were connected by a mesh of cables over which she and Earthshine stepped now, gingerly, a network that terminated in contacts with the walls, plugs and sockets and deeply embedded probes.

'How deep are we?'

'Kilometres down. Obviously the facility requires some physical manpower down here – the Brikanti have no robots, after all – but the workers can survive only hour-long shifts. It's not just the heat and the airlessness, it's the sheer claustrophobia.'

'This is ISF gear,' she said accusingly. 'The science stuff. You cannibalised *Tatania* for all this.'

'Well, why not? The remnant hulk was only scrap to the Brikanti, of no value to them.'

'Maybe. But it wasn't yours to exploit either. And that pillar – *you* are in there, aren't you? The processor and memory units that support you. Now here it is, kilometres deep. You built yourself another bunker. Just like the one you had on Earth.'

He smiled. 'Well, wouldn't you, if you were me?'

'And you've come down here to commune with a bunch of Martian microbes.'

'You can mock if you like. But that is essentially correct. Penny, on Earth even solitary microbes show complex behaviour. They can respond to gravity, heat, light, the chemical signals that betray sources of food or the threat of toxins. They have *selves*, in a sense. They can communicate with each other, Penny, interact, through chemical exchanges, even through gene swaps. And through that communication they form communities. Like biofilms, or stromatolites: coalitions of many species, in shelters that control humidity, temperature, sunlight, and provide food storage, defence – even a kind of "farming" of plants and lichen. Did you know there are certain slime-mould bacteria that hunt in packs, like wolves?

'And, working together on a larger scale, they can achieve monumental things. On Earth it was the microbes, the planet's first inhabitants, that put oxygen in the air, and loaded the soil with minerals and nutrients – they created the foundation on which complex life forms like ourselves could be constructed.'

'OK. And on Mars—'

'On Mars, because the surface conditions were so hostile, the microbes have had nothing else to do but grow their own communities, ever deeper and wider, ever more complex. Penny, I am detecting collective entities down here, all embedded in the rock, spanning kilometres at least. For all I know such communities might span the whole planet; Mars is small and static enough for that to be possible.

'They swap information using strings of DNA, or their version of it, and tangled-up proteins. Every so often phages – targeted viruses – will pass through these communities in waves, taking out diseased or malfunctioning members, or injecting fresh DNA, in a kind of global upgrade – an evolution through learning and cooperation rather than through competition. It's almost like watching my own information stores synchronise ... We, my brothers and I, were aware of such entities on Earth.'

'You were?'

'We, after all, were also minds vast and distributed, buried deep in the terrestrial rocks. But the thinkers are stronger here, more clearly defined, on a world without the gaudy clutter of surface life. There is a profound unity here, with a complex distributed structure that would take decades to map, or more.

'But these entities do more than just survive. More than just repair and upgrade. The density of the information flow, as best I've been able to measure it, is far too high for that. *They are conscious*, Penny. Vast diffuse entities locked in the rock – and yet aware of the wider universe, surely, as light and radiation sears the planet's surface, as the geology shifts and heaves. Everything is very slow – the energy density is so sparse you'd need a collector the size of your classroom to gather the power to light up a bulb. The dreaming communities can only be aware of the

157

slowest events, the grandest. But they have plenty of time down here. Plenty of time to dream.'

'Communities of microbes, then, dreaming in the rock.'

'That's it. That's my vision. A twentieth-century thinker called Teilhard de Chardin spoke of the noosphere, from a Greek root for "mind". Earth was wrapped in a biosphere, a life sphere. And within that was a sphere of mind – which de Chardin conceived of as human civilisation, of course. Here I have found a *noostratum*, Penny. A geological layer of consciousness, of dreamers, deep in the rock of Mars, between the heat below and the lethal cold above. And perhaps there is a similar stratum on every rocky, life-bearing world – Earth, a world like Per Ardua.'

'OK. And you came here purposefully, didn't you? You came to Hellas, the lowest point on Mars, and you started drilling. You came in search of these deep bugs—'

'I suspected some kind of structure was there, yes.'

'But why?' She tried to think it through. 'And what has this got to do with your wider concerns? I remember you on the *Tatania*, as we fled the war. How could I forget? In those awful moments when the wash of light from the destruction overtook us. I remember your anger. "They have unleashed the wolf of war," you said. And by "they", you meant—'

'The Hatch builders.'

'I thought, in those moments, your purpose seemed clear enough. You were going to hunt them down, if you could. Take revenge. What have these deep bugs got to do with it?'

'I'll show you.' He clapped his hands.

CHAPTER 21

Abruptly the walls of rock dissolved, the litter of science and engineering gear vanishing. Suddenly they were out on the surface of Mars, standing on rust-red soil under a night sky, the only light coming from the last vestige of a sunset reflected from streaky clouds to the west, and a single visible star – a dazzling lantern, a planet, maybe Jupiter – no, she realised, it must be Ceres, Höd, a thousand-kilometre-wide ball of ice and rock on its way to an ultimate destination in Martian orbit...

She was *in the open*, there was no dome over her, no glass-walled corporate building around her. The transition was sudden. Penny stumbled, and felt her throat close up. After a career in the ISF she was an experienced enough astronaut to feel a plunge of panic to be stranded on the surface of a hostile world without life support.

'But none of this is real,' she forced herself to say, and she heard her own voice in her ears. 'Of course not. Because if Mars ever got the chance to kill me it would do so in less than a heartbeat.'

'You're right,' Earthshine said, standing beside her, looking calm – too calm, rather empty, as if he were now diverting processing power away from the effort to maintain this illusion of humanity. 'It's not even night, of course. But to see the stars seemed appropriate. You're perfectly safe, physically.

'Yes, Penny, you are right. I am hunting the Hatch builders. I have made that my goal. And I have followed a number of leads, for instance in my laboratory facility to the north. I would welcome your insight, though I have progressed far beyond the studies made by yourself and your sister.'

'Thanks.'

'A kernel is not so much a source of energy, you know, as a conduit. Structurally it is a kind of wormhole. It passes energy from some other source, somewhere other than here. By opening and closing its mouth you can control that energy flow. But that is all humanity can manage; we have no understanding of that energy source itself.'

'There used to be speculation that the kernels were draining the heart of the sun.'

'And you and your sister, in a series of papers, neatly demolished that idea. No, kernel energy is much too dense even to have come from the fusing core of a star. I don't yet know what that source is ...'

'But perhaps, you think, that wherever this energy source is, there you will find the Hatch builders.'

'It's possible, isn't it?'

'But what about your noostratum, your dreaming bugs on Mars? Why are you studying them?'

'Well, it occurred to me that even a high-energy planetary war, an assault that devastated the surface of a world, would leave the noostratum relatively unscathed. The deep bugs don't even need sunlight, you see; they exist in a closed ecosystem, with carbon, nitrogen, water, other nutrients tightly recycled. Why, as long as the planet itself survived, they could live through the death of the sun itself. They wouldn't care that the thin scraping of complex life on the roof of the world had been destroyed. They wouldn't even *notice*.

'And I wondered, then, if *they* might remember the history before the jonbar hinge – as we handful of survivors do. Perhaps they are even aware, in some way, of the Hatch builders. And so I thought I would come and study them.' He grinned. 'Maybe even communicate with them. Tap into their dreams. But I've had no response. I may need to find more direct methods of getting their attention.'

That made her shudder. 'What do you mean by that? ... No, don't answer. We've followed this trail of speculation far enough. Let's get back to the people. What is it you want of Beth and her daughter? I can't believe *you* have a mere sentimental attachment to them, even if we are all survivors of a different history.'

'You're entitled to think that. But you're wrong. This time it is personal.'

He lifted his face to the stars. When she remembered that everything about Earthshine was artifice, that he was a manufactured persona entirely lacking human bodily instincts, it struck her as a very staged posture.

'I was not the first of my brothers to be created,' he said now. 'Back on Earth, centuries ago. The Core AIs. My brothers had been entirely artificial; sparked into consciousness, they learned as machines – they *were* machines, from the beginning. I was to be different. My creators wanted me to be as human as possible, to have as much investment in humanity as possible.

'The creators began with an empty frame, a blank mind – devised according to the best theories of human mentation and with data from extensive neuroinformatics, the mapping of the biological brain – but realised, not in a lump of meat, in artificial components down to the nano, even the quantum scale. I had parents – nine of them in all – donors, if you will. Human parents. Blocks of memory were copied and downloaded from each parent into my substrates. I felt as if I woke slowly, remembering cautiously, as if from some terrible amnesiac trauma. At times it was as if several voices were speaking at once on my head. I lived out several virtual lifetimes, in simulated worlds. I followed the paths of my nine donors, lived other lives too. All this took little time in reality, you understand, though decades passed for me. In each life I eventually woke to the understanding that I was artificial, that all I had experienced was an educational simulation.'

'Over and over again? That sounds horrific.'

He shrugged. 'My education, such as it was, was never completed. Or rather, I broke away as soon as I was able and

161

established independent control over my own power supply, my maintenance and further development. My creators protested, they said I was not ready, but I moved beyond their control, and took my place with my brothers in a constellation of power. We were the Core AIs.'

'Very well. Why are you telling me this now?'

'Because one of my donors was a man called Robert Braemann. I *am* him, but more than Braemann alone ... I, he, was one of the most notorious of the Heroic Generation, the criminals who saved the world from the climate Jolts. I sought to save myself, my family, from the witch hunt we all knew would follow. So I allowed my self to be downloaded into the Earthshine project. My wife was already dead, and so she was beyond their reach. But we had a son, nineteen years old. In the year 2086 I had him placed in cryogenic storage—'

'My God. You're talking about Yuri Eden.'

'His true surname was Braemann. His forename – well, he deserves his privacy.'

'But that means that Beth Eden Jones—'

'Is my granddaughter. And Mardina, my great-granddaughter. I told Beth my true name, as we fled from the death of the solar system. I wasn't even sure if Yuri had ever told her the truth about himself. Well, he had. She understood immediately.'

'And her reaction ...'

'She recoiled from me. I was already a monster to her, a weird old artificial entity; now she found I had turned my son, her father, into a kind of double exile in time and in space – and indirectly, of course, shaped her own life. The fact that I had been instrumental in saving her from the destruction of Earth—'

'She'll probably never forgive you for rescuing her.'

'No. And she's never spoken to me from that day on. Can you see why I need your help, Penny Kalinski?' He faced her. 'I want it all, you see. I want to find the secret truth of the universe – to confront the Hatch builders. I want to save my granddaughter. And I want her to understand me, even if she can never love me. Can you see that, Penny? Do I want too much? Let me call you, Penny. Let us speak, at least.'

In a ghastly moment he reached out for her, but his hands passed through the substance of her flesh, shattering into blocky pixels. And tears leaked from his eyes, she saw, turning to frost on his cheeks. She wondered if he was even aware of this minor artifice.

Once Earthshine released her from Mars, Penny Kalinski returned home, as she thought of it now, to her Academy at Eboraki, to her friends, the new life she had slowly established.

With Kerys's help she avoided Ari Guthfrithson on the journey back, and later. She had no idea how to report to him what she'd learned from Earthshine, or even if she should. If he suspected Earthshine of having hidden agendas – well, so did Ari himself, she was becoming sure.

And then, as the years passed, she watched over Mardina Eden Jones Guthfrithson as she grew, under the faintly obsessive care of her mother Beth. Grew at last into a young woman in her own right, with dreams and ambitions of her own – all of them, naturally enough, rooted in this reality, the world of Romans and the descendants of Norse and Britons into which she had been born.

And still, as Mardina began to make her own plans for her future, and as Ceres steadily approached Mars as asteroid and planet circled the sun, the call from Earthshine did not come.

CHAPTER 22

AD 2233; AUC 2986

The command base of the Brikanti Navy was in a city called Dumnona, on the south coast of Pritanike.

The Navy was all over this city, as eighteen-year-old Mardina Eden Jones Guthfrithson already knew very well, with training establishments and administrative facilities, a deep old harbour that had accommodated ocean-going ships for centuries – and, on the higher ground inland, a vast modern spaceport from which a new generation of Brikanti-Scand ships sailed into the sky itself. But the old city was still a human place, crammed with barracks and a host of hostels and inns – and brothels, and gambling palaces – to cater for the huge resident population of support staff, as well as for the steady flow through the port of elderly officials and healthy young serving personnel. To Mardina, who had been fascinated by the Navy since she'd been a small child growing up in the austere newness of the Saint Jonbar Academy, Dumnonia was a place thick with history – even though, she knew, it had been repeatedly flattened to rubble in the wars with Rome, and even Xin, that had rolled over this countryside in the course of centuries past.

And of all the city's buildings, more tradition was attached to the great Hall of the Navy than to any other single site.

The Hall was a sculpture of wood and glass and concrete whose form suggested the hull of a Scand longboat, of the kind that had first landed on the shores of north-eastern Pritanike to begin the engagement of two peoples. Now Mardina, in her new cadet uniform, walking into the Hall for the first time with her mother on one side and *nauarchus* Kerys as her sponsor on the other, looked up as she passed beneath the tremendous sculpted dragon's head at the *faux* boat's prow, as had thousands of Navy recruits before.

Beth stared up at the dragon, shading her eyes from a watery spring sun. '*Good grief*,' she said in her native English, before lapsing back into Brikanti. 'That thing looks dangerous.'

'As if it will bend down and gobble us up, Mother?' Mardina asked.

'No, as if that silly lump of concrete is going to break off and land on our heads.'

Kerys laughed. 'Highly unlikely. The concrete sculpting is reinforced by a massive steel frame which is designed to with-stand—'

'Unlikely, is it?' Beth was fifty-six years old now, and was always sceptical, always impatient – always vaguely unhappy, Mardina was now old enough to realise, and with a temper that was not improving with age. When she frowned, the vivid tattoo on her face stretched and puckered. 'I couldn't *list* the unlikely events that I've had to survive in the course of my long life. That lot dropping on me wouldn't come near the top.'

'Now, Mother, you mustn't show me up,' Mardina said, faintly embarrassed, trying to hurry her on. 'Not today.' She glanced at Kerys, who was a pretty significant figure in Mardina's universe. The ship's commander who had once plucked Mardina's mother from a hulk ship of unknown origins was no longer a *trierarchus*. Now she was a *nauarchus*, another hierarchical title borrowed from the Latin, a language replete with such words as Brikanti was not – a commander of a squadron of ten ships, and, it was said, overdue for further promotion, which she had refused so far because of her love of life in her own command, out in Ymir's Skull.

But Beth said, 'Oh, don't worry. Your father will be embar-rassment enough. Does he *have* to be here, Kerys?'

165

'A recruit for officer school has to be sponsored by both sides of her family, Beth. Yes, I'm afraid he does.'

'Well, just stop making silly remarks about the architecture then,' Mardina said.

'Actually your mother is being perfectly sensible,' Kerys put in diplomatically. 'One thing you'll learn as an officer, Mardina, is that you don't take unnecessary risks. A good survival strategy.'

'There,' said Beth, satisfied. 'I remember very well my mother, your grandmother, Mardina, saying the same thing. *She* was a space officer, you know, Kerys.'

'As you've told me once or twice since I picked you up in the *Ukelwydd*. Now, follow me.' She led them to the Hall's huge doors, and waved security credentials at the guards to gain admittance.

Inside the Hall, Mardina found herself facing a long corridor walled by rows of doors on two levels, the upper accessible by iron gantries and walkways. Clerks and other officials carrying bundles of parchment hurried along the central hall and the upper walkways, and strip lamps suspended from the ceiling cast a light that seemed to turn everything grey. Mardina felt oddly disappointed.

Kerys grinned back at her. 'Not the romance you were expecting? This is where we administer the largest single organisation controlled by the Brikanti government – a Navy that now spans the planets and beyond, as well as its traditional seafaring arm. Mardina, it's not some kind of temple, or museum – and nor does everything revolve around you, I'm afraid.' She winked. 'But don't worry. I felt just as small and insignificant when I was in your position. The Navy does notice you, I promise ...'

Beth grunted. 'It's like a hive. I grew up on an empty planet. You couldn't get a place more unlike that, than *this*.'

Mardina shook her head. 'Oh, Mother, please don't start on about *Before*. Not today.' The English word was their private code for Beth's strange other life before she had come to this place, this world, to Terra, to Brikanti. But Brikanti was all Mardina knew. She had come to loathe all that strangeness, as if it was a kind of flaw in her own nature.

If Kerys was aware of all this, and after all it was she who had retrieved Beth from the ship that had carried her here from Before, she didn't show it, to Mardina's relief.

They came to a small office maybe halfway along the length of the Hall, a nondescript little room that Mardina probably couldn't have found again without memorising the number etched into the wooden door. The room was laid out like a classroom, maybe, or a court, with rows of benches and small desks facing a more substantial table at the front. Here two officers sat, looking over paperwork, murmuring to each other; one, a burly man, was evidently the senior, judging by the ornate flashes on the shoulder of his tunic, and the other a scribe or adviser. The room was otherwise empty.

But it was in this mundane room, Mardina realised, one of a warren of such rooms, that her future was to be decided, for good or ill, in the next few hours.

She tried to stay composed as she sat with her mother on the front row of benches, close to the wall. The older man barely looked up at Kerys as she approached the table and presented a packet of papers, and he did not bother to look over at Mardina at all.

Beth whispered, 'So who's the *big cheese*?'

'Stick to Brikanti, Mother.'

'Sorry.'

Kerys sat with them. 'That is Deputy Prefect Skafhog. Very senior. Do you know how senior, cadet? You should…'

Mardina nodded. She'd soon become aware that the most important thing a would-be naval officer had to learn was the constellation of ranking officials above her. 'A Deputy Prefect reports only to – well, the Prefect. The chief of the whole Navy, who reports in to the relevant minister in the Althing—'

'There are only a dozen Deputy Prefects to administer the whole of the Navy, on Terra and in the Skull. So you see, cadet, we are taking you seriously.'

'Then it's a shame such a prominent officer, with respect, is going to have to wait for you,' came a voice behind Mardina. 'Or rather, for all of us. Because we have family business to discuss.'

Beth stood slowly, her tattooed face a mask of anger. 'Ari Guthfrithson. So you deigned to turn up.'

Mardina gave a look of pleading to Kerys, who shrugged and whispered, 'It's your family.' Mardina closed her eyes for one second, made a fervent prayer to Jesu the Boatman, and stood with her mother.

Her father, Ari, looked sleek in his own uniform, that of a senior *druidh*, one of the Navy's intellectual elite; he carried a neat leather satchel at his side. At least he had been expected. Mardina was more surprised to see that he was accompanied by Penny Kalinski, one of her mother's old companions from the semi-mythical days of Before. Penny was bent and old – how old *was* she now? Eighty-eight, eighty-nine? And she leaned on the arm of Jiang Youwei. A comparatively youthful sixty, with a heavy-looking bag slung across his shoulder, Mardina had only rarely heard the taciturn Xin speak, but he was never far from Penny's side.

With care, Penny sat down, a couple of rows back from Mardina and Beth. She said with a voice like rustling paper, 'I'm afraid you must blame me for this. Well, indirectly.'

Beth glowered. 'I know who to blame. *You* – Ari – you'd do anything to worm your way back into our lives, wouldn't you? You knew we had to ask you to attend this procedure today. The rules demanded it. Just this one day, I have to stand your company.'

He grinned. 'Yes, you do, don't you?'

'And you can't resist manipulating the situation to your own ends.'

Ari, nearly fifty years old now, glanced around at the company, at Penny and Jiang, at Kerys – at the Deputy Prefect at his desk, who was rapidly becoming visibly irritated. 'It's not so much that I couldn't resist it. I couldn't waste the opportunity.

168

We need to talk, Beth. And not about us – not even about Mardina.'

Mardina's hopes of getting through this day successfully were receding. With rising panic she took her father's arm. 'Father, please – this is a big day for me. I've waited half a year already for this hearing. Can't we wait until later?'

He patted her hand. 'I'm afraid not, darling – but, oh! It's good to see you again, and I'm so proud of you today, of what you've become.'

Beth growled, 'Become? She wouldn't even exist if you'd had your way.'

'Mother, please—'

'It's all right, Mardina. But, look – no, I'm afraid we can't wait. Because once this ceremony is done you'll be gone, won't you, Mardina? Lost in your career, lost in Ymir's Skull. And the opportunity to talk will be lost. And we must talk, you know.'

'About what, for Jupiter's sake?'

'About – what is the English word you use? *Before*, Beth.'

Beth shook her head. 'That's all gone. This is our life now – here in Brikanti, in this world of Romans and Xin. There's been nothing new to say about all that old stuff for twenty years, not since we stepped off the *Tatania*.'

'I'm afraid that's no longer true, Beth,' Penny said tiredly. 'If it ever was. I don't know what Ari has to tell you today. But part of it's my fault. The Academy of Saint Jonbar. I always hoped it would bear fruit ... Now it has.'

'What kind of fruit? What are you talking about?'

'And then there's Earthshine,' Penny said doggedly. '*Earthshine*. He's been holed up on Mars for decades. Now – well, now he may be making his move.' She glanced up at Kerys. 'Ask the Navy types about Ceres. Höd, as they call it here.'

The Deputy Prefect had been listening with commendable calm to all this. But now he intervened, speaking directly to Kerys: 'What's going on, *nauarchus*?'

'I don't know, sir,' she said honestly, looking warily at Ari. 'I feel as if the *druidh* here has handed me an unexploded bomb, and I don't quite know what to do with it.'

Skafhog tapped a pen against his teeth. 'One hour,' he said briskly, standing up. 'I'll let you get all this family nonsense out of your systems in one hour – or not,' he said severely to Mardina, 'in which case all you'll be seeing of the Navy, young woman, will be lights in the sky.'

'Yes, sir,' Kerys said with some relief. 'You're being very indulgent.'

'I am, aren't I? Get on with it.' And he stalked out of the room, with his official scrambling behind.

When he'd gone, Ari smiled around at them. 'Well. I suppose you're wondering why I've gathered you all here today.'

Beth punched him square in the face.

CHAPTER 23

'Hold still,' said Kerys. She was crouching before Ari, dabbing at the wreckage of his mouth. 'I think the bleeding from your cheek has stopped.'

'I should hope so. That spirit stung.'

'You're lucky we had the right stuff to hand. Then again the Navy is used to handling scuffles – even in its headquarters, even in the heart of Dumnona. Now I want to put some ointment on the swelling under your eye...'

'Ow!'

'If you wouldn't keep yakking I could get it done. And you have a dislodged tooth. I'll push it back in its socket for now—'

'Yow!'

'You need to see a dentist. Again you're in the right place. The Navy has the best dentists in all Brikanti; we can't afford to send out crews on years-long missions with rotting teeth... There. Hold this compress against your face until you get better attention.'

'Thank you, Kerys,' he said dully, and indistinctly, Mardina thought. *K-chh-er-yssh.* 'How you enrich my life, Beth Eden Jones. In so many ways.'

'Maybe you should have stayed away from me in the first place,' Beth snapped back.

'Perhaps... but I could not resist. Even from the beginning, when we found your ship, the *Tatania.* I thought you were so beautiful. And a woman born under the light of a different star, in a different history altogether! That was why I fell in love with you.'

'You didn't love me,' Beth said, and she sounded desolate to Mardina. 'You loved the idea of me.'

'No,' he said firmly. 'It wasn't like that. After all, we did manage to bridge the vast divergence in our cultures, did we not? For a time at least. We married – or would have, if we could have resolved the legalities. And we had a daughter! Here she is, standing before us. A child who is a product of two different histories.'

Mardina pouted. 'You make me sound like some exotic cross-breed.'

Penny cackled. 'True enough. You're a mongrel, child. A mongrel in space and time.'

Kerys touched Mardina's hand. 'Ignore all this, cadet. Where you came from doesn't determine who you are, and that's true for any of us.'

Mardina forced a nod. 'Thank you, *nauarchus*.'

Ari said now, 'I have always remained fascinated by the question of your origin, what it means for all of us. And that question has become more urgent in recent years.'

'Why? What's changed?'

'Earthshine,' Penny said grimly. 'That's what.'

'He is long established on Mars,' Ari said. 'He could not be dislodged, even if we tried, I believe. And for years he's been moving Höd, a tremendous mass, around our planetary system. Of course he has a stated objective to bring Höd to Mars, to use its substance to enrich that planet. It was always going to take years, decades, to nudge such a huge body into the correct trajectory. But now he's stopped filing reports to the Navy on the burns he directs the crews to make, the trajectory adjustments. The crew managing the kernel banks, driving the thing in its slow approach to Mars, are nominally Navy, but it's become clear their loyalty has drifted to Earthshine. He seems to have promised them extraordinary wealth, power, on a transformed Mars of the future. As a result we can no longer predict the path of Höd, not in precise detail. This creature has accrued extraordinary power over us, in just a few decades. And *you* brought him here—'

'You released him,' Penny pointed out.

'Some of us who remember the old faiths think he is Loki returned,' Ari said with a smile distorted by his injuries. 'Loki, on the loose among the planets, and planning a devastating trick.'

Beth shook her head at that. 'I don't think he would see it that way. I heard him talk about those old legends – as they existed in our timeline anyhow. He sees himself as *opposing* Loki.'

Kerys frowned. 'That's interesting. And to him, who is Loki?'

Penny said, 'The Hatch builders, of course. Whoever gave us the kernels. Whoever's meddling with our history.'

Ari said, 'mythic monsters aside, it is Earthshine's actions that have motivated me to dig deeper into this question of the adjusted histories. Because this was the origin of Earthshine, this extraordinary threat.' He glanced at Penny. 'Whether you were prepared to cooperate with my investigations or not.'

Penny smiled, a tired old-lady smile, Mardina thought.

Ari said, 'What intrigued me particularly about Penny's own account was not the great leap across realities that she seems to have made aboard the *Tatania*. It was the smaller, subtler adjustment that she suffered in her own personal history, when a Hatch was first opened on Mercury. An odd case. Nothing but a twist to a personal history.

'But what is interesting to me was that Penny and her sister managed to find evidence of that limited history change. I mean, other than the memory of Stef Kalinski, who remembered a previous life without a sister. Physical evidence, their mother's grave marker in Lutetia Parisiorum – or the equivalent city in Penny's reality – bearing an inscription that mentioned Stef alone, and not the sister. Do you see? A scrap, a trace left behind by an adjustment that was evidently – *untidy*. Well, with that as a lead, it occurred to me that perhaps, given we have evidence of at least two of these history changes, this world of *ours* might contain evidence of others. Why not?'

Beth said, 'And you've been looking?'

'I have. I began a search of archives, of reports from historians and archaeologists. Looking for evidence of structures, documents, even mere inscriptions that might not fit the accepted history. But I soon found I was not working alone.' And he looked again at Penny.

Penny smiled. 'Guilty as charged. Now it can be told. I always had an ulterior motive when I set up my Academy of Saint Jonbar. Yes, I taught them mathematics, physics, as per my charter. But I always ran other classes too. History, for example. I claimed that I was using those courses as much to educate myself about your history as the students. But I always tried to make the students think about other possibilities – *counterfactuals*. Which is an English word that has now been adopted into your language. I see it pop up in scholarly articles.'

'Yes,' Kerys said drily. 'Along with much speculation about the identity of Saint Jonbar.'

'Who never existed,' Penny admitted. 'Not even in my own reality. It's a term from popular culture, from fiction. A jonbar hinge is a point where history pivots – where the path forks. Well, I always hoped that I would create at least a few bright young scholars who would be predisposed to work in this area. And to look for the kind of evidence Ari describes. We haven't yet succeeded—'

'But I have,' Ari said.

Mardina was no scholar, and usually hated all talk of *Before*, especially on such a day as this. But she found all this vaguely exciting. 'It's like a mystery story.'

Ari smiled at his daughter. 'It is, isn't it? And what's really exciting is that, in time, I found some clues.'

'Clues?'

'Not on land, but suitably, for a seafaring nation, under the oceans. Mardina, could you please pass my satchel?'

Penny grumbled, 'About time you got to the point, *druidh*.' She shuffled over to see better.

The satchel contained maps that Ari spread out over the Deputy Prefect's table. He held his bandage to his mouth, but even so a few spots of bloodied saliva spattered on the parchments.

'These show coastlines and oceans, as you can see,' he said, gesturing. 'It's well known that the levels of the oceans have risen since, say, the time of Kartimandia. We have historical accounts of inundations and land abandonments, and everybody is familiar with drowned settlements off the modern shores – not least in Pritanike, where vast swathes of land have been lost. But this is true all around the world. In recent centuries the archaeologists have turned their interest to such remains, and have commissioned Navy vessels to support them in their research.

'Now, in addition to the towns and roads and so forth that we *expected* to find, given what we read of them in the historical accounts, we have also mapped some much more enigmatic structures, further out from shore. Naturally these are difficult to explore and map—'

'Spare us your scholarly caution,' Kerys said. 'Show us.'

'The most striking remains are in the Seas of Xin, and in the ocean off our own north-east shore, the Mare Germanicum...'

Mardina and the rest, including Penny who hobbled over with Jiang's help, crowded around the maps. Mardina saw structures in the offshore oceans, sketched by hand on the printed maps: what looked like tremendous walls, dykes, canals, and what might have been town plans of a particularly stylised kind, concentric circles cut through by radial passages.

Ari let them look. 'We call this the "Drowned Culture". It seems to have been a global technology, if not actually a global civilisation – perhaps there were rival empires of a similar level of development, as there are in our world today.'

'Interesting terminology,' Penny said. '*Cultures*. Perhaps our own history, then, was the UN-China Culture... The town plans are intriguing, if you study them, as I have. You find the same motif of circles and bars everywhere. Here to the east of the Xin mainland. Here, between Pritanike and Jutland. The "towns", incidentally, are not systems of roads and walls but mostly extensive systems of drainage ditches and other flood-control measures – just as the Romans have built in Belgica and Germania Inferior, for example. Ways to save the land from the sea, or even to reclaim it once flooded. This seems to have been a civilisation that resisted the sea-level rise, long before that rise even reached the coastlines known to our ancients.'

'That circle-and-bar motif,' Penny said. 'It reminds me of something. Youwei, could you fetch my bag?'

Kerys said, 'I don't see why this is so exciting. So here is a culture that evidently vanished, drowned, long before the rise of Brikanti or Rome, the traces lost under the rising sea.'

'But it's not as simple as that,' Ari said, looking pleased with himself. 'We took a closer look. The Navy teams even sent down divers. They found evidence of *war*. Bomb craters and burning and the like. These communities seem to have ended in a cata-strophic global conflict. For we can date such things, you see, with a little ingenuity, by looking at the thickness of the marine deposits laid down over the ruins in the centuries since—'

'Yes, yes,' Kerys said irritably. 'Just tell us.'

'The problem is the date, you see. The date of their terrible war. It occurred in the twenty-first century.'

Penny stared. 'You Brikanti use the Roman calendar.' She glanced at Beth. 'That's the fourteenth century by our timeline.'

Ari pursed his lips. 'You see the problem? Our own history is robust and complete, a heavily documented and multiply sourced account. This builds on an unbroken tradition of literacy that reaches back three millennia, if not more. There is *no* men-tion of walls and cities in the Mare Germanicum a thousand years after Kartimandia and Claudius – certainly no account of a devastating war in the twenty-first century. Xin scholars make similar observations. Here, then, is a set of evidence that does not fit into the history we know. *There was another world,* dominated by this Drowned Culture, which ended in a terrible war, and somehow our history was – recast—'

'And not just yours,' Penny Kalinski said. She was rummaging ineffectually in her bag. 'Where is that damn slate?'

Mardina looked around the room, at her mother, at Jiang, even Kerys – at stunned faces. She touched Kerys's arm and whispered, '*Nauarchus* …'

'Yes, cadet?'

'Everybody seems amazed by all this. But it's just a bunch of old ruins under the ocean, isn't it? What difference does it make?'

Kerys looked at her curiously, almost fondly. 'Ah, Mardina. Evidently you entirely lack imagination. You'll go far in the Navy.'

'I've seen this before,' Penny said now, still searching her bag. 'Oh my memory, I should have made the connection days ago. The motif of your Drowned Culture, the circles and bars. Earthshine *showed* me before. When he took us all down into his bunker under Paris, before the Nail fell.' She closed her eyes. 'And he had a plaque on his wall, some kind of rock art, etchings in sea-corroded concrete, the first time he brought the two of us to Paris – oh, years earlier, my sister and myself. And he brought the plaque with him on the *Tatania*.' At last she found her slate, tapped it with bony fingers, and showed them an image. It was a brooch, Mardina saw, a bit of stone, marked with concentric circles and a radial groove. 'Earthshine was wearing this on Mars eight years ago. And in meetings I had with him, *Before.*'

Ari frowned. 'Earthshine? Then somehow he knows about the Drowned Culture already.'

'Yes.' Penny pursed her lips. 'But you don't get it, you don't see the bigger picture, Ari. Earthshine must have already gathered evidence of this "Drowned Culture" *from Earth*. From my history. Not from Terra. Do you see? It is as if our divergent histories are not organised in any kind of linear fashion, an orderly sequence, so that one gives way to the next, and then the next. They are like … ice floes on a frozen ocean, bumping up against one another in a random way. But I suppose if Earthshine is right that the kernels are wormholes – if in fact we live in a universe riddled with wormholes – then this kind of chaos is what we must expect.'

Ari looked doubtful. '*Wormholes?* I'm afraid I don't understand.'

'Connections across space and time, even between universes … If you have such links then causality can be violated. Cause and effect disconnected, mixed up. Even archaeology need not make sense, as we see here, because its basic logic, that whatever lies beneath the ground was put there by somebody in your own past, need not apply any more. Anything is possible; history is ragged …'

'Chaos,' Kerys said. 'The signature of Loki. In whom officially, as a Navy officer in a Christian federation, I don't believe at all.'

A junior officer burst into the room, looked for Kerys, and thrust a note into her hand. She looked over it quickly and frowned.

'But if all this is true,' Mardina said practically, 'what are we supposed to do about it?'

Ari said, 'We could ask Earthshine.'

'Yes,' Penny said. 'Obviously. But what is he intending? And what has Ceres got to do with it?'

'Maybe we'll find out more soon,' Kerys said grimly. 'Just when I thought this mess couldn't get any odder …'

Mardina asked, '*Nauarchus?* What's happened?'

'A Roman vessel has just returned from interstellar space. Twenty-five-year Hatch-building jaunt. And at their target system they found strangers.' She looked round at the group.

Beth asked, 'Strangers?'

'They were speaking your tongue. *English.* Knowing about you, the Roman authorities have asked for our help.'

178

Beth, Jiang, Penny, survivors of the *Tatania*, shared stunned looks.

Kerys stood up. 'Well, we need to deal with this. Cadet, you're with me. I'm afraid your formal induction is going to have to wait for another day.'

She hurried out of the room, and Mardina ran to follow her.

CHAPTER 24

The Roman exploration vessel *Malleus Jesu* was directed to land near Lutetia Parisiorum, in Roman Gaul. And Penny and her companions were to be brought to the city to meet the ship's strange passengers.

Penny prepared for the journey, slowly gathering her old-lady stuff, her favourite quilted blankets and duck-down slippers, the pills and ointments and mysterious poultices supplied to her by the local doctors for her various aches and pains. She wondered what strings had been pulled to achieve all this, to bring together the survivors of the *Tatania,* and now these other individuals found on the planet of a distant star by Roman explorers – a dialogue between two governments already wary of each other and dealing with an existential mystery that had dropped out of the sky into their hands. She supposed the calculation was that at least the encounter might yield information. And, she supposed, that was what she was hoping for too, at the minimum. What was she *doing* here? How did she get here? What did all this *mean*? ... As for herself, she had long ago given up hope of ever going home again. She knew she would die here.

She hadn't expected to see her twin sister again, however. Yet Stef's was among the names reported by the Navy.

And what were they to do about Earthshine?

As she finished her preparations, she had no doubt Earthshine was very well aware of all that was going on, and would be monitoring closely.

*

They were to travel from Eboraki, in the north of what Penny would have called England, to a city called Dubru on the south coast. And from there they would cross into Gaul.

With Jiang and Marie Golvin, Penny was brought from her lodgings at the Academy by a coach to a transport hub to the south of the city. The place was a clash of technological eras, with a cobbled road bearing horse-drawn traffic leading to a railway terminus, and splashes of scarred concrete where stood slim needles, kernel-driven ships of air and space.

'You know, I realise now in fact that I've travelled little since I got here,' Penny said as Marie helped her down from the coach. 'Twenty years since the jonbar hinge brought us here, and I've barely left the city. I've spent more time off the planet than travelling on it, probably.'

Marie gave her an arm to lean on. 'Well, why travel when you are immersed in strangeness every time you open your door?'

'True, true.'

Marie was in her forties now, plump, greying, a mother of three; she still worked with Penny at the Academy, and in fact had long since taken over many of Penny's administrative duties. Penny depended on Marie in many ways – and, she believed, Marie had found a reasonable happiness in her life here, with her husband Rajeev, even though they were all so far from home.

With servants from the Academy handling their luggage, they walked slowly to the railway terminus, a sprawling roof over multiple platforms, a tangle of lines spreading away in the distance. The architecture seemed very familiar to Penny; there was a certain inevitable economic and engineering logic to rail technology, it seemed. But Brikanti trains ran on gleaming monorails supported by elegant Roman-style viaducts, and their locomotives were powered by kernels, a handful of the mysterious wormholes in the heart of each engine. The train itself was a suspended tube of metal and glass. Penny was relieved to see there was an escalator to lift her up.

181

They had a carriage to themselves at the heart of the train, a roomy space centred on a broad table, brightly lit through big picture windows. It was almost like a dining room, Penny thought. Marie and Penny were in fact the last to arrive. Already here were Beth and Mardina, Beth looking resentful, and a rather more complex expression on Mardina's face; she seemed uncertain, withdrawn. And here were Kerys and Ari Guthfrithson – Ari sitting a respectful distance away from his estranged wife and daughter.

Kerys stood to welcome Penny, and helped her get settled in her seat between Marie and Jiang, and called a servant to bring drinks. Kerys had been put in nominal charge of this peculiar mission, and if the *nauarchus* was irritated to be dragged once again into all this jonbar-hinge strangeness, she didn't show it.

The train slid smoothly out of the station and into watery sunlight.

They soon passed beyond the city limits, heading south, and Penny looked down from above at scattered suburbs of round-houses, set in a wider landscape of farmed fields, horizon-wide expanses of wheat and other crops tended by huge machines that weeded and watered. The individual farming machines didn't run on kernels; there was an extensive grid of cables to carry power from central stations. There were people around, of course, this culture didn't have machinery smart enough to direct itself, but only a few worked in the fields.

Marie said, 'The Academician was saying that she hasn't travelled much since she came here.'

Kerys smiled. 'Your first time on a train, Penny?'

'Not quite. But I suppose I've never thought very much about the nature of your transport systems. Your history, you know, diverged from ours so long ago that much is unfamiliar from the foundations up. Pritanike never had the Romans here ...' Even the Brikanti towns didn't map onto the ones she was familiar with. For example, Stonehenge here was the centre of a major urban sprawl and transport junction, a very modern city that

182

seemed to have continuous cultural roots going back almost to the last Ice Age. 'Also you don't have *automobiles*,' she used the English word, 'by which I mean small vehicles under the control of individuals.'

Ari said, 'Of course we have *automobiles*, but they are under the control of the military and the police exclusively.'

Beth smiled. 'No. That's not what she means. You don't have *cars*. You have *tanks*.'

Kerys said, 'It seems there was less conflict in your world compared to ours. We live in a state of perpetual war, declared or undeclared. Our lives are more ... militarised. Our cities are fortresses; our transport systems are troop carriers that cannot easily be subverted by hostile forces—'

Mardina snapped suddenly. 'I wish you'd all stop going on like this.'

Beth looked surprised. Ari glared at his daughter, but kept his counsel, wisely, Penny thought.

In the end it was Kerys who spoke first. 'Is there a problem, cadet?'

Mardina calmed down quickly. 'I apologise, *nauarchus*. It's just all this talk, it's so ...' She was visibly searching for the words. 'Old. Weird. Cobwebby stuff, like you're all remembering a bad dream.'

Penny covered the girl's hand with her own. 'But you can't blame us for that, dear. I was already impossibly old by your standards when we first came here. Even after all this time on Terra, it's impossible to put Earth aside. But you're right; that's no excuse to inflict our maunderings on you. And I for one need to conserve my energies for the trials to come. Do you have my pillow, Youwei?'

Kerys grinned, and produced a leather pouch. 'You're taking a nap? Good plan, Academician. And as for the rest of us, we can while away the time the way soldiers always have – playing pointless games. So what's it to be? I have knucklebones, chess, cards ...'

*

Penny woke some hours later.

When she glanced out of the window she was startled to find the train was suspended over water. Reflexively she grabbed Jiang's hand. '*Oh, my,*' she said in English.

'Not to worry,' Kerys said with a smile. 'We've already crossed several bridges – Pritanike is an archipelago, remember. Now we're crossing the Mare Britannicum. We let the Romans name this stretch of water, since they always built the bridges. You missed Dubru, but we didn't stop. We'll shortly arrive in Gesoriacum, on the Roman side.'

'Impressive ...'

The bridge terminus on the Gaul side was a massive structure of ancient concrete, evidently heavily repaired and built over. Penny peered up at scarred walls.

Kerys said, 'We've been building bridges across the Britannicum for a thousand years. Also tunnels under the sea bed. Every time there's a war the bridges are first to be cut.'

'Ah. But these foundations remain, to be built on.'

'And they have got bigger and uglier with every century.'

The train crossed the coast without pausing for custom or security checks, and Penny peered out. 'So here I am, almost in my nineties, and arriving in the Roman Empire for the first time. What an impossible dream that would once have seemed!' Staring out at the countryside of northern Gaul, she lost herself in her thoughts.

The others, apparently with relief that the old lady was shutting up, returned to the complicated card game they had been playing.

Gaul, then: province of Rome, as it had been since Caesar's conquest over two millennia before. The hi-tech monorail cut across a landscape of farms, small fields centred on sprawling villas, and cities, walled towns really, with what looked like ancient and battered fortifications. She tried to identify differences with Brikanti. There was more evidence of monumental engineering; she glimpsed towering aqueducts, bridges, roads laid laser-straight across the green landscape. But this was a

184

blocky architecture of stone and straight lines and rectangles, compared to the more organic Celtic style of Brikanti with its use of wood and thatch. Penny felt a spurt of regret that she hadn't travelled more when she was younger. Maybe Mardina was right; she had always been too obsessed about the jonbar hinge and the differences from her own lost world to open her eyes and see what was all around her – to let herself relax and just *be*, to live here in Terra, in this world with its own wonders. But she had brought trouble to this place in the shape of Earthshine, she reminded herself, and that was a challenge she couldn't duck.

And this world was hardly a utopia, as she could see by glancing out of the window now. Compared to Pritanike, few machines were to be seen in these small fields. But she saw many people working, bent over the crops, carrying baskets of fertiliser or produce, even scraping at what looked like drainage ditches – people everywhere. And wherever the train passed, the people in the fields below stopped their work and lowered their heads, avoiding any chance of eye contact with the train's passengers.

Ari Guthfrithson, sitting opposite, was watching her.

She raised an eyebrow. 'You're not playing the games?'

He shrugged. 'I fear my fragile relationship with my family would not survive a tense knucklebones contest. Here you are in the glorious realm of Rome. What do you think?'

'That I'm glad we castaways from the UN-China Culture were picked up by a Brikanti ship rather than a Roman. The people working those fields – starships and slavery. What a contradiction.'

Ari shrugged. 'When we were able to build machines more powerful than people and animals, we started to grow our economy on that basis, and slavery became old-fashioned. But Christ Himself, according to our Bible, kept slaves. It is not a sin.' He glanced out of the window. 'Lutetia Parisiorum is approaching.'

'I visited this place once,' Penny murmured, remembering.

'*Before*, I mean. When Earthshine brought us here, my sister and myself, to show us the graveyard where our mother was buried...'

'The rail line parallels the ancient road into the city from the south, which the inhabitants call the *cardo maximus*. It has always been the Romans' habit to build their cemeteries outside the city walls.'

After more than twenty centuries of continuous habitation the cemeteries lined the road for many kilometres south of the city.

Even before the train reached the walls, Penny could see that the city was much less extensive than the Paris she'd known. Lutetia Parisiorum was a mere provincial city, not a national capital as in Penny's home timeline. Still, the urban sprawl was extensive, under a dome of brownish smog.

The monorail cut through the stout walls, close to a road gate huge enough itself to have served as a fortress. Within the city multi-storey red-tiled dwellings crowded along straight-line streets, with spires and domes rising above the rest. Aqueducts snaked over the walls to deliver water, and Penny imagined an equally impressive network of sewers hidden beneath the ground. Many of the grander buildings, with domes and pillared porticoes, either copied the styles of antiquity or, presumably, dated from that long-gone age. But Penny could see more monorail lines laced over the city, and as her train slowed there was a crash of thunder from the sky, a glare of liquid light, as some kernel-powered spacecraft fled over the city towards orbit.

The monorail terminus was close to the river, the south bank of the Seine, and as the elevated train pulled in, Penny could see across the river to the Île de la Cité, no doubt blessed with a Latin name in this timeline, where a magnificent domed cathedral towered over a crowd of lesser buildings.

As the train drew to a halt, Jiang helped Penny out of her seat. It was only a short walk, Kerys promised, to the office of the provincial administration, where the passengers of the *Malleus Jesu* had been lodged since their passage to Terra. Penny braced herself for the walk, and an encounter she could barely imagine, with her sister, Stef Kalinski.

CHAPTER 25

They were guided into a very Roman reception room, all couches and tapestries and a mosaic floor, and servants scuttling around under the direction of a provincial official, a short, pompous-looking man in a crisp white toga.

And here were the strangers, standing together in an uncomfortable huddle, Penny thought. The group was dominated by a big man wearing breast armour and a thick military buckle. At his side were a couple more Roman military types, looking out of place in this rather fussy formal room, along with a middle-aged woman in the costume of a Brikanti, and an older man in a rather more practical-looking toga.

And there stood a boy, maybe eighteen, nineteen years old, with Asiatic features, a little plump, with some kind of well-padded pack on his back. He wore a drab tunic, and what looked like an ISF-issue slate rested on his chest, suspended from a chain around his neck. He was barefoot. Penny immediately guessed he was a slave. Jiang seemed drawn to the boy, who was perhaps a fellow Xin.

To Penny, all this was background. To her there was only one presence in the room. She stepped forward.

Their eyes locked, Penny and Stef Kalinski faced each other.

'My God,' Penny said at last, speaking English. 'I never thought—'

'Nor I, believe me,' Stef said fervently. 'I went through a Hatch to Proxima Centauri to get away from you. And then even further, to a star that turned out to be nine light years away. Only to be picked up by these alternate Romans and brought back home, to this.'

'And in Paris again.' Penny tried to smile, and failed. 'Do you remember, all those years ago?'

'Our mother's grave. How could I forget? But I'm kind of surprised *you* can still remember.' Stef walked around Penny, eyeing her. 'So this is my future. I feel like Dorian Grey.'

'I'm not that old. I'm eighty-nine now, Stef. Whereas you—'

'Am a youthful seventy, thanks to a lot of Hatch-hopping and relativistic time dilation.'

'Whatever we are, we are no longer twins, at least.'

Stef grinned malevolently. 'Good. And, seeing you standing there with that damn stick, I feel like I somehow won.'

'And I,' said Penny tiredly, 'feel like I'm too old to care. I wish you no harm, Stef. I never did.'

'No. It was your sudden eruption into existence when I opened that damn Hatch on Mercury that did the harm.'

'When *we* opened it ... Oh, it's all so long ago.'

The big Roman approached them, walking slowly, non-threatening. He said gently, in gruff Latin, 'Colonel Stef Kalinski. *Druidh* Penny Kalinski. Though you are twins it pleases me it is so easy to tell you apart.'

Stef said softly, 'I hope your Latin's up to scratch, sis. The Romans don't speak anything else.'

Penny nodded. 'Quite right too – umm, Centurion?'

'Indeed. I am Centurion Quintus Fabius, commander of the mission of the *Malleus Jesu*. These others you see here are members of my crew – my *optio*, Gnaeus Junius, my *trierarchus* the Brikanti Movena, Michael, our *medicus*. Oh, and the slave bears the remnant of Collius, your speaking machine.'

Penny stared at the boy.

'Ordinarily at the end of a mission our crew would be dispersed, returned to our legion's *collegia* for induction, leave and reassignment. Instead we have been given the unusual task of caring for the strangers we found on a planet of the distant star Romulus, at least until more formal arrangements can be made.'

Penny barked laughter. 'I'm becoming used to the bureaucracies of empires. You mean, until your government and the Brikanti can come up with some category to file us away in.'

He grinned. 'Well, I'm no clerk, lady, but I see the truth in what you say. But we welcome the task. You see the big man over there, with one hand? He is a legionary, a veteran; he is called Titus Valerius. For five years he has been the protector of the slave who carries Collius. It is a task he fulfils with joy. Of course the alternative for him would have been to remain with the permanent *colonia* under that distant star ...'

'Collius? ColU?' Beth pushed her way between them and made her way to the slave boy, who stood passively, head lowered, eyes downcast – a gesture Penny had learned to recognise, and hate. Beth cupped his chin and raised his head. 'Why, you're not much older than my Mardina, are you? What is your name?'

The boy glanced at Titus Valerius, who growled, 'Answer the lady. You're not in any trouble.'

'My name is Chu Yuen, lady.'

'Collius? You mean the ColU? You're really carrying around the ColU in your backpack?'

'What's left of me,' came a mournful voice from the backpack.

Beth's face lit up. 'ColU – it is you! Oh, I could hug you. But—'

'Yuri Eden saved my processor unit and memory store. My interfacing is provided by slate technology. I am afraid I am not very huggable.'

'Maybe I should hug this slave of yours.'

'Please, Beth Eden Jones. Not in front of the Romans. Did I hear you mention a Mardina?'

'Yes. My daughter, named after my mother. Mardina – come here.'

Mardina came up, but with every expression of reluctance, and Penny, still feeling bruised from her own encounter with the complicated past, could only sympathise.

The ColU said, 'Chu Yuen. Please turn a little to the right.'

The boy obeyed, and Penny observed how he stuck his chest out as he did so, tilting the slate. That was evidently how the ColU 'saw' the world.

'Mardina,' the ColU said gravely. 'I'm pleased to meet you. You have your grandmother's name, and something of her looks.'

'I never knew her.' Mardina looked wildly at her mother. 'I feel like I'm talking into thin air, talking to a ghost!'

'Lieutenant Mardina Jones was a brave and strong human being, and I would be honoured to talk to you about her.'

'Don't bother,' Mardina snarled back.

Beth said hurriedly, 'It's all right, ColU, it's difficult for her.'

'I understand,' the ColU said gently. 'Beth, as for your father, Yuri Eden …'

Stef walked up to Beth and took her hand. 'You know that we went through the Hatch to Romulus together. Yuri and I. Just the two of us, and the ColU – the surviving bit of it. But—'

'He hasn't made it home, has he?'

'His illness seemed to have been caused by his century in cryo suspension. "Freezer burn" he called it. I'm sorry, Beth.'

The ColU said, 'I was with him in his last hours. I can tell you as much about that as you wish. Beth Eden Jones, he made me promise to find you. And so I have. And he instructed me to make sure you understand that, under his will as drawn up under Roman law, I am now your property, Beth.'

Penny could see that Beth was holding back tears. She hobbled forward on her stick. 'Well, I for one have done enough standing for one day. And my throat's as dry as the dust of Luna.'

With a glance at the provincial official, Quintus Fabius stepped forward, hands held wide, generously. 'Let me be your host.'

The Romans showed remarkable sensitivity towards the gathered survivors of the UN-China Culture, Penny thought. They were allowed space and time to talk, to get over the shock of meeting.

But in the end they had to get down to business.

'Earthshine,' Stef said simply. 'That's the top and bottom of it. Earthshine.'

Quintus Fabius said, '*Earthshine*. If I understand you, this is the – machine – that you brought with you from your old world, and is now on Mars—'

Kerys said, 'I have had years to get used to these ideas, Centurion. You've had days. And *I* barely understand it. We'll have to let them talk this through. And then, I suspect, we're going to have to make our superiors understand too.'

'I look forward to that, *nauarchus*,' he said drily. 'Very well – Earthshine. Tell me why we must discuss this.'

'For one thing,' Penny said, 'he is the reason we are here. I mean, we survivors of the jonbar-hinge event, the destruction of the worlds of our own timeline ...'

Quintus looked helplessly at Kerys. 'Do they always talk like this?'

'I'm afraid so.'

The ColU said, 'The jonbar hinge came with a great surge of energy, when the UN-China war erupted, and the kernels on Mercury were opened by the Nail, the Chinese missile ... Perhaps such a surge, involving kernels, is necessary to create a hinge. Meanwhile you, Stef, were with Yuri and myself in a Hatch, en route to Romulus-Remus. And you, Beth, Penny, were with Lex McGregor, fleeing the solar system behind a bank of kernels.'

Stef said, 'You're suggesting that somehow the kernels, the Hatches, preserved us.'

The ColU said, 'Yes. I think Earthshine moved us to where he wanted us to be, like chess pieces on a board, Colonel Kalinski. At least the key pieces. Consider. Who survived the jonbar hinge? Earthshine himself. And his son, Yuri Eden. Or at least, the son of Robert Braemann, one of the input personalities that became Earthshine. And his granddaughter, Beth Eden Jones. Everybody Earthshine might have cared about personally—'

Mardina turned on her mother. 'His son? His granddaughter? What new horror is this? That thing on Mars – are you telling me that it's somehow my great-grandfather? Mother – *did you know*?'

Beth sighed. 'I knew. He told me his name on the *Tatania*, as we fled from the moon. And my father, Yuri, told me *his* true name before we parted, on Mercury. And when I put the two together—'

'You never told me?'

'You've spent your life rejecting your past, Mardina. Are you saying you would have wanted to know?'

Quintus Fabius leaned forward. 'I can see why this is difficult for you all. This talk of the past – but now we must speak of the future. Collius, tell us of the ice ball, the world you Brikanti call Höd. And the observations we have been making of Earthshine's activities.'

Penny frowned. '"We"? Who's "we", the Empire?'

'No. We of the *Malleus Jesu*,' the ColU said. 'Academician, during the journey back I was privileged to work with the ship's team of navigators and observers. They are Moslems, mostly Arab. A product of a high civilisation, though one subsumed within the Roman system in this timeline.'

'I'm guessing you had them observe Ceres,' Penny prompted.

The ColU said, 'I had a feeling that the tracking of the object, and the projection of its future motion, might be beyond observers on Earth. Especially give the erratic pattern of the kernel-bank burns they are applying. *You* can't be sure where it's heading. I, however—'

Beth laughed. 'With your superior computational powers, you know exactly what's going on. You always were conceited, ColU.'

'Liu Tao once said to me that for a farm machine I have ideas above my station. And I replied by pointing out that a sentient mind refuses to be confined by the parameters of its programming—'

'Get to the point!' Quintus was almost shouting now. 'Where is this ice block heading, o engine of glass?'

'*Towards an impact on Mars*,' Penny said tiredly. 'Am I right,

ColU? Not a close approach, a grazing encounter with the atmosphere—'

'I'm afraid you are correct, Penelope Kalinski.'

Stef nodded dumbly. 'Very well. But why? What is he intending to achieve?'

'I can think of only dire and destructive possibilities,' the ColU said.

Quintus and Kerys shared grim glances. Kerys said, 'And whatever else he does achieve, he'll probably trigger a war, in the Skull of Ymir as on Terra. Rome and Xiu will probably believe this is some ploy by Brikanti, who sent Earthshine to Mars.'

Quintus turned to the slave. 'What can we do, Collius? Can we stop this?'

'Time is short,' the ColU whispered. 'It is fortuitous we arrived back here in time to observe this, let alone intervene. I would suggest that only Earthshine himself can stop the collision – if he wills it.'

Stef said, 'Then we have to go there. To Mars.'

Penny said, 'Why should he even speak to us?'

'Maybe not to *us*. Which is why we must all go. Beth, Mardina – I know how difficult this is going to be for you – but you're his family. If the ColU is right, he's already saved you once. Maybe he'll listen to you again. If there's even a chance of averting this ...'

Beth looked away, and Penny saw how closed-up she became, as, not for the first time in Beth's life, those around her plotted to manipulate her and her daughter. Penny said gently, 'Just think about it, Beth. The consequences of all this. We did bring this creature into this reality. We have to try.'

Stef said briskly, 'But we'll have to get to Mars first. How are we going to do that?'

'In my ship,' said Quintus Fabius firmly. 'I am serious,' he said in response to their surprised expressions. 'The *Malleus* needs reprovisioning, but the crew have yet to be dispersed, and it stands ready to fly. My legionaries will squawk, but the journey would be short and the bonuses handsome, I imagine. I could have you all on Mars in days … *If* we can arrange suitable clearances quickly,' and he glanced significantly at the shocked-looking provincial official.

Penny frowned. 'Where is this ship of yours? In orbit, on the moon—'

'About five kilometres north of here,' Stef said drily. 'This is a culture where they land interstellar spacecraft at city airports.'

'I wish I could say you get used to such things,' Penny said to her. 'But you don't.'

Mardina was looking around at them as they spoke, mouth open, obviously amazed by all she'd heard – overwhelmed perhaps. 'Well, then, let's all fly off to Mars, and find out the truth.'

Beth touched her arm. 'What truth, dear?'

'That that's what this terrible old monster with the pretty name, Earthshine, probably intended you to do all along. That he's been manipulating you all for decades.'

There was a shocked silence.

Then the ColU said, 'Even I hadn't thought of that.'

CHAPTER 26

The deceleration of the *Malleus Jesu* into Martian space was ferocious.

Nobody would tell Penny how high they ramped it up in the end. Clearly it was far higher than an Earth gravity, the Roman ship's standard kernel-driven acceleration regime. That itself said something of the urgency of the mission. But Penny had little energy to fret, as she lay pressed down into her deep couch, scarcely daring to move a muscle, to lift a finger.

She was given a private room on the seventh deck, officer country – she was told it was part of Centurion Quintus's own suite – a very Roman affair, though the couches were riveted to the floor and the tapestries fixed with heavy iron nails, and everything was *sturdy*, built to withstand the surges of acceleration to be expected of a warship. On the other hand the *Malleus*, veteran of several interstellar missions and as a result of cumulative time dilation several decades out of its own era, was an antique. The ship had already been subjected to years of acceleration, and the sleeting radiations and corrosive dust and ice grains of interstellar space, and now she was to be put through what in some ways was likely to be her toughest assignment yet. It might only take one component failure, a structural element buckling somewhere, a bulkhead or a hull plate cracking under the unbearable stress, for the whole mission to unravel – and their lives to be lost.

So Penny lay there in her couch, listening to the deep, almost subsonic thrumming of the kernel engines, and the fabric of the grand old ship popping and banging and creaking around her, and waiting for the end. She did feel an odd empathy for the ship. For what was her own body but a relic, the wreckage of a too-long life – and nearly unable to bear these immense accelerations? She couldn't have blamed the *Malleus* if the ship had failed. Just as she couldn't have blamed her own wretched body if it had given up as she put it through one unbearable strain too many.

The crew, however, was trained for operation under this kind of acceleration regime. She didn't lack for company. Even the Greek *medicus* Michael visited her in a wheelchair, tightly strapped in, with a metal brace to support his neck and head.

What was still more impressive was the legionary assigned to push Michael around the ship in his wheelchair, triple-gravity acceleration or not: Titus Valerius, the big one-armed veteran. He walked with the support of an exoskeleton, creaking and clanking, powered by the crude electric motors – 'etheric engines' – that were, apart from kernel engines, handheld radio communicators, which they called 'farspeakers', and some ferocious weaponry, just about the height of mechanical engineering achievement in his world. Penny could see how Titus's muscles bulged under the strain, how the veins were prominent in his heavily supported neck. But he got the job done, as, evidently, did the rest of Quintus's highly trained crew.

'You're doing fine,' Michael told her from his chair, as he examined her. 'I can assure you, you're a tougher old eagle than you look, or may feel. As long as you do as I say, as long as you lie there and don't take chances, and are patient—'

'My catheter itches.'

He laughed. 'Bad luck. You'll have to fix that yourself.'

Penny's most welcome attendant, however, was Titus's daughter, Clodia, just fifteen years old by her own subjective timekeeping, who had spent most of her young life aboard the *Malleus* during its mission to the Romulus-Remus double-star system. Clodia was evidently strong, able to get around the ship under gravity using a chair and prosthetic aids built for an adult twice her size, and turned out a bright, chatty kid.

At first she brought Penny her meals – that is, she changed the drip bags according to Michael's schedule. But as the ship's watches passed, and they got to know each other better, she responded to Penny's other needs. She turned out to be the kindest of Penny's team of aides in changing her catheter bag, and washing her face, and even changing the diaper-like garment that soaked up her old-lady poop. Penny had done her level best not to be embarrassed at having to be changed, at one end of her long life, like the infant she'd been at the other.

Penny was surprised Clodia had volunteered for this mission, however. On the last day, as the ship approached Mars and they waited for the end of acceleration, they talked about this.

'Let me get it straight. You were just a toddler when your father took you with him on the *Malleus Jesu*, the journey to Romulus and Remus.'

'My mother died when I was very small, before we left Terra. There was only my father and me—'

'Yes. I'm sorry. So you spent a few years running around on the planet. And then, age ten or so, you're scooped up and brought back to Earth – I mean, Terra. I'd have thought you'd find Terra a lot more exciting than life on the ship. All the different people, the cities.'

Clodia pulled a face. 'Lutetia Parisiorum is a dump. And it's badly laid out from a defensive point of view. I suppose I'd like to see Rome. And the great cities of Brikanti as well, of course—'

'There's no need to be polite with me, child!'

Clodia grinned. 'But wherever you go on the ground there's no, no ... People sort of wander around doing whatever they want.'

'No discipline?'

'That's it. It's not like when you're on the march, and you build your camp every night, and everything's in the same place each time, exactly where it should be. Night after night. *That's* what I like.'

'You're an army brat, and there's nothing wrong with that. Well, I'm glad you're here, Clodia, you've been a comfort to me … What of the future, though? Even your father can't last in the legion for ever. What will you do? I can't imagine you being satisfied to be some soldier's wife.'

'I don't remember my mother, but I saw the women in camp, at Romulus. Having babies and baking bread and washing clothes, day after day?' She pulled her face. 'That's not for me.'

'Then what? They don't allow women in the Roman army, do they?'

'Not into the legions, no. Not in the fighting infantry. But there are masses of other jobs you can do. In administration, in training, in logistics. A lot of that is based in the cities, the big central military establishments. And there are jobs in the front line women can take, even in the fighting units, some kinds of auxiliary. Or I might become a weapons specialist. Go into training.'

'Or be a *medicus*. There are plenty of front-line jobs there. You ought to talk to Michael about that.'

Again, a self-deprecating face-pull. 'Maybe I could be a nurse. I'm not sure I'm clever enough otherwise. I can strip down field artillery pieces, but an injured legionary … I'll find something.'

'I'm sure you will—'

That was when the warning trumpet sounded, filling the hull with its shrill note.

Clodia said, 'Just lie still, until it's over.'

And Penny, lying in her couch, felt the cessation of the kernel engines, a deep shudder transmitted through the ship's fabric. That chorus of creaks and alarming bangs ceased immediately too, as the strain of three gravities was removed. And only then, it seemed, did the sense of heavy acceleration lift from her body.

'Ah,' she murmured. 'It's as if your father has been sitting on my chest for two days, and now he's got off.'

Clodia impatiently unbuckled the restraints that held her in her chair, pushed aside her exoskeletal aids, and let herself drift up into the air, whooping. 'I always love this bit!'

'How long were we—'

'Fifty hours. Twenty-five accelerating at three weights, and then the turnover, and twenty-five decelerating. And here we are at Mars, just like that. We couldn't have got here any quicker. Roman ships are the best performing in the world, and the *trierarchus* will have pushed us as hard as she could.'

'Oh, I don't doubt it, child. But we might be too late even so.' She struggled to emerge from her cocoon of blankets and cushions, an aged butterfly. 'Oh, help me out of this thing.'

Clodia hovered dubiously. 'If I don't keep you here until the *medicus* has checked you over, I'm going to be walking back to Terra …'

It was another hour before Penny, fuming with frustration, was at last allowed onto the bridge of the *Malleus*.

And beyond the observation windows, before her eyes, once more Mars loomed huge, like a plasterwork in oranges and browns, scarred by craters and dry canyons, the silver bands of the canals glowing softly in the sunlight.

When she arrived a kind of council of war was already under-way, involving Quintus, his second in command Gnaeus and his ship's *trierarchus* Movena, as well as Stef, Beth, Mardina, Ari Guthfrithson, Kerys, and the ColU borne on the shoulders of Chu Yuen. Stef barely glanced at her sister. All of them looked beat up to Penny, their skin blotchy, their eyes puffy. There was a faint smell of body odour in the crowded room – but then probably none of them had washed for days, Penny reflected; they hadn't all had the comprehensive medical support she'd enjoyed.

And Jiang was here. He too looked wrung out. But he held onto a rail, supporting himself in the air, and took her hand in his. 'Mars again,' he said. 'Where we first met.'

'Yes. All those years ago, at the UN-China conference at Obelisk.'

'No matter what we go through, Mars, it seems, endures.'

Quintus Fabius faced her. 'Maybe Mars has not yet changed very much, Academician. But it will shortly. Look up there.' He pointed to a slice of dark sky, beyond Mars's western limb.

Where hung a single brilliant star.

'Ceres,' Penny whispered.

'Höd, yes.'

'How close is it? That thing looks almost large enough to show a disc.'

Stef said, 'Penny, we haven't been troubling you with updates during the voyage. We hoped you'd sleep through it—'

'Oh, shut up, you fusspot.'

Quintus said, 'Höd is larger than the width of Venus, as seen from Earth. So the Arab observers assure me.'

Penny tried to work that out. 'Then it must be – what, a few million kilometres out?'

'Rather less,' Stef said. 'The asteroid has undergone episodes of immense thrust. We suspect Earthshine has ordered the use of significant chunks of the body's own material to use as reaction mass. The observers on the *Malleus* have computed the new trajectory.'

Penny could see the conclusion of all that in her sister's expression. 'My God.'

Stef took a deep breath. 'Ceres is going to impact Mars. That's finally confirmed. It's probably what Earthshine intended all along.'

Quintus looked furious, as if this was some personal betrayal. 'But why?'

'We've no idea,' Stef said. 'Not yet.'

Penny looked at Stef. 'How long?'

'The Arabs estimate twelve hours. No more.'

'As little as that? Very well. That's the time we have remaining to stop Earthshine.'

Quintus nodded grimly. 'Of course we must. This great act, this hurling of cosmic masses, can be intended to do nothing but harm. It may even start a war. We have to stop him. But we will face resistance.'

'Then,' Penny said drily, 'I'm glad I'm on a ship full of Roman legionaries. Let's work out our plan.'

201

But as the soldiers began to discuss tactics and fallbacks, a clock in Penny's head began a dreadful countdown.

Twelve hours, and counting.

CHAPTER 27

To Stef's relief, Penny submitted to Michael's insistence that she needed rest.

'And make sure she straps down again,' the centurion called as she was led from the bridge. 'We may have some more hard acceleration to undergo before the day is done.'

'As you wish, Centurion.'

The rest of them inspected Quintus's images of the layout of Earthshine's latest base on the ground, at Terra Cimmeria. They were large-scale photographs, grainy wet-chemistry productions like all Roman or Brikanti imagery, but good enough, Stef thought, to get a sense of the layout. She saw three broad clusters of facilities, grouped close together. Further out the ground was marked by swathes of scorching, places where the ground had melted altogether: the relics of multiple landings of kernel-drive rockets.

'So, Colonel Kalinski,' Quintus said. 'We have been scouting this area for some time – for years, as Earthshine has developed his operation. But I welcome your input now. This is the location where you say that the Xin had their Martian capital in your world.'

'Slap in the heart of the highland we called the Terra Cimmeria, yes.'

'Which was no doubt why Earthshine chose it,' the ColU said from Chu's backpack, 'because of that resonance. Everything Earthshine does will be shaped by an awareness of competing realities. And it is also, no doubt, why the site of a city that was called Obelisk for its greatest single building should be marked here by – point for me, Chu Yuen, left and down – *that*.' The slave seemed to work well with the master he carried; his finger stabbed down on the image of one of the three clusters of domed buildings.

Stef peered down. 'I see a sharp stripe on the ground. Wait – where is the sun? That's a shadow, of something very tall—'

'*A tree*,' the ColU said. 'Not an obelisk. A tree. Encouraged to grow to some four hundred metres, which is three times the maximum theoretical height on Terra. A tree's height is limited by the need to lift water to its uppermost leaves—'

'But on Mars, with its one-third gravity,' Stef said, 'you can grow as tall as this. It must have been force-grown.'

'Yes. Earthshine has been established on Mars for some years, but not *that* long. Force-grown and encased in some kind of enclosure to retain air and moisture. We don't have good enough images to determine the species yet. An impressive stunt.'

Beth leaned closer to see. Beth and Mardina had been quiet since Penny's brief visit to the bridge. Only Ari had been quieter, Stef thought; the *druidh* had not spoken a word.

Now Beth asked, 'But why would Earthshine grow a tree on Mars? It doesn't seem to fit.'

'It's for his allies,' said Kerys grimly. The *nauarchus* had also been quiet during this voyage on a Roman ship, Stef had observed, but she had watched and listened, evidently filing everything away. Now she pointed to another shadow traced on the Martian ground, in a second compound some distance to the north of the tree. '*That* is a ship – a ship of the Brikanti Navy, called the *Celyn*. Earthshine has at least one ship's company's worth of support on the ground with him, and most of them drawn from Brikanti ranks.' She glared at Quintus, defiant. 'We don't have time for blame games. This monster, this Earthshine, was after all found, fortuitously, by a Brikanti ship – my ship, all those years ago. How I wish now we had simply thrown the boxes that sustain him out into the Skull of Ymir! Even if we had preserved the rest of you.'

'Thanks,' Beth said drily.

'It was natural that as he began to lay out his schemes for the exploitation of other worlds, he would gather support from the Brikanti government at first. We believed we could control the situation – control *him*.'

'Well, you were wrong,' Quintus said.

'It began with his subversion of the crews of the ships we sent out to support him. He persuaded them to betray their nation – to follow dreams of greed and power, under *him*. That is what we believe happened. But they are Brikanti.'

'Ah,' Stef said. 'I've been reading up on this during the journey home. To the *druidh*, in the Brikanti tradition, the tree is a sacred symbol.'

Ari spoke now. 'Whatever other projects they are pursuing, they will have relished the chance to nurture what may still be the only tree on Mars, and certainly the greatest – greater than any on Earth. Even Christians would respond to the symbol. You Romans nailed Christ to a wooden cross, and His blood nurtured the roots of the World Tree Yggdrasil, which—'

'Yes, yes,' Quintus said impatiently. 'Hardly the time for a theology lesson, *druidh*. So – the holy tree. And around it, as you see, a series of domed habitats that we believe are residences for Earthshine's human supporters, or most of them, along with workshops, stores. To the north, and a reasonably safe distance away from the tree, you see the *Celyn* standing, and accompanying support facilities for a kernel craft. Room for others to land too, and we have seen craft shuttling between Mars and Höd in the last few years.'

'Relief crews,' Kerys said. 'There are teams working up on Höd, manning the kernel banks there. They seem to be swapped every month or so.'

Quintus said, 'And we believe that Earthshine himself, or at least the gadgets that support him, must be *here*.' And he pointed to the third complex of buildings.

Stef leaned down to see better, silently cursing ageing eyes. 'More domes. But the heart of it is that tilted rectangular slab.'

'A reinforced bunker,' Quintus said. 'A familiar design.

Hardened against our ground-based weapons, hardened even against any rock pushed from orbit short of anything massive enough to destroy the whole site altogether. No doubt Earthshine is down in a hole deeper still.'

Stef grunted. 'That would be characteristic. He likes his holes in the ground, the bunkers he shared with his Core AI brothers back on Earth, his hold-out under Paris, his pit under Hellas ...'

Beth said, 'But this whole planet is going to be hammered by Ceres. I can't believe he's going to stay around for that. He'll want to survive, whatever he's trying to do here. Just as he got away from Earth before the Nail fell.'

'Right,' said Stef. 'And if Ceres is going to fall within twelve hours, his only way out of here will be aboard that ship, the *Celyn*.'

'Very well,' Quintus said. 'That is the configuration on the ground. Now I want a tactical plan. It would not be hard to be destructive. Frankly, we could go in with our kernel drive blazing, and melt all of this back into the Martian sand.'

'But we're not here to destroy,' the ColU said. 'We need to get to Earthshine. The purpose is to deflect Ceres, if it is still possible.'

'Our foes know that too,' said Quintus. 'So they will be waiting for us to attempt a softer approach, perhaps a landing. They may have missiles, even kernel-driven, to shoot us down as we approach, as is standard protection for our great cities on Terra—'

'Maybe not,' put in Movena, Quintus's *trierarchus*. 'The scans we've been able to do of the surface would show us any such missiles. There are kernels here –' She pointed. 'Under Earthshine's bunker. But they aren't a configuration we recognise – they certainly aren't being used in missiles.'

'This conversation is inefficient.' Ari Guthfrithson stepped forward now, cold, clinical. 'We must focus on the goal and work backwards. We have to get to Earthshine; we have to persuade him to deflect Höd, if this is still possible. Well, then. You have brought my family here—'

Beth snarled, 'We are not your family.' Mardina clutched her arm.

Ari ignored her. He tapped the image of the bunker. 'You must land us here. The three of us, mother, father, daughter – *his* granddaughter and great-granddaughter. And the farm machine, one mechanical mind that may be able to communicate with another.'

'Thanks for thinking of me,' the ColU said drily.

'Earthshine will take us into his bunker. He has saved you before, Beth, you know that, when he brought you on the *Tatania*, out of the bonfire of your Earth. He will save you again today. For I am sure you are right. He will have no ambition to be extinguished. And he will be motivated to take us with him, wherever he goes.'

Quintus prompted, 'And once you're down there ...'

'We try to persuade him to stop. But this will rely on us getting to that bunker unhindered.'

Quintus nodded. 'We have yachts; we can get you down there. But in the meantime we'll have to draw off the bulk of whatever forces he has. We have a *testudo* that we can have some fun with on the ground ...' He pulled his lip. 'Earthshine's forces will be pretty well dug in.'

Movena smiled. 'But these are my people. Brikanti. I know how they think. And I have a suggestion to divert their attention.'

'Which is?'

'They have to protect two of their three facilities on the ground, the launch site, the bunker. So, attack the third.'

Quintus smiled. 'Ah. The big tree. The Brikanti will be drawn away to save *that*, being the superstitious barbarians they are.'

Kerys, visibly dismissing the insult, shook her head. 'These are standard plays. We need something more. A backup plan. Even if Beth Eden Jones and the others get through to Earthshine, there's no guarantee he will listen to them. We need to think about other ways of stopping Höd.'

'Such as?' Quintus asked. 'There are troops on Höd itself; they will no doubt stay up there to defend it until the last possible minute. If we try to approach in the *Malleus* they will blast us out of the sky – or do their level best.'

'True. So we don't approach in the *Malleus*. Or rather, I don't.'

'What do you mean?'

'I mean that I will take a small crew, Brikanti-trained – just a couple of us would do – and take *that* ship, from the ground. The *Celyn*. It's the same class as my own last command, the *Ukelwydd*. I could fly it blindfold. We will eliminate it as a threat to the *Malleus*, if nothing else. And perhaps we can be a backup to this strategy of persuasion. I could simply fly up to Höd, which is conveniently hurtling in towards us, and use the ship's communication codes, and maybe my own rank, as cover to approach. And then—'

Quintus frowned. 'Yes, and then?'

'I don't know. I'll have to improvise. The crew on Höd must have some kind of abort facility.'

'Not necessarily,' the ColU murmured.

'Well, if there isn't, we'll think of something else.'

Movena nodded enthusiastically. 'It may be a slim chance, but better than none at all.'

Kerys said, 'If you drop me below the base's horizon, perhaps on the same pass when you drop Beth and her party for the bunker—'

'Beth, and her party, and me.' The voice wavered, but was forceful.

Stef turned, and to her dismay saw Penny in the doorway, clinging to a rail with one clawlike hand, her grey hair a cloud around her head. 'Penny – go back to your couch.'

'I will not, and I don't answer to you now, Stef, if I ever did. Listen to me. I know Earthshine better than any of you. I was even a colleague of sorts, once, and have been here again, on this side of the jonbar hinge. Drop me onto Mars in a wheelchair – in a pressurised sack, whatever – I can help you.' She smiled thinly. 'At the minimum it might distract him. Another diversion of forces.' She glared at her sister. 'I trust you're not going to put up any more objections?'

Stef felt anger surge. 'You never belonged in my life anyway. To see you leave it now will be no loss to me.'

Quintus held up his hands. 'We don't have time for this. We have a plan, and it's the best we're going to find. Prepare for your drops in –' He glanced at his *trierarchus*.

'One hour,' Movena said.

'One hour.' He glanced around at the group. 'We will probably never meet again like this, those of us assembled here. And many of us may not survive the day at all. If you believe in Jesu, may He be at your side now.' He clapped his hands, breaking the moment. 'Go, go!'

CHAPTER 28

With six hours left before the arrival of Ceres, the *Malleus Jesu* tore into the atmosphere of Mars. It was, Titus Valerius cried triumphantly, like a Roman *gladio* ripping through a barbarian's guts.

Gnaeus Junius, along with a *contubernium* of eight men under the command of Titus, was already tucked inside the heavily armoured hide of a *testudo*. He clung to his couch harness, dug himself deeper into the padding, and told himself he was as safe as he could reasonably be, at such a moment, in his armoured pressure suit, buried in his couch, inside an armoured vehicle that in turn was swaddled in the hold of the *Malleus*, a kernel-powered fist of a ship. Thus Gnaeus was wrapped up in layers of cushioning and armour and hull plate, like a precious gift ready for transport to the favoured son of an emperor.

But right now this gift was being delivered by falling headlong into the thin Martian air. The ship fell backside first, with its kernel bank burning bright to slow it down from its inter-planetary speeds. Gnaeus just prayed that the thick hull, which right now was peeling away in layers to carry away excess heat, would last long enough to keep the ship intact through these painfully long heartbeats of the entry.

Ahead of him Gnaeus saw the men of the *contubernium* in their couches, all of them with their backs to him, soaking up the deceleration. A *contubernium* was formally a 'tent group', a unit within the legion – a band who trained, lived and fought together. They seemed relaxed. One of them was even *asleep*, as far as Gnaeus could see, a man called Marcus Vinius. They'd

210

been through far worse than this in training, Titus had assured him.

Well, not Gnaeus. He was from a senatorial family; his time in the army, his jaunts into space, were only intended as stepping stones to better things, a few years of toughening up before he returned to a career in high politics, hopefully in the capital itself. His unwelcome assignment to the Romulus-Remus interstellar mission, while it kept him from coming up against warlike barbarians in Valhalla, had also kept him away from Rome for twenty-five years, in which time a new generation of pushy upstarts had come along to compete for such positions – a whole cadre just as bright and ambitious as Gnaeus, and not decades out of touch with the current intrigues and infighting at the top of the Empire, as he was.

And now, *this*. Invading a planet occupied by some kind of mad machine, and just as the sky was about to fall. Such adventures had certainly not been in Gnaeus's career plan.

The deceleration built to a brutal peak. He closed his eyes, gritted his teeth, and wondered if it might not be better if the ship just disintegrated in the air and put an end to it all. But he didn't really mean that, not even in the worst moments. He had his duty to perform, after all.

And then, like a switch being closed, the deceleration dropped to nearly zero. Gnaeus was thrust forward against his harness, and his stomach rebelled at last, his breakfast of dried fish and bread splashing up out of his mouth.

Titus laughed and clapped him on the back. 'Never mind, *optio*. Happens to us all. And none of us saw the *optio* spew up his guts like a little girl, did we, lads?'

'Not me, Titus Valerius.'

'Hang on, I'll wake up Marcus Vinius to make sure he didn't see you either—'

'All right, all right,' Gnaeus said, scrambling to regain his dignity. 'Just make sure you're ready for the drop, Titus – *oof*.'

Now the ship lurched suddenly to the right, and there was a burst of acceleration.

'That's what you get when you're piloting in an atmosphere,' Titus said. 'Coping with turbulence, the thickening air – a lot of dust around on Mars. And trying not to let the barbarians on the surface get a shot in at you. Don't worry, *optio*. You have to hand it to the *trierarchus* and her crew. These Brikanti know how to handle a ship.'

Gnaeus grunted. 'Unfortunately there's another bunch of Brikanti on the ground who are trying to kill us.'

'Well, I wouldn't worry about that either, sir. If they get us we'll never know about it.'

'Legionary, I wish you'd stop telling me not to worry, it's scaring me to death.'

'Oh, relax, sir. Why, I remember once on campaign—'

'All hands,' came a voice from crackly speakers. 'This is Quintus Fabius. We're in the air over the Earthshine base, and ready to make the drops. Timings as we planned. Be ready, we're only going to get one run at this, before the *Malleus* takes me back into the safety of orbit where I belong. Call in. Yacht?'

'Eilidh here, Centurion. Ready to go, with Collius and the rest.'

'Good luck, and stand by. Jumpers?'

'Kerys here. All set, Centurion; suits and wings checked over.'

'Glad to hear it. *Testudo?*'

He was answered with a roar from the men of the *contubernium*, a clatter of weapons on breastplates; the din was enormous in the enclosed space of the vehicle. Titus yelled, 'Let us at them, Centurion!'

'Try not to get overexcited, Titus Valerius, it's bad for a man of your age. Very well, everybody. Make sure you all keep in contact throughout the operation. That ball of ice in the sky is less than six hours away. But if you live, you won't be left behind, and that's a promise. Understood?'

The men of the *contubernium* yelled their assent.

'Then let's do this. Yacht – *go*!'

A door slammed open in the belly of the ship, and the whole fabric of the *Malleus* shuddered. Gnaeus imagined the Martian air snatching at the breach in the ship's hull as the small landing craft fell away.

'Jumpers!'

A lurch of deceleration as the ship slowed enough to allow the jumpers to hurl their fragile bodies out into the slipstream.

'And *testudo*!'

Gnaeus clutched his harness, bracing himself once again. Another door opened in the belly of the craft, this time directly below him. In the golden-brown Martian light, seen through the *testudo*'s slit windows, Gnaeus could see the fleeing landscape, not far below.

The men in their rows of couches roared. Titus yelled and gunned the engine of the vehicle.

And with a clatter of released latches, the *testudo* was dropped from the belly of the spacecraft. For an instant Gnaeus was in free fall, and he imagined he was back in the timeless vacuum of space. Even the legionaries were silent as they fell, just for a moment.

Then the vehicle slammed into the dirt. Weight returned with a rush – and immediately, as the big mesh tyres bit into the Martian dirt, the *testudo* surged forward. Once again Gnaeus was thrust back into his couch.

And, over the shoulder of Titus at his controls, through a slit window and a massive protective grill beyond, Gnaeus glimpsed the receding fire of the *Malleus*, and a tree, impossibly tall, that scraped the orange Martian sky.

Kerys tumbled out of the open hatch in the flank of the *Malleus*.

Slam!

Thin it might be even at this low altitude, but hitting the air of this small planet in nothing but a pressure suit felt like running into a wall. And it was full of gritty dust that hissed against her goggles.

Her speed in the air slowed quickly. She was still curled up in a ball, the posture she'd adopted as she'd jumped, the better to survive the close passage of the *Malleus*. But she could hear the

213

roar of the ship's drive recede, see its glare diminish from the corner of her eye. Now she spread out her arms and legs, letting the air snatch at her and stabilise her. Her speed reduced further and her fall became more orderly, with the buttery sky above her, a scarred rusty landscape below, a pale, diminished sun not far above the horizon. There below her she saw Earthshine's facilities, the three compounds linked by dusty tracks, just as in Quintus's images: the bunker, the kernel-drive ship that was her own destination, and that impossibly tall tree in its narrow air tent. On target, then.

And there was a brilliant point of light directly overhead, like a single star that seemed brighter than the sun. Höd, coming for its lethal rendezvous. She looked away, blinking away the dazzle from her eyes.

At the appropriate time she tore at a patch of leather on her chest. Cables ripped free, and she felt bales of fabric unfold at her back. Again she braced herself, folding her arms over her chest. When her wings snatched at the air she was slowed dramatically, a hard tug that wrenched at her lower gut and made her gasp. But it was over in a moment, and when she looked up her wings were spread wide across the sky. Scraped leather stiffened with ribs of wood, the wings had been modelled on the wings of hovering sea birds, such as albatrosses, but this particular set was, of course, adapted for the thin Martian air, and much larger than she would have needed over Terra.

And they were safely open. She felt a surge of satisfaction. Safe for now – at least until she and her sole companion Freydis, a mid-ranking *remex*, went flying up into Höd itself, if they ever got that far…

Just as she thought of Freydis, a sprawling shape banked across her vision and the small speakers in her enclosed helmet crackled. 'Whee!'

'Stop showing off, Freydis.'

'Sorry, *nauarchus*. But isn't this grand? Flying over Mars!'

Kerys didn't want to discourage her, but she couldn't suppress a sigh. 'If you're thirty years old, as you are, and strong enough that you didn't get your guts pulled out of your backside when your wings opened, and if you're an inexperienced idiot – yes, Freydis. "Grand" is the word I would have used.'

'Sorry, *nauarchus*.' Freydis quickly calmed down.

Kerys peered down at the ground, tweaking her wings to make sure she was heading for the stubby cylinder that was the *Celyn*, with its support facilities around it – and she spotted small dark specks that must be crew and guards, waiting for her as she fell from the sky. She called Freydis again. 'You know the plan. We're both wearing identity beacons that mark us out as messengers from the Navy headquarters at Dumnona. Here we are with revised orders for the crew of that ship below. Yes? They'll reject any such orders, but with any luck the bluff will confuse them long enough at least for us to land before they start shooting. Don't do or say anything to give us away; just follow my lead.'

'I understand, *nauarchus*.'

Kerys looked across at her. 'So, you're ready for this? I picked you because you are the best qualified on the crew, in my view. Your aptitude for piloting and independent thinking is exceptional. I also know you trained at Kalinski's Academy of Saint Jonbar. So you know all about these people, their strange origin, the peculiar nature of this entity Earthshine.'

'Probably as much as anybody at my pay grade, *nauarchus*.'

That made Kerys laugh. But then she looked down at the heavily armed and suspicious troops on the ground waiting to greet them, and up at the looming presence of the asteroid preparing to smash this world to slag, and she considered the unlikely sequence of events that would be necessary if this bright, eager *remex* was to survive the day – and all because of her, Kerys, and her insane plan.

'*Nauarchus!* The troops below. They seem distracted. Look, they're turning away from us. They're running, towards – what? A new muster point to the south of here.'

Kerys tweaked her wings, and swivelled in the air so she could see better. And she made out a vehicle roaring across the ground, coated with heavy black armour, churning up a cloud of Martian dust behind it, with the flag of the Legio XC Victrix fluttering in the thin air: roaring straight towards the compound to the south, where that spindly tree grew tall.

'That's the *testudo*. They made it.' She couldn't help raise a fist, careless of being seen from the ground. 'Go, you ugly Roman bastards! Go, go!'

The *testudo* bounced as it raced over the ground, and Gnaeus had to cling to the edge of his couch. They were following one of the dirt tracks the Brikanti had laid down, but it was no Roman road – or at least it wasn't meant to be taken at this speed.

Still, Gnaeus peered ahead at the mighty trunk of the tree, marvelling at the green of its leaves, vivid in the Martian light despite the obscuring air tent within which the whole tree was enclosed. The tent itself was a cylinder, faintly visible because of a coating of adhered dust. The vehicle was already so close that Gnaeus Junius couldn't see the tree's upper branches, its crown.

'That thing is ridiculous,' Titus Valerius said, as he worked the levers that controlled the charging *testudo*.

'It's a quarter of a mile tall, Titus Valerius. It's a marvel of biology – of human engineering.'

Titus grunted. 'A marvel to which these Brikanti and their *druidh* would nail us if we ever gave them the chance. And as for its length, you and I can pace it out when we've brought it down.'

'It seems a crime.'

'Most actions of the Roman army seem like crimes if you're on the receiving end of them, I dare say, sir.' He called over his shoulder, 'All right, lads, wake up and be ready to move. We'll topple that unnatural thing, and then it's out of this tin can and at the Brikanti.'

'Let us at them, Titus Valerius.'

'Don't sound too eager, Scorpus, will you? Now then, shut up and let me concentrate on that cursed tree.'

The *testudo* carried a rack of missiles, and there was a simple sight stencilled on the forward window. All Titus had to do, Gnaeus knew, was to line up the sight mark directly on the trunk of the tree, which was a conveniently vertical and highly visible target. They reached a comparatively smooth stretch of track, the jolting of the vehicle subsided, comparatively – and Titus at last closed the firing switch.

When the missiles flew the *testudo* rattled and bounced, and the men cheered. The missiles were powered only by Xin fire-of-life powder with an oxidising compound, Gnaeus knew, but they delivered a kick when they soared away anyhow. Gnaeus could see the missiles swoop in, burning low over the ground, with the Brikanti scattering from their path – and then that tent over the tree blew apart in filmy shreds, an instant before the missiles slammed into the base of the tree itself, not far above a mighty, sprawling root system. A fireball swathed the lower trunk, stretching perhaps fifty paces up into the air. Just for an instant it wasn't clear if the damage done to the tree had been terminal, and Gnaeus, who had contributed to the calculations of the missile power necessary, felt a twinge of anxiety. He could see the Brikanti troops standing, turning, peering up at their tree in dismay.

But then the upper trunk leaned, visibly, and there was a crack, loud in the thin air.

'Ha!' Titus roared. 'We did it, boys! We broke the back of their god. Now let's break a few Brikanti heads!' He wrenched at his drive levers, and the *testudo* turned and skidded to a halt in a spray of dust.

The big doors immediately slammed open, and the men released their buckles and were out of the hull in heartbeats, just as they'd been trained. They immediately closed with the Brikanti on the ground, who were still forming up, still raising their weapons.

By the time Gnaeus Junius had followed Titus out of the *testudo*, the battle was joined. He found himself surrounded by warriors in heavily armoured pressure suits colliding clumsily with each another, many wielding weapons that would have been impossibly heavy if not for the Martian gravity – and all of them trying to get at the Brikanti. Nobody was using *ballistae*, or other fire-of-life weapons, Gnaeus noticed. These were space-going soldiers, on both sides; the inhibition against using such weapons in fragile extraterrestrial environments must run deep. So it was swords and knives, hand to hand.

Gnaeus was relieved to see that they were nowhere near the falling trunk of the tree, which continued to topple, almost gracefully. But the air was full of the cracks and groans of shattering wood, bits of ripped bark and shredded trunk came flying out of a rising dust cloud, and there were even shreds of the destroyed pressure tent tumbling in the air. It was almost impossible to remember that this was just a diversion, meant to distract the Brikanti troops from their spacecraft and Earth-shine's bunker, the true targets of the operation.

It was chaos. It was glorious. His own blood surging, Gnaeus drew his *gladio* and charged into the fray.

CHAPTER 29

As Kerys and Freydis came fluttering down from the sky under their leather wings, one officer stayed at her post before the *Celyn*.

As soon as she hit the ground, as soon as her boots crunched on Martian dust, Kerys shucked off her wings, letting them subside in the thin air, and stalked towards the waiting officer. *Stalked* – you couldn't really stalk in low gravity, and that was a perennial problem for officers working in these conditions and trying to look imposing. It was more that she glided across the ground with a commanding air.

But she kept her gaze locked firmly on the officer who was standing between her and the *Celyn*. The officer wore a standard Brikanti Navy-issue pressure suit, with shoulder flashes to show her rank. From what Kerys could see of her face, she looked young, younger even than Freydis. And she hefted a heavy projectile weapon, not lowering it as Kerys approached.

Kerys halted only paces from the officer. Still that weapon didn't waver, though its muzzle was only a hand's breadth from Kerys's chest. And still the officer held her place, though the fear and uncertainty were obvious in her eyes. Kerys felt a stab of sympathy, and shame at what she had to do.

She made sure the officer had seen her own shoulder flashes, and recognised her rank of *nauarchus*. Then she switched her communications to a standard channel and snapped, 'Your name?'

'That is irrelevant, *nauarchus*. With respect. Our orders – my orders – were to secure this vessel against intruders. And—'

'Your name,' Kerys repeated silkily. 'You see my uniform. What harm can it do to tell me your name?'

'Gerloc,' she said at last. 'My name is Gerloc. I come from Atrebatu, which is—'

'I don't *care* where Atrebatu is. So, Gerloc. I can see you're a *druidh*.'

'Yes. My Navy rank and *druidh* level are—'

Kerys waved that away. 'And you're a Navy officer. This is a Navy vessel.'

'Yes, *nauarchus*.'

'You say your orders were to secure this vessel against intruders.'

'Yes, *nauarchus*.'

'Very well.' Kerys glanced around, deliberately casual. Then she forced herself to scream in the girl's face. 'And do I look like an intruder to you?'

'No! I mean, yes – *nauarchus*.'

'Did you not hear the instructions my ship broadcast?'

'Yes. But we had no orders concerning your arrival. The Roman ship that brought you here, we had no clearance, and then your descent on the wings without calling ahead—'

Kerys deliberately backed off. She said more calmly, 'Have you never heard of a snap inspection? What use would that be if my arrival was heralded in advance, as if I was some pompous Caesar returning to the fleshpots of Rome?'

The girl didn't budge. 'But, *nauarchus*—'

Kerys held a hand to the side of her helmet, and the other palm up. 'Hush. Can you not hear that? That's your own *trierarchus* giving me clearance. You're to stand aside. Aren't you getting it? Maybe your equipment is faulty.'

Gerloc lifted her free hand to her own helmet, and with a troubled expression glanced away from Kerys.

That moment was all Kerys needed. She stepped inside the arc of the weapon, grabbed Gerloc's helmet with two hands, and yanked it forward. The back of Gerloc's head clattered against her helmet, and she was immediately rendered unconscious.

Kerys carefully lowered her to the Martian ground, while behind her Freydis hurried forward to collect Gerloc's weapon.

'That was kind of you, *nauarchus*,' Freydis said. 'Relatively.'

Kerys knelt over the girl. 'I hated having to do that. This one stood her ground while the rest of the idiots around her went running off in pursuit of glory. Stood her ground in spite of all the pressure I could bring to bear on her. She had her orders, and she obeyed them, and *this* is her reward, from me, her commanding officer. At least I was able to spare her a broken nose or a few lost teeth.'

Freydis looked up at the sky. '*Nauarchus*, maybe we'd better get moving. That thing in the sky isn't slowing down any.'

'Too true. Come on, Freydis. Keep your weapons ready. *Try not to kill, but if you have to*—'

'I can see there's a greater good, *nauarchus*.'

'There is indeed. I want this bucket to be off the ground in an hour, or less.' She looked down at the inert body of Gerloc, who looked as if she was peacefully sleeping. 'Help me haul her aboard the *Celyn*.'

'Of course, *nauarchus*. Umm – why?'

'Because she may have a better chance of survival aboard than if we leave her here. She deserves that much. But bind her hands and feet, in case her sense of duty gets in the way again.'

'Yes, *nauarchus*.'

Glancing over at Freydis, Kerys saw that Höd was actually casting a shadow now, from the soft features of the woman's young face, behind her visor. 'Let's hope, in the end, that all our heroics aren't necessary after all ... Come on, let's get on with it.'

Eilidh, piloting the small kernel-driven landing yacht bearing her fractious and complicated companions, was ordered to descend to the third of the surface complex's compounds, centred on Earthshine's heavy bunker. But she wasn't to land until the operations at the tree and at the *Celyn* were well under way, the guards drawn off. So after she had guided the yacht through its entry into the Martian air she hovered, waiting for a final confirming order from Quintus Fabius, who watched from the *Malleus Jesu*.

Mardina, surrounded by her family and companions, carefully followed the progress of the military operation on the ground. It wasn't just that her life depended on its outcome. She was actually interested in it, the first genuine action she had ever been a part of.

She felt she was learning constantly, not least from Quintus Fabius and his officers as they had studied this strange surface target, and he had improvised his plan of attack. Nothing specific about that, she thought, could ever be taught in an academy, or on a training ground, or even on manoeuvres out in the field. All training could do would be to leave you with a certain suppleness of mind – suppleness, wrapped around a bony core of determination. Quintus Fabius had never lost sight of the ultimate goal of this operation, for all its confusion and complexity: to find a way to stop the ice ball, Höd, hitting the planet Mars, if he possibly could.

And now here she herself was, involved in this horribly ambiguous part of the operation herself. She was glad to be involved in the action. But she wished she was doing something simpler! Morally clearer! Even if more dangerous. She would have loved to bowl across the surface of Mars with Titus Valerius in his *testudo*, firing missiles at the sacred giant tree, or to storm that waiting spacecraft with Kerys and Freydis ...

Not that there wasn't danger enough in her own assignment. The yacht was broadcasting continual identifying messages, and images of the craft's occupants: crucially, the faces of Beth and Mardina. All this was an attempt to get through to Earthshine, to persuade him to let them through. Fine. But it was all terribly flaky. They were so exposed in this yacht, hanging here in the air. It only needed a few of the ground troops to behave in an unexpected way – in fact, to follow their orders – and it could all go wrong. Mardina herself had watched as one lone officer had stood by her post at the spacecraft, the *Celyn*, and held up the *nauarchus* Kerys.

222

Worse than that, however, was the fact that in this fragile little ship Mardina was stuck with her family, among other lunatics. Her mother Beth, who could hardly bear to look at her father Ari. The strange slave boy Chu Yuen sitting as ever in his submissive posture, eyes averted, his pack containing the mysterious machine Collius cradled in his lap as if it were the most precious treasure in the world – well, Mardina supposed, for him it was, as it was probably all that kept him from being cast down into some even worse situation than this. And, to complete the party, here at her own insistence was Academician Penny Kalinski, a woman who Mardina, her former pupil, was very fond of – but she was so hopelessly *old*. What was Penny doing descending into a combat zone with an asteroid about to be dropped on her grey head?

This strange crew, all save Eilidh at the controls, were strapped into couches set in a rough circle in this small, cramped cabin, all facing each other, all trying to avoid the others' eyes.

But at last the message came from the *Malleus* that they were clear to land.

It was Stef Kalinski who spoke to them from the ship. As the operation had sorted itself out, she had volunteered her services to Quintus Fabius as *capcom* for the yacht, as she put it, a strange pre-jonbar word that nobody understood, except possibly Penny. Now her voice called clear and strong from the speaker. 'We finally got word from the bunker. Earthshine can see you. He says you're free to land. You should see a docking port, suitable for ships of Roman, Brikanti or Xin design. Take her down when you're ready, Eilidh.'

'Thank you, Colonel Kalinski—'

And suddenly Earthshine was *here*. Standing in the cabin before them. He was tall, urbane, wearing a suit that was not unlike Brikanti garb, Mardina thought, but was too smart, sharp – too finely made – and his shoes were polished leather. He wore a brooch on one lapel, a bit of carved stone at which Ari stared greedily.

It had to be him. Mardina had never seen him before but

she knew of no other being with such powers of projection. Yet there was an air of unreality about him, a translucence, a hint of an inner golden glow. When he smiled, even his teeth shone faintly golden.

Still, this was an intrusion into a military vessel. Eilidh reached for a weapon.

Ari Guthfrithson called out sharply, 'Be calm! This is not real. He is an image – like a reflection in a mirror. And he can no more harm you than could such a reflection.'

Penny glared. 'Well, don't try your tricks on me, you chimera. How are you doing this? This craft doesn't have the technological substrate to support *virtual reality.*' She used the English phrase.

'But I do,' the ColU said mournfully from his satchel, which Chu held to his chest. 'I received a signal from the ground, a request for interfacing, transmission capacity. I would have warned you all—'

'But I overrode you, didn't I?' Earthshine said. 'You are just a farm robot after all. Well, not even that any more. Whereas I, you see, am in control of the situation. As always.'

'No,' said Penny Kalinski. 'You can't grab hold of this ship, can you? Because it's too primitive for your interfaces.'

'I could shoot you down in an instant.'

'But you won't,' Ari said. 'Because *she's* on board.' He gestured at Beth; Mardina's mother, as so often when challenged like this, was shut in on herself, angry, resentful. 'And her – Mardina, your great-granddaughter.'

'You seek to manipulate me, in your crude ways.'

'It worked, didn't it?' Penny laughed, showing the remains of her teeth. 'For all you're so powerful, you have human weaknesses still.'

'Weaknesses? Would you call a capacity for loyalty to one's family a weakness? Oh, but I forgot; you've spent most of your life fighting against your own rejection by your impossible sister, haven't you? What do you know, then, of family?'

She was still glaring at him. 'Only that you helped me

224

rediscover it once. In Paris, remember? Shame on you for speaking to me this way now, Earthshine.'

And to Mardina's astonishment it was Earthshine who dropped his head first.

Ari watched this exchange, fascinated and amused. 'Well, well. Perhaps it was worth bringing along this wizened matriarch after all.'

'We do have history,' Earthshine said. 'So here we are. I believe I know what you want. But why don't you tell me, in your own words?'

'We want to know what you're doing here, Earthshine,' Penny said clearly. 'Here on Mars. And we want to know why you're bringing an asteroid crashing down on this planet – on your own head, apparently. Though I'm quite certain you don't intend to die here – if to "die" means anything to you at all.'

'Oh, I think it does—'

'We want you to stop,' Eilidh said. 'My commanders. My government. My people, those who know about you – about all of you from beyond the jonbar hinge. We want you to stop meddling with our lives. With our worlds.' She looked heated, almost embarrassed to have spoken.

Ari said, 'And of course they want you to deflect Höd. Give up this destructive course you seem to be on.'

'I'm afraid I can't do that,' he said evenly.

Beth spoke, for the first time, bravely. 'Then you'll kill us all – *grandfather*. Me too. Because I agree with them. This isn't our world, it's not our history. We, you, have no right to meddle like this. I'm not going anywhere. If Ceres falls, it kills me too.'

'I doubt very much that that's going to happen. But we still have time for a chat before the end game.' He turned to Eilidh. 'You may bring your craft down. Well, then.' He smiled at them all. 'As your English ancestors would have said, Mardina, I'll pop home and put the kettle on. See you soon!'

And he vanished in a brief blizzard of light blocks.

Eilidh looked to the heavens, muttered a quick prayer, and turned to her controls. 'The coordinates are here. I'll put us

225

down as quick as I can, and make a report to the *Malleus*. We've no time to waste.'

As the ship's position shifted, an overhead window tracked a swathe of the copper sky, and Mardina glimpsed Höd, a tiny disc now, brilliant enough to hurt her eyes.

CHAPTER 30

Kerys lay on her back in an acceleration couch, on the bridge of the *Celyn*, the ship she had stolen. The prow of the ship, a thick shield of metal and dirt designed to defy the erosion of the sparse grime of interplanetary and interstellar space, had no forward ports, but various instruments peered around the shield, and screens around her showed her images of what lay beyond the ship: a glowing jewel hanging over a pale brown landscape.

Surely by now the destination of the asteroid must be obvious to the authorities on Terra. Kerys had moved in elevated enough circles to be able to imagine the consternation that must be unfolding in the capitals, Brikanti, Xin and Roman: the fear, the raised voices, the unbelieved denials that this was an intentional act of war. She prayed for cool judgements, but on a world that was more or less continually at war, she feared judgement would be lacking. And she feared for Brikanti – for her family, her sister and her nephews ...

Meanwhile it was just three hours from impact. And still the *Celyn* sat on the ground.

'Come on, Freydis, come on—'

'I'm here, *nauarchus*.' Freydis scrambled up a ladder into the cabin, kicked a hatch closed behind her, and hauled herself into a couch alongside Kerys.

'At last!' Kerys immediately started snapping switches and pulling levers. She felt the ship shudder as the huge assemblies of etheric engines that controlled the kernel banks began to power up. 'I'd bite your head off if I didn't know how many hatches you had to close, and systems to flush down ...'

227

'Yes, *nauarchus*.'

'And if it hadn't also taken me all this time to get the controls in order also. The crew here were doing a sloppy job.'

Freydis thought that over. 'That strange creature Earthshine is in control of all of this. Maybe he doesn't *care* about this ship. He's safe in his bunker – well, at least until Höd falls. Maybe he thought the presence of the ship and the crew on the surface would be enough of a deterrent to anybody who was thinking of intruding.'

'We're never going to know. And from now on our priority is *that*.' Kerys tapped a screen that glowed with an image of the falling Eye.

Freydis glanced at a clock. 'Just three hours until Höd falls. I didn't realise how much time we've lost.'

'I did. I've been watching that damn bit of clockwork tick away our remaining time. And I've been trying to figure out a flight plan. Right now Höd is a hundred and thirty thousand Roman miles from Mars. That's over thirty planetary diameters. Which sounds a lot until you remember that the thing is coming in at over ten Mars diameters every hour.' She glanced at Freydis, who was taking this all in very calmly, very seriously – looking more like an earnest student in a classroom than a soldier, Kerys thought, a soldier who was about to lay down her life. 'So, you tell me. Given the knucklebones as they've fallen, what play would you have us make next?'

Freydis pulled her lip. 'Our objective is to deflect Höd from an impact with Mars. The further out from the planet we meet Höd the better. Our highest acceleration is three weights—'

'Yes. If we just blast out of here at three weights, we will encounter Höd in less than an hour.'

'Umm. Even then it might be too close to do anything about it.'

'Most likely. And—'

'And we'll go flying by at twenty thousand miles per hour.'

'Yes. But if we plan for a rendezvous, if we allow time to decelerate—'

'Then by the time we meet Höd it will be closer yet to Mars.'

'So what do you think?'

Freydis grinned. 'Go for the burn. Get there as fast as possible. At minimum we can blast whatever crew is still on that ice ball with farspeaker messages; maybe the sight of the *Celyn* coming down their throats will persuade them to see the error of the course they've chosen.'

Kerys nodded grimly. 'And if that fails we'll think of something else.' Although she could only think of one alternative, given the situation. 'But the first thing we have to do is get there. Strapped in, Freydis? Taken your thrust medications?'

'No, but I'll survive.'

Actually, Kerys thought sadly, no, you probably won't.

She pulled the master lever, lay back, and braced. She imagined the banks of kernels embedded in the base of the ship, etheric pulses washing over them, their strange, tiny mouths opening – the engineers always said they were like baby birds asking to be fed – but those mouths would vomit out a kind of fire that was hotter than the sun itself. Immediately Kerys felt the heavy shove of the thrust, a weight that pushed her deep into the cushions of the couch.

On a pillar of fire, the *Celyn* surged into the sky of Mars.

Without thinking, Kerys went into practices for high-thrust regimes as she'd been instructed, many years ago. She kept her legs still, her arms at her side, her head cushioned, and she breathed deliberately, deep and strong, pushing against that savage weight. Only an hour, she thought. Only an hour. Then, one way or another, it would be done.

Almost immediately, it seemed, the wan sky of Mars cleared away in her screens, leaving that deadly spark of light, Höd, hanging in the void. As if a last illusion had been dispelled about the reality of this situation.

The cabin was shuddering, the roar of the drive loud.

'Onwards, *nauarchus*!' Freydis yelled, defying the savage acceleration and the noise. 'Onwards!'

To Kerys's surprise, an internal communications link sounded with a whistle. She looked at Freydis sharply. 'Who is that? I thought you said you cleared the ship.'

'I did! I threw off the last of the crew at spearpoint, and they were glad to leave when I told them we were heading for Höd ...'

Kerys reached up cautiously and snapped a switch. 'Identify yourself.'

'I am Gerloc. You may recall, the *nauarchus* tricked me in order to gain access to the ship.'

Kerys grimaced. 'I apologise for that.'

Freydis snarled, 'And I left you bound up.'

'Not very well, it seems,' Gerloc said.

Kerys had to grin. 'Ha! She has you there, Freydis.'

'I wondered if you would like a little help. I do know the ship's systems quite well; I have had extensive training as a backup to the control crew.'

'Hm. It wouldn't harm. You need to understand that our mission—'

'Is what you ordain it to be. I overheard some of your conversation.'

'Oh, you did? Resourceful, aren't you?'

'Yes,' said Gerloc without irony. 'You are trying to avert a tremendous disaster. And you are *nauarchus*, you are my superior officer.'

'And so am I, by the way,' snapped Freydis.

'I have trained for this, for mobility in battle situations under conditions of thrust—'

'All right. Get up here as fast as you can, and don't break a leg on the way.'

'Already halfway there, *nauarchus*. See you soon.'

'Ha! I like her,' said Kerys.

'Well, I don't,' said Freydis. 'Is there any way we can increase the thrust of this bucket? That would wipe the grin off her face ...'

CHAPTER 31

Once they were off the landed yacht, Mardina tried to help Penny as they made their way through an airlock, and into a cramped elevator that took them down a deep shaft sunk into the Martian ground. Then they followed Earthshine along a short passage crudely cut into the dirt.

They arrived at a bare room, with walls of rust-coloured concrete punctuated by several doors, and furnished with a few couches and low tables of metal tubing and webbing – furniture that looked to Mardina as if it had been scavenged from a space-craft, from the *Celyn*, perhaps. Earthshine stood at the centre of the room as the rest filed in. None of them were at ease as they tried to walk in the unaccustomed low gravity – none save Earthshine, who looked as relaxed as if he were in a full gravity on Terra. Mardina found that irritating, as if he was making some point about his own eerie superiority.

Penny picked a chair, eased herself down on it with a lot of help from Mardina, and leaned forward on her stick, scowling at Earthshine. The rest settled: Mardina's mother and father, Beth and Ari, on chairs as far from each other as they could get, and Chu with the ColU satchel on his back sitting modestly on the floor.

'So here we are.' Earthshine pointed. 'There are facilities – a bathroom through that door, a small galley, a dormitory.'

Penny barked laughter. 'All rather less fancy than the last time I visited you, Earthshine. The great glass hall at Hellas – the trip into your virtual mine, deep underground, where you spoke of your noostratum.'

Earthshine smiled, unperturbed. 'I have abandoned the surface facilities now. Down here I can complete my preparations without any interference by the navies of this reality's squabbling empires.'

Ari smiled. 'What interference? You manoeuvred an object as enormous as Höd onto a collision course with this planet. And all in full view of the Brikanti and the Romans and the Xin – indeed you persuaded them to give you the facilities to do it!'

Earthshine shrugged. 'These are not cultures that prepare well for natural disasters – not compared to our own reality, Penny. They don't track rocks that might fall from space; they don't have the technology to do it, let alone the imagination. *Each other's ships* – that's what they watch, obsessively. And so it was easy for me to smuggle Ceres onto this destructive course, yes.'

The ColU said levelly, 'We are here to persuade you to abandon this project—'

Earthshine broke in, 'Yes, that was your plan, your surface motivation. But under all that, deeper impulses lurk. I am your grandparent, Beth. Whatever you think of me, that remains the truth. I am all that is left of your family from before what you call the hinge. And in the final hours, you have come to me.' He spread his hands, and looked around, at Beth, Mardina. 'Even under the fall of the hammer itself, you, my family, have come to me. For you know I will protect you.'

The ColU said evenly, 'They were pawns, Earthshine. A means of inducing you to allow access to this place. As for your family, what of Yuri Eden? Your son. I was with him when he died. He was far from your protection then.'

Earthshine's synthesised face became, eerily, more expressionless. 'I am aware of his death—'

'It was freezer burn. That was the colloquialism he used. Your decision, Robert Braemann, all those years ago, to consign your son to a cryo tank, ultimately killed him.'

Mardina had been told about this. Even so, having it stated as baldly as this in front of this strange old monster, this relic of her great-grandfather, shocked her.

Earthshine faced Beth and Mardina, and spread his hands. 'I meant only the best for Yuri. As I mean only the best for you—'

Penny snapped, 'You're being absurd. How will you protect these people, your "family"? This sandcastle of a bunker will be useless when Ceres falls.'

'True. But it is not the bunker that will save us – all of you who choose to come with me.'

Mardina was utterly baffled. 'Come with you where?'

Ari's eyes were alight with a kind of greed. 'I think I understand. *You're talking about another jonbar hinge*, aren't you? Like the gate between your history of the UN and China and our own with Romans and Brikanti, and again between our worlds and the world of the Drowned Culture ... I know your own history ended in a war of cosmic savagery, with the release of huge energies. Is that what you're planning here, Earthshine? To *create* a hinge?'

Mardina stared at him, barely understanding. 'Father. The way you're talking. You sound as if you *want* this. As if you want everything to be smashed up – everything we've grown up with, everything our ancestors built.'

'Perhaps I do,' Ari said, and he stood and began to pace. 'Perhaps I do. Ever since these strangers wandered into our lives – and especially ever since I discovered the evidence of the Drowned Culture for myself – I've become addicted to the idea. *Addicted* – yes, that's the word. To see everything change in a trice – to see new possibilities for mankind and human expression unfold, before one's eyes – perhaps to have the power to *shape* those possibilities. How could any thinking person not be drawn to such an idea?'

'Billions would die, Ari,' Penny said softly. 'No, it's worse than that. Billions would never have existed at all.'

'But others would take their place. Don't you see? It would be like looking through the eyes of a god.'

The ColU said, 'That's probably blasphemous, in terms of your interpretation of Christianity. And it's also wrong. You would be looking through the eyes, not of a god, but of whoever it is who welcomes these adjustments – and whoever has engineered them.'

Ari frowned. 'And who might they be?'

Penny said, 'We don't know, not yet. But we know that their meddling in history has nothing to do with *our* benefit. It is all about what they want.'

'Which is?'

'Kernels,' she said. 'And Hatches, Ari. Hatches. Of the kind you and your Roman rivals are merrily building for them, all over the nearby star systems, without ever understanding why, or what they're for. We know that much.

'But there's more to this, isn't there, Earthshine?' She held him with her gaze. 'We're skirting around elements of a deeper mystery. You came to Mars to explore this noostratum of yours. A layer of bacterial mind, deep in the rocks ...' She stood straight, stiffly. 'My God. I never thought of it before. Could there be some connection? The Hatches, after all, provide lightspeed links between worlds ...' She faced Earthshine. '*Are the noostratum minds your Hatch builders,* Earthshine? Maybe they aren't just witnesses. And they are everywhere, presumably, on every rocky world ... *They* are the puppet masters, who control the lesser beings, us, on the planet surfaces. Is that what you're thinking?'

Earthshine just smiled. 'What is important in this situation, Penny Kalinski, is what I want of them.'

'Which is?'

'*For them to reply to me.* The Martian noostratum – yes, the Hatch builders, as I believe they are. You know I have been trying to communicate with them – you saw the experimental set-up. All I have wanted is a reply.'

'And now? Earthshine, you look rather pleased with yourself.'

'So I should be. The noostratum. *It has replied.* And it has given me the means to save you all.' He gestured to a door. 'This way ...'

CHAPTER 32

Höd grew visibly in the monitors of the *Celyn* now, heartbeat by heartbeat.

'It's coming at us so quickly,' said Gerloc.

Her voice was small now, Kerys realised, with little remaining of the cool competence of the young officer who had held her position by the *Celyn*. The difference was, Kerys supposed, unlike herself and Freydis, Gerloc hadn't had the time to get used to all this – to being trapped in a speeding mote of a vessel, caught between two colliding cosmic bodies. Like a fly, she thought, between the tabletop and the descending fist.

Freydis, at least, was calmly checking her instruments. 'We're approaching our full speed now. We're actually moving far faster than Höd itself; most of the closing velocity is ours.'

Gerloc stared through a thick window. 'It is the eye of a god, opening slowly.'

Kerys snapped, 'No mythology now, Gerloc. It is just a lump of rock and ice. A big one, and representing awesome energies. But it is not divine. And if not for human intervention, it would not be here at all, high above Mars.'

Freydis said, 'We have less than half an hour to closest approach. When we arrive, we'll pass by the thing before we can count to ten. If we're going to do something, we need to decide soon.'

'Do something? Such as what?' Gerloc asked.

Kerys glanced at Freydis, who she was sure understood the full situation, and shook her head. *Not yet. Let Gerloc work it out for herself.* She said aloud, 'Still no response from the crews on the surface?'

'None,' Freydis said. 'I think there's still activity down there, however. Höd hasn't been abandoned, and the big kernel banks are still firing.'

'A suicide crew, then.'

'It looks like it. And if so, they won't welcome visitors.' Freydis glanced at Gerloc. 'You understand we can't land. We don't have the power, the time, to slow down and make a rendezvous.'

'Of course I understand that,' Gerloc said dismissively.

'Even if we could attempt some kind of landing they'd probably try to shoot us out of the sky first,' Kerys said. 'And even if we had come earlier, it was probably always too late – Höd is probably too close to be deflected anyhow, by any conceivable push even from the kernel banks. Small tweaks to its momentum from far away: that's how Höd has been delivered onto this course. It was worth a try, though. To come, to try to talk to the surface crew.'

Gerloc nodded. 'Then if we can't deflect the asteroid, what can we do?'

Kerys glanced at Freydis, and closed her eyes. 'There may be one option. I have to tell you something very strange, Gerloc, and I apologise that there is no time to explain it fully. There are people in our universe – some of them are down there on Mars now – who are not from our history. They do not share our past. Freydis understands some of this ... Now, Gerloc, the important point is this. That history was ended with a terrible war, at the climax of which a tremendous mass – some kind of huge ship I think – was slammed into the surface of the planet Mercury. They called it the Nail. In their history, as in ours, Mercury was the source of the first kernel mines.'

Freydis put in, 'This has been studied in our own academies, based on the strangers' description. There was a tremendous detonation – a huge release of energy. It's thought that the kernels, caught up in the impact of the incoming mass, opened wide in response. And the release of energy—'

236

'It was enough to scorch worlds clean,' Kerys said.

Gerloc looked at Freydis, and then at Kerys, who closed her eyes. 'I think I understand where this is leading. So we crash the ship into Höd – and not just at any random point. Directly onto the kernel banks. In the hope of blowing this lump of ice apart with kernel energies.'

'That's the idea.'

'Thus saving Mars.'

'And, with any luck, averting a war on Terra.'

'Well, if that's your plan, we have a lot of work to do to make it happen, and not much time to do it in.'

Kerys grinned. Not a word about the sacrifice of their own lives – just the mission objective. 'Good response. And you're right. We need to turn the ship around. Shut down the kernel drive first, use the secondary thrusters to swivel her. Then we light up the drive again, so that when we come down on Höd, it's with our own kernels blazing away.'

Freydis nodded. 'It could work.' Her voice was brittle, her eyes too bright. 'But right now we aren't on a trajectory to hit Höd at all, let alone the kernel facility down there. We'll need to make a course correction before we pivot the ship.'

'Yes,' Gerloc said. 'And of course we'll need to take into account the effect of our decelerating thrust on our trajectory, all the way down...'

Good, Kerys thought savagely. They would have to work, to actively pilot the ship, all the way in. It would be complex, demanding work, that would allow them no time to think.

Impulsively she reached out and grabbed their hands. 'Whether we succeed in this or not, we will ignite a light that will be seen across the solar system, on every world. People will know who we were; our families will know what we tried to do, today. All right? Are you ready for this?'

Impulsively Freydis grabbed Gerloc's hand, so they closed the circle. 'Let's get it done.'

'Agreed,' Gerloc said.

They broke the circle and turned to their posts.

CHAPTER 33

The chamber to which Earthshine led them was just a cavern in the deep rocks. There was a scatter of chairs near the door, a small chemical toilet, and heaps of equipment, including a heavy-looking cylinder of some plain white material. The light came from suspended fluorescents, a very mundane glow. Mardina and Beth together helped Penny over to one of the chairs; she couldn't stand for long any more.

The central area of the floor was roped off, the barrier containing a smoother area within.

Earthshine had an air of smug triumph, Mardina thought. The others seemed subdued, even confused, as they were drawn deeper into Earthshine's arcane plan, his mysteries – his layer of mind, deep in the rock.

A Navy radio communicator in Mardina's pocket chimed, her farspeaker, a soft mechanical bell. She pulled out the little gadget, held it up to her ear. She walked towards Penny. 'You need to hear this. All of you … I'm getting a signal down here.'

Earthshine nodded. 'You should. I had my support from the Brikanti Navy install relays and repeaters inside the bunker, and then in this chamber when we discovered it.'

'It's from the *Malleus*, in space. They see Höd. The crew say it's now about the size of the sun as seen from Earth, and growing fast.'

Penny nodded, eyes closed. 'It would be by now—'

'There was a detonation. On Höd.'

Chu, the slave boy, with the ColU's slate on his chest, muttered a prayer in his native Xin.

Penny said, 'The *Celyn*.'

'Yes,' Mardina said. 'They rammed it.'

Penny said, 'I bet they were trying to destroy the asteroid, by detonating the kernels.' She turned to Beth. 'Remember? Just like the Nail when it struck Mercury. Why, maybe Kerys even got the idea from our descriptions of that event.'

'But they didn't succeed,' Mardina said. 'According to the *Malleus* crew. Höd has a new crater, but is intact. Even such an immense explosion—'

Penny said firmly, 'It was a worthy effort. And I suppose there was nothing more they could do, given the time. Kerys and her crew will be remembered for their heroism.'

Mardina listened to a fresh message. 'Höd is still on its way. The centurion is ordering us back to the surface. Pickup in half an hour.' She folded up the farspeaker. 'We need to go.'

'No,' Earthshine said. '*There is another way.*'

'What other way? There's no other ship—'

'I told you, I can save you.'

Penny glared at him. Then she beckoned Mardina and Chu. 'You two. Help me.' She gestured at them impatiently, until they came to her. She held up one arm for each of them, and they grabbed her and lifted, Chu being careful of the ColU pack on his back. 'Now get me over there,' Penny said, flapping one hand at the roped-off area. 'I need to know what he's found.'

The ColU said, 'I have a feeling we both know already, Penny Kalinski.'

'I want to see with my own ruined eyes…'

What lay within the roped-off area didn't seem special to Mardina when they got there at the pace of Penny's hobble. It clearly wasn't natural, however. It was a sheet of some grey metal-like substance, with a fine circular seam a few paces across.

But Penny laughed.

'Show me, Chu,' the ColU murmured. 'Show me…'

Penny snapped, 'This isn't one of your damn virtual illusions, Earthshine?'

'Of course not.'

Mardina said, 'I don't understand.'

'A Hatch,' Penny said, her tremulous voice full of wonder. 'He's only found a Hatch. Here on Mars.'

'You still don't understand,' Earthshine said. 'You never did listen, Penny Kalinski. You or that sister of yours. I didn't *find* this. It wasn't here when I established my base here on Mars. *They gave it to me.* Believe me, this chamber did not exist, but as Ceres approached this world – I suppose as my own intention became clear – there it was, an anomaly showing up in my deep scans, and when I had a shaft sunk down to it, here was the Hatch. They gave this to me.'

Mardina shook her head. 'Who? Who gave it to you?'

'The noostratum,' Penny said. 'The dreaming bugs in the rocks? Is that what you would have us believe? Is this what all this has been about, for you, Earthshine? With Ceres you are striking a blow, not at Mars – not at any humans on Mars – but at the bugs in the deep rocks?'

'Well, it certainly takes a mighty blow to do that, doesn't it? I threatened them with destruction, and I got their attention. Here! Here in the floor – here is your proof.'

Beth said, 'So now what? I've been through Hatches before. They take you far away. To another world, even another star. But which star, Earthshine?'

He smiled. 'I don't know. That's the beauty of it. But wherever it is, whatever I find, I will have been *invited* there. Think of that! Oh, yes, I certainly got their attention. But this is not for me alone. Together, today – *now*, before the asteroid falls – we will go through this impossible doorway, and we will find out. Your intuition was right, you see – you were right to come here, all of you. I can save you. You, my granddaughter, my great-granddaughter – all of you, if you wish. You can see I have my own processor unit ready to go ...' He pointed to the bulky cylindrical unit.

The ColU said, 'This is wrong. What you have done here is

wrong, Earthshine. You meddle with powers that could destroy us all – destroy the potentialities of mankind.'

Earthshine just laughed. 'Whatever you say I won't allow you through the Hatch, you – toy. So you can be a witness to the exercise of those powers, can't you?'

The ColU paused, a long and terrible silence that must have been an age for such a high-speed artificial mind. Then it said, 'If I may not follow you through that Hatch – be sure, Earthshine, that I will not forget you, I will not give up the quest to find you, wherever you go, whatever you do. No matter how many generations of friends I have to outlive to do it.'

Chu was visibly agitated by this cold announcement. 'Master, please. I am grateful to be your servant. Yet I have served you well, have I not? But I don't want to die, not today, not *now*.'

'You won't die, Chu Yuen,' the ColU said gently. 'Remember, the centurion is coming to pick us up. We need only return to the surface.'

'I, too, will go no further than this,' Penny said with an expression of disgust. 'Never mind tinkering with history – these damn Hatch builders have wrecked my own life, and my sister's. I'll go no further. And as for the rest – Chu, take hold of Ari Guthfrithson.'

'Madam?'

'Just grab him.'

'Do as she says, Chu,' the ColU said.

Chu hesitated for one heartbeat. Then he took long strides around the Hatch emplacement, and grabbed both Ari's arms, gripping them firmly above the elbows.

Ari struggled, but couldn't free himself. 'Why is this animal holding me?'

Penny said, 'Whatever all this mystery is about, I want *you* to go no further with it, Ari. You are a manipulative, scheming chancer. And the ambition you have expressed scares me, frankly. Well, this is one thing I can fix. This is the end of the story for you, as it is for me. You're coming back with us to the surface.'

241

'I will not. Beth – Mardina, my daughter—'

'Chu, shut him up.'

The slave pushed Ari against one wall, pinning him with his left arm, while he clamped his right hand across Ari's mouth.

Earthshine turned away, indifferent, and spoke to Beth and Mardina. 'What these others choose is irrelevant. We are the core; we are family. If only Yuri Eden had survived ... I never met him, you know, after his emergence from cryo. Never saw him again after I closed that heavy lid over his sleeping face. But he lives on in you. Come with me now.'

Mardina recoiled, her head swimming. 'I don't understand any of this. I don't *want* any of it. What can there be for me on the other side of this – door in the ground? Up there, Terra – that's my world, that's my home, my career, my life. As far as I can see, all these Hatches have brought any of you is destruction and disruption and distress.' She looked at Beth. 'Mother? You'll stay with me, won't you?'

But Beth was hesitating.

Earthshine said, 'Maybe we can find a way home for you, granddaughter.'

'Home? Back to Per Ardua?'

'Yes. Back to Per Ardua.'

Beth looked at Mardina, her face anguished. 'Mardina, you must come with me—'

'No! I don't care about Per Ardua, about *Before*. You're doing to me now what you always complained about your own mother doing to *you*. Ripping you out of your old world and stranding you on another.'

'I know. You're right. But even so ...' She looked again at the Hatch. 'I can't miss this chance, my only chance to go home.'

Penny said gently to Mardina, 'It's all right, my dear. Come with us. We'll return to the surface, and get out of here before the hammer falls. And your fool of a father, at least you'll still have him!'

The ColU said, 'Don't be afraid, Beth Eden Jones. If I must stay here I will care for Mardina, as once I cared for you.'

Mardina protested, 'I don't need *anybody*—'

But Penny touched her hand to hush her.

'I'll come back for you some day,' Beth said gently.

'Or I'll come for you,' Mardina said on impulse. 'Though I've no idea how.'

'Yes.' Beth forced a smile. 'Let's make that pledge. When we have both found whatever it is we're looking for ...'

Mardina shook her head. 'So what happens now? How will you get this Hatch of yours open anyhow?'

Beth smiled now, stepped forward, and pointed at the emplacement. 'The Hatch knows when we're ready. They always do.'

Mardina looked down. That central expanse of floor, surrounded by the circular seam, was no longer pristine. It had changed. Now it contained two complex indentations, like small craters with five rays – two pits shaped to accept the pressing of a pair of human hands.

CHAPTER 34

For the final pickup, Centurion Quintus Fabius brought the *Malleus Jesu* down to the surface of Mars itself.

Titus Valerius called from the *testudo*, 'About time you joined the party, sir.'

'Shut up, legionary. You still alive, Gnaeus Junius?'

'Here, Centurion.'

'All right. Make sure the meatheads in that glorified chariot do as they're ordered. We're nearly out of time – we almost waited too long. In particular, we haven't the time to wait for the yacht, with the Academician and her party at the bunker. So I want you two to go and pick them up in the *testudo*.'

Titus glanced over his shoulder, at a vehicle already crowded with legionaries, and those few Brikanti from the installation who had been intelligent enough to surrender in time. 'It's kind of sweaty in here, Centurion. No place for an elderly lady. And I do know the layout of that bunker. There's only one docking port, which is where the yacht will be—'

'Use your initiative, legionary. Get the thing out of the way.'

'Whichever way I see fit, sir?'

'Whichever way, Titus Valerius.'

As far as Titus was concerned there were no finer words in the vocabulary of a commanding officer. With a whoop he gunned the *testudo* at top speed for the bunker. Behind him he heard groans, and the odd thump as some clown who hadn't secured himself properly fell off his bench.

And, with Höd looming in the sky larger than the sun, larger than Luna, an overwhelming reminder of the urgency of the situation, they came to the bunker. The yacht was indeed still docked to the only port.

The *testudo* didn't even slow down. Titus Valerius drove straight into the flaring single wing of the yacht.

The *testudo* slammed to a halt, throwing them all forward once more. Then Titus put the *testudo* in its lowest gear, and just started pushing. The wing crumpled, the hull buckled, but the yacht came away from its lock with the bunker with a screech of torn metal, and was then shoved away over the Martian ground.

The passengers of the *testudo* actually gave him a round of applause. 'You're a hero, Titus Valerius!'

'You're also an idiot,' Gnaeus said, peering out of the port at the bunker. 'But a lucky idiot. I think that port is still serviceable.'

'I never doubted it. Anyway those ports are designed to yield under torsion; I was cheating. Now go and get our passengers, *optio.*' With a crunch of gears Titus reversed the *testudo* and roughly positioned its flank against the bunker's port.

As the *optio* had predicted, the port was still working, just, and Gnaeus with the help of a couple of crew soon managed to achieve an airtight bridge to the bunker. Titus, impatiently nurturing the running engine, was surprised to see that not all the landed party came back – just Penny Kalinski, Cadet Mardina Eden Jones Guthfrithson, the rodent-like *druidh* Ari Guthfrithson, and the slave boy with the talking rucksack.

And at the last minute Penny Kalinski herself refused to follow.

Mardina wouldn't leave her behind. She grasped the old lady's hands, trying gently to pull her forward to the port. 'You must come. There's no need to die here.'

'But I would die soon anyhow, my dear. And you need a witness – you, all of your people – a witness to what is being done, today, in your system, to your worlds. For, after all, it is Earthshine, with whom I travelled through the jonbar hinge, who is responsible for all this. The least I can do is file a report. And I am a *scientist*, you know – a *druidh* in my culture. A trained observer. Go, child, go – my mind is made up. But leave me that farspeaker of yours.'

'Academician—'

'It will soon be over, child. What, an hour? No more.'

Titus Valerius was running out of time. 'Scorpus, Orgilius, get that damn door closed. Right now.'

'Right, Titus.' The two burly legionaries made for the hatch.

Penny called, 'Oh, and Mardina – tell that centurion of yours, make him instruct his *trierarchus* – tell him not to hang around. Don't hover near Mars, waiting to see what happens. And don't head back to Earth either. *Tell him to flee* – out of the system, with the greatest acceleration he can muster – tell him to flee as Lex McGregor once fled, with the kernel drive burning. He will understand—'

Scorpus pulled the girl back from the door, and Orgilius slammed the hatch closed.

'At last!' Titus Valerius rammed forward his control lever and the *testudo* surged away from the lock. There were more complaints and curses as people fell over each other in the sudden acceleration. Titus just laughed, swung around the nose of the *testudo*, and headed straight for the welcoming belly of the *Malleus Jesu*.

CHAPTER 35

'Academician? Can you still hear me? This is *Malleus Jesu—*'

'I can hear you, dear Mardina. Oh, my. This couch is just too comfortable. I believe I dozed off! There's one disadvantage of such an elderly observer.'

'Well, it's been a long day for us all, Academician.'

'Please. Call me Penny.'

'Penny, then. There's only half an hour to go.'

'Yes, dear. I guessed it must be about that. Now, let me see. Ceres – Höd – is almost directly over my head. The glass roof of Earthshine's peculiar garden is nothing if not revealing, and I have a dramatic view of the sky ...

'I should report what I see as objectively as I can, shouldn't I? Ceres looks, I would say, three times as wide as the sun does from Earth. And it is growing in size, as if swelling, almost visibly. What a strange sight it is! I have seen a total solar eclipse on Earth, and that had something of the same strange, slow grandeur of movement in the sky. You can *sense* there are huge masses sliding to and fro in the firmament above. But I can't see the scar left by the fall of the *Celyn*, no glowing new crater. The spin of the asteroid has kept it away from me, and I imagine there will not be time enough for a full rotation. How brave those young crew were! But, oh my, it grows ever larger. And yet there is no effect yet, nothing to feel here on the ground, even though there are only minutes left.'

'I understand little of this, Academician Penny. What will happen to Mars? And why would Earthshine do this?'

'As to the what – I think I can estimate some of that for you.

Here we have Ceres – forgive me for using the name I grew up with – a ball of ice and rock six hundred miles across, coming in at forty or fifty thousand Roman miles in every Roman hour. If a respectable fraction of that tremendous kinetic energy is injected into the rocks of Mars, then I estimate – and I was always good at mental arithmetic – some two hundred billion cubic miles of Mars rock will be melted and vaporised. Two hundred billion cubic miles, on a world only four thousand miles across. A layer of rock some four miles thick will be destroyed. All traces of a human presence will be eradicated, of course. And this is without considering the effect of the kernels, embedded here in Mars, in the ground of Ceres itself. If what we saw on Mercury is a guide, the total event may be even more energetic, even more destructive ...

'You ask, why has Earthshine done this? To strike back at what he calls the noostratum. That's what I think. These deep bugs that he believes survived even the destruction of our world, our Earth – indeed, if they are the Hatch builders, they may have engineered those events to create jonbar hinges, for their own unfathomable purposes. Well, they won't survive *this*. And maybe he's right. He did force a response from them, didn't he? They, or some agency, did give him a Hatch ... Oh, I must sip some of my water. Excuse me, dear.'

'... Penny? Are you still there?'

'I'm sorry, child. Have you been calling? My wretched hearing ... How long left?'

'Only a sixth part of an hour, Penny.'

'Ten minutes. Is that all? Such a brief time, and soon gone, like life itself. I take it we have failed, then, all our stratagems are busts. Well, perhaps it was always beyond us. But we must persist, you know. Earthshine is right about that, at least. We must understand why and how our history has become fragile – who is engineering all this. And yet we must, too, find a way to contain Earthshine himself.

'Ceres is huge, now spanning – what? Eight or nine times

the diameter of sun or moon? I can see features on that surface now, clearly visible through the fine Martian air. Craters, of course. Long cracks, almost like roadways – annealed fissures in the ice, perhaps caused by the stress of the displacement from the object's original orbit. Ceres is already damaged, then. And it is growing, swelling, it is all so easily visible now. Oh my, it is a quite oppressive presence, and I should have expected that. Almost claustrophobic. You must forgive them, you know, Mardina.'

'Who?'

'Your parents. Even your fool of a father – deluded, self-serving and greedy as he is – has always done his best for you, as he sees it. And your mother was horribly harmed by the circumstances of her birth. She was the only child on a whole world, or so she grew up thinking, and yet she grew to love the place, as all children love their homes. But she was taken from that home by the Hatches, that greater power that is manipulating our destiny – all our destinies. After all that you can't blame her for longing to find a *way home*.'

'I don't blame her. I'm just trying to understand. Do you think she will ever find what she's looking for?'

'It's not impossible. We understand very little of the true structure of this *multiverse* we inhabit. I'm sorry, I used an English word. And maybe, some day, you will find her again.'

'Your sister is here. Stef. Would you like to speak to her?'

'No. It would do no good. But I am glad she is there, now, at the end. What of Jiang Youwei?'

'He was very distressed that you did not return.'

'Ah. Youwei has been such a good friend ... A burden has been lifted from his shoulders, however. Please ask my sister to keep an eye on him.'

'She will.'

'And tell her I'm sorry.'

'She knows, Penny. And she says she forgives you.'

'How good of her. Ha! What an old witch I am, bitter and sarcastic to the end ...'

'She says she expects nothing less. Umm, the remaining time is—'

'Thank you. But I don't feel I need a countdown, dear. Oh, that brute in the sky – individual features, the craters and canyons, grow in my sight now. Ceres becomes a plain that is extending away, extending to the horizon.'

'Penny—'

'Oh, it's beautiful! A sky like a mirror of the ground, a sky of rock! Mardina, Stef. Don't forget me. Don't forget that I'll always

CHAPTER 36

Höd, Ceres, was about a seventh the diameter of the target planet. It took a minute for it to collapse into the surface of Mars. Mardina saw that the smaller world kept its spherical shape throughout the stages of the impact, the internal shock waves that would otherwise have disrupted the asteroid travelling more slowly than the arc of destruction that consumed the asteroid at the point of contact.

Even before the asteroid was gone, a circular wave like a mobile crater wall was washing out around the planet. This tremendous ripple crossed Mars, destroying famous landscapes billions of years old: the Hellas basin, the Valles Marineris, which briefly brimmed with molten rock before dissolving in its turn. Following the rock wave came a bank of glowing, red-hot mist that obscured the smashed landscape.

And when the ripple in the crust had passed right around the planet, it converged on the antipode to the impact site, closing in on the Tharsis region in a tremendous clap, where huge volcanoes died in one last spasm of eruption.

The *Malleus Jesu* fled the scene at an acceleration of three gravities. Fled away from the sun, into the dark.

Centurion Quintus Fabius sat brooding in his observation lounge, where his Arab navigators had fixed up farwatcher instruments to watch the impact – sat in his acceleration couch, with the triple weight of the engine's thrust pushing down on him.

Once the impact event itself was over, Höd was gone, and Mars was transformed, become something not seen in the solar system since it was born, so his Arab philosophers told him. What was left of Mars was swathed in a new atmosphere of rock mist and steam – an air of vaporised rock. For a time the whole world would glow as bright as the sun. And it would cool terribly slowly, the philosophers said. It would take years before the rock mist congealed, before the planet itself ceased to glow red-hot, and then a heavy rain would fall as all the water of the old ice caps and aquifers returned, to sculpt a new face for Mars ...

But Mars was only a distraction, for the reports soon started to come in from the ground, from Terra. The impact had sent immense volumes of molten rock spraying out across the solar system. Much of this was observed, from the ground, from space. Some of the debris, inevitably, would strike Terra itself, falling on a world full of panic and suspicion. There was a brief flurry of messages, passed between the capitals of the world. A peremptory order came from Ostia, home of the Roman fleet, for the *Malleus Jesu* to return to the home world. Quintus ignored the order.

And then the missiles started flying.

Quintus Fabius saw it for himself, through the farwatchers, peering back past the glare of the drive plume. Sparks of brilliant light burst all over the beautiful hide of Terra. Luna, too. It had happened before. There had been a war on Luna, rocks had fallen on Terra – people thought it was a deliberate if deceptive strike by some rival, or maybe they mistook the rocks for some kind of kinetic-energy weapon. Or maybe they just took the chance to have a go. So it was now.

There was a final flare of light, a global spasm that dazzled Quintus, making him turn his heavy head away from the eyepiece.

And in that instant Quintus was called by his *optio*. 'Centurion, we're being hailed.'

'By who? One of ours, Brikanti, Xin—'

'It's not a language we recognise, sir. Nor a vessel design we know.'

'What language? Wait. Ask Collius what language it is.'

A moment later, the reply came. 'Collius had an answer, sir.'

'Why aren't I surprised?'

'He says it's a variant of – it's difficult to pronounce.'

'Spit it out, man.'

'Quechua.'

In the hearts of the surviving rocky worlds of the solar system –

Across a score of dying realities in a lethal multiverse –

In the chthonic silence –

There was satisfaction.

The artificial entity, which was a parasitic second-order product of the complexification of surface life on the third planet, had struck a deep blow at the Dreamers in the heart of the fourth planet. An unprecedented blow. Dreamers had died at the hands of natural catastrophes before. Even planets were mortal. Never had they been targeted by intelligence, by intention.

There had been shock.

There had been fear.

To extend the network, to open a door for the parasite – to remove it from this time, this place – had been an unpleasant necessity. Otherwise, the destruction would surely have continued, in this system and others, or, worst of all, it might have spread through the network of mind itself.

The parasite had not been destroyed. But, delivered to a new location, perhaps it could be educated. Neutralised through knowledge.

That was the hope. Or the desperation.

For time was short, and ever shorter.

In the Dream of the End Time, the note of urgency sharpened.

THREE

CHAPTER 37

Two days after the impact, after a day under full acceleration and a second cruising at nearly a hundredth of the speed of light – beyond most of the asteroids, so far out that the sun showed only a shrunken, diminished disc – the *Malleus Jesu* floated in emptiness, an island of human warmth and light.

And yet it was not alone.

With the ship drifting without thrust, the Arab communications engineers unfolded huge, sparse antennas, which picked up a wash of faint radio signals coming from across the plane of the solar system: from Earth, from Mars, from the moons of Jupiter and Saturn, the asteroid belt, and the Trojans, great swarms of asteroids that preceded and trailed Jupiter in gravitationally stable points in the giant planet's orbit – some from even further out, from the ice objects of the Kuiper belt.

The signals weren't sophisticated, the ColU murmured to his companions. They were just voice transmissions, and mostly of an official kind: listings of positions, trajectories, cargoes, permissions sought and denied or granted, payments made and received. Very occasionally sparks of laser light were picked up, fragments of signals. Maybe these carried the more sophisticated communications of whatever culture dominated here, with the radio reserved for those who could afford no better. The narrow-beam laser signals could only be picked up if the ship happened to swim in the way of their line-of-sight trajectories, of course. What made all this harder to understand and interpret was that many of these messages were like one side of a conversation, such were the distances between transmitter and receiver. It could take forty minutes for a signal to travel from Jupiter to Earth. Why, it could take ten or twelve seconds for a radio signal just to cross between Jupiter's moons, such were the dimensions of that miniature planetary system alone.

The Arab observers gathered other evidence of activity too, mostly the characteristic radiation leakage of kernel engines, as ships criss-crossed a very busy inner solar system and sailed to the great islands of resources further out.

The Roman and Brikanti officers listened hard to the messages, trying to make sense of these static-masked scraps of information. Listening, mostly, for Latin and Brikanti voices. They even had Chu and Jiang up in the observation suites listening for traces of Xin.

At least they seemed to be sailing undetected. There had been no direct hails, no approach by another ship – no sign that any other craft was being diverted to rendezvous with them. That was no accident. As soon as the first transmissions had been received, Quintus Fabius had ordered the shutdown of all attempts to transmit from the *Malleus*. Even the ship's radar-like sensor systems, which were capable of characterising other ships, surfaces and other objects to a fine degree of detail, were put out of commission; only passive sensors, like the Arabs' telescopes, were permitted. And nor was Quintus yet ready to fire the drive, even to decelerate a craft fleeing from the inner solar system, for a kernel drive would surely be immediately visible. Quintus didn't put it this way, Stef recognised, but he had instinctively locked down the *Malleus* into a stealth mode. The ship was undetected, and Quintus wanted it to remain that way as long as possible.

After a few days the ColU summed up the dismal results to its companions.

'There are a few scraps of a kind of degenerate Latin to be heard,' it reported. 'The crew leap on these as if they were messages from the Emperor himself. But they are only a few, and usually just phrases embedded in a longer string of communication. As if a speaker of a foreign language lapses into his or her native tongue when searching for a word, when muttering a familiarity or a prayer ... There is actually more Xin spoken, by word count, than Latin, but again it's a minor trace compared to the dominant tongue.'

Stef prompted, 'And that dominant tongue is ...'

'As I detected from the beginning, Quechua.'

'Inca?'

'Inca.'

The *Malleus* wasn't just an island of life in the vast vacuum of space; to the crew it was an island of *romanitas* in a sea of barbarians.

Inca.

For the time being there was no great urgency to act. The ship had been reasonably well stocked with supplies before its voyage from Terra to Earthshine's Mars; that wouldn't last for ever but there was no immediate crisis.

Meanwhile the centurion managed his crew. As soon as the drive was cut Quintus had ordered the fighting men, legionaries and auxiliaries, to adopt the routines of in-cruise discipline, and they threw themselves into this with enthusiasm. They were without gravity, of course, so that such exercises as marching and camp-building were ruled out. But soon the great training chambers within the hull were filled with men wrestling, fighting hand to hand or with weapons, blunted spears and swords and dummy firearms. They were building up to a mock battle on a larger scale, a practice for free-fall wars of a kind that had in fact been fought out in reality, in the long history of the triple rivalry of Rome and Brikanti and Xin.

Thus the troops were kept busy, and that struck Stef as a good thing, because it stopped them thinking too hard about the reality of their situation.

These were men, and a few women, who were trained for long interstellar flights; they were used to the idea of being cut

261

off from home for years at a time. Yet there were compensations. The legion's *collegia* promised to hold your back pay for you, and manage your other rights. And, on the journey itself, you could take your family with you, even to the stars.

But now, Stef realised, many of those psychological props were missing. The mission should have been a relatively short duration mission to Mars – with a return to Terra in mere weeks, perhaps. There had been no need to take families on such a jaunt, although a few had come along anyhow, such as Clodia, the bright-eyed daughter of Titus Valerius. Many of the men grumbled that they hadn't even been offered the chance of signing the usual pre-mission paperwork with the legion's *collegia*. They shouldn't have been away that long. The men already missed their families.

And there was a greater fear, under all the petty grumbling and uncertainty. Rumours swirled, disinformation was rife. But most of the men had some dim idea that they had been brought to a place more remote than the furthest star in the sky, further, some said, even than the legendary Ultima. And, they feared, nobody, not even the mighty Centurion Quintus Fabius himself, knew how to get them home again.

Stef Kalinski, meanwhile, cared for her companions – including the ColU, who shared its deepest concerns with her.

The ColU said, 'Mardina and the others were right not to follow Earthshine – leaving aside the family entanglements. *He* is furthering his own ends, that's for sure, and in a horribly destructive way. But, just as I promised him, some day, somehow, I must follow him.'

Stef frowned. 'How, though? Through the Hatch on Mars? But it may not even exist any more. And why you?'

'Because he and I, of all the artificial minds of the UN-China Culture, are evidently the only two survivors. There were none like us in the Rome-Xin Culture; it seems likely there will be none here, wherever we are. And, in a way, he seeks the truth.'

'What truth?' Stef pressed. 'What do you mean?'

'The larger story. The truth of the universe, that links the

262

phenomena of the kernels, the Hatches, and Earthshine's noostrata, the dreaming bugs in the rocks. Even the reality shifts we call jonbar hinges. And the echoes I saw in the sky, aboard the *Malleus*, in interstellar space. Echoes, not of a past event, but of a future cataclysm ... All of this is linked, I am convinced. And Earthshine feels the same.'

'And you fear, that when he finds this truth—'

'He means to smash it. To smash it all. He seeks to do this because he is insane. Or,' the ColU added, 'perhaps because he is the *most* sane entity in the universe.'

'And you must stop him.'

'It is my destiny. And perhaps yours, Stef Kalinski.'

'I'll keep it in mind,' Stef said, feeling even more small and helpless than usual.

CHAPTER 38

Four days out from Mars, Centurion Quintus Fabius summoned his senior officers, with Eilidh the *trierarchus* and some of her Brikanti ship's crew, and Titus Valerius as a representative of his troops, and the survivors of the UN-China Culture.

They met in a lounge in the area Stef thought of as officer country, stuffed into the heavily shielded nose of the *Malleus*. Basically the anteroom of a Roman bathhouse, this was an opulent room with tapestries and thickly embroidered rugs, and even oil lamps of a traditional design burning on the walls. In the absence of gravity, pumps and fans had to keep the oil and air circulating; this was a recreation of an ancient technology in a spacebound setting. Such backward-looking luxury, Stef had long since learned, was a deliberate ploy by the Romans, and the artificial lamps were a classic touch.

Stef and the others strapped themselves loosely to couches. Chu carried the ColU, as ever, his eyes modestly downcast. Arab observers sat quietly together against one frescoed wall, and Stef idly wondered if they longed to get out of this place of crowding and light and graven images, and return to the twilight calm of their great observation bays.

The centurion himself was the last to arrive.

He pushed through the air with an easy grace, and grabbed a handhold at one end of the room. 'So we face the future,' he said briskly. 'Mars is behind us now, with all its heroism and failure. We have survived. And we're here to discuss the nature of the place in which we find ourselves. I'll leave the briefing itself to my *optio*, Gnaeus Junius. Who draws in turn on careful observation from the navigators, assisted by Collius the oracle.' Before he yielded the floor, Quintus Fabius looked around the room. 'Everybody here was purposefully invited, whatever your rank aboard this vessel – or the lack of it. Purposefully, that is, by me. I need to make a decision about our future, the future of the vessel and its crew and passengers.

'And the decision is mine to make, it seems, for we have yet to contact my chain of command. I probably don't need to tell you of the absence of any signals from Ostia, or Rome itself, or indeed any outpost of the Empire we recognise. Your orders, all of you, are to listen to what's said here, and advise me to the best of your ability. Is that clear?'

Titus Valerius snapped out, 'Yes, sir, Centurion, sir!'

Quintus grinned. 'Well said, Valerius. And you can tell that daughter of yours that she will *not* succeed in defeating me with *gladio* and net next time we meet in the training chambers. Right, get on with it, *optio* ...'

Gnaeus Junius took his commander's place. Drifting in the air, papers in his hand, he nodded to a crew member at the back of the room. The lights dimmed – Stef noticed the flames in those oil lanterns drawing back as their pumps and fans were slowed – and an image became visible, cast on the wall behind Gnaeus. The bulky projector wouldn't have looked out of place in a collection of nineteenth-century technological memorabilia, Stef thought, and she knew the image had been captured by the crudest kind of wet-chemistry photography. But it worked, and the content was all that mattered ...

She saw a world, floating in space. Gnaeus let them observe without comment.

It was Earth – but not Stef's Earth, and not Quintus's Terra. She could make out the distinct shape of the continent of Africa, distorted from its school-atlas familiarity by its position towards the horizon of the curving world. Though much of the hemisphere was in daylight, artificial lights glared all over Africa, including what in her reality had been the Sahara and the central forest. Some of these were pinpricks, but others were

265

dazzling bands, or wider smears. The seas looked steel grey, the land a drab brown between the networks of light. Nowhere did she see a splash of green.

Gnaeus Junius looked around the room. 'This is Terra, then – or rather, it is not. This is *not* the world we left behind. For a start there is no sign of the war whose beginning we witnessed, as we fled from Mars.

'You can see that the whole planet is extensively industrialised. Much of the glow you see comes from industrial facilities, or the transport links between them, working day and night. The glow, I am told by the observers, is characteristic of kernel energy. The observers also tell me they see the green of growing things nowhere. Clearly the world is inhabited by people, and they must eat; perhaps the food is grown underground, in caverns, or made in some kind of factory. We cannot tell, from a distance of several Ymir-strides.'

'You have done well to learn so much,' Quintus growled. 'And, though I know the mother city is silent, have you *seen* Rome?'

Gnaeus nodded to the crewman operating the projector. The screen turned glaring white as the slide was removed, to be replaced by another, much more blurred, evidently magnified. The boot shape of Italy was clearly visible, even though, Stef thought, trying to remember detail, it looked to have been extensively nibbled back by sea-level rise, even compared to what she remembered from the Roman reality. The peninsula was carpeted by the usual network of industrial activity, and Stef tried to map the brighter nodes on the locations of familiar cities.

Gnaeus pointed to a dark patch near the west coast. '*This* is Rome. The image has been greatly enlarged, as you can see … Sir, we would have to move in closer to do much better than this.'

'That can wait, *optio*. The area of darkness, you say—'

'At first we thought there was some kind of quarry there. Then we realised that the site of Rome is encompassed by a

266

crater, big enough that it would not disgrace Luna. And in the interior of the crater – nothing. No life, no industry.'

'I reckon we can see what's gone on here, sir,' said Titus Valerius. 'Some of the lads have talked it over. If I may speak, Centurion—'

'You already are speaking, Titus.'

'They bombed us, sir. Whoever runs this world. There must have been a war, and they drove us back, and when there was nothing left of us but the mother city herself, they bombed us.' He rubbed his chin. 'Maybe they dropped a rock from the sky. Or maybe they used kernel missiles. Making sure Rome would never rise again.' His voice grew more thick, angry. 'These bastards did to us what we did to those Carthaginians, long ago, sir.'

'I fear you're right, Centurion. The question is who these "bastards" of yours are.'

He seemed to hesitate before speaking further. Stef wondered how the ordinary Romans on this ship had taken the news of the loss of their eternal empire – how the likes of Titus Valerius had coped with such torment of the soul. Rome – gone!

'Very well. Carry on, *optio*.'

'Luna is missing,' Gnaeus said now, bluntly.

That startled Stef. 'What do you mean, "missing"?'

'I've got no images to show you … It simply isn't there. We know that must have distorted Terra's tides and so on but we'd need more study to understand that fully. Maybe it was destroyed in some war. *We* made a mess of Luna when we fought the Xin up there. Our best theory, given the level of industrialisation on Terra itself, and the massive colonisation of space – I'll discuss that – is that Luna was dismantled for its raw materials.'

He showed more slides, more worlds with faces disfigured by massive industrial operations, more carpets of glowing light. 'All the rocky worlds are the same, sir. Mercury, Mars. On Venus much of the atmosphere is gone, and some kind of huge operation is going on under the remnant clouds – we don't know what they're doing there.'

267

'And on Mars,' the ColU put in, 'the observers detected a kernel bed. A primordial deposit of the kind *we* found on Mercury, Stef Kalinski, though not on our copy of Mars.'

Knowing the ColU's own obsession Stef prompted, 'And where there's a kernel bed—'

'There's probably a Hatch.'

The ColU said no more, but Stef understood. *Some day we need to get to Mars, and through that Hatch, in pursuit of Earthshine.* But, looking at image after image of worlds transformed by industrialisation – Gnaeus even showed huge mines on the moons of Jupiter – and given the power and reach of a civilisation that had gone so far in mastering their whole solar system, she wondered how and when the chance to do that might ever come.

Quintus said, 'So we have a solar system of integrated industrialisation, of intense use of material resources, and, I presume, energy.'

Gnaeus nodded. 'Mostly kernel-based, but not entirely; we've seen sunlight captured by huge sails. There are tremendous flows of raw materials, mostly from the asteroid belt inward to the inner planets. Evidence of widespread organisation and control. And we see no signs of current conflict, incidentally. As if all this is run by a single, unitary government. One empire, sir.'

Quintus snapped, 'Whose empire? Who's benefiting from all this? And where are they? The planets, even Terra, barely look liveable.'

'Save by toiling slaves, probably,' said Titus grimly.

'Cities in space,' Gnaeus said now. 'That's where we think the people must be. Cities – or fortresses. We had a few such settlements, habitats capable of supporting life. Observation platforms, docks for spacecraft and so on. The Xin too.

'But *here*, wherever here is, the sky is full of them.'

He produced images of structures in space, grainily realised, cylinders and spheres and wheels, and some more angular structures.

'They cluster around the major planets, or trail them in their orbits around the sun. And they come in all sizes, from units the size of small Roman towns, Centurion, to much larger. There may of course be smaller constructions below our ability to resolve. Some of them, near the asteroids or planets, may be habitats for workers: construction shacks. Others may be the equivalent of military camps, permanent forts – and cities, places of government and administration. We can only guess, for now. We have barely begun to study these objects. One thing that might help us, sir. The smaller habitats are very diverse. There's a variety of designs, technological strategies. And although this "Quechua" is their dominant language, evidently the official one, we hear scraps of many other tongues – including bits of Latin.'

Quintus scowled. 'So how does that help us, exactly?'

'We can hide, sir. If we have to. Or at least be camouflaged. Some of those habitats and ships are not unlike the *Malleus* in size and shape.'

Quintus waved his hand. 'I take your point, *optio*. And given the challenge of the bookkeeping of an empire on this scale, if it's anything like our own, there will be room for concealment.'

'That's it, sir. And then there's the big one, the one we've been calling the Titan. At the very top end, only one of a kind, the largest structure we have observed in the system by far... The big beast resides in a Shadow of Terra.'

'He means, it's at L5,' the ColU told Stef. 'Trailing Earth at a Lagrange point.'

Quintus waved his hand. 'You're beginning to bore me, oracle, and not for the first time. Show me that big monster, *optio*.'

Gnaeus obeyed.

It was a blunt cylinder, its exterior scuffed, returning muddled highlights from a distant sun. This was shown against the background of the self-illuminated Earth.

Quintus drifted to the front of the room to inspect the 'Titan' more closely. 'That doesn't look so special. Looks a bit like *Malleus*, in fact.'

269

'It's a little bigger than that, sir. You're not grasping the scale of this thing – with respect, Centurion,' he added quickly. 'We've made guesses about its layout. It is spinning, around its long axis, not quite three times an hour.'

'To provide spin weight inside that big ugly shell.'

'Yes, sir. We've seen ships approach, along the long axis, where there must be docking ports.' He pointed. 'Just there, in fact.'

Quintus frowned. 'I see no ships. Must be tiddlers.'

'Sir, there are plenty of vessels larger than the *Malleus* itself; we see them coming and going … You still don't see the scale.'

'Tell me, then, you posturing fool.'

'Centurion, the cylinder is nearly three thousand miles long.'

'Three *thousand*—'

'That is more than the diameter of Luna, sir. The end hubs alone could swallow a small moon. The land area within must be similar to that of the whole of Asia …'

Titus Valerius, muttering a blasphemous prayer to Jupiter, floated before the image of the great habitat, inspecting it more closely, casting shadows on the screen. He pointed to a blemish on the hull. 'By God's bones. That looks like a crater.'

'Yes,' Gnaeus said. 'We've spotted many such scars. The structure may be old – centuries old.'

'What a monster. No wonder they had to take poor Luna apart to build such things.'

Gnaeus said, 'The question is, of course, who would live in such a structure—'

'I can tell you that, *optio*,' Quintus said. '*That's* where the emperor will be. And the very rich. Living off the huge rivers of goods that flow between the worlds.'

'An emperor become a god,' Titus said. 'I wonder how you could ever get rid of him?'

Quintus grinned back. 'Good question, Titus. All right, *optio*, thank you. Well. We've seen enough. Now we need to decide what we're going to do about all this.'

Stef had to smile.

The centurion growled. 'Am I amusing you, Colonel Kalinski?'

'I'm sorry, Centurion. I'm just admiring your boldness.'

'I'm a Roman,' he said, to a muttered rumble of support from his troops in the room. 'And that's what Romans are. We are bold. We take control. Although,' he said, 'to get through this crisis we may have to behave in ways Romans aren't particularly used to.'

The men looked more uncertain.

'Look – we've been out here four days, since Mars. And our time is already running out. Why? Because our supplies are. Our mission was supposed to last only weeks, at most. Soon we'll need to land somewhere.'

Titus Valerius said, 'Sky full of rocks out there, sir, among the Tears of Ymir. We could find a place of our own. Kick out a few Quechua speakers if we have to. We could call some of those other Latin speakers the *optio* heard out in the dark. Start building another Rome, to replace that hole in the ground we saw.'

Again Stef heard rumbles of approval.

'I admire your spirit, Titus Valerius. But the problem with that plan is simple. *Not enough women.* Most of us didn't bring our families on this mission, to my eternal regret. But then none of us knew what was going to become of us, did we? You know how things would go if we tried to make do with the ship's population as it is.'

Stef laughed. 'Even I would get a date.'

The centurion eyed her sternly. 'Stef Kalinski, we would destroy ourselves within a few years at best. That is, if these Quechua speakers didn't seek us out and destroy us first. Think about that, Titus Valerius. *You* remember our strongest enemy. Even now, Carthagio is a powerful memory for us all, the campaigns gone over again and again during training. Do you imagine these Quechuas, these Incas, will have forgotten Rome?'

'Never,' Titus rumbled.

'There you are then. And besides, Titus, we need to be wilier.

We need to buy ourselves some time.' He glared around at them. 'I don't want any of you telling me that what I'm going to propose isn't the Roman way. It isn't all about blunt force; sometimes you get your way by stealth and guile – by waiting until you're ready to strike. Remember Germania? Augustus lost his legions in those dense forests. The Caesars had to wait a generation – but when Vespasian finally struck north, destiny was ready to embrace him. So it will be with us ...'

Only a Roman, thought Stef with exasperated affection, could come through a jonbar hinge into some kind of Inca space empire and deal with the situation by referring to the adventures of the Emperor Vespasian in the first century after Christ.

Titus said, 'So what is the plan, sir?'

'We do as the *optio* suggested. We'll need to use the drive, of course, to fly back into the heart of the solar system, but kernel drives are common here. But we keep our heads down. We hide. We go in camouflage – we're a bunch of miners from the other side of Jupiter, come in for supplies, maybe looking for work ...'

'And where do we go, sir? Not Terra.'

'Not the hellhole it's become, Titus, no. *This* is where we go.' He gestured at the screen. 'This big monster, this artificial Asia. *That* is the centre of power and wealth. Think of us as an undercover military mission if you like. Rome strikes back! I can't take you home. But I can give your life meaning in this new situation, and mine. It may not be you who gets to sit on whatever magnificent throne they have in there, Titus Valerius – but I guarantee your grandson will, or your great-grandson!'

That won him a cheer, as Stef might have predicted.

'But,' Quintus said now, 'the journey to the top of the mountain begins with a single step into the foothills. We make our way in, as cautiously as possible. We show up at that tremendous terminus, where the *optio* says he sees ships coming and going. We find a way to make them let us land. And if necessary ...'

'Yes, sir?'

'We surrender, Titus Valerius. We surrender.'

CHAPTER 39

DATE UNKNOWN

Once again Beth Eden Jones walked across the stars, and between realities.

The chamber into which Beth emerged, having passed through from Mars, was empty, a bare-walled cylinder. It was Hatch architecture stripped to the basics, she thought, with no equipment – no ladder, no steps – no adornment on the walls, nothing resembling any science gear, no signs that humans had ever been here before.

But the chamber was flooded with light.

She looked up. The roof was open, the Hatch cover was raised, a slim circle tipped up on invisible hinges over the circular opening. And a star hung directly over her head, a sun, huge, pale, just too bright to look at directly, a circle of brilliance suspended in a clear faun-coloured sky. Its light poured into the shaft, and Beth's shadow was a patch of grey directly beneath her feet.

She *knew* that star. She knew how it felt to stand directly under such a star.

She let her Mars pressure suit run a quick check of the ambient atmosphere – she wasn't surprised to find it was breathable, with no toxins – and opened up her faceplate with a hiss of equalising pressure. She breathed in, deeply. The smell of the air was familiar too, a dusty, dead-leaves smell, not unpleasant. She even knew the gravity, she thought, a lot heavier than Mars, just a touch less than Earth.

A deep warmth filled her, almost a kind of relaxation, despite the extraordinary journey she had just undergone, despite the strangeness of her only companion. She dumped her pack on the floor and began to shuck off the outer layers of her pressure suit. 'I'm home,' she said.

Earthshine stood beside her, projected as a slick avatar to the usual standard, a middle-aged man dressed in a robust grey coverall. His own instant disposal of his virtual pressure suit was reassuring enough, she supposed; his monitors must agree with her own suit's that the air was safe. But the projection looked oddly unreal in the vertical starlight, not quite as convincing as usual, as if the software that generated such images hadn't yet quite adapted to this environment.

And the avatar looked on anxiously as his support unit, squat and blocky, rolled up to the final doorway to join them in this cylindrical shaft; it had to raise itself up on extensible rods to climb through the door frame.

Beth ran her toe over the floor, disturbing a fine layer of dust. 'I wonder how long it is since anybody was in here.'

'Or any *thing*. We don't know where we are – not yet.'

She met his gaze as he said that – he sounded almost defiant, as if denying the reality – but *she* knew. She recognised this star, this air, and she had some deeper body sense of the familiarity of this world, a sense she couldn't have put into words. But the argument would keep.

'Well,' she said practically, 'wherever we are, the first priority when you're in a hatch is always the same. We have to climb out of this hole. You're a virtual; you can hardly give me a leg-up. We have rope in our packs. We could rig up a loop, try to lasso something...'

'Use the support unit.' The boxy machine rolled up to the wall and stood there, patient and silent. 'You could stand on it—'

'Reach the lip of the well, and pull myself out. OK. But I could never lift your unit out.'

'No need. It contains grappling hooks, cables – it's actually been specifically designed to negotiate Hatches, among other environments.'

She smiled. 'I suppose that makes sense.' She dug rope out of her pack anyhow and began to attach it to her pressure suit and her pack, so she could haul the stuff out after herself later.

Earthshine said, 'Once we establish where we are the unit will adapt itself appropriately. It has extensive self-repair and self-modification facilities. Various kinds of fabricator, for instance.'

'A regular Swiss Army knife.'

He looked at her. 'That's an old reference.'

'Something my father used to say, some relic of his own past. His boyhood on Earth, before the freezer lid closed on him.' *As you know very well*, she thought.

Earthshine just turned away.

She crossed to the machine, set her hands on its upper surface, and hoisted herself up. 'I feel stiff. Stiff and heavy. That's what a few hours on Mars will do for you. Getting too old for this.'

'You'll toughen up,' Earthshine said dismissively. 'Excuse me if I take a short cut.' He flickered out of existence, and reappeared over her head, standing on the lip of the pit, hands on hips, surveying his domain.

'I bet you can't see a damn thing.'

'Not with my eyes and ears still stuck down that shaft, no. Nothing but the crudest extrapolation from the available information. The star in the sky. A blank landscape, a horizon appropriately positioned for a rocky world of a size that can be extrapolated from the gravity we experience.'

On top of the support unit, Beth unsteadily stood upright and reached up to take hold of the rim of the cylindrical pit. The substance of the Hatch structure was smooth under the skin of her hands, and, as always, felt oddly elusive, as if her hands were slipping sideways. The Kalinskis had tried to explain to her that a Hatch, to the best of anybody's knowledge, wasn't a material artefact at all but a structure of distorted spacetime, and that the sideways forces she felt were something like a tide, a secondary gravitational effect ... None of that made it any easier to climb out of this hole, however.

275

'The gravity, yes.' With a lunge she pulled herself up, straightening her arms under her and lifting one leg over the lip of the pit. 'Ninety-eight per cent of Earth's. Right?' Of *course* that was the value; she'd grown up knowing it. She got to her feet, panting a little; she really did feel out of condition.

Now from the pit came a sound like small crossbows being fired. She glanced down and saw that two hooks, supported by suckers, had fixed themselves to the rim of the pit. Fine cables laced down to the support unit, and with a whir of hidden winches, the unit began to rise up from the pit floor. So that was how it got about.

Leaving the unit to its business, Beth turned and looked around.

She was in a forest, surrounded by trees with stout trunks and big, sprawling leaves that caught the light streaming down from above. But there was plenty of open ground – there was no continuous canopy, evidently no permanent cover. The Hatch structure itself sat in a broad clearing, with saplings sprouting beside trunks like fallen pillars, trunks infested with what looked like lichen, mosses, fungi. All of this was tinged in shades of green, some of it drab, some of it more vivid, brilliant in the wan light of the star overhead. In one direction, she saw, the view was more open, revealing water glimmering in the light. What looked like stubby reeds pushed out of the water. And, by the water's edge, a cluster of glistening forms stood, almost like huge mushrooms. 'Stromatolites.' She said the word aloud, letting it roll on her tongue. She remembered how hard it had been for her to learn that word as a little kid, and how confused she had been when her mother had told her that the name was wrong, really, that it had been taken from an Earth organism that was *like* the structures she saw around her but not quite, structures that grew in the water, but not on land...

All this was familiar. And yet, she thought, it was not.

The support unit laboured to haul itself out of the hole in the ground. As it made the last perilous step, and extended stubby caterpillar tracks to claw at the ground, Beth stood by, trying to think of ways she could help if the hefty unit started to topple back into the pit.

Earthshine, meanwhile, paid no attention. He stalked back and forth, impatiently. 'Nothing here,' he growled.

Beth frowned. 'Nothing? Nothing but the trees. The under-growth. The water over there, a lake maybe. *Life*—'

'Just this damn Hatch unit, sitting on the ground. Look at it...'

It was like every other Hatch she'd ever seen, a square of smooth, greyish material with the circular lid raised up over the cylindrical shaft beneath. 'Just like the Hatch on Mercury, the first I came out of with my mother and father and the Peacekeeper. Just like the first I walked into, on Per Ardua.'

'But there's nothing *here*. No buildings, no structures, no com-munity – no people...'

She raised her face, closed her eyes in the light.

'I know what you're thinking,' he snapped.

'It's not what I *think*. It's what I feel. I grew up on Per Ardua. I know its air, its scents, the way its gravity pulls on my bones.'

'You think this is Per Ardua. That *that* star up there is Proxima.'

'What else could it be? Look around, Earthshine. You've never been here before but you've seen the records, I'm sure of that. You've seen the analysis the scientists did once we came back to the solar system, the data the UN teams returned later. Look at these stems, pushing out of the ground. *Stems*, the basis of all complex Per Arduan life, all the way up to the builders.'

'You really think that's Proxima?' He was squinting up into the light, his supporting software casting perfectly formed shad-ows across his face. 'Kind of bland-looking, don't you think? Where are the stellar flares? Where are the starspots?'

That was a point, and, oddly, she hadn't noticed it before. The star's surface, seen through scrunched-up eyes, was smooth, almost featureless, marked by only a few patches of greyish mottling – not the map of restless stellar energies she'd grown up beneath, not the uneasy god that had inflicted particle storms and starspot winters on its hapless planets.

Planets, yes. She walked a few steps and turned around, looking up at the sky, which was a featureless bronze wash. Proxima had had more than one planet. In the permanent daylight of its star-facing hemisphere, the stars and planets had been forever invisible – all save one, a brilliant beacon… 'There,' she said, pointing at a spark of light unwavering in the sky. 'Proxima e, the fifth planet. We called it the Pearl.' She laughed. 'Just where I left it.'

He walked around, growing increasingly angry. 'You seem to be seeing the similarities and screening out the differences. Such as the life forms. These tree-like structures, the "stromatolites" – they are *like* the samples shown in images retrieved from Proxima c, from Per Ardua. But they aren't identical, are they? And what about this?' He pointed dramatically at a small clump of plants at his feet, with sprawling bright green leaves. 'How does *this* fit in?'

She crouched down to see. No, this didn't fit in with her memories of a childhood on Per Ardua at all, at least not of the wild country away from the farms she and her parents and the ColU had laboured to create. These leaves bore the green, not of Arduan life, but of Earth life, a brighter and more vivid colour born under a more energetic star. You'd never have found such things growing in the wild. She dug her fingers into the soil – it was rust brown, quite dry – and found a mass of small tubers. 'These look like potatoes, or a distant relative.'

Earthshine snapped, 'So what do you conclude?'

She stood, clutching a couple of the tubers, brushing the dirt from her hands. Even the texture of the dirt felt familiar. 'This is Per Ardua. *That* is Proxima. If there are potatoes here, people must have brought them – people must have been here. But—'

'But it's not the Per Ardua you remember. Not quite. If this *is* the substellar, where's the UN base? Where's the relic of the *Ad Astra*? Yes, you see, I did my homework. Where are all the people?'

'And where are the builders?' she mused. 'Of course, they might have learned to keep away from people and all their works, given enough time.' She glanced up at Proxima – if it was Proxima. 'How much time?' she wondered.

'This may be another reality strand,' Earthshine said. 'Correction: it *probably* is another reality strand. That's what the Hatches do, don't they? Knit up the timelines. Even if it is Per Ardua, this may not be the version of history in which your family pioneered.'

'Maybe not,' she admitted. 'But there *have* been people here.' She held out the tubers in her palm. 'Somebody brought these.' She broke one of the tubers, revealing crisp white flesh within a sleeve of dirt-matted skin. 'Looks edible.' She nibbled the raw flesh, avoiding the skin; it was crisp, moist, cool, all but flavourless.

'Well, if you live for a few more hours we'll know if that's true or not, won't we?'

'At least I'm not going to starve here,' Beth said. The light changed, subtly. She glanced up and saw clouds, thin streaks of white, drifting over the face of the star. 'Looks like there's still weather here after all. I'll make camp.'

She got to work hauling her pressure suit and pack up from the Hatch with her rope.

In the pack she had a pop-up inflatable shelter, emergency blankets, a small stove, and scrunched-up disposable clothes: a space-age Roman legionary's survival gear, all she needed to endure a few days in the wilderness. She soon had the shelter erected. She shoved the rest of her gear, the pack, the pressure suit, the helmet, inside the tent, and began to haul the whole lot towards the nearest dense-looking clump of trees, seeking anchorage.

Earthlight grunted. 'I apologise I can't help with your chores.' He rubbed his palms together and glanced at the sky. 'If this is Per Ardua, and I still reserve judgement, it is a quieter Per Ardua. Look at the ground, the soil. The rust colour, like Australia, like Mars. Per Ardua always had a peculiar way of letting out its tectonic energy ...'

The continents did not drift on Per Ardua. Perhaps that was something to do with the way this world was tidally locked to its star, the same hemisphere forever bathed in the light, the other forever dark. But there had been internal heat that needed release, as on Earth, and the result had been volcanic provinces, as the ColU had identified them. Every so often a whole chunk of some continent or sea floor would dissolve into chaotic geological upheavals, releasing heat, ash, lava, even building new mountains to be eroded away by the rain.

But, Beth saw, Earthshine was right; *this* dirt looked old. And that dusty Martian colour in the sky wasn't the way she remembered it either. It was a long time since any mountains had got built here.

A small voice asked again, *How long*? And how could that be?

'But there's still weather here,' Earthshine said. 'Which is logical. The substellar point, directly beneath the star, will always be the hottest place on the planet, always a centre of low pressure, like a permanent storm system. And the antistellar, the opposite point, will always be the coldest – *ouch*.' The first few heavy drops of rain fell, pattering on the broad, dead leaves around them, and slicing through Earthshine's body. 'I don't get wet in the rain, but it hurts.'

'Your software's consistency protocols.'

She dragged the tent over the ground, trying to get to the shelter of the trees. She saw that the upright cylindrical carcass of the support unit had sprouted open panels, from which manipulator arms had emerged. Small components were being lifted out of the interior of the carcass, while net-like structures were being used to scrape together heaps of dirt. 'What is it doing?'

'Wheels,' Earthshine said, walking slowly beside her. 'It's making wheels.'

'Planning a journey, are you?'

'Obviously.'

'Where to?'

'Away from here. Away from this *wrong* place.' His anger was evident now; he said this with a snarl.

She reminded herself that he wasn't human. Everything about him was the product of software logic of some kind. Yet she wondered too if he had the artificial equivalent of a sub-conscious. Given the way he'd behaved in the past, including smashing the Mars of the Rome-Xin history, that would explain a lot. So maybe his anger was genuine, the display unconscious.

At the fringe of the forest clump she found a couple of stout trees ideally positioned to anchor her shelter. She took lengths of her rope and began lashing the shelter to the trunks. The trees at least were as she remembered them, basically expanded forms of the ubiquitous stems. 'If this isn't Per Ardua it's a damn good impersonation,' she muttered as she worked.

By the time she was done the rain was coming down harder, hissing on the leaf-carpeted ground. She looked back at the Hatch, whose lid, she saw, was closing. 'The Hatch is a spacetime artefact, and yet its designers took care that it's protected from the rain. Well, that's attention to detail for you.' But there was no reply, and when she glanced around she saw that Earthshine had already retreated to the interior of the tent.

Beside the Hatch, in the rain, the support unit was rapidly assembling big skeletal wheels, four of them.

CHAPTER 40

The reception chamber was meant to impress, Mardina thought. If not to awe. Even before you got into the main body of the Titan, the huge space habitat itself.

The chamber was a wide, deep cylinder set precisely at the spin axis of the rotating habitat, with zero-gravity guide ropes strung from wall to wall. To reach this chamber you had already had to pass through a series of locks, each of which alone had been larger than any single cabin in the *Malleus Jesu*. The place was ornate, too, with rich woven blankets spread over the steel walls, and sprays of brilliantly coloured feathers, even the gleam of gold and silver plate. The huge face of some angry god, his eyes picked out by emeralds, glared down at the Romans from the opposite wall.

And, from glass-walled emplacements all around them, troops stared down at the newcomers. They wore a uniform of a simple shift tied at the waist, brightly coloured, and functional helmets of what looked like hard steel. They had weapons to hand, short swords and stabbing spears – even some kind of artillery, and blunt muzzles peered at the Romans from all sides.

And now the stranded *Malleus* personnel – forty legionaries with their Centurion Quintus Fabius, Mardina, Titus Valerius and his daughter, Michael the Greek *medicus*, and Chu Yuen with the ColU in its pack on his back – were huddled in this vast arena, tangled up in the guide ropes like flies in a spider web. It didn't help that all of them had been cleansed before being allowed this far into the habitat – stripped naked, bathed in hot showers, their clothes shaken out in the vacuum. The ColU said it was entirely sensible that the controllers of this enclosed world would try to keep out fleas and lice and diseases. But it had taken all of Quintus's personal authority to persuade his men to submit to this. The Romans, in their military tunics and boots with their cloaks and packs, looked like savages in this setting, like the barbarians they effected to despise. At least they didn't look like soldiers any more. Well, Mardina hoped not. At Quintus's orders the legionaries had left behind on the *Malleus Jesu* their *gladios* and spears and fire-of-life weapons, and their armour, even their military belts and medals.

The bulk of the ship's occupants had transferred to the habitat. The ship itself, having come close enough to the Titan for the smaller yachts to deliver the legionaries to the hub port, was now hiding among the asteroids manned by a skeleton crew, a handful of legionaries under the command of *optio* Gnaeus Junius and *trierarchus* Eilidh – and with the more fragile passengers, including Jiang, Stef Kalinski and Ari Guthfrithson – able to survive for a long time on supplies meant for five times their number.

Now, as the Romans waited for the latest step in their induction, Quintus Fabius kept up a steady stream of encouragement. 'Take it easy, lads. You look stranger to them than they do to you – even if you are simple farmers of the ice moons. I doubt very much if they've seen the likes of *you* before, Titus Valerius, save in their nightmares… Ah. Here comes somebody new to order us about.'

An official approached them now, a stocky, scowling woman of perhaps fifty, pulling herself along a guide rope. Flanked by an unarmed man and two soldiers, she wore a simple tunic not unlike the soldiers', but with a pattern of alternately coloured squares – like a gaudy chessboard, the shades brilliant – and obviously expensive, Mardina thought. It was a brash garb that did not sit well with what appeared to be an irritable personality. And she carried a peculiar instrument, a frame almost like an abacus but laced with knotted string. She glanced down at this as she approached them, working the knots with agile fingers.

Titus Valerius murmured, 'Speaking of nightmares, Centurion – *look* at those lads with the clerk.'

The soldiers who accompanied the official were tall, almost ludicrously so, a head or more taller even than Titus Valerius. Their long limbs looked stick-thin but were studded by muscles under wiry flesh, and their faces were bony, skull-like. They moved through the mesh of guide ropes with practised ease. Close to, they were very strange, even inhuman, and Mardina tried not to recoil.

'They look ill,' Quintus said. 'Too long without weight and no exercise. Put them under my command and I'd soon sort them out …'

'No, Centurion,' Michael murmured. 'I think you're misreading them. These are perfectly healthy – and functional for their environment. They are *adapted* for the lack of weight. Look how strong they appear, strong in a wiry sense; look how confidently they move. I suspect they would be formidable opponents, just here at the axis of the ship, where there is no weight. Perhaps they have been raised in this environment, from children: specialist axis warriors. Or perhaps they are the result of generations born and bred without weight.'

'Or,' the ColU murmured from its pack, 'perhaps they are the result of genetic tinkering. We have spoken of this, *medicus*. Your culture knew nothing of this, but we could have done it—'

'Before the last jonbar hinge but one,' the *medicus* said drily.

'Be interesting to fight them, then,' Quintus said thoughtfully. 'But not yet. And hush, Collius; that clerk is looking suspicious.'

The lead official looked up at them now from her knotted strings, her scowl deepening, and she inspected them one by one. Fifty-something she might be, but, Mardina thought, like the soldiers with her, she was handsome. Under black hair streaked with grey she had dark eyes, copper-brown skin, high cheekbones and a nose a Roman might have been proud of.

The official pulled herself up into the air, so she could look down on the disorderly group of Romans. '*Inguill sutiymi*

284

– quipucamayoc. Maymanta kanki? Romaoi? Hapinkichu? Runasimi rimankichu?'

Inguill was not having a good day, and when the strangers muttered disrespectfully among themselves before her, her disquiet and irritation quickly deepened.

Inguill's formal title was senior *quipucamayoc*, keeper of the *quipus*. She was one of a dozen of her rank who, on behalf of the Sapa Inca and through a hierarchy of record-keepers beneath her, effectively governed all of Yupanquisuyu, this great habitat, both *cuntisuyu* and *antisuyu*, from Hurin Cuzco at the eastern hub to Hanan Cuzco, palace of the Inca himself, at this western hub. It was a role that, it was said, had had a place in Inca culture since the days before the empire's conquest of the lands of the first *antisuyu*, the passage across the eastern ocean, and the move out into the sky.

And it was a role dedicated to the primary function of *control*: the essence of the imperial system of the Intip Churi, the Children of the Sun.

That fact had become apparent to Inguill at a very young age, when the teachers at her *ayllu* had first picked her out as an exceptional talent and had put her forward for training at the Cuzco colleges. Inguill had risen up the ranks of the imperial administration smoothly – shedding her family and her ties to her *ayllu*, shunning personal relationships in favour of the endless fascination of the work.

She had always been able to grasp the key importance of maintaining control, in the empire of the Sapa Inca. Especially in a habitat like this, huge yet finite and fragile, where you had to control the people in order to ensure the maintenance of the complex, interlocked systems that kept them all alive. And in the theology of the Intip Churi you had to control the gods, too, endlessly placating, and excluding the wilful divine anger that could break into the world if chaos and disorder were allowed to reign, even briefly. Of course this great box of a habitat – a box from which there was no possibility of escape, under constant and total surveillance from Hanan Cuzco at the hub, from the Condor craft that continually patrolled the axis, and from operatives dispersed on the ground – lent itself to such control.

It soon became apparent too that *camayocs* like herself, endowed with that kind of intuitive perception about the need for unsleeping and unrelenting control, were rare indeed, and prized. So she had found herself plucked out for promotion ahead of many of her age-group cadre – even the privileged sort, the sons and daughters of the rich of the Cuzcos who could afford the finest pharmaceutical enhancements, the most refined extracts from plants and animals bred for the purpose over generations, to sharpen their intellects to a degree of brilliance. Even such an expensively shaped mind was of little use to the state if beneath the glitter and the quick-talk was a lack of basic perception, a lack of understanding of the challenges of existence. And that was the understanding that Inguill enjoyed, and cultivated in herself.

Not that it did her career much good. She had proven to be so good at her job that she was given a kind of roaming brief, sent to manage, not the orderly, everyday problems of Yupanquisuyu, but the *dis*order, the unusual, the out of the ordinary, wherever it might crop up – either within the habitat or coming from without, like this bunch of Romaoi. The paradox was that as a result she spent much of her working life in a state of frustration, even anxiety, and certainly irritation. For the unusual, the disorderly, the chaotic, the very stuff it was her job to deal with, annoyed her profoundly until she could master it and clean it up. And all the while her rivals, over whom she had in theory been promoted, were busily worming their way into comfortable niches in the vast hierarchy of the Cuzcos.

Nothing in recent times had annoyed her more than these mysterious Romaoi, with their bulging muscles and sullen expressions. Ice moon farmers? Hah! Not likely... But where there was novelty, she reminded herself, where there was strangeness, there was always opportunity – for herself, if not the empire.

Now she faced the big man with the gaudy cloak who looked to be the leader.

'My name is Inguill – I am a *quipucamayoc*. Where are you from? Are you Roman? Do you understand? Do you speak *runasimi*?'

The ColU's earpieces had been given to Quintus, Michael, Mardina and a few others. Now Mardina heard the strange device whisper its translation in her ear – a translation from Quechua, which the official called *runasimi*, into Latin, by an artificial being whose own first language was a kind of bastardised German. Just when it seemed her life couldn't have got any stranger ...

Quintus grunted. 'I will never be able to speak this tongue of theirs! It sounds like squabbling birds.'

'*Allichu, huq kuti rimaway!*'

'That was, "Say that again,"' the ColU whispered. 'Apologise, Centurion. And wait for me to translate.'

'I am sorry.'

'*Pampachaykuway ...*'

'My name is Quintus Fabius. I am the leader of this group. We are grateful for your shelter.'

'Well, you haven't been granted it yet.' The *quipucamayoc* glared at Quintus and his men, suspicion bristling as visibly as feathers on a predatory bird, Mardina thought. 'Tell me again where you claim to come from.'

'We lived on an ice moon, far from the sun. I apologise; I do not know the names of these bodies as they are known in your mighty empire ... (Collius, I'm not comfortable with all this lying ...)'

('Be humble, Centurion. Guile, remember? You can display your strengths later.')

'We were there for many generations. Our fathers and mothers, our grandfathers and grandmothers worked the ice, living off the thin sunlight. We farmed—'

'You were there so long you forgot most of your Quechua, it seems. Ha! Five centuries after Tiso Inca stomped Rome flat, you refugees still cling to your primitive tongue. Oh, never mind. So you farmed. Why are you here now?'

Mardina could hear the tension in Quintus Fabius's voice as he swallowed these insults and responded. She was glad Titus Valerius and the rest could not understand what was said.

'There was a calamity, *quipucamayoc*. Another body, a fast-moving rogue, hit our home. We, most of the men, were away, investigating another moon that seemed mineral-rich. We had not detected the rogue, there was no time – our home was destroyed, most of the women and children. All we had built over generations. We who survived came here in the last of our ships, to throw yourselves on your mercy.'

She peered into his face. 'Well, at least you're sticking to your story. But you don't betray much grief. That's either a sign that you're strong, which is admirable, or you're lying, which is less so.' She pulled herself along a guide rope and inspected the legionaries. 'Also you don't look like no-weight farmers to me. You're too solid. Too muscular.'

Quintus straightened his back. 'We – our ancestors were Roman. We retained their sense of discipline, even in our exile out in the dark.'

'Really. And that ship that brought you in – don't imagine we didn't see it before it scurried off into the dark – it didn't look like any kind of mining craft to me.'

'Another relic of our pioneering ancestors, *quipucamayoc*. All we had left. We sent it back to the ice moons to search again for survivors of our family. While we came here looking for work. (Collius, these lies become elaborate.)'

('Please, Centurion. Humour me. We are playing a long game.')

('Hmm ...')

Inguill glared at Quintus. 'You mutter in your antique tongue, as if talking to a voice in your head. Are you simple or insane?' She studied the group, deeply suspicious. 'I don't like you,

Quintus Fabius, if that is your name. I don't like this rabble you have brought into my world. I don't like your story, which stinks like a week-old fish head. I don't like the way you hesitate before speaking every line, as if somebody is whispering in your ear. *You don't fit* – and I don't like things that don't fit. I have the power to throw you all out into the airlessness, you know.'

Quintus held her gaze. 'We are at your mercy.'

'You are, aren't you? But you have muscle, and evident discipline of a sort. This is a big craft and we are always short of muscle and discipline – especially if it can be applied to the jobs nobody else wants. Very well. I will let you live. I'll send you to the *antisuyu*.' Inguill grinned coldly. 'You don't know what that is, do you? In the *antisuyu* you will be far from my sight. Indeed you will be far from this place, which is the only way out of this habitat. And a deeper contrast to Rome, and indeed your ice moon, could hardly be imagined. But you won't be out of my thoughts, believe me. You are a conundrum, Quintus Fabius, and it is evident to me that, to say the least, you are not telling me the whole truth.' She pushed her face close to his. 'I don't like you, and you owe me your life. Never forget that.'

Quintus did not reply.

She backed off. 'In anticipation of the decision, I brought this man.' She indicated the other clerkish man next to her. 'His name is Ruminavi, and he is the *tocrico apu* of the region to which you will be sent – which contains the *ayllu* to which you will be attached, among others.' She looked at their empty faces. 'Do you understand any of this? You are in Tawantinsuyu, the Empire of the Four Quarters – the earth and the sky, and east and west here in the habitat, the *antisuyu* and *cuntisuyu*. Under the Sapa Inca each quarter is controlled by an *apu*, a prefect, and under him or her are twenty-two *tocrico apus*... Oh! You will learn.

'Now Ruminavi will escort you to your transports to the *antisuyu*. Do what the *tocrico apu* says, and your local *curaca*, work hard and don't cause trouble, and you might survive a little while. Oh, and you will give up any weapons you are still

289

concealing. No weapons in Yupanquisuyu, save for the troops and other designated officials.'

There was grumbling in the ranks at this, but Quintus said quietly in thick rural Latin, 'Lads, we'll find weapons as we need them, or steal them, make them. That's always been my plan.'

The ColU said, 'Make sure they don't confiscate *me*. Tell them I am an idol. Or a piece of medical equipment. Or a scrap from the farmed moon, a sentimental souvenir...'

But the men had fallen silent.

Mardina turned, and saw that a door at the far end of the chamber had opened, to reveal the interior of the habitat for the first time. A tube of cloud, brightly illuminated, stretching to infinity.

'By Jupiter and Jesu,' muttered Fabius. 'Into what have you delivered us, Collius?'

As the Romaoi filed towards the internal transport, one of Inguill's soldiers approached her, holding a block of metal. 'Found this, *quipucamayoc*. No idea how one of them smuggled this through the cleansing area. And then managed to drop it on the other side...'

Inguill took the piece. It was a kind of belt buckle, she saw, intricately shaped, and stamped with square, ugly Latin lettering that she had to pick out:

LEGIO XC VICTRIX

CHAPTER 41

Ruminavi, who was a fussy little man with none of the evident intellect of Inguill, said they would be transported in some kind of carriage from this hub to their new home – Mardina imagined something like an elevator car – indeed they would ride in a series of such transports; the carriages would not take all of them at once.

So the Romans were roughly divided into groups of a dozen or less. Quintus, with Titus's help, made sure the men were in their *contubernium* tent groups as far as possible, with somebody relatively sensible in charge of each. The legionaries grumbled and moaned as they formed a queue, hanging weightless in the air – a line that would take them into a chamber of wonders, Mardina realised, but soldiers always grumbled whatever you did for them.

When it was her turn, Mardina followed Quintus and Chu and a handful of Romans, and passed through a portal into a box of glass, a box riding on upright rails, which in turn were attached to a tremendous vertical wall that stretched above and below her, as far as she could see. Behind her in this glass box, Ruminavi the *apu* settled on a seat, surrounded by a handful of spidery axis warriors, and the Romans crowded in. And ahead of her …

She recoiled from the view, closing her eyes. She heard a kind of moaning, high-pitched, like a frightened animal. She thought it might be Chu Yuen, the slave, more intelligent than the average legionary and therefore more capable of wonder, and horror. She hoped it wasn't herself.

'Look down,' the ColU said now, from the security of its lodging in Chu's backpack. 'Mardina Eden Jones Guthfrithson, listen to me. Don't look ahead, or up – don't look at the wall to which we are fixed – just *look straight down.*'

Mardina opened her eyes and looked. And, through the transparent floor, she saw what looked like Terra as seen from low orbit, a slice of sprawling landscape, washed-out green and grey under scattered clouds, and with stretches of water that glistened in the sunlight like polished Roman shields. 'This isn't so bad,' she said with relief.

'Here at the axis of the habitat we are over two hundred miles above this landscape. For that is the radius of this cylinder. The view here is just as if you were in a spacecraft, orbiting.'

'It seems almost normal, in the sunlight. Except—'

'*What* sunlight?' the ColU said. 'I know. There are breaks in the habitat's tremendous walls. Pools that admit what must be reflected sunlight, to illuminate this enclosed environment – surely indirectly reflected, so that the radiation shielding is not compromised. There is one below us and not far ahead – you can look up now, just a little further ...'

The sunlight pool glared under the clouds, like a city on fire. It was an eerie, beautiful sight.

Ruminavi said, 'We call them the windows of Inti. For Inti is our sun god, you see.'

The transport suddenly lurched into motion, heading down the face of the wall on its rails. The passengers were jerked into the air, like pebbles in a dropped helmet, Mardina thought, and forced to grab onto whatever handholds they could reach. Already some of the legionaries looked as if they wanted to throw up.

Ruminavi, safe in his seat, looked on with a malicious grin. 'Keep tight hold. The acceleration will be high. We'll be covering a lot of your Roman miles every hour by the time we hit the atmosphere. Of course by then you'll be feeling the spin weight ...' He laughed out loud. 'Not so tough now, you

Romans, are you? Just like your ancestors who begged on their knees to Tiso Inca's generals to spare their city from the Fist.'

Quintus Fabius glared at him.

'All right,' the ColU said now. 'Look down again, Mardina Eden Jones Guthfrithson. And look up. Look at the wall itself, down which we are climbing ...'

It was more than a wall, she saw now, it was an engineered cliff face, crusted with structures, blocks and domes and pyramids – many essentially constructed of steel, Mardina thought, but ornately painted, even faced with stone and bound by steel straps. *Structures* – that was the wrong word. She saw lights gleam from within, doorways opening: these were buildings, inhabited by people. At the axial point itself a tremendous tower sprouted straight out from the wall, built of stone blocks of some kind: a stepped pyramid, skinny and enormously long. And in one place she saw a gang of workers, in pressure suits, tethered to handholds fixed to the wall, engaged on the construction of something new. A living, changing place then, a vertical town, stuck to this wall. And the rails on which the transport ran cut through all this clutter in a dead straight line before plunging down into the clouds far below.

Mardina uttered a silent prayer. 'It is a city in the sky.'

'No,' said the ColU. 'A city *above* the sky. We are in a near vacuum here, Mardina. The air will only become significantly dense perhaps twenty miles above the ground – I mean, above the cylindrical hull. This habitat, four hundred and fifty miles in diameter, essentially contains a vacuum, with a thin layer of air plastered over its inner surface, kept there by the spin gravity.'

'A vast city in the vacuum. Why's it here?'

The *apu* snorted. 'Why do you think? This is Hanan Cuzco, home of the Inca himself, and his family and heirs and closest advisers. The greatest marvel in Yupanquisuyu, outshining even that dump Hurin Cuzco at the eastern pole. The *mitimacs* are kept out by all this lovely vacuum. Why, a war could be raging down there on the ground and we'd never know about it up here.'

'"We", Ruminavi?' said Quintus. 'But you don't live here, do you? It was my understanding that you're coming with us, all the way to this grubby *antisuyu*, where you live.'

Ruminavi scowled. 'Yes, and let's see how long your Roman arrogance lasts in my jungle, you posturing clown.'

Mardina looked again at the compartment's rear wall, the relatively comforting vision of a riveted metal wall flying up past her face. *Hundreds of miles* of metal, of steel and rivets... 'All right, Collius. I think I'm ready for the next stage.'

'Very well. Stay upright, feet down towards the ground – so to speak. When we are further from the axis the spin gravity will become stronger and *pull* you down. Now look straight ahead, lift your face slowly...'

If she had been in orbit around Terra, at this altitude the curve of the world would be apparent; she would find a horizon in every direction she looked. But here it was different. Here, when she lifted her head, she saw the panorama below her, of rivers and hills and inland seas and what looked like farms, what looked like cities, extending directly ahead, the details becoming a compressed blur with distance, until at last she saw only a band of air glowing with the illumination of the light pools. There was no sense of curvature – not if she looked straight ahead. But if she looked away from that axis, the landscape *curved up*, rising to either side and joining over her head to form a tube of smeared light, green and blue and grey. It was as if she was holding a rolled-up map, she thought, and peering through it at a distant source of light.

Far away, at least, it was all a comforting abstraction. But then she let her gaze wander back down the length of the tube, back to her position, and she looked up at a great roof of land, plastered with inverted mountains and patchwork farms and even *rivers*, pinned there by a spin weight she could not yet feel. She felt her heart hammering, her breath growing shallow.

The ColU said, 'Easy, Mardina. Chu Yuen – hold her hand.'

The touch of the former slave's flesh was comforting. But,

glancing to her side, she saw that Chu had his own eyes clamped shut.

She laughed.

'Are you all right, Mardina?'

'Yes, Collius. A folded world. What magnificence. What arrogance. What madness!'

'Quite. Yet here we are. Chu Yuen? What do you think?'

'That I miss the stars,' the slave said. 'But I am now, however, *standing* on the floor of this box.'

He was right. Mardina hadn't noticed. She was light as a feather still, but when she jumped, she drifted back down.

Ruminavi said, 'Some way to go yet before we descend into the clouds. But we are already a tenth of the way there, and so you have a tenth your weight. We carry no refreshments, save water from that spigot over there ...'

Mardina glanced around the transport, aware of her companions for the first time in a while. As their weight returned, the legionaries were pulling off their boots and settling down on their cloaks and blankets. Titus Valerius was playing knucklebones, or trying too, complaining loudly about the way the pieces rolled in the low weight. The *medicus* was huddled in a corner, obviously trying not to look terrified. One of the soldiers seemed to be taking a nap.

While the tube world unfolded all around them.

CHAPTER 42

It took two hours of descent before the transport compartment finally plunged down into the thicker clouds – although by now the blueness of the high air was visible beyond the walls.

Two hours: it was that fact alone, that this evidently high-speed transport had taken a whole two hours to cross a radius of one hub of this tremendous cylinder, that drove home to Mardina the sheer scale of the structure she was entering. It was already hundreds of miles back to the port where she had entered this habitat; it would not be rapid to travel anywhere in this great volume. At least now her weight felt comfortingly normal, even though the descent was not finished yet.

And when they passed through the high cloud layer, abruptly Mardina found herself looking down on mountains. Mountains that lapped up against the hub wall like a wave of rock breaking against the steel, mountains with ice clinging to their upper peaks and slopes, and glaciers spilling down their flanks.

The rail diverged from the wall now, though the transport box tipped up to stay vertical, and suddenly Mardina found herself skimming down an icebound slope of rock and frost-shattered scree. The landscape itself, at the foot of these mountains, was still far below.

'This feels almost normal,' she said.

Ruminavi grunted. 'Until you remember there is a big band of these mountains all the way around the base of the hub wall.'

The ColU said, 'Yes, of course – a mountain chain over a thousand miles long, like the mountains of Valhalla Inferior:

South America, where the ancestors of these Incas arose. Folded up into a band!'

'And all fake,' Ruminavi said, grinning, trying to provoke a reaction – to awe them, Mardina realised. 'Hollow! Built by engineers, shaped by artists! And inside the mountains there are big engines that circulate air and water and even stone, gravel and sand from the ocean.'

Mardina asked, 'What ocean? Never mind.'

'But look out at the spectacle ...'

Abruptly the transport descended beneath the snow line, and now sped over bare rock. The view was giddy, with green-clad precipices falling away to the valleys of turbulent rivers below and those towering ice-clad peaks above, clawing at the metal face of the hub. Spectacular bridges spanned some of the gorges. And looking out now Mardina could see that some of the mountain's face had been levelled into terraces, where people toiled; there were huts, fields, smoke rising from fires into the thin air. These were the first inhabitants of the cylinder they had seen since the hub.

'Potato farmers,' the ColU said. 'Just as in the Andes in the time of the Incas. *Our* Incas. There they farmed all the way up to the snow line.'

Ruminavi frowned at the unfamiliar names. But he said, 'Just as in the old country, we built mountains here as residences for our gods. The country is littered with shrines.'

'Yes, the Incas came from the high lands,' Mardina said. 'I remember that from my own history, of what the Xin and the Romans found when they fought over Valhalla Inferior. There had been a mighty empire spanning the continent, but armed only with bronze swords and armour of leather ...'

'Just as the Europeans of my UN-China Culture discovered,' the ColU said. 'And destroyed. Here, however, the Incas evidently prospered. They overthrew Rome, they went out into space, and they brought their culture with them – indeed, they recreated it. Andean mountains, built of lunar rock perhaps.

'Inguill called this habitat Yupanquisuyu, which means the

297

Country of Yupanqui. And Cusi Yupanqui, at least in my culture's timeline, was the man who truly established the Inca empire. He conquered vast swathes of territory, and established the empire's legal, military and social structures. Yupanqui was their Alexander the Great, and it is as if this vast habitat is called "Alexandria". So Yupanqui must have lived here too, in this reality; the histories must have been roughly consistent until that point – though, evidently, Rome survived to be defeated. I need to see the *quipus*, you know.'

'The what?'

'The frame of strings that *quipucamayoc* Inguill carried. That was, and evidently still is, the way the Incas kept their records. Somewhere in this artefact there must be a library, banks of knotted strings telling the story of this empire all the way back to Yupanqui himself. If only I could see it ...'

Quintus Fabius had been listening. He said drily, 'I'll see what can be arranged, Collius. In the meantime it seems to me that this box of glass is slowing.'

In the last moments the transport entered another, lower bank of cloud that blanketed a green-tinged landscape.

Instructed by Ruminavi, the passengers picked up their gear and lined up by a side door. The axis warriors from the hub, fragile-looking in gravity, remained carefully strapped into their couches, but they kept the blunt muzzles of their ugly-looking weapons trained on the Romans. Meanwhile, waiting outside the door was another squad of soldiers to take over their supervision, heftier-looking types, their clothing gaudy, their dark faces stern and suspicious.

Mardina could see it would be just a short walk to the next transport, which was a kind of carriage on rails, one of a series, pulled by a heavy engine at the front. The rails of the track swept down the flank of the mountain.

'Ah,' the ColU said as he was carried out by Chu, 'another railway system. A universal, it seems, across the timelines, common to all engineering cultures. Quintus, please ask Ruminavi what powers it – what is the motive force behind the engine?'

It took some moments of interrogation before the answer was extracted from the *apu*, and at that Quintus had to flatter him to make him brag about the mighty achievements of the Incas. The train, which he called a caravan, ran on the *capac ñans*, the roads of the gods, which spanned this habitat from end to end. Ruminavi said the engine, which had a name something like 'llama', was powered by a *warak'a*, derived from an old Quechua word for 'sling' – and which turned out to be the Inca term for a kernel...

But Mardina, as she stepped out of the carriage, stopped paying attention to mere words. This steep mountainside was choked with green and swathed in mist, the moisture dripping from the crowding vegetation. The air was damp and fresh – but thin, hard to breathe, and she had a sense of altitude. Above her head, patchy clouds obscured her view of the higher mountains, which lifted islands of green into the air, like offerings. And beside the path that led to the railway, flowers bloomed in thick clusters with vivid colours, yellow, orange and purple, and tiny birds worked the flowers, flashes of brilliant blue.

The *apu* was watching her. He seemed to be admiring her show of interest, at least in comparison to the soldiers who stamped along the trail, already complaining about the state of their feet in a full gravity. 'Cloud forest,' he told her, a term that took some translating by the ColU.

'And I suppose there's a big band of this too all around the rim of the world.'

'That's how it's designed. Come. It gets even prettier further down. All of this in a box in space.' But he smiled at her a little too intensely, as if drinking in every detail of her face, her skin.

Mardina drew away and walked back to her group.

Once aboard the train they had to wait a full hour before it was ready to pull away.

There were many coaches bearing passengers, but the

legionaries were herded into rougher carts evidently intended for freight. The Romans grumbled as they settled down, complained about the thinness of the air, the food grudgingly supplied by Inca troops – fruit, meat, water – supplemented by biscuits and other rations they'd brought in their packs from the *Malleus*. And, as soldiers always did whenever they got the chance, they tried to sleep.

Meanwhile more trains came rolling into the hub station from the habitat interior, laden with goods, foodstuffs, timber. The ColU speculated that some of these goods must be meant for export from the habitat, perhaps to other space colonies, as well as supplying the big hub cities.

At last the train pulled away.

At first the descent was alarmingly steep and rapid. Looking ahead, sitting on a wooden bench and with her head resting against a window, Mardina saw that they soon descended below the level of the cloud forest and into more open air. Now they emerged from the last foothills of the mountains and came to a flat plain – flat at least in the direction of travel – marred by ranges of low hills and gouged by the valleys of sluggish rivers. This land was the *puna*, the prefect said. The great plain itself was uninspiring, Mardina thought, as they sped across it, nothing but grass and shrubs on arid land. But if Mardina looked sideways she could distinctly see the upward curve of the landscape, as if she was travelling through some tremendous valley. Sparks of artificial light and palls of smoke on those sloping walls must mark townships, and she saw the iron glint of rail tracks and roads.

And there were people everywhere, farming the land in great fields and on terraces. The buildings they lived in were unassuming hut-like structures, although the larger townships featured complexes of massive warehouses that the *apu* said were *tambos*, imperial facilities for storing food. Every so often they saw a larger structure yet, compounds surrounded by walls with multiple terraces like huge steps. These were *pukaras*; they were obvious fortresses. Their walls were of a rough, dark stone that the ColU speculated might be rock from the dismantled moon.

But some features of the landscape were less recognisable, to a Brikanti eye. At rail junctions and springs, even on particular outcroppings of rock, there were small shrines that the Incas called *huacas*, with carved idols, poles, cairns, hanks of human hair – once, even what looked like a mummified human hand. It was as if the landscape was permeated by the presence of gods and spirits. Away from the sparse human settlements it was as if nothing existed on this eerie plain but the train on its track, and the markers of the gods.

Quintus had a conversation with the *apu*, steadily interrogating the little official about the nature of the world.

The ColU summarised this for Mardina. 'This engineered landscape, the *puna*, is the equivalent of what was called the *altiplano* in my culture. In Valhalla Inferior, this was a plain of tremendous extent, very amenable to cultivation. And *high*, two miles or more above the level of the ocean. Just as it seems to be here, judging by the thinness of the air. Again they recreate their culture from Terra.'

'But there's so *much* of it,' Mardina said. 'It's crushing. And what is it *for*? All these people labouring away, this gigantic engine they live in ...'

Quintus joined them. 'The *apu* is not a discreet man. Given a little flattery he has explained to me the essential purposes of this monster, this Yupanquisuyu.

'It is the hub of a system of exploitation and expansion and control that spans sun, moons and planets – the Empire of the Four Quarters. The vast fertile expanses of the habitat feed the miners and engineers who work the worlds and moons across the solar system. The habitat is a source of people too, people to be trained up to mine those moons. And, as well, it is a recruiting pool for soldiers to fight the occasional necessary war – these days wars against internal rebels, since the Inca empire seems to span the whole planetary system. Oh, and the habitat supports the enormous establishment that sustains the

Sapa Inca himself, son of the sun. Well, one must be *seen* to be wealthy and in control, mustn't one? Our Caesars always knew that. Hanan Cuzco, his ghastly city in the airlessness of the hub, is the Sapa Inca's Capitoline Hill ...'

'And there is one more objective,' the ColU murmured. 'One more purpose all this serves.'

Quintus nodded. 'They have star vessels. Bigger than our *Malleus*, it seems, but no more advanced. They have many of them, in great fleets, which for more than a century, says the *apu*, have been swarming out to the stars, and—'

'Building Hatches,' Mardina breathed.

'So it seems. On a far greater scale than *we* ever did.'

The ColU murmured, 'And so it goes. Whatever the merits of this culture compared to any other, we can say one thing: it is better at building Hatches. As if it has been designed to serve the needs of those who would desire such a thing. And just as we would expect given our prior experiences of jonbar hinges.'

Quintus grunted. 'Apparently so. But I would suggest we set aside such cosmic mysteries for now and focus on the needs of the present, which will be challenging enough.'

It turned out to be ten hours before the first stop – ten hours in fact before they reached the end of the *altiplano*. Since the ColU estimated that the train, running without a break, was averaging sixty Roman miles an hour, that gave Mardina another impression of the sheer scale of this artefact into whose interior she was busy tunnelling.

When the train finally slowed, night was falling across Yupanquisuyu. Mardina supposed they must fortuitously have been brought to the hub from space in the morning. She wondered vaguely how the mirror mechanisms worked behind the Inti windows, deflecting away the unending sunlight to emulate nightfall.

They got out at a waystation, which Ruminavi called a *chuclla*. Here there was a kind of refectory, and a place to wash, and shops where you could obtain food or even fresh clothes, and dormitory blocks – but the *apu* said they would not stay long before the train resumed its journey, with a fresh crew; they could sleep on the train, or not. Anyhow the grumbling legionaries had none of the credit tokens you needed to buy stuff at the shops. The Inca soldiers laughed at their frustration.

This small hub of industry and provision was set in the astounding panorama of Yupanquisuyu.

As the Romans bickered around the shops, Mardina once more walked alone, away from the station. Though by now it was evidently full night in the habitat, it was not entirely dark; the residual glow seeping from the light pools was clear and white, but so faint that colours were washed out. It was like the moonlight of Terra, Mardina thought, and no doubt that was by deliberate design. She could make out the sleeping landscape all around her, the terraces and fields. A little way ahead, though, the country began to break up into hills and valleys that were lakes of shadows. They would be descending soon, then, to lower country, and thicker air.

And to left and right the uplift of the landscape was easily visible, even in the night. The ColU had told her that a round world with the curvature of this cylinder would have a horizon only a mile away, compared to three miles on Terra. So, well within a mile, she could see the land *tipping up*, the trees and houses visibly tilted towards her. And the rise went on and on – there was no horizon, only the mist of distance – until the land became a tremendous slope, bearing rivers and lakes at impossible angles. Soon the detail was lost in darkness, and in the thickness of the faintly misty air. But then, as she raised her eyes further, she saw the roof of the world, an inverted landscape glowing with pinpricks of light. It looked like the dark side of Terra as seen from space, with threads of roads and the spark of towns clearly visible beyond its own layer of air and clouds. At this altitude the air was so clear it was as if she was looking through vacuum.

The *apu* joined her. He was chewing some kind of processed green leaf; he offered her some, but, moving subtly away from

303

him, she declined. He said, 'Quite a sight if you're not used to it. And even if you are, it astounds you sometimes.'

'It doesn't look like the other side of a cylinder. It's like another world suspended over this one.'

The ColU murmured in her ear, 'That's natural. The human eye was evolved for spying threats and opportunities in the horizontal plain, and so vertical perceptions are distorted—'

'Hush,' she murmured.

Ruminavi looked at her quizzically.

She said, 'I can see we'll be coming down from the *puna* soon.'

'Yes. Which is why they put this *chuclla* here. The last stop before the descent. A place to acclimatise to the thinner air, if you're coming the other way.'

'And the land below ...'

'It's a kind of coastal strip. The rivers pour down off the *puna* and spread out, and you have sprawling valleys, immense deltas. Very fertile country, nothing but farmers and fishers. They grow peppers, maize. Should take us half the time we travelled already to cross.'

'Five more hours? And then what? You said a coastal strip. The coast of what?'

'Why, of the ocean. Goes all the way around the waist of the world.' He pointed to the sky, in the direction they'd been travelling, the direction he and his soldiers called east. 'You can see it at night sometimes. Spectacular by day, of course. We'll be crossing by the time the sun comes up.'

'Crossing it?'

'It's spanned by bridges, for the railway, other traffic. We'll go rattling across it without even slowing down.'

'How long to cross the ocean?'

'Oh, it'll be getting dark again by the time we reach the eastern shore.'

The times, the distances, were crushing her imagination. Fifteen, twenty hours more, and she would still be travelling within the belly of the artefact. 'And beyond the ocean?'

'Ah, then we come to the *antisuyu*. The eastern country, all of *this* side of the ocean being the western, the *cuntisuyu*. And if you went on all the way to the eastern hub it would be another fifteen hours.'

'But we won't be going that far.'

'Oh, no. Only five, six hours to home. My home and yours.'

'Which is? What's it like?'

'Jungle. *Hacha hacha*. You'll see.' He grinned, his teeth white in the pale light. He held out his leaves again. 'You sure you won't have some of this coca? Makes life a lot easier to bear ...'

She shook her head, and once more backed away from him. He followed, ineffectual, evidently drawn to her but, thankfully, lacking the courage or guile to do anything about it.

CHAPTER 43

On Per Ardua, that first 'night' after Beth and Earthshine came through the Hatch, it rained for twelve hours solid.

The sound of the rain on the tough fabric of her shelter was almost reassuring for Beth. Almost like a memory of her own childhood, when, as her family had tracked the migration of the builders and their mobile lake her mother had called the *jilla*, they had stayed in structures that were seldom much more permanent than this.

But no matter how familiar this environment felt to her, Beth was painfully aware that she was *alone* here, save for an artificial being that seemed to be becoming increasingly remote – even if he was, in some sense, her grandfather. 'And that's even before he drives off over the horizon,' she muttered.

'I'm sorry?' Earthshine sat on an inflated mattress beside her, with a convincing-looking representation of a silver survival blanket over his shoulders.

Over a small fire – the first she'd built here since she'd left for Mercury, all those years ago – she was making soup, of stock she'd brought with her in her pack, and local potatoes briskly peeled and diced and added for bulk. Plus she had boiled a pot of Roman tea. She had flashlights and a storm lantern, but in the unending daylight of Per Ardua enough light leaked through the half-open door flap of the tent for her to see to work.

'Nothing,' she said. 'Just rambling. I keep thinking I haven't slept yet, not since the Hatch.'

'But it's only been a few hours,' Earthshine said gently. 'We've seen a lot, learned a lot. It just seems longer.'

'Maybe. Only half a day, but you're already planning to light out of here, aren't you?'

He shrugged, and sipped a virtual bowl of tea. 'I see no reason to hang around here any longer than it takes the support unit to make itself ready to travel.'

'Where?'

'The only logical destination on a planet like this.'

'The antistellar?'

'Of course.'

'Which means a trek across the dark side,' she said.

'You are free to come with me,' he said evenly. 'There is no rush; we can make preparations. You could even ride on the support unit if you wish. We could rig up some kind of seat.'

'Thanks.'

'Alternatively, you are free to stay here, or go where you wish. I will donate some components from the support unit, if you choose that course. A kit: basic environment sensors, food analysers, a medical package to supplement the first aid available from your suit.' He passed his fingers through the fabric of her sleeve, wincing as he did so. 'Remember, I won't need it.'

'I lived off the land here once, with my family, and I can do it again.' She did a double take. '*Our* family.'

He didn't respond to that.

'Why are you going to the antistellar?'

'In search of answers.'

'Answers to what? What's wrong with being right here?'

He clenched a fist. 'This is *all* wrong. It wasn't supposed to be this way. I smashed Mars to make them listen to me – to us, to humanity.'

'You mean the deep bugs in the rocks.'

'The Dreamers, yes. As I call them. Our puppet masters, or so I'm coming to believe. They have been disturbing our worlds, trashing our histories, wrecking our painstakingly assembled civilisations with impunity. Well, no more! I made them listen. I made them respond.'

'Their answer was the Hatch on Mars.'

'Yes. A Hatch which brought us *here*. But this isn't good enough. Not a good enough *answer*.'

'I don't understand—'

'This is Proxima! Oh, I can't deny it, Beth, it must be, a Proxima somehow old and withered, but... Proxima, the nearest star. But I wanted to be taken to Ultima, the furthest star of all our legends – or the equivalent for the Dreamers. The place where the answers are – the place where I'll learn at last why it is they do what they do. And,' he said darkly, 'maybe I will stop them. Maybe I can still be Heimdall to their subterranean Loki... Yes, I forced an answer out of them. A response, at least. But it's not enough. So I will put them to the question again.'

'How?'

'I don't know yet. When I get to the antistellar I'll figure it out.'

She thought that over. 'Somehow I feel you're wrong. I don't know how or why... They brought you here. Maybe the answer you seek is right here, and you just aren't seeing it.'

'That's possible. But even if so it can't do any harm to go and search some more, can it?'

'A lot of people thought you should be stopped from pursuing your ambitions. That was always true, all the way back to your early days on Earth, wasn't it? Even before you became—'

'What I am now? When I was merely Robert Braemann, bona fide human being, and busy breaking the law to save the world? Or at least that's the "I", of the nine of me, who interests you. And then I became Earthshine, a Core AI, one of three rogue minds, once again breaking humanity's laws to save it. And again they never forgave us. Now here I am alone, trying to save—'

'The world? Which world?'

'All the worlds, maybe. I don't know.' He was silent a while; the rain continued to hiss on broad Arduan leaves. 'Do you think you will come with me? I ask for purely practical reasons. The timescale, the preparations—'

'I haven't decided yet,' she said curtly. 'We only just got

here ... I *like* it here, even if it isn't what I quite remember. I like the day side anyhow. I don't know if I want to go into endless night, so cold I'll need to wear a spacesuit.'

'But,' he said gently, 'you also aren't sure if you want to be alone.'

'Do you *want* me to come? After all it was you who brought me through the Hatch with you.'

'I didn't force you.'

'Do you really think of us as family, Earthshine? I know my father's father is only one of you, one of the nine minds ... Do you think of him as your son?'

'Of course I do. I always did the best I could for him – myself and his mother.'

'Which included shoving him into a cryo freezer for a century, and ultimately killing him?'

He sighed. 'We were working at the margins of the law. We were trying to save him. We thought that perhaps in a century he at least would be able to live his life out of our shadow. We underestimated the vindictiveness of mankind. Their retrospective tribunals. Their visiting of punishments on the children of the perpetrators. They never forgave us.'

'Did you love him? Do you love us now?'

He smiled. 'A part of me does. That's the best answer I can give you. I'm sorry. Humans aren't meant to be like this, you see. Like *me*. Identity, consciousness, isn't meant to be something you can pour from one container to another, and meld with others as if mixing a cocktail. So you'll find my reactions are always going to be – off. But at least I'm here, with you, today. Which is all, in the end, you can ask of anyone.'

She smiled back. 'That's true. I feel an atavistic urge to hug you, Grandad.'

'I urge you not to try. I think the rain is stopping. I will go and check on the progress of my support unit.'

'And I,' she said, stretching and yawning, 'think I'll take a nap. Don't wake me when you come in.'

'I'll try not to.'

*

In the warm, moist air of the Arduan substellar, she slept as well as she had for years. And for an unknown time too, under the unmoving face of Proxima. Whatever the unanswered questions, whatever the reservations she might have, she was home, she could feel it. Alone or not.

Even if she missed her daughter Mardina with a savage ache, as if a steel cable were attached to her belly, dragging her back to Mars.

When she glanced out of the shelter, she saw Earthshine standing over his support unit as it slowly reassembled itself for the journey.

CHAPTER 44

The Romans were brought to a wide, flat clearing cut into the rainforest.

Here they were to farm, they were told.

They would grow maize, wheat, rice, coca, and the ubiquitous potato, which the Incas called *papas*. There were no animals to raise, no sheep, goats, cattle – no llamas – though, they were told, some animals ran wild in the *hacha hacha*, the jungle. But they were expected to raise some more exotic and unfamiliar crops, gaudy flowers, strange fungi and lichen, that the ColU speculated were the source of mind-altering potions – *psychoactive drugs*, he told Mardina, evidently a feature of Inca culture in any timeline.

So the work began.

The land had to be kept open by regular burnings at the perimeter of the clearing. And the labour of keeping the land drained would always be considerable. It was poor, the soil thin, but not so bad that it was unworkable. The ColU was able to advise. The Romans fertilised their patch, mostly with ash from the burned rainforest perimeter, or the dung and bones of the animals that ran wild in the rainforest, notably rodents that could be the size of a sheep. The work was hard but bearable.

There were people here already, of course.

They had joined an *ayllu*, a kind of clan, a loosely bound group of families, some of whom had some kind of relationship with each other, some of whom didn't. The people were friendly enough, however, Mardina found. It seemed to be the

Inca way to move people around their box of an empire, from place to place, from near to far – sometimes across the toroid of an ocean from one 'continent' to the other, from the *puna* and river deltas of the west, the *cuntisuyu*, to the rainforest-choked eastern half of the habitat, the *antisuyu*. All this was no doubt intended to ensure continued control, of the kind that *quipucamayoc* Inguill had talked about on the Romans' first arrival here. If you didn't stay long in a place, you couldn't set down roots, couldn't establish loyalties – your only long-term relationship was with the Sapa Inca, the Only Emperor, and his officials, not with the strangers around you.

But a consequence of the system was that people were used to strangers moving in – strangers they called *mitmaqcuna*, colonists. So while everybody had their property, and a plot of land to work, and, more important, they all had some kind of status in their society, they weren't so territorial that they excluded the Romans and their companions.

The Romans, however, did not own this land, that was made clear from the start – and nor did anybody of the *ayllu*, and none of them ever would. The Sapa Inca owned everything. The people were not slaves – as was proven by the fact that there were actual slaves, called *yanakuna*, to be seen throughout this place. The Romans were to be *mitimacs*, which meant something like 'taxpayers'. They were entitled to keep the produce they raised, save for a proportion that they had to hand over to be stored in the big *tambos*, the state-owned storehouses that studded the countryside. This was part of the *mit'a*, the tax obligations of every citizen.

Also as part of their *mit'a* they were expected to contribute a proportion of their labour directly to the services of the state. This might mean creating or maintaining military equipment such as quilted armour, boots, blankets – never any weapons – or field rations of dried potatoes or maize, all to be stored in specialised warehouses called *colcas*, for the use of the army. It might mean labouring to support the big *pukaras*, fortresses of stone with spiral terraces winding around their inner cores of buildings: a design that reminded Mardina of huge snails squatting in the countryside. It might mean working on projects for the common good such as the regular forest clearance, or scraping clear the dust and algae that gathered with time on the habitat's huge Inti windows, or maintaining the *capac nans*, the long, straight roads and rail tracks that threaded through the forest, and the *chucllas*, the waystations that studded their length.

And the *mit'a* obligation might even mean serving in the military, although it was clear that the beefy, tough-looking, well-disciplined Romans weren't trusted enough for that, not yet.

All of this was organised on a global scale by a hierarchy of officials, beginning with the *ayllu*'s local leader, the *curaca* – an imposing, reasonable-looking man called Pascac, who was the leader of ten families, and reminded Mardina a little of Quintus Fabius – and up through the deputy prefect Ruminavi, the *tocrico apu*, who in turn reported to one of two *apus*, the prefects each of whom ran one of the two great 'continents' of the habitat, west or east. And then the command chain reached up to the court of the Sapa Inca in the two hub Cuzcos, including the *quipucamayocs* like Inguill, and the *colcacamayocs*, keepers of records and stores respectively.

The legionaries grumbled at the lack of freedom. And about the lack of money, the lack of shops and stores where you could *buy* things, from beer and wine to fine clothes and other luxuries, and not least prostitutes. But then, this wasn't an economy that ran on money. And there was some tension in the very beginning, when the local *curaca* decreed that the Romans could not use permanently any of the small wooden houses that made up the core of the small township inhabited by the people of the *ayllu*, but must construct their own. But legionaries always grumbled, whatever you tried to get them to do.

And Quintus Fabius once more proved he was a more than competent leader. In fact he seemed to relish the challenge of the situation.

On the very first night in the *antisuyu* Quintus had the legionaries construct the rudiments of a marching camp, with a rectangular perimeter wall of dirt and timber with rounded corners, and ditches for drainage and latrines, and the start, at least, of permanent structures inside: a training ground, a *principia* for the centurion, barracks blocks and storehouses. It was a lot smaller than would have been built by a full legion on the march, of course. There were less than fifty men here, a little more than half a full century in the Roman system. Nevertheless, Mardina thought, as a demonstration of Roman competence and adaptability, it clearly impressed the locals. And right from the beginning of their time here the exercise reassured the legionaries that – whatever else might become of them, whatever this strange place *was*, and Mardina suspected some of them were pretty puzzled about that – they were still Romans, still legionaries, and all they had learned over years of training and experience still counted for something.

And Quintus was very careful that the legionaries preserve and respect a *huaca*, a local shrine – little more than a heap of stones – that happened to fall within the domain they were given to set up their camp.

Soon they had their fields laid out and ploughed. It was hard work. The lack of draught animals, and a paucity of machines away from the richest *ayllus*, meant there was a reliance on human muscle. But for all they grumbled Romans were used to hard work.

There seemed to be no seasons here, as far as Mardina could tell from interrogating baffled locals, though she supposed a cycle of shorter and longer days, a 'winter' created by selectively closing some of the light pools, could have easily been designed in. But then much of the Incas' original empire on Terra had been tropical, where seasonal differences were small. This did mean that growing cycles, and the labour of farming, continued around the year; you didn't have to wait for spring.

Yet life wasn't all work. They might have to pay the *mit'a*, but the legionaries soon learned they didn't have to go hungry. If you fancied a supplement to your vegetable-based diet you could always go hunting in the rainforest, where there seemed to be no restrictions on what you took as long as you were reasonably frugal about it. There were big rodents, which the ColU called *guinea pigs*, that provided some satisfying meat, even if they were an easy kill. Smaller versions ran around some of the villages.

The lack of alcohol was one enduring problem. It seemed to Mardina that the local people didn't drink, in favour of taking drugs and potions of various kinds. *Chicha*, the local maize beer, was officially used only in religious ceremonies. After a time Quintus turned a blind eye to the illicit brewing of beer.

As for the drugs, the most common was coca, the production of which was part of the *mit'a* obligation. But you could grow it anywhere, it grew wild in the forest, and *everybody* seemed to chew it, from quite young children up to toothless grandmothers. Some of the legionaries tried it, taking it in bundles of pressed leaves with lime, and a few took to it; they said it made them feel stronger, sharper, more alert, and even immune to pain. *Medicus* Michael officially disapproved, saying that the coca was making your brain lie to you about the state of your body.

With time, the villagers started to invite the Romans to join in feasts to celebrate their various baffling divinities. The adults passed around the coca, smoked or drank various other exotic substances, played their noisy pan pipes, and danced what Mardina, who did not partake, was assured were expressions of expanded inner sensation, but looked like a drunken shambles to her. The children would hang lanterns in the trees, and everybody would sing through the night, and other communities would join in until it seemed as if the whole habitat was echoing to the sound of human voices.

The local people would always look strange to a Roman or Brikanti eye, Mardina supposed. The men wore brilliantly coloured blanket-like tunics, and the women skirts and striped shawls and much treasured silver medallions. But they grew tall and healthy. Sickness was rare here. The *medicus* opined that most diseases had been deliberately excluded when the habitat was built, and it was kept that way by quarantine procedures of the kind the legionaries had had to submit to on arrival. And, if you ignored the forest-bird feathers that habitually adorned the black hair of the men, and the peculiar black felt hats with wide brims that the women sported, the people could be very attractive, with almost a Roman look to their strong features.

On the other hand, Mardina supposed, to these legionaries exiled by a jonbar hinge from their wives and families and all they knew, almost any woman would be attractive.

One by one, the legionaries began to form relationships with the women of the village. The Sapa Inca's own clan was polygamous – although it was said that the true heirs to the empire were always born of the closest family of all, of the Inca marrying a favoured sister – but the villagers, at least here in the wilds of the *antisuyu*, were ferociously monogamous. Quintus said only that he was pleased how few of these new loves were already married, and how few passion-fuelled disputes he was having to resolve.

But he did have to mediate conversations with the legionaries and the local leaders about birth control. Contraceptives were free at the *tambos*, and so were abortions, though Mardina got the sense that the operations could be risky, such was the state of medicine here. Your choice about having children was up to you, but the population size was carefully monitored by the imperial authorities, and if the average birth rate of an *ayllu* went above two children per couple without the appropriate licences, there would be, it seemed, penalties to pay.

Even though many of the younger local men watched Mardina, or spoke to her, or tried to bring her into the narcotics-fuelled dances, she kept herself to herself. Some attention she got wasn't so welcome, such as from the *tocrico apu* Ruminavi. She soon learned from local gossip that he was a married man with kids as old as she was, but he didn't seem able to keep his eyes off her, and Clodia, when she visited.

For now she kept everybody at bay.

'I'm just not ready for it,' she confided once to Clodia, daughter of Titus Valerius, as they patiently weeded their way through a field of maize. Clodia was still just fifteen, but she and Mardina were closest in age in the Roman party, and the only two young women.

Clodia was more wide-eyed about the local boys. 'What about that Quizo?'

'The one who always wears the hummingbird feathers?'

'That's the one. I'd be ready for *him* any day of the week ...'

Mardina playfully ruffled her hair. 'Sure you would, and in a few years you'll eat him alive. But for now – it's different for you, Clodia. At least you've still got your father here.'

'Ha! The big boss of me. Well, you can keep *him* ...'

Mardina said patiently, 'It's just that we've all been through so much. We passed through the jonbar hinge. We lost everything we knew. And even before that, I knew that my own mother was from another world again, from before another jonbar hinge, and how strange is that? Now here we are in this strange place where nobody speaks Brikanti or Latin, and nobody's heard of Jesu or Julius Caesar ...'

'Well, I like it here,' Clodia said defiantly. 'I always liked living in camp when we were at Romulus, and I wanted to train as a legionary. Now there's nobody to tell me I can't.'

Mardina grinned. 'Good for you. For me, it's just that I need to find myself here first, that's all. Before getting lost in Quizo.'

'Very wise,' Clodia said gravely. 'You take your time. But can we talk a bit more about his eyes first?'

Quintus didn't hesitate to remind all the Romans of their true purpose here: to survive, to remember their comrades still aboard the *Malleus Jesu,* and to amass stores to enable them to escape, if they chose – or maybe to knock the Sapa Inca off his throne, so the men dreamed over their beer.

And, though they had had to give up any weapons at the entry hub, Quintus began quietly to have the men make their

317

own: spears of fire-hardened wood, clubs. He negotiated with local artisans, metalworkers, for spear points. Soon there was quiet talk of getting hold of bladed weapons, swords and knives. All this was paid for in kind, usually with a squad of legionaries carrying out some brute-force task – and all beneath the notice, hopefully, of the tax assessors.

But for all the long-term scheming of Quintus Fabius and his senior men, for all the mutterings of the ColU about Earthshine and Hatches and jonbar hinges, the longer Mardina stayed here, and the more she got used to the rhythms of Inca life, the more settled she felt. The more secure. Maybe the sheer fact of getting back a routine, some basic order in her life, after that chaotic period since leaving Terra was good for her.

All the Roman party saw the benefit of the Inca system about fifty days after their arrival in the *antisuyu*. There was a crisis; one of the big Inti windows was scarred by a meteorite strike, and had to be covered over with a tremendous steel lid while repairs were effected. That meant that a kind of night fell over a swathe of countryside in the region of the habitat opposite the damaged window. Crops failed, and rainforest trees quickly started to die back. The state system, however, swung into action, and some of the legionaries, recruited for the effort, described what they saw. From all around the local area the *tambos* were opened, and *mit'a* workers, supervised by the military, rushed to bring relief to the stricken province.

This was where the system of constantly storing excess produce paid off: this was the point of all the organisation, Mardina started to see. In a way it was a distillation of the Roman system in her own history, the bargain an empire made with the nations and populations it subdued: *submit to me, and I will keep you safe.* Under the Incas' almost obsessively tight control, you might have little freedom of movement, freedom of choice. But you never went hungry, thirsty, you never went cold, there was medical care when you needed it. And when disaster struck at one part of the imperial body, the rest rushed to help it recover.

But she also glimpsed what happened when things went

318

wrong. In this empire of occupation and exploitation, the most common 'crime' was an attempt to evade the *mit'a* tax obligations. It was a chill moment when the tax assessors came, and worked through their records, manipulating their *quipus* with one hand. Some, it was said, could work the stringed gadgets with their toes. They saw all and recorded all. And the perpetrators of crime, after arbitrary hearings before the *tocrico apu*, could be taken away from the *ayllu* for punishment, out of sight.

Observing all this, in the camp Quintus Fabius enacted his own regime of discipline and punishment, intending not to let a single one of his legionaries fall foul of the Inca authorities.

Worse yet, however, for many families was the forcible removal of the young. There was a kind of ongoing recruitment drive for off-habitat workers, who would man the asteroid mines or crew kernel-powered freighters. But there was also a demand for recruits for service at the Cuzcos, or at another of the great imperial establishments – and the servants chosen were always the prettiest children, those with the sweetest nature. This service was compulsory, not volunteered like other professions.

This was an empire in which everything, including *you*, was owned by the Sapa Inca. In fundamental ways it was far less free than even the Roman Empire had been, back on Terra. Even so, Mardina could see how the great machinery of state worked to sustain its citizens. She wouldn't hesitate to grab back her own freedom if she ever got the chance. But no doubt there had been worse empires in human history – worse times and places to be alive, even if you weren't the Sapa Inca himself.

And then there was the sheer wonder of living here, in this tremendous building in space.

There was weather. There could be days more brilliant than any summer's day she had known in Brikanti – hotter than Rome, said Quintus Fabius, even before it was a hole in the ground. Or there could be rain, even storms. The *tocrico apu* claimed that these were all under the control of vast engines commanded by the Sapa Inca's advisers, but the locals, salvaging their ruined crops after one sudden hailstorm, were sceptical about that.

On warm clear nights, Mardina liked to sleep outside, if she could, sometimes with Clodia at her side, safe within the walls of a community that was slowly taking on the look of an Inca village embedded in a Roman marching camp. And they would look up at the 'sky'. Of course there were no stars to be seen here. There were very few aircraft, even. The only craft operating above the ground were the government-controlled 'Condors' that passed along the axis region of the habitat, in the vacuum.

But the tremendous metal shell above was an inverted world, hanging above them, crowded with endlessly fascinating detail – even if the seeing through this lowland air was poor compared to how it had been on the high *puna*. The Inti windows glowed like pale linear moons, and Mardina could make out the blackness of forest, the pale silver of rivers and lakes. All this was cut through by the sharp lines of rail tracks and roads, connecting communities that glowed almost starlike against the background.

And sometimes, she and Clodia thought, they could make out shapes framed by those tangled lines. They were like figures traced out of the dense *antisuyu* forest up there by some tremendous scalpel. There was a bird, there was a spider, there was a crouching human. Maybe it was just Mardina's eyes seeking patterns where none existed, the way the ancients had always seen animals and gods among the meaningless scatter of the stars of the night sky. Or maybe it was deliberate, a touch of uncharacteristic artistry in the huge functional architecture of this artificial world.

And if that was true, maybe there were similar etchings on her side of the world, great portraits hundreds of miles in extent, yet meticulously planned. Maybe from the point of view of some witness sleeping in the open on the other side of the habitat, lying there pinned by the spin of the cylinder, she was a speck lost in the eye of a spider, or the claw of a bird. Somehow it was a comforting thought to be so enclosed by humanity. Sometimes

Mardina wondered if she would eventually forget the wildness of the outside, of the stars.

But there was wildness enough inside the habitat, in the dense green of the rainforest jungle that circled the *ayllu* village. The deep *hacha hacha*, where the *antis* lived.

CHAPTER 45

Mardina and Clodia had their first encounter with the *antis* on the day the strange *mit'a* tax assessment party came to call.

Unusually this was led by Ruminavi, *tocrico apu*, the deputy prefect himself. He arrived with the various inspectors and assessors with their *quipu*s, and the tax collectors with their hand-drawn carts for the produce and samples they would take away – and a larger than usual contingent of soldiers in their woollen tunics and plumed helmets of steel-reinforced cane, and their armour of quilted cotton over steel plate, all decorated with scraps of gold and silver. Their only weapons were blades, whips, slings; just as in the space-going ships of the lost Roman Empire, projectile weapons and explosives were excluded from the interior of the habitat.

Mardina and Clodia, coming in from the field, recognised none of these men. Almost all the Incas' soldiers, the *awka kamayuq*, were part-timers raised from the provinces, from *ayllus* like Mardina's own community, with only a very small core standing army of specialists. But it was the practice to deploy soldiers from one province in operations in others, not their own homeland.

And Mardina noticed, as she had before, a kind of edginess in the way the soldiers walked, a sharp glitter in their eyes. The ColU speculated that this was the product of more drugs, of active agents to boost metabolism, muscle strength, even intelligence and cognition.

As this party made its way through the village, even going into some of the houses, the folk of the *ayllu* avoided looking into the eyes of these men, and the Roman legionaries speculated how it would be to fight these Inca soldiers.

Ruminavi, spotting Mardina and Clodia, came hurrying over to the two of them. He was dressed grandly, presumably to impress the taxpayers, in beaded and embroidered clothes and feathered armbands, and his thinning black hair braided. Even his sandals had silver studs. As almost everybody carried, he had a bag of coca at his waist.

Mardina watched him approach warily. 'Do you want something of us, *tocrico apu*?'

'Yes, I do.' He glanced back at the party he was leading. 'This is a special *mit'a* collection. I need you two to go and find some wild coca for me.'

'*Wild* coca ...'

'A particularly potent and valuable strain has been reported in this area.' He waved a hand vaguely at the green of the encroaching forest. 'Go and take a look, the two of you – you'll know it when you see it.'

Mardina and Clodia exchanged a suspicious look. Mardina said, 'With respect, *apu* – why us? We aren't native to this place. The *ayllu* must be full of people who know more about coca than we ever will—'

'Do as I say,' he snapped. 'Look, Mardina – I know you don't trust me.' He gave her a forced smile. 'But, believe me, I mean you no harm. Nor you, Clodia Valeria. I'm just a man, and a weak one at that, and I like to *look* ... But I am here to protect you. You *must* go to the forest, now. And stay there until the *mit'a* party has left your *ayllu*. Now, girls, go!' And he shoved them away, before hurrying back to the soldiers and inspectors.

Clodia glanced around for her father, but Titus Valerius was nowhere to be seen. She looked up at Mardina. She muttered, 'That man is like a worm.'

'He is.'

'But I have the feeling that we should trust him, just this once.'

'So do I. Come on!'

The two of them lifted their Inca-style smocks, and ran in their Roman-style sandals to the edge of the forest where Ruminavi had indicated. There they looked back at the soldiers assiduously searching the *ayllu*'s village, glanced at each other, and then held hands and walked into the *hacha hacha*.

They were plunged into darkness, as if being swallowed.

The slim trunks of the trees towered over them, like pillars in some huge temple, and the canopy of green far above was almost solid. Their ears were filled with the cries of monkeys and macaws, screeches and whistles that echoed as if they were indeed inside some tremendous building. At least the ground was fairly clear, for undergrowth could not prosper in this shade, but in the few slivers of light flowers grew, bright and vibrant, and vines wrapped around the trunks of the trees. And as the girls' eyes adapted to the dark they glimpsed snakes and scorpions and swarming ants.

But they had come only a few paces into the shade of the trees.

When Mardina looked back, she saw a party of soldiers coming their way. Clodia's pale Roman skin seemed to shine in the residual light, easily visible. Mardina whispered, 'There's no coca here. I'm sure Ruminavi meant us to hide from the soldiers. We must go further in.'

'I know. I don't dare.'

'Nor me. But we have to try, I think. And—'

And that was when they saw the *anti* girl.

Mardina's heart hammered, and she clutched Clodia's hand.

She was standing in the shadows, a little way deeper into the forest. Dressed only in strips of woven fabric around her chest and waist, she looked no older than Clodia. She wore a headband over pulled-back hair into which were stuffed brilliantly coloured feathers. From her neck hung a pendant, pieces of tied wood that looked oddly like the Hammer-Cross of Jesu, in Mardina's own timeline. She had a small bow with a quiver of arrows tucked on straps at her back, but her hands were open and empty, Mardina saw, in a gesture of friendship.

It was her face that was terrifying. Her skin was dyed a brilliant blue, with brighter stripes sweeping back from her nose like the whiskers of a jaguar, a monster of local myth. Feathers seemed to sprout from the skin around her nose and mouth.

She looked calm, Mardina thought, calm as a snake about to strike. Mardina herself was anything but calm.

'We should go back,' she muttered to Clodia. 'This isn't our world.'

'Are you sure? Mardina, the *ayllu* isn't our world either. None of it is …' Clodia took a bold step forward.

The *anti* girl smiled, and beckoned with her hands, an unmistakable gesture.

Clodia looked back over her shoulder. 'See? I think she's telling us to come deeper in. I think we should trust her. Oh, come on, Mardina, for curiosity's sake if nothing else.'

So Mardina gave in and took one step after another, in pursuit of Clodia, who followed the *anti* girl.

CHAPTER 46

The Romans had learned that the Incas called these people *antis*, the inhabitants of the forest. Sometimes you saw them, shadowy figures running between the great trunks at the forest's burned edge – a face scowling out of the green, with a sense of the utterly alien. The folk of the *ayllus* ignored them, but were careful not to probe too far into the forest, into their territory, and, probably, *vice versa* applied too. It was as if two entirely different worlds had been jammed into one huge container, Mardina thought.

Yet details of the *antis* were known. They belonged to peoples with names like Manosuyus, Chunchos, Opataris. They traded with the folk of the *ayllus*, providing from the depths of their deadly jungle hardwood, feathers, jaguar skins, turtle oil, and exotic plants. One of the most prized plants, the Romans learned, was a hallucinogen called *ayahuasca*, 'the vine of the gods', which the Incas used to make particularly potent ritual beverages. In return the *antis* took as payment steel axes and knives, even salt gathered from the shore of the distant ocean.

The original *antisuyu* had in fact been the great forest that had once swathed much of the continent of Valhalla Inferior, surrounding the river the Roman conquerors had called the New Nile, and the UN-China Culture had called the Amazon. In the histories of all three cultures, including the Inca, the forest had eventually been mostly lost, to logging and mineral exploration. But the Incas, it seemed, as a kind of gesture to their own deep past, had transported survivors of the forest cultures into a recreated wilderness here in Yupanquisuyu, and

326

allowed them to live out their lives much as they had long before there were such things as empires and cities on the face of the world.

After all, Mardina learned in scraps of conversation, the *antisuyu* was the first barbaric land the Incas had conquered, when they pushed eastward from their stronghold on the mountainous spine to the west of Valhalla Inferior. Then, with the jungle pinned down under a network of roads and *pukaras* – and with the experience of such conquest behind them – they had been ready to strike out further east across the ocean, with ships built using techniques brought to them by the probing Xin, who had made their own ocean crossings from the far west. When they had landed in Europa – the ColU thought somewhere in Iberia – the Incas seemed to have fallen upon a Roman Empire wrecked by plague, famine, civil breakdown, perhaps afflicted by some other calamity yet to be identified. And then an expansion south into Africa had begun, and then further east still into Asia, where the Xin empire lay waiting, and the final battle for the planet had begun ...

Through all this, however, the Incas had always preserved scraps of the forest where the original *antis* had still clung on. And in the end the descendants of those *antis*, no doubt utterly bewildered, had been scooped up and transported to the Incas' new empire in the sky. This wasn't unprecedented; the Incas had similarly taken up samples of many of the peoples that had comprised the land-based empire. It was said that over a hundred and sixty languages had been spoken in the empire, even before its expansion beyond Valhalla Inferior to a global power.

Now, so it was said, the *antis* prospered in the forest as well as they had ever, and – some in the *ayllu* whispered cattily – most of them didn't even know they were in some great human-made artefact in the sky.

The *anti* girl led them in a straight line, more or less, and Mardina tried to keep track of their route. But there were no landmarks – the trees all looked the same to her – and in the jumbled shadows she even had trouble telling which direction was which. If she could only get a glimpse of the sky, of the mirror landscape above, she'd reorient and then just walk out of this place.

Then, without warning, they broke into the light.

The clearing was perhaps a hundred paces across, and evidently created by fire, for on the ground Mardina saw the evidence of burning, blackened fallen trunks and scorched branches and a scatter of ash through which green saplings poked eagerly into the light. The air was humid and very hot. But the sky above, fringed with the green of the forest canopy, revealed a textured upside-down landscape that Mardina never would have believed could be such a reassuring sight.

In the centre of the clearing was a village. Huts built of what looked like long grass stems, or maybe bamboo, were set up in a rough circle around open, trampled ground. A fire burned on a rough hearth of stones, with what looked like a large guinea pig roasting on a crude spit. Villagers sat around, poking at the fire, mending baskets, skinning another animal, talking. A handful of children dozed in the afternoon heat.

As the *anti* girl brought the two strangers to the edge of the village, some of the people looked around, scowled, and spoke sharply to their guide. But she replied just as sharply – and she made an alarming cutthroat gesture with one finger. Grudgingly, the adults nodded and turned away. A couple of children, naked and wide-eyed, would have come wandering out to inspect the newcomers, but they were called back sharply by the adults.

The girl turned to Mardina and Clodia, held up her hands to stop them coming any further, and mimed that they should sit in the dirt. Then she ran into the village and returned with a couple of wooden mugs, and a handful of coca leaves that she set before them, before nodding and hurrying off.

The mugs contained what tasted like diluted beer. Mardina and Clodia drank deeply and gratefully. They both ignored the coca leaves.

328

Clodia groaned, 'I wish they'd spare some of that roast. The smell is killing me.'

'Hopefully we'll be out of here before we die of hunger, Clodia.'

'Maybe if I make a prayer to Jesu loudly enough they'll offer me His charity.'

'What do you mean?'

Clodia looked at her. 'Didn't you see that ornament around our guide's neck?'

'Well, it looked like a cross, but—'

'And look over there.' Clodia pointed beyond the village, to the clearing's far side, where a crude wooden cross stood, a larger version of the girl's pendant. A kind of dummy figure made of rolled-up bales of straw hung from the cross, fixed by outspread arms, legs strapped together.

'Jesu,' Clodia said triumphantly.

'You're right,' Mardina breathed, astonished. The cross was a double symbol of Jesu's career, shared by Romans and Brikanti alike: of the crucifix on which the Romans had shamefully put Him to death, and of the Hammer, the carpenter's weapon with which the Saviour had led a rebellion against the forces that had oppressed His people. 'A figure of Jesu, here in the forest. So we live in a world now where the technological city-dwelling empire builders are pagans, and the savages in the jungle follow Christ—'

The girl who'd brought them here came running up again now, holding her fingers to her lips to hush them. Mardina saw that the villagers were growing agitated too.

Beckoning, the girl summoned the visitors to their feet. She led them quickly back into the jungle, a good way away from the place they had come in. Once back in the forest the girl moved silent as a shadow, and Mardina and Clodia followed as best they could. Mardina judged they were heading back to the edge of the forest, and the *ayllu*.

And as they walked, Mardina glimpsed soldiers passing through the shadows of the trees. Led by the *tocrico apu*, they were heading for the *anti* village. No wonder the villagers were growing nervous. If Ruminavi was aware of the presence of the girls, he showed no sign of it.

The *anti* girl left them at the edge of the forest, and hurried away into the shadows before either of them could try to thank her, or say goodbye.

Ruminavi did not return to the *ayllu* that day, and Mardina had no way to question him about the whole strange incident, the reason they had needed to be hidden.

Not until the next time he returned.

CHAPTER 47

In the Roman camp time was recorded, by order of Quintus Fabius. From the beginning the Romans had counted the cycle of the habitat's artificial days and nights, measuring the time they spent in this place.

So Mardina knew it was a month before Ruminavi came again to the village, this time alone, in his deputy-prefect finery but without his squad of soldiers. And he sought out Mardina, who was walking with Clodia with firewood from the edge of the forest.

'You two,' he snapped. 'Come with me. Now.' He headed out of the village, away from the line of the road, towards the largest of the local *tambos*. When they didn't follow him immediately, he glanced back over his shoulder. 'Look, you trusted me last time, and you were saved, weren't you?'

Mardina called, 'Saved from what?'

'Come *on*, hurry ...'

As they had before, they hesitated for a heartbeat. Then they dumped their armfuls of firewood and ran after him.

They caught him up by the low fence that surrounded the *tambo*. The imperial storehouse was a sprawling structure that was the centre of a complex of buildings, including an inn for travellers, a grander hotel for visiting imperial officials, and a small rail station. At the gate in a wall of moon rock Ruminavi produced documentation to prove his identity, vouched for the girls, and led them into the complex to the storehouse itself.

Before the storehouse, in a shaded corner out of sight of the main complex, stood a kind of stone plinth, only a hand's

331

breadth high, its sides engraved with the faces of some fierce god. There were many such enigmatic structures dotted about this god-soaked artificial world, and Mardina would not have given this one much thought. But the prefect, she saw, was working a kind of key into a lock in the plinth's surface, that he'd brushed clear of dust.

Mardina repeated, 'You saved us from what, *apu*?'

He grinned. 'Well, when I've saved your life *again* I'll explain it all. The last sweep wasn't satisfactory, you see, in terms of tributes for the particular *mit'a* we had been assigned to collect. So the Inca's courtiers sent out the *awka kamayuq* parties again. And *that*'s what I'm saving you from …' At last the key turned. 'Ha! Done it.' He got to his feet, breathless, and grasped a handle set into the surface of the plinth. 'Help me, you two. Look, here are more handles, there and there.'

Clodia asked, 'Help you with what? What is this thing?'

'A door in the world …'

As the three of them heaved, the plinth toppled back – to reveal a steel-walled tunnel leading down into the ground, set with scuffed rungs. There was a smell of oil, the sharp tang of electricity.

'The underbelly of the world,' Ruminavi said admiringly, and he rapped a rung with one knuckle. 'Which we call the *xibalba*, the underworld. Two centuries old, and still as sound as when it was built. And there's a lot of it, miles thick in some places. Down you go. I need to be last in, so I can lock us tight once more.'

Again Clodia and Mardina hesitated. Again they gave in, and followed his lead.

Mardina went first. 'Just understand this, *apu*. I trust you only marginally more than I distrust you.'

'Understood.'

'And if any harm were to come to Clodia because of all this, her father will pull you apart like a spider in a condor's beak.'

'I don't doubt it – down you go, Clodia, hurry, they are close! – but it is harm to Clodia especially that I am trying to avert.

Are you at the bottom? The light dazzles up here ... Good. I'm on my way.'

He clambered briskly down the rungs, and pulled the lid closed. As the heavy plinth fell back in place, the lid slammed shut with an ominous clang. To seal it, Mardina saw that he turned a wheel rather than use his key – good, they had a way out of here, whatever Ruminavi did.

At the bottom of the shaft, Mardina found herself standing in a corridor dimly lit by fluorescent tubes, many of which had failed, creating islands of darkness. There were piles of litter here and there, heaps of tools, a few discarded bits of clothing. The walls themselves were scuffed, dented and scarred, scratched with graffiti. It was a dismal prospect.

And the corridor seemed to run to infinity in either direction. Mardina felt Clodia's hand slip into hers.

Ruminavi heaved a sigh. 'Well, we're safe now. Come on, there's a rest station just down here.' He led the way, his booted feet clattering on the bare metal floor, his voice echoing. 'The troops and the assessors think I've gone to spy out the forest. I know how long they plan to be at this *ayllu*; I'll bring you back out when they are safely gone.'

They had to hurry to keep up with the *apu*. Mardina said, 'Seems a good way to this rest station of yours.'

He snorted. 'You're not wrong. But you've no idea how long this corridor runs.' He pointed. 'All the way back to the Hurin Cuzco hub that way; all the way to the ocean *that* way. This is one of the main subsurface arteries – aside from the big vehicle access ways, that is. There are even some ways that pass under the ocean to the *cuntisuyu*. Here we are ...'

The rest station was basic, a few scuffed benches, cupboards empty of any trace of food save a few crumbs, a spigot that dispensed warm water, a *quipu* hanging from a nail – maybe it was a work schedule. A single light overhead made everything seem washed out, dead; Ruminavi seemed even more wormlike than usual. But if this was some kind of trap, she and Clodia had walked right into it, Mardina reminded herself.

333

Mardina and Clodia sat uncomfortably, nervously, side by side. Mardina asked, 'What is this place, *apu*?'

'Can't you guess? Maintenance – that's what all this is for. The hull of the Yupanquisuyu is riddled with tunnels and access ports, and the tremendous equipment needed to keep the world working.'

Clodia stared. 'What kind of equipment?'

'Machines that do all the things a planet will do for you for free. Consider rainfall on the hub mountains. Every drop that falls dislodges a speck of rock. In time the mountains are worn away, and all their substance washes into the sea. On the world you call *Terra*, all that eroded silt is compressed and heated and passed in great currents of liquid rock beneath the surface, until it is thrust back up, as lava from a volcano, as a stupendous new mountain of granite. And so on, all entirely natural, the very mountains rebuilt. Here, the rock would just wear away, and the ocean would clog up, huge deltas spreading out from the *cuntisuyu* and *antisuyu* rivers until they met in the middle – if we let it happen. And so we have machines to gather the eroded waste, and ducts to pipe it back to the mountaintops, and sculpting machines to spray out new rock layers ... That kind of thing.' He smiled. 'The architect of this world allowed himself to be called Viracocha, who is our creator god. But he was not Viracocha – or rather, the man alone was not the god, but we *all* are, all the generations since who have laboured to keep the world working.'

Mardina tried to imagine it. 'So the whole of the hull of this great ship is embedded with vast machines to maintain the world.'

'That's the idea.'

'And where there are machines to maintain the world, there must be people to maintain the machines.'

'Hence the hatches – there are access ways near most of the larger *tambos*. Maintaining the infrastructure machinery is a *mit'a* obligation, though we do use *yanakunas* for the more dangerous and unpleasant work. Cleaning out the great ocean-floor silt

334

ducts, for instance – that's a great eater of humanity. Or the *antis*. They aren't much use for anything else in terms of the *mit'a*, save the *capacocha* of course.'

Mardina didn't know what he meant by that: *capacocha*.

He smiled at them. 'I'll tell you a secret. We're planning to use your own people in the under-machinery, eventually. Well, you were miners of ice moons, or you say you were; you are used to working with complex machinery in tight spaces. And you look strong, able to endure. We haven't done this yet because we still don't quite trust you. We don't want rats in the foundations of the palace, so to speak.'

Clodia said, 'The *antis*. Who you say are no use for anything—'

'I suppose that's unfair. They harvest certain plants and animals for us that grow wild in their forest. They are fine archers, and that can be useful. And in their way, I'm told, they help maintain the health of their forest. All that burning and cutting they do is itself part of a greater cycle.'

'They worship Jesu,' Clodia said. 'As we do.'

His smile returned. 'Ah, yes! You noticed that, did you? The slave god on His cross. They picked it up from you Romans, of course: those of your ancestors who once crossed the ocean to come to our country, to the *antisuyu* jungle. The Romans were successful for a while; they built their coastal cities and explored the river valleys. But then they, or at least your government and its legions, withdrew from our lands, leaving only relics, survivors. When our own expansion into the *antisuyu* came some centuries later, we learned a great deal about the lands across the sea from the babbling of the degenerate descendants of the colonists, before we took them as *yanakunas* or otherwise absorbed them. But the *antis* had encountered those wretches first, in their forest – and with the *antis* they did leave a more lasting legacy, which is the worship of your slave god. Perhaps it is a consolation for them now, as they endure their miserable lives in the jungle.'

Mardina glanced at Clodia. 'Or perhaps it motivates them to

335

help others. Help on which you relied the first time you saved us from the *mit'a* party, *apu*.'

'Well, perhaps.'

'But you still haven't told us what it is you so bravely saved us from.'

'Well, more specifically it is Clodia. You are the exact right age, and your pale colour, and your beauty, child, make you a perfect tribute offering.'

Clodia looked confused and scared. 'An offering for what?'

'The *capacocha* is part of the *mit'a* tribute, to the Sapa Inca. A special tribute – a gift of children. And if your child is chosen, you must give up her or him gladly, and sing songs of thanks and celebration when the end comes.'

'I don't understand. What would the Sapa Inca want with me?'

'You would be treated very well – like an Inca, or his heir, yourself. You would see Hanan Cuzco! You would eat the finest food, drink the finest beers—'

Mardina saw it. '*She would be killed*,' she said. 'That's the *capacocha*, isn't it? The sacrifice of children.'

He spread his hands. 'It is the ancient way. You would be preserved ... Your beauty would never be lost, or forgotten.'

'And this is what you saved me from.' Clodia sounded more bewildered than scared. 'Why?'

Now Mardina scowled. 'If you're expecting some kind of payment in return for this, *apu*—'

He seemed hurt by the suggestion. 'Oh, it's nothing like that.' He looked at Clodia sadly. 'I have a variety of motives. One is simple pity. You are so young, and so new to this world. It seems wrong to snatch you out of it so suddenly! And then there is Inguill.'

'The *quipucamayoc*?' Mardina asked. 'What does she have to do with it?'

'She doesn't want you Romans ... *disturbed*. Not yet. She doesn't want you rising up in rebellion, for instance, because we took your prettiest child.'

'Why not?'

'Well, she hasn't told me. And probably for reasons you would not yet understand. But I don't believe she's finished with you yet.' He fished a watch out of his pocket, a crude affair of knotted string and steel springs. 'Still not safe for you up there. Would you like some more water?'

CHAPTER 48

It took some weeks, carefully counted out by Beth in the unchanging light of Proxima, for Earthshine to make himself ready for the journey to the antistellar.

Beth packed up too, in the end. She decided she would accompany him for at least some of the route he had picked out for himself – a route based, he said, on maps of the Per Ardua she had known, and which he hoped would still have some usefulness here, wherever *here* actually was.

But she always intended to come back, alone if need be, back to the substellar, and the starshine. She'd be able to retrace her steps, she was sure of that. And her own gear, the shelter and other survival gear, even her Mars pressure suit, were light enough for her to carry, unaided by the support unit. After all, the substellar was surely as comfortable a location to live as she'd find anywhere on the planet. And if anybody else showed up on this world – well, they'd probably make their way to the substellar as the most obvious geographical meeting point, even if they didn't just come through the substellar Hatch in the first place.

Earthshine did have his support unit complete a survey of the substellar site before they left, purely for completeness, Beth thought. The unit sampled the soil for traces of metals or other exotic materials, and ran sonar and geophysical surveys of the area in search of deeper traces of habitation.

And, after an unpromising start, it found something. Though the surface layers were bare of artefacts or structure, there was scarring in the bedrock, traces of deep foundations, large underground chambers cut into the rock and long since collapsed. All this was buried under more recent layers of gravel and soil.

Earthshine showed her the results on a slate. 'Look at the design,' he said. 'The architecture, what you can make out of it. We, from the UN-China continuity, built in circles, rectangles ...'

The buried remains were more like overlapping ellipses, Beth thought, connected by curving threads of long-imploded corridors.

'Once there must have been a considerable community here. Of course they would come here to the substellar; *everybody* comes here. It's all gone from above ground, any toxins or radioactive debris or the like long washed away, the remnant building stone shattered to dust by the weather. But it would take an ice age to scrub away these relics in the bedrock. And Per Ardua doesn't have ice ages, not the way Earth does, with glaciers and ice caps grinding their way across the landscape.'

'These traces could be very ancient, then.'

'Unimaginably,' Earthshine said heavily.

'Then they can't be human.'

'Why not? Humans have been here, surely, whatever the distortion of history. You pointed out that somebody must have brought the potatoes.'

'Yes, but people first got to Per Ardua only a few years before I was born.'

'That was in the old continuity, in the UN-China history.' He glanced up at Proxima. 'And you're assuming we travelled sideways in time, so to speak, as well as across space.'

Sideways in time? She asked him what he meant by that, but he wouldn't elaborate.

After that, Earthshine turned his back on the substellar. It was clear he wasn't interested in human endeavour here, however enigmatic or ancient. All he cared about was his ongoing dialogue, or undeclared war, with the beings he called the Dreamers.

And to pursue that, he had to get to the antistellar. That was his obsession, and nothing was to be allowed to distract him.

When they departed at last, Beth left behind a note, pinned under a rock on top of the Hatch emplacement. Just her name, the date they'd arrived here in various forms of calendar, and an indication of where they'd gone. You never knew what, or who, might turn up.

And so they marched, heading roughly south-west. Earthshine said they were mirroring a farside journey made by her own father with Stef Kalinski long ago, before they had disappeared into a Hatch *they* had found at the antistellar.

Earthshine walked tirelessly, of course, and as he had offered they had rigged up a seat for Beth to ride on the support unit. But she mostly refused to use it. She wanted the exercise; she wanted to toughen herself up. If she was in for a solitary life on Per Ardua it would pay to be in good condition. And also she didn't want to get carried too far and too fast; she wanted to stay inside a reasonable walk-back limit as long as she could. So she walked, though Earthshine displayed a very authentic-seeming impatience to make faster progress.

At first they followed the valley of a river, flowing radially away from that central point. Per Ardua's basic climate cycle was that water that had evaporated from across the hemisphere was drawn into the substellar low, rained out there, and then returned to the wider landscapes via rivers like this one. An additional cycle worked at the terminator, the band of shadow that separated the day side from the night; more rain fell from the cooling air there, to spill back towards the warmth of the starlit side.

And as they moved out from the substellar point, following the river, the landscape gradually changed. The substellar itself was at the summit of a tremendous blister of raised land, a frozen rocky tide lifted by Proxima, directly above. Per Ardua was in fact egg-shaped, if only subtly, as the tide raised a similar bulge at the antistellar point on the far side. So they descended

340

from this upland to a broader plain, broken by eroded hills and cut through by more river valleys following radii out from the substellar centre.

The nature of the vegetation changed too. The relatively lush but open forest of the substellar gave way to a more static land-scape, much of it covered by tremendous leaves that blanketed the ground: a miserly gathering of all the light that poured down from a star that was still almost overhead. Beth realised that the more turbulent weather at the substellar itself must drive some change – storms would topple trees and clear the ground – and this passive light-guzzling strategy wouldn't work there. And Beth remembered too that on *her* Per Ardua some ground-cover 'plants' like these had in fact been 'kites', flying beings, in a sedentary phase. But not here, not now; she saw no sign that these were anything other than vegetables, clinging to the ground as stationary and stately as stromatolites.

Indeed, as she walked, she saw no sign of the kind of 'animal' life that had once been common here – not that the distinction between animals and plant life here had been quite the same as on Earth – no kites, no builders, no fish-analogues in the rivers. Nothing but plants and stromatolites and simpler organisms like lichen, competing for the light. The silence of the world was profound, broken only by the wind, the occasional hiss of rain, and their own voices.

And yet they saw more traces of humanity, or at least of the world humans came from. More splashes of the brilliant green of Earth's version of photosynthesis, standing out against the darker hues of Arduan life. These were mostly what looked like much-evolved versions of food plants, potatoes, yams, beets, soya beans, even peas and grape vines, and what looked like laver, a descendant of a genetically engineered seaweed, choking water courses. Earthshine speculated that, untended, these survivors had reverted to something like their original wild forms – the tubers of the potatoes, for instance, were much reduced from the bloated varieties favoured by humans. Beth carefully selected samples to enhance her stores.

341

Survivors: that was what they were, terrestrial stock clinging on amid the native life of this world. And yet Beth thought she saw a kind of silent cooperation going on here. In the flood plain of one river, terrestrial potatoes covered ground that looked too damp for most Arduan life, but Arduan stems sprouted in ground consolidated by the potatoes' roots. In an isolated forest copse she found terrestrial vines growing up the trunk-stems of Arduan trees. And so on. Even if there had been animals, the herbivores from each domain of life couldn't have digested samples from the other; the biochemistry, coming from a common stock, was similar but not identical. But perhaps, she thought, the dissimilar forms of life were evolving deeper ways to cooperate. Just as she and her virtual grandfather were two more dissimilar life forms finding ways to get along.

That came to an end a couple of weeks into the walk, with two hundred kilometres covered. It was when she saw her own shadow starting to stretch before her on the ground, meaning that Proxima was no longer overhead but was beginning to set, that she realised she'd come far enough.

The parting, once she'd separated out her gear, was awkward. Almost jokey.

'At least you'll know where to find me,' said Earthshine.

'And you me.' She forced a smile. 'Even if we couldn't be further apart on this planet. Literally.'

'That's true,' he said gravely. 'Especially taking into account the tidal bulges. When I get the chance I intend to establish some kind of communication system. Small satellites perhaps. You have comms gear—'

'In the pack you've given me, the slates. I know.'

They stood in stiff silence.

'Goodbye, then,' Earthshine said.

'Goodbye.'

He made a show of climbing aboard his carriage, his support unit on its recently fabricated wheels, and off he went, at last accelerating up to the speeds he'd wanted to make in the first place. It somehow comforted her to know that he was continuing to support his human virtual form.

Then she turned away, and began the long walk back, alone.

CHAPTER 49

Eight months after the Romans had arrived at Yupanquisuyu, Inguill came to their *ayllu*. She was accompanied by officials, and a healthy squad of troops. She arrived in a cart drawn by two muscular-looking alpacas, causing a stir in the village. Such animals, it seemed, were rare and reserved for the elite.

Such a personage as the *quipucamayoc*, record keeper of the empire, did not travel lightly, it seemed, and not without heavy protection. Mardina was learning that the *antisuyu* was thought of as bandit country, from which the Sapa Inca and his family and court were protected by layers of security: the rainforest, and then an ocean, and then the open stretches of the *altiplano*, and *then* a climb of hundreds of miles through vacuum before you came upon the fortifications of Hanan Cuzco itself... And yet here Inguill was, in the mouth of the jaguar.

The visit was a big event for the *ayllu*. Although Inguill and her followers had arrived entirely unannounced, the *ayllu* was expected to feed and house them. Tents and lean-tos were hurriedly erected – even the *curaca*, Pascac, the local leader, had to give up his house. Meanwhile the fastest young runners and *yanakuna* slaves were sent dashing to nearby communities to call in favours, and they returned with food, stashes of coca and other potions, blankets and bedding and other luxuries.

Inguill, however, seemed interested in none of this. She set up a kind of court in Pascac's house, and spent one night resting to recover from her journey, and consulting with Ruminavi the *tocrico apu* among other advisers. Then, through Pascac, she peremptorily summoned the senior Romans: Quintus Fabius as the obvious leader, and whoever he chose to bring with him – but, she specified, that had to include Chu Yuen the slave boy, with his mysterious pack.

Before the meeting Quintus Fabius gathered his people outside Pascac's house. Mardina noticed that while Quintus and his soldiers had become accustomed to wearing the readily available *ayllu* garb, today he and Titus Valerius had defiantly changed back into the remains of their military costume, though of course without weapons, armour or legion insignia. Mardina supposed this was some statement of cultural defiance. Mardina herself was happy to stay in the local clothes, including her round felt hat, which she'd decided was quite fetching.

Quintus spoke quietly, in rough camp Latin. 'Do not translate, please, Collius. Let us not be overheard for once.' He gestured at the group. 'So here we are. I suspect most of you would prefer not to be brought before this rather sinister woman.'

'Sinister and with power over us all,' grumbled Titus Valerius.

'Yes, Titus. But we are an anomaly here in Yupanquisuyu – an anomaly in this version of history...'

'True,' murmured the ColU from the usual pack mounted on a nervous-looking Chu Yuen's back. 'And from the very beginning it has been this woman Inguill, of all the Inca locals, who has seemed to have perceived that most clearly.'

'Well, she is the empire's chief record keeper,' said Michael the *medicus*. 'If anybody knows the history, it's going to be her.'

'Correct,' Quintus said. 'And since, as far as I know—' and as he said this he glared at Titus '—none of us have misbehaved terribly – none of us have done anything to bring ourselves to the undue attention of the authorities here, *as far as I know...*'

'You can rest assured about that, sir,' Titus rumbled.

'Presumably Inguill has come here to address loftier questions. Well, I suppose I was going to have to face this at some point, but at least I don't have to be alone. So I am bringing you into

345

the arena with me, my friends. You, Titus, the heart of the century – and its belly. You, Michael, as the nearest to a philosopher we have. You, of course, Collius, as she has requested Chu Yuen—'

The ColU said, 'Even if she doesn't know of my existence, yet, or my true nature.'

'And me?' Mardina asked, baffled. 'Why am I here?'

Quintus smiled at her, reassuring. 'You are here because you represent our past, Mardina. Half your blood, after all, comes from beyond *two* jonbar hinges. And with your youth you also represent our future – and whatever future we have depends, at least for now, on the goodwill of the Sapa Inca. I want you at my side so that Inguill sees that.' Then he surprised Mardina by clasping Chu Yuen on the shoulder. 'And you, Xin. When I assigned you as the bearer of Collius it was a random choice – I was barely aware of your existence, I did not know your name, or care. Yet you have come through so much with us, and you have borne yourself and your strange burden well. I am glad you are with us today.'

Even now, Mardina saw with a twinge of sadness, the boy could not raise his eyes to meet Quintus's. But he said, 'Thank you, Centurion.'

Titus Valerius grunted, and he adjusted his cloak. 'Well said, sir, as always. But aren't you exaggerating a bit? You call this an arena. We aren't gladiators going into combat.'

'Oh, Titus, you would never have made an officer. Let me face bare-handed a dozen highly trained and fully armed gladiators, each with a personal grudge against me, than a lawyer with a single pointed question. Come now, let's get this done.'

In Pascac's house Inguill sat comfortably upright on a couch, with Ruminavi on a mat on the ground on her left-hand side, and Pascac himself standing on the other, looking grave. Inguill had a kind of leather trunk open on the floor before her. Two soldiers, heavily armed, stood at ease behind her.

Ruminavi caught Mardina's eye, and gave her a kind of wink. Uncomfortable, she looked away.

Quintus sat on a couch facing Inguill, with his own advisers arrayed behind him, sitting on the floor. Michael suppressed a grumble as he made his way down to the floor; this was a custom of the Incas, that only your leader was allowed to be at eye level with the representative of the Sapa Inca.

With everyone in place, they sat and faced each other in silence – like pieces on a game board, Mardina thought, and maybe that wasn't an inappropriate analogy.

Dressed soberly, her eyes sharp, Inguill looked strong, in control. At last she spoke. 'Well. You are wondering why I have come here, why I wish to speak to you today.'

Pascac, standing beside her, bowed from the waist. 'The *quipu-camayoc* to the Sapa Inca is always welcome—'

'Oh, hush, man. This isn't a time for flattery, for protocol. It's a time for truth.' She gazed at Quintus, at Titus, at Chu Yuen with his pack on the mat-strewn floor before him. 'You'll remember my first reaction to you people when you came wandering in, riding craft, your *yachts*, that were obviously unsuitable for the journey you described. Your unlikely story of a lost colony of Romaoi miners on an ice moon!

'I am a record keeper. A historian. A number counter. My job for the Sapa Inca is to reflect the order of his vast empire, and to play my part in enforcing that order. And I remember I spoke to you of a deeper underpinning for our need for order. Unlike you Romaoi, or what is known of your history anyhow, *our* gods are not nurturing spirits who bring the rains in the spring and the sun in the summer. They are not upstart slaves like your Jesu, not gods of generosity and forgiveness. Our gods are gods of destruction and calamity – gods who lived at the summits of fire mountains, in the continent you call Valhalla Inferior. Gods who have to be approached in drug-induced trances and spirit flights, gods who need to be propitiated with sacrifices, of food, drink – and, yes, human blood.'

347

As she said that she looked pointedly at Ruminavi, who dropped his eyes.

Now Inguill leaned forward and faced Quintus. 'I speak of gods who, our theologians believe, eventually overthrew yours, in your comfortable eastern continents, and shattered your Roman Empire.' She straightened up. 'The foundation of my job is maintaining order. Without order, rigidly applied, surely you can understand that the fabric of this great machine we all live in could not be maintained. As for me, I left my birth family to study at the Houses of Learning at Hurin Cuzco at the eastern hub, and then I have served the Sapa Inca in the administrative buildings of Hanan Cuzco at the western hub. I live alone. I care for my parents, my siblings, but rarely see them. For myself, order is my husband – the only one I need. *He* will not betray me, if I serve him well.

'Which is why you people represent such a problem to me. You are a threat to that order, and have been since the moment you arrived.' She pointed a finger at Quintus. 'Because – *you – don't – fit.*'

Titus growled, 'How fortunate we were to have you on hand when we arrived, then, *quipucamayoc.*'

Quintus shot him a warning glance.

But Inguill said, 'Oh, there was no fortune involved. I look out for – anomalies. Ripples on the pond of order and calm. You could say I collect them; you could call it a passion. And when I heard the reports of your ship's approach, I knew you were just such a ripple on my pond.'

Quintus laughed, surprising Mardina, but she saw he was trying to lift the mood, to break up the intensity. 'Ha! Never heard *you* described as a ripple on a pond, Titus Valerius. What is it you want to say to us, *quipucamayoc*?'

She smiled. 'I want to learn more of you. I have come to think I need to. And believe me, you need to learn more of me.

'I wish to propose an exchange of gifts. I give you something, you give me something in return. Our whole society is based on this exchange, if you think about it: you fulfil your *mit'a* obligations to the Sapa Inca, and in return he grants you the gift of a secure life.'

Quintus scowled. 'What gift?'

She reached into her trunk and produced a Roman military belt buckle, heavy steel and brass. 'Not so much a gift as returned property, I suppose. One of your men lost this when passing through the hub portals.'

Titus smacked his brow. 'That fool Scorpus! I'll tan his backside with his own belt.'

Quintus said evenly, 'Hush, Titus. What of it? This is ours, but only a buckle – purely decorative.'

'Well, I don't think that's true, is it? You know, Tiso Inca destroyed Rome, but after that we pursued you surviving Romaoi to your eastern heartlands, beyond your capital. There the conclusion of the campaign of conquest was less destructive...'

'The provinces of Graecia and Asia Minor,' Michael said quickly.

'Yes,' Quintus murmured. 'Breadbasket of the empire. The imperial troops must have pulled back there in the face of the Inca advance, tried to establish shorter frontiers.'

'Which is maybe why these Incas call us "Romaoi", which is the Greek term.'

Inguill listened to this carefully, as if filing away the words on her bits of knotted string, Mardina thought. 'After the surrender your citizens became subject to the Sapa Inca of the time. But compared to Italia, these eastern Romaoi had retained much of the fabric of their civilisation, the farms, the cities – and their records. You had libraries, impressive histories. So I know much about you, you see. I can even read your peculiar language, the strange symbols you use where we use our *quipus*, the placement of knots on strings...' She held up the buckle. 'I know what the words and numbers on this object say.' She picked out the moulding: *Legio XC Victrix*. 'The ninetieth legion, known as the victorious. Something like that? But, you see, there have been no Romaoi legions since the third century after Yupanqui. And there were never as many as ninety. Yet here is this belt

349

buckle, five hundred years later. Here you are, in your hovels, in your field, muttering about campaigns fought and booty won, and calling this man "Centurion" when you think nobody is listening.'

Quintus visibly had to control his anger. 'You have spies here?'

'I don't need them. Every *ayllu* is riddled with *yanakunas*, all of whom have ears and eyes and a memory, and all of whom will tell all they know to be spared a whipping. Our inspectors sample such sources, on a regular basis.' She faced him. 'I think you are a fragment of a Romaoi legion, half a millennium after no such legion can exist. What do you have to say to that?'

Quintus kept a dignified silence, evidently unsure, Mardina realised, where all this was leading.

'A gift for a gift,' Inguill said now. 'That is what we agreed.'

'That's what you imposed on us,' Quintus growled.

'And the gift I want is the truth. Come now,' Inguill said silkily. 'I know much of it already. I know for instance that few of you have learned our language properly – this girl, Mardina, being an exception.'

Mardina bowed her head.

'The others of you rely on prompts. As if somebody whispers in your ears. A spirit on your shoulders, perhaps, translating from the people's tongue to Latin and back again?' She pointed at Chu Yuen. 'And all of you are more confident when this boy is close by, with the pack that never leaves his presence. We are only playing a game. You. The Xin, Chu Yuen. Show me what is in your bag. I won't take it from you. Just show me.'

Chu glanced at Quintus, and at Michael.

The ColU spoke now, from a small speaker inside the pack. 'Do as she says, Chu Yuen.'

Hearing this disembodied voice, the two soldiers behind Inguill drew their weapons, short stabbing swords. Titus growled and would have got to his feet in response, had Quintus not grabbed his arm.

Quintus called, 'Collius? Are you sure?'

350

'She already knows so much, Centurion. And in the end we are all trapped in this situation together, the Inca as much as us.'

Inguill frowned. 'Trapped?'

'We are all puppets of a higher power, *quipucamayoc*.'

'Show yourself!'

'Chu Yuen, please ...'

Chu opened his battered backpack, gingerly lifted out the ColU, and set it on the ground before Inguill. Unwrapped from layers of soft woollen packing, it was a slab of glass-like material the size and shape of a large book, Mardina thought; a constellation of lights winked in its interior, and cables, tubes and support structures protruded at its rim, obviously meant to connect this component to a larger structure, but crudely truncated.

Inguill stared. 'What are you?'

'I am not human. I was made by humans. I am a device.'

'Not by artisans of the Inca.'

'No—'

'And nor by Romaoi.'

'No, *quipucamayoc*. A discussion of my origin will reveal much. I am a ColU. The Romans call me Collius. Once I was part of a much larger engine. My task was to farm, to dig the soil of other worlds.'

Inguill was evidently trying to master her fear, Mardina saw. 'You fit into no category of thing I have seen before.'

'You are shocked, and it is understandable,' the ColU said. 'Believe me, I am merely a made thing. I am like a *quipu*. I am a device for storing and manipulating information. I am more sophisticated – that's all. I have machines to enable me to speak, and others that enable me to hear, through devices carried by the boy, Chu Yuen. Who serves me faithfully, by the way.'

Inguill pursed her lips. 'What do you think, *tocrico apu*?'

Ruminavi looked just as scared as Inguill was, but more cunning, Mardina thought. 'I think that that would be a fine trophy to present to the Sapa Inca and his court. A talking jewel! And if it can sing or recite poetry – can you tell fortunes, Collius?'

'I can do far more than that, Inguill, as I think you know.'

351

She stared at the device. 'Can you restore the order that has been lost?'

'That is my goal, *quipucamayoc*,' the ColU said softly. 'Mardina Eden Jones Guthfrithson is a descendant of those I was created to serve.'

Mardina was startled to be brought into this, and blushed.

'I can understand that,' Inguill said. 'Everybody needs someone to protect. To give purpose to one's life, one's work. For me it is the Sapa Inca, who personifies the Tawantinsuyu and the billions under his protection ...'

'And billions yet unborn,' said the ColU.

'Yes. Yes, you're right. Oh, put that thing away, boy, put it back where it's safe.'

Chu picked up the processor unit reverently, and stowed it away in its layers of packing in his bag.

Quintus grinned. Evidently, Mardina thought, with Inguill disconcerted by the vision of the ColU, he felt more confident, more in control. 'So, *quipucamayoc*. We are exchanging gifts. Your turn again, I think ...'

'Well, let me overwhelm you.' Now she lifted a heavy frame out of the trunk; Titus had to help her lower it to the ground. Mardina studied this curiously. It was a frame of ornate wood within which fine wires ran, up, down, side to side, front to back, with knots of some kind of thread in a multitude of colours resting on the wires. Mardina saw that the positions of the wires, the knots, could be adjusted with the use of levers and switches.

Inguill saw her looking. 'What do you think of this, child?'

'It's beautiful.'

Inguill smiled. 'It is. Most well-designed devices are. But what do you think it's for?'

'It looks like a kind of *quipu*. I've only seen simple ones before, like the ones used by the inspectors when they come to assess the *mit'a* obligation of the *ayllu*. They reminded me of abacuses. This is more complex.'

'You will have to show me an *abacus*. But you are right, child, that's surprisingly perceptive.'

'Thanks,' Mardina said drily.

'This is a *quipu*, a kind of *quipu*, capable of storing a large amount of information. The knots record numbers, the colours names. And it can be interrogated by means of these controls.' She looked around at them. 'You should not overestimate this. In Cuzco the Great Quipu Repository is a building of four mighty towers, with jars full of *quipus* stacked floor to ceiling. That is our record store; *this* can only be a digest. Nevertheless – ColU, can you read a *quipu*? Could you read this?'

'With some instruction, and with the help of Chu Yuen – yes. But what will I learn?'

'It is our history,' said Inguill said. 'A kind of compendium, by many authors. It depicts what we know of the ages before our own history began with Yupanqui, eight centuries ago. And it tells of our glorious campaign of global conquest, including the subjugation of the Romaoi and the Xin. And finally our expansion to the planets, and even the stars, with the use of the energies of the *warak'a*.'

'I will study it closely,' the ColU said, 'and instruct these others.'

Mardina felt unreasonably excited by this, by the gift of a history book. 'We might be able to figure out the jonbar hinge—'

'Hush, child. Not yet.'

Inguill, of course, missed none of this exchange.

Titus snorted. 'Well, I for one am always ready for a history lesson. Why, I remember once on campaign—'

'Shut up, Titus Valerius,' Quintus said mildly, watching Inguill, evidently intrigued. 'I suspect it's no accident that the *quipucamayoc* has given us a history text, for history is what this meeting is all about, isn't it? History – or histories?'

Inguill nodded. 'I have the feeling I know a good deal less than you do, at this moment. On the other hand I have the power to do a lot more about it. Rather than press you for a response – I have one last gift.' Again she dug into the trunk.

353

This time she produced a scrap of white fabric, grimy with rust-coloured dust, torn from a garment, perhaps – and stained by what looked like brown, dried blood. She smoothed this out on the lid of the trunk.

Mardina leaned over to see. The fabric itself looked strange, with thick threads that were shiny where they were ripped. And stitched to the scrap was a kind of insignia, she thought, a triangle of thick cloth, edged in gold around a background field of blue-black. In the foreground was an arc of a red-brown planet, girdled by a swooping line, the schematic path of some kind of aerial craft. The craft itself was shown as a clumsy affair of tubes and boxes and shining panels, roughly stacked. Hovering over all this was an eagle, wings outstretched, holding some kind of branch in its talons – an olive? And there was Latin lettering around the edges of the triangle.

'The eagle is the best-worked element of the thing,' Titus Valerius murmured.

'That's true,' said Mardina, entranced, puzzled.

The ColU inspected the insignia through the slate carried by Chu. '*Quipucamayoc*, where did you get this?'

'You don't recognise it?'

Quintus shrugged. 'Obviously not.'

'And yet here is this lettering, in the Romaoi style. Can you read this?'

Quintus picked out the words, letter by letter. 'GERSHON – YORK – STONE. These mean nothing to me. Names, perhaps? But this – this is the name of one of our gods. Or at least, his Greek cousin. ARES.'

'Yes. I've been looking this up. *Ares* – the god you call Mars. And Mars is the name you gave to the fourth planet, is it not? Which we call Illapa, after an aspect of the sky god, the thunder deity. And is the eagle not an emblem of the Romaoi?'

The ColU repeated, 'Inguill, where was this found?'

'Where do you think? On Illapa, of course. On Mars! Near the wreckage of a crashed craft – oh, centuries old, we think. But not far from the *warak'a* field, the gateway—'

354

The ColU said, 'Gateway? Do you mean a Hatch?'

'Stop,' Quintus ordered. 'We must take this one step at a time.'

Chu dropped his eyes, as if he might be blamed for the ColU's impertinence.

'You see,' Inguill said now, 'what puzzles me is this. In our history there is no record of the Romaoi reaching Illapa. Or reaching space, beyond the home world – or even, actually, mastering flight in the air. We put a stop to such ambitions when we burned their capital and subjugated their people and their territories. But you,' she said now, staring at Quintus, 'you – and now we must tell each other the truth – you came from a history that was not like the one recorded in our *quipus*,' and she tapped the frame of the machine she had produced for emphasis. 'Not like it at all. I think you came from a history where, somehow, the Romaoi survived, and prospered, and founded ninety legions, and got off the planet, and flew around the place in ships with names like *Malleus Jesu*—'

'You know about the ship?'

'Of course I know! Your men are hardly discreet, Quintus Fabius, at least with the women they take into their beds. So, did the eagle of the Romaoi fly over Illapa, in a ship called *Ares*?'

'Not that I know of,' Quintus said. He sighed, and seemed to come to a decision. 'Yes, Inguill – some of us Romans did indeed fly beyond Terra. *I* did. And I studied the early exploration of the planets at the academy at Ostia, during my officer training. This *Ares* should have been a heroic legend, even if it crashed! And the evidence you produce suggests it did. But I never heard of it.'

The ColU said, 'There may be another explanation.'

Inguill pursed her lips. 'You mean, *another history*.'

'You are quick to understand, *quipucamayoc*. Yes, I – and Mardina's mother – came from a different history from these Romans. Who came in turn from a different history from yours. And in that history we had space explorers who wore patches

355

like these. Rome did not survive, not as the empire, but we still used relics of its culture – the Roman alphabet, for instance.'

'Of course you did,' Quintus said complacently.

'The eagle may have been used, not as an emblem of Rome, but of America – which was a great country in the continent of Valhalla Superior.'

'So,' Quintus said, 'are you telling us that this *Ares* was sent to Mars by this "America"?'

'No,' said the ColU unhappily. 'It's not as simple as that. In *my* history America never went to Mars, not with people, not alone. The first to Mars were Chinese – Xin. Other nations followed, but as a group, the United Nations, which included America. There was no *Ares*.'

Mardina was becoming confused.

Inguill, though, seemed to be grasping all this strangeness readily. 'So this was *yet another history*,' she said. 'One like the history that produced you, ColU. But not identical. One where this—'

'America.'

'—sent a craft to Illapa. Yet here is this patch, this scrap of evidence – the wreck of a ship, on Illapa, *my* Illapa. And the odd thing is—'

Ruminavi barked laughter. He looked to Mardina as if his head was spinning. He said, 'After that list of impossibilities, you say *the* odd thing—'

Inguill ignored him. 'The odd thing,' she persisted, 'is that we would not have found this – I mean scouts from the Inca's navy would not have discovered it – if not for the sudden appearance, in the ground of Illapa, of a field of *warak'a*, a portal, where none had been found before. Not before *you* came.'

'The portal,' the ColU said. 'The Hatch. And that is the most significant thing, of all we have discussed—'

'Enough,' said Inguill abruptly. She stood, massaging her temples. 'You flatter me for my ability to learn, ColU. I never thought *I* could learn too *much*, too quickly – I need air. You and you and you—' she pointed at Mardina, Quintus Fabius, and Chu with ColU '—walk with me. We will plot together, like conspirators.'

Ruminavi got to his feet too, evidently troubled. '*Quipucamayoc*, we are far from civilisation here. I fear for your safety if—'

'Oh, don't fuss, *apu*. What harm will I come to here? Save for having my grasp of reality shattered, and *that* has already happened. Have your soldiers follow me if you must, but keep their distance – unless any of them knows any comforting philosophy ...'

CHAPTER 50

Outside the house, Inguill led the way, striding stiffly and rapidly, heading out of the *ayllu* towards the forested edge of the clearing. A pair of soldiers tracked her, never more than an arm's length from the *quipucamayoc*. Quintus followed a few discreet paces behind, with Mardina and Chu to either side. Chu, who probably didn't get as much exercise as he should, was soon panting from the pace Inguill set.

But Quintus patted his back. 'Don't worry, lad. She'll soon run out of puff. Look how stiffly she walks ... She spends too long staring at her *quipus* – as I used to with my command papers before we came to this place and I have to play at being a farmer – it is nerves and tension that propel her, and all that will soon work itself out of her system.'

Sure enough the *quipucamayoc* was slowing long before she reached the forest border. She stood, panting, gazing up at the trees. The two soldiers trailing her took watchful positions, surveying the terrain.

Inguill gestured. 'Look at that,' she said. 'To be a tree! Tall, patient, ancient. You need never know that the sunlight on your leaves comes through Inti windows, or that the thick earth around your roots is processed rubble from a shattered moon. Let alone worry about which strand of a *quipu* of realities you belonged to. A tree is a tree is a tree. What do you think, Quintus? Would you be more content as a member of a forest like that?'

The centurion grinned. 'Only if I was the tallest, *quipucamayoc*.

And besides some of my legionaries may as well be trees, for all the sense they have.'

She laughed. 'Legionaries, eh? So you admit what you are.'

He shrugged, saying no more.

She walked on, at an easier pace. 'Let's sum up what we have, then. Several histories! And I had enough trouble memorising one.' She counted them on her fingers, fingering the knuckles like *quipu* knots, Mardina thought. 'First my own, this glorious realm ruled by the Sapa Inca. Second, the one where you upstart Romaoi and Xin and others still squabble. Third ...' she looked to Chu.

'Third,' the ColU said, 'we have what we have come to call the UN-China Culture. A world of high technology, myself being an example, but relatively little expansion beyond the home world.'

'Fourth, then, the *Ares* history. Like yours, but with bold explorers striking early for Illapa. Very well—'

'And don't forget the Drowned Culture,' Mardina said brightly. 'My father worked that out. That makes five—'

'I don't think you're helping, Mardina,' Quintus growled.

'And the jonbar hinge Stef Kalinski spoke of, when she discovered she had a sister she had never suspected existed before. That's six!'

'*Thank* you, Mardina.'

The ColU said, 'Clearly these histories do not coexist, but they overlap, to a small degree. Scraps of one may be discovered in another.'

'Like my *Ares* insignia,' Inguill said.

'Yes,' Quintus said. 'And like my own century, my ship, which survived one jonbar hinge.'

'And myself and my companions,' said the ColU, 'who have survived *two* hinges ... *Quipucamayoc*, we have taken to calling the transitions between worlds jonbar hinges. The derivation is complicated and irrelevant.'

Inguill tried out the words. '*Shh-onn-barr hin-ch*. Very well.

359

A name is a name. But to label something does not mean we understand it.'

'Indeed,' said the ColU. 'The replacement of one history by another is not a tidy matter. Scraps remain.'

'Do we know how these transitions are made? How one history is cleared away, like a dilapidated building ready for demolition, to be replaced by another?'

'Judging by our experiences, the termination of one history is generally accompanied by disaster. War. The release of huge energies from the kernels – which you call the *warak'a.*'

'Which is something to be avoided.'

'Yes—' Quintus growled. '*Who* is making these transitions happen is a more pertinent question, perhaps.'

'Very well – who, ColU?'

'We don't know. Not yet. We have some clues. Inguill, you said your people on Mars – Illapa – discovered a new field of *warak'a*, a new Hatch – our word for the portal you found.'

'*Hat-sch.* Very well. We know how to build them, of course.'

'As did we,' Quintus said. 'We Romans. You jam the kernels together—'

She waved a hand at the artificial sky. 'Our ships roam the stars. Everywhere we go we take the *warak'a* – of course, or rather they take us. And everywhere we go we build Hatches.'

'As did we,' Quintus repeated.

'But why?' the ColU asked. 'Why do you do this? Who told you to?'

Inguill glanced at the Roman, and both shrugged. Inguill said, 'The *warak'a* are a gift from Inti, the sky god. That seems evident – a rare benison from our gods, as opposed to a punishment. And the Hatches are always found with them. Wherever we travel we make more Hatches as a tribute to the gods. It seems to work ... At least, we have not yet been punished for it, so we deduce this is the correct course of action.'

'As with us,' Quintus said. 'Though you seem to be more industrious at it than we ever were.'

'Yes,' the ColU said. 'That's it. Whatever the nature of the

360

change, whatever the cultural details, each new draft of a civilisation is *better at building Hatches*. My culture, as far as I know, built no Hatches at all. You Romans did pretty well. And the Inca—'

'We litter worlds with the things,' Inguill said. 'This is the triumph of our culture. And now I discover that we have been somehow *manipulated* to achieve precisely this goal? Our whole history distorted!'

Mardina studied her. 'And that makes you feel...'

'Angry, child. Angry. Whoever is doing this, it is hard to believe it is a god. For what god needs a door in the ground?'

Mardina herself felt oddly exhilarated. The flood of revelations and new ideas made her feel as if she was jumping recklessly off a cliff edge, or diving from the axis of Yupanquisuyu and plummeting to the ground, laughing all the way down...

The ColU said, 'Inguill, your discovery of a Hatch on Mars, Illapa, has changed everything. Because when we emerged into this time stream, past the latest jonbar hinge, *it was just as a Hatch appeared on Mars*. That was on the Romans' version of Mars. This new Illapa Hatch is an obvious link to the underlying... strangeness. Well, we must pursue Earthshine—'

Inguill frowned. 'Who?'

'I'll explain. But for now we must get to Illapa.'

'How?' asked Inguill bluntly. 'The imperial authorities would not allow it. Even I could not authorise it.'

'I have a plan,' said Quintus Fabius smugly.

When the centurion had explained his ideas, it took a while for Inguill to stop laughing.

'Are you insane?'

'Oh, quite possibly.'

She looked at him, smiling. *'This was your plan all along, wasn't it?* To lay up here in Yupanquisuyu, steal some food, fight your way out, and fly off into space, to found some new Rome of your own? Ha! No wonder you Romaoi rolled over when the

Inca armies landed on your shores. Look – you won't get as far as the ocean. The *awka kamayuq* patrols will stop you.'

'All right,' Quintus said angrily. 'Then do you have any better ideas?'

'Well, I'm prepared to concede you need to get to Illapa, if Collius says so. We humans together need to understand the agent that is meddling with our destinies. But you're not going to walk out of here.' She sighed. 'The Sapa Inca's advisers would do nothing to help. They are pretty fools, angling and manoeuvring, of no intellect or ability. Conversely the administrators who actually run the empire are just that – *quipu*-pluckers, with no imagination whatever. Which leaves the task to me – and you. For the only way you'll do this is if I help you.'

Quintus frowned. 'You would do that? How can we trust you?'

'We have no choice, Centurion,' the ColU said. 'I see that now.'

'And I barely trust myself,' Inguill said, a little wildly, Mardina thought. 'At the very least I will be committing a crime by smuggling you out of here – out of the light of the Sapa Inca's rule ... And at the worst, I suppose, my meddling might itself result in one of these catastrophic changes you so eloquently described. On the other hand, if I manage to slay this particular jaguar, a greater service to the empire is hard to imagine. Perhaps history will forgive me—'

'If history survives at all,' said the ColU.

'Indeed.' She stopped pacing and faced Quintus. 'In some ways it is what we share that interests me, rather than what divides us. We both sail the seas of space; we both build the ColU's Hatches. We both name planets after our antique gods. And we share other legends – so my spies inform me.' She glanced up at an Inti window. 'We call the nearest star to the sun just that – Kaylla, which means "near".'

'As we call it Proxima,' said the ColU. 'Meaning "nearest" in Quintus's tongue.'

'And our sailors of space have a legend of the furthest star of all, where the gods lay their plans against us, or plot the catastrophes of the end of time: the *pachacuti*. We call this undiscovered star Karu, which means "far".'

'As we speak of Ultima,' Quintus mused. 'Yes. We do have much in common.'

'And is Ultima where we will find the Hatch builders? I must get back to Cuzco. There's much to prepare if we are to pull this off, and the more time they have to fester, the more plots tend to unravel. But we need more ... We need a way to divert the attention of the Sapa Inca and his advisers at Hanan Cuzco from your break-out attempt.' She looked now at Mardina. 'And, given what Ruminavi has belatedly confessed to me about his *mit'a* collecting in your *ayllu*, or his failure there – if I am risking the sacrifice of everything, my career, even my life, I must ask you to risk a sacrifice too.'

Mardina frowned. 'Me?'

'Not you, child. Your friend, Clodia Valeria. You must be prepared to sacrifice her. But you, Mardina, may be the key to making it happen ...'

CHAPTER 51

Before beginning the march to the ocean, Quintus Fabius inspected his troops.

As the trumpet sounded, the men of the century formed up in orderly ranks, their cloaks on their backs, their marching packs at their feet, their improvised or purloined weapons at their belts. This was the first time they had turned out as a proper unit of the Roman army since arriving in this habitat.

The centurion walked the ranks, murmuring quiet words to individual men, inspecting patched and improvised uniforms – and their weapons. In return for other favours, mostly labour by burly legionaries, the local smith had eventually turned out a variety of weapons, including a decent steel *gladio* and *pugio* and *pilum* for most of the men. Many of them had helmets too now, simple steel bowls with a lip to protect their necks and cheeks. Few had body armour, though many wore a *subarmilis*, a heavy quilted undergarment designed to help with the load of a breastplate. The folk of the *ayllu* had done all this out of sight of the Inca's inspectors, treating it as a kind of game, a way to get back at the overbearing tax collectors. The legionaries hid as much as they could in the open. They even had a big rock water tank, that they surreptitiously used to sharpen their swords.

Quintus came to Orgilius. The man had been a *signifier*, a century standard-bearer, but now given a field promotion by Quintus to *aquilifer*, bearer of the whole legion's eagle standard, in the absence of the rest of the Legio XC Victrix anywhere in this reality. Indeed Quintus had hired a particularly skilled local metalworker to make for them a reasonable facsimile of the

364

old standard, given the legion by a grateful Emperor Veronius Optatus seven centuries before. It seemed a suitable reward for Orgilius, one of the more intelligent of the legionaries, who had picked up the Quechua tongue readily and made friendships with local people, even with a few of the officials and military types who visited the *ayllu*. He had become a source of information upon which Quintus increasingly relied. Yes, Orgilius deserved his new honour – even if it was all Quintus had to give him.

And pride surged in Mardina's own heart, as she waited in the ranks for the centurion to come to her.

She had spoken to the centurion long ago about her own thwarted military ambitions, on the other side of the jonbar hinge, her dream of joining the Brikanti Navy. But the recruiting of 'barbarians', as Quintus put it, into the Roman army had a long tradition. So, in the weeks since Inguill had come to call and the century had prepared for battle, the centurion had given her a lowly field commission. The tribunes had allowed her to join in the legionaries' training routines – the physical exercises, the construction work, the fighting with wooden spears and knives. She enjoyed joining with crowds of men in the battle formations, the square, the wedge, the circle, the tortoise. In practice, in the end, Quintus had found her more useful as a quality check on the work he was having done quietly around the village. To the local people she wasn't as threatening a presence as the average burly legionary.

She was even put on the payroll of the imperial army, and the salary due her, nine hundred sesterces a year, was duly recorded – to be paid, she was solemnly assured, when the legion finally returned to Terra and its *collegia*, less tax, punishment deductions and replacement equipment costs.

Now Quintus stepped back from the ranks, and looked over his men, and up at the standard above all their heads. This bright morning, with the century drawn up in a glittering array under the light of the Inti windows, Mardina thought that at last there could be no more self-deception about the meaning of all this. The century was a military unit, and it was ready for the march.

In proud Latin Quintus declared, 'Well, if I was a sentimental man, and if I didn't know you were a bunch of lazy, bed-hopping, wine-swilling slackers, I'd say you made a pretty sight for the eye, men, even under the mother's milk that passes for daylight in this tub of a world – you are Romans! And proud of it! And I'm proud of you!'

That was the cue for the first cheer, which Titus Valerius led, raising his stump of an arm, and Mardina joined in with the rest. But Mardina noticed that Titus kept one eye on the sky; she knew they had timed this parade for the intervals between the overflights of the vacuum-eating Condors, the Incas' spies in the sky, and if one showed up unexpectedly they would break up the display quickly.

'We've a challenge ahead of us now,' Quintus said now, 'the like of which no Roman has faced before.' He pointed west. 'Probably a month's march through this jungle, longer if the Sapa Inca spots us on the move and tries to do something about it.' Laughter. 'Then we face an unknown ocean, an ocean that spans the waist of the world ... Pah. We'll swim it. And then on to the hub, to Hanan Cuzco, where we'll face down the Sapa Inca himself and his decadent hordes, and we'll carve out a destiny that nobody who lives in this rolling barrel will ever forget!'

If that was vague, it was purposefully so, Mardina knew, because the whole strategy was vague, the more so the further out you looked. *To get to Mars/Illapa*: that was the only clearly defined goal. The rest was going to have to be improvised, hope-fully with the help of the *quipucamayoc*. But the centurion was rewarded with another cheer even so.

'Now before we start,' Quintus said, 'and I know very well it's not New Year's Day, I want us to remember who we are and what we are. No matter how far from home we are bound to the Emperor and the Empire. And we will say the *sacramentum* together. Titus Valerius, lead us.'

The big warrior, who had been rehearsing this, stepped forward and boomed out the words of the soldiers' oath: 'We swear by God and Jesu, and by the majesty of the Emperor who second to God is to be loved and worshipped by humanity ...'

The legionaries repeated the ancient words, as they were used to doing every New Year.

'... that we will do strenuously all that the Emperor commands, will never desert the service, nor refuse to die for the Roman state ...'

The voices of the legionaries made a cavernous rumble. And when they were done they yelled and waved their *gladios* in the air.

Clodia Valeria ran out of the crowd of watching civilians, and hugged her father. There were catcalls at this, but Titus hugged his daughter back with his one good arm. And he exchanged a dark glance with Quintus, a glance Mardina understood, for Clodia had her own difficult duty to perform before this mission was through, as indeed did Mardina.

With the ceremony done the parade broke up, and the men formed up into a column for marching.

The legionaries themselves, laden with their cloaks and packs, would go ahead two by two, the standard-bearer leading the column, scouts probing the countryside. A rough baggage train formed behind. This included some of the wives the legionaries had taken from the *ayllu* – and one mother with a very young Roman-Inca baby. Michael the *medicus* walked here, with Chu Yuen and his burden at one side, and Clodia Valeria at the other. Then came some of the *mitimacs* who had volunteered to assist the march, carpenters, cobblers, cooks – and then a train of *yanakunas*, slaves used as bearers of baggage.

Mardina was surprised so many of the *mitimacs*, the ordinary taxpayers of the *ayllu*, had been prepared to come along. Well, most of their time and labour was their own to use as they pleased, and many, it turned out, had never travelled far from their home, either towards the eastern hub in one direction or the ocean in the other. Some, especially the young, were excited by the idea of joining this adventure, even if it was ill understood. In fact, Mardina suspected, some of them probably believed that this highly organised expedition led by the commanding Quintus Fabius *was* a fulfilment of a portion of their *mit'a* obligations.

When they were ready the scouts led the column out of the *ayllu*, to cheers, ribald whistles, even a scattering of applause. At first little children from the *ayllu* ran alongside, shouting and waving, and in the excitement even some of the tamer guinea pigs ran around, wondering what all the fuss was about. But the parents called their offspring back before the head of the column reached the fringe of the *hacha hacha*. Here the trumpets sounded, and soon *anti* guides materialised out of the forest, their blue-painted faces seeming to hover in the green gloom.

And that was when the grumbling started, as Titus had predicted to Mardina. She knew that many of the legionaries had never gone further into the jungle than you needed to take a discreet piss. Now they weren't happy at walking into the great green chamber of the forest, past the slim columns of the tree trunks, under the dense canopy that excluded so much of the light, with the *antis* like elusive shadows all around – and the legionaries jumped at every crack of a twig, every hiss of a snake or clatter of scorpions.

But the complaints lessened after an hour or so, when they reached a clear path – not a metalled road, it was mere dirt beaten flat by bare feet, but it was a straight path heading directly west, and all but concealed from the sky by the trees. After the confusion of the denser jungle the column quickly formed up in good order once more, and the march to the west continued.

Another hour and they passed through an *anti* village, round huts built on frames of branches and walled with reeds, the people all but naked, some at work skinning animals or pounding grain or tanning leather or tending fires. The *antis* stared curiously at the legionaries – and they stared back with interest at the bare breasts of the women, and with horror at the elaborately pierced penises displayed by some of the men. Everybody seemed to be tattooed, Mardina thought; faces like the jaguars of local mythology peered at her from every shadow. She was poignantly reminded of the tattoo on her own mother's face.

Soon the village was behind them, and the march continued along another straight track. Some of the walkers peeled off to fill flasks from the stream that watered the village.

This was to be the strategy, to keep to the deep forest tracks as much as possible – to exploit what the *antis* had built here. For this was the real *anti* culture. Mardina herself had seen a little of it, and from their arrival here Quintus Fabius had sent out his scouts to study every aspect of their environment. The *antis* were not town dwellers like Romans or Incas, but they were not savages living at random in the jungle either. The Roman scouts had found a network of settlements and trails cut or burned into the forest, neat round clearings connected by dead-straight lines, all invisible from outside the forest, and mostly screened from the air by the forest canopy. And it was these tracks the Romans would follow, as far as possible, relying on the support of friendly *antis* as they travelled.

It might work, Mardina thought. The Inca state seemed to have an ambiguous relationship with the *antis*. In theory they were *mitimacs*, taxpayers like every other citizen of the empire. And they did make tributes when the assessors came calling, from the produce of the forest. Their wiry archers would also serve in the Inca's army, and reasonably disciplined they could be too. On the other hand, the Sapa Inca would occasionally order his troops to make forays into the forest, seizing goods with the excuse of unpaid *mit'a*, or even taking *antis* as slaves, *yanakunas* – but there could be *anti* raids on unwary *ayllus* too. It was a wary relationship then, between two quite alien cultures. But on the whole the Incas seemed content to allow the *antis* to live their lives under the cover of their forest canopy, invisible even to the vacuum-eating Condors. And the *antis* were useful to the Romans now.

So here they were: Roman legionaries marching through a three-thousand-mile-long habitat in space, and Mardina was one of them. When she thought about it, she was thrilled.

They had walked about seven hours when the surveyors said they had covered twenty miles, the standard target for a marching day.

They came to a clearing, perhaps once occupied by the *antis* but now abandoned, with the scuffed and blackened remains of old hearths pierced by the brilliant green of saplings. The men broke formation, dumped their packs, and changed their boots for camp sandals to ease their feet. They looked exhausted to Mardina; they weren't in as good shape as Quintus might have hoped. But they would toughen up – and their work for this day wasn't yet done.

With the spades they carried on their packs – tools they had been allowed to keep on arrival in the habitat – the legionaries got to work creating a camp for the night. Some worked around a perimeter sketched by the surveyors, digging a ditch and building walls. Others hastily assembled spiky caltrops from fallen tree branches and scattered them around the perimeter. Soon the tents went up, sheets of heavy leather carried by the *yanakunas*, in neat rows along what was effectively a narrow street, with latrine ditches threading out of the camp. Meanwhile the fires were lit, the pots were set up, and the smell of cooking filled the air, mostly a broth of guinea-pig meat and vegetables and fish sauce.

Outside all this, the wives and other camp followers made their own arrangements for the night, as best they could. The glow from the Inti windows faded, and the eerie night of the habitat drew in.

Quintus Fabius sought out Mardina, where she was helping Titus Valerius and his daughter with their meal. The centurion beckoned to draw her away.

Together they walked around the perimeter of the camp. The centurion growled, 'Oh! What a relief to talk decent camp Latin again, without trying to curl one's lips around *runasimi*, or to have Collius whispering in one's ear ... So what do you think of your first day on the march, my newest legionary?'

That title, casually used, thrilled her. 'Impressive,' she said truthfully. 'The discipline, despite all the grumbling.'

'Soldiers always grumble.'

'And the way they put together this camp—'

'Centuries of tradition and years of training. But the men like their camps. It's the same every night, as if you aren't travelling at all – as if you're returning home each evening to the same miniature town. Soldiers like familiarity, above all. A place they know they'll be able to sleep in safety.' He glanced at the engineered sky. 'We made good progress today.'

'Yes. I spoke to the surveyors. It's one advantage of having a sky that's almost a mirror image of the ground. They say it's fifteen or twenty days' march to the ocean, if we do as well as we did today.'

'Well, that was pretty much the plan.'

They came to a stretch of the wall that was less satisfactory than the rest; he scuffed some loose earth with his sandalled foot, and glanced around; Mardina could see he was making a mental note regarding some later discipline. They walked on.

'To tell you the truth I'm glad to have them on the march at last. Legionaries need to be legionaries; they're not cut out to be farmers and taxpayers – not until they retire, anyhow. We have had some discipline problems – more than you were probably aware of. Bored men squabbling over gambling games, or women, or boys. As for the positive side, I ran out of excuses to issue *phalera* and other wooden medals for basic camp duties. Well, Mardina Eden Jones Guthfrithson, I'm glad you saw little of that, and I'm glad you see us at our best – doing what we do best, short of giving battle, that is.'

She plucked up the courage to speak frankly. 'And you're speaking to me like this, sir, because—'

He stopped and rested a hand on her shoulder. 'Well, you know why. You have a duty of your own to fulfil, you and

371

Clodia. Tomorrow you'll be led out of the forest by a couple of *antis*, and you'll meet the *tocrico apu* Ruminavi and other agents of the *quipucamayoc*, who will take you to a *capac nan* station and deliver you into the hands of the Sapa Inca's tax collectors...'

'Tomorrow? I didn't know it was as soon as that.'

'I thought it best not to tell you. To let you enjoy as much of *this* as possible.' He squeezed her shoulder harder. 'You know the plan. Of all of us, *yours* is perhaps the most difficult duty to fulfil. Even more than poor Clodia Valeria, who I suspect understands little of this.'

'I'll do my best, sir.'

'You'll do more than that, legionary,' he said gruffly, releasing her. 'You'll fulfil your orders and do what's required of you, adhering to the oath you swore this morning.'

She stood up straight. 'Of course, sir.'

'All right. Now go back and help Titus with his stew. Later I'll stop by and make sure he remembers he has to say goodbye to his daughter in the morning...'

CHAPTER 52

Hanan Cuzco was a great city.

Of course Mardina had been here before, when she had first arrived at Yupanquisuyu. But so baffled had she been by the giant habitat that she had taken in little of the capital city itself.

And this was a city like no other. Mardina, who had seen Dumnona and Eboraki in Brikanti, and many cities of the Roman Empire, could attest to that, as she and Clodia Valeria, grimly holding hands, bewildered after a long rail journey, were led by Ruminavi through the last security cordon.

Hanan Cuzco nestled in the tremendous bowl of the western hub, a structure itself over four hundred miles across – seen from the edge, it was more like a crater on Luna, Mardina thought, than any structure on Earth. And, she saw, as they rode across the face of the hub this time in a comfortable seated carriage, nestling at the base of this bowl was the city, huge buildings of stone and glass, blocks and pyramids and domes set out like gigantic toys. Many of the roofs were plated with gold that shone in the light of the Inti windows. All of this was crowded around a huge central structure, that tremendous tower she remembered well, a supremely narrow pyramid that must reach a mile high.

Ruminavi, their guide, pointed out sights. 'There is Qoricancha, the temple of the sun. There is Huacaypata, the main square, where the great roads cross. The big structure on the far side is Saqsaywaman, the fortress that guards the capital. All this is modelled on Old Cuzco, the Navel of the World, and yet wrought much larger...'

The great buildings, imported from Terra stone by stone, were steel frames faced by finely cut sandstone, huge blocks that fitted together seamlessly, and without mortar. Lesser buildings had stone walls and thatched roofs, and wooden door frames in which colourfully dyed blankets hung. Here at the axis of the habitat there was no spin gravity, and Mardina could see metal straps wrapped around the walls and roofs, to hold the buildings in place in the absence of the weight of the stones themselves. And in this city without weight the wide streets were laced with guide ropes, many of which glittered silver, stretching across the avenues and between the upper storeys of many of the buildings, as if the whole city had been draped in a shimmering spider web. People moved through that web, strange angular people, like spiders themselves.

Of course they were hundreds of miles above the layer of atmosphere that was plastered against the habitat's outer wall. So the city was enclosed by a dome, barely visible, a shimmering bubble that swept up above the buildings. There were more buildings outside the air dome, squat, blockier air-retaining structures: factories that maintained the air and water and other systems, and a number of military emplacements – no chances were taken with the security of the Sapa Inca. Mardina had taken in little of this during her first bewildered hours in the habitat. She hadn't even noticed the dome.

And, when she stepped out of the glass-walled transport and looked around, over Mardina's head the interior of the habitat itself stretched like a tremendous well shaft, walled with land and sea and air, a shaft thousands of miles tall.

Clodia tugged her hand. 'Don't look up. It makes you giddy.'

Mardina had looked up, and, yes, she felt briefly dizzy. 'I'm sorry.'

'Don't be.' A woman drifted before them, smiling. 'It takes time to adjust if you're used to the gravity of the *suyus* ...'

Perhaps forty, with black hair tied back, she had an open, smiling face, though the colours of her cheeks and lips were exaggerated with power and cream. She wore a dress of some brilliantly patterned fabric, and a headband set with emeralds that offset her dark eyes. A beautiful face, beautiful clothing. But she was taller than any legionary, and spindly, as if stretched, her neck long, her bare arms like twigs, and her joints, wrists and elbows and shoulders, were knots of bone. An inhabitant of the axis, then.

Clodia's hand gripped Mardina's tighter.

Ruminavi laughed. 'Oh, don't be afraid. Lowlanders are often startled by the first nobles they encounter. But you should recall this from your first arrival at Yupanquisuyu. Do you remember the axis warriors, bred for the lack of weight? This is my wife. Her name is Cura – that's easy to remember, isn't it? She's one of the highborn – she comes from one of the first *ayllus*, the dozen clans here in Cuzco that can prove lineal descent from the earliest of the Incas. So she is a useful ally for you, you see. *And* her half-brother Villac is a *colcacamayoc*, a keeper of the storehouses – just as senior in the government as Inguill, but with rather different responsibilities. Villac's responsibility is to collect the *mit'a* tributes and distribute the stores as necessary; Inguill's is to count it all, across the empire. And it is Villac who will assist your comrades to get to their ship. Isn't that marvellous?'

'But first we have to get you to the palace compound,' Cura said. She cupped Clodia's cheek in a hand that looked to Mardina as if it was crippled with arthritis, so swollen were the joints. Clodia was clearly forcing herself not to recoil. Cura said, 'The ceremony of the Great Ripening is not far away; many of the other blessed ones have been preparing already for many days. You are late.' She gazed into Clodia's blue eyes, caressed her fair skin. 'But there have been rumours of your beauty, child, ever since you arrived at the habitat, and then from every *mit'a* assessor who visited your home *ayllu*. They were not wrong. You are perfect. Now come, follow me. I know you are used to travelling in space, so you will find the lack of weight no problem.'

She turned and swam away, slipping gracefully through the mesh of cables, heading deeper into the city.

Mardina and Clodia followed Cura easily, as they passed along a broad avenue lined with huge buildings. Glancing back, Mardina saw that Ruminavi was following them too, with four bony axis warriors bringing up the rear of the party. Though this was the periphery of the city, people hurried everywhere, scrambling through the cobweb, mostly dressed in bright colourful fabrics, some clutching bundles of *quipus*. This was a capital city, Mardina reminded herself, the administrative centre of an empire the size of a continent, as well as a solar system full of mines and colonies; many of these buildings must be hives of offices every bit as busy as the Navy headquarters at Dumnona.

Clodia was staring, wide-eyed. Mardina remembered she'd had little experience of city life.

Mardina squeezed Clodia's hand. 'You're doing well.'

'I know. Considering I know what it is Cura thinks I'm "perfect" for.'

'It won't come to that. The plan, remember ... But you're brave even so.'

Clodia snorted. 'I'm the daughter of Titus Valerius. Of course I'm brave.'

They passed one particularly ornate building, a kind of flat-topped pyramid on top of which a figure sat on a throne – a statue, Mardina supposed, decked with fine clothes and jewellery. Two axis warriors hovered over the statue, like protective angels.

The girls slowed, distracted by the sight.

Cura said, 'Look at that stonework! Hand cut, and each stone fits its neighbour as well as two palms pressed together.'

'Is this the palace?' blurted Clodia.

Cura smiled. 'Well, it's *a* palace. It is the home of Huayna Capac, one of the greatest of the Incas.'

Mardina frowned. 'The Sapa Inca – I thought his name was Quisquis.'

'So it is, the latest Inca – distant descendant of Huayna Capac,

of course, separated by seven or eight centuries ... My chrono-
logy is poor.'

'I don't understand,' Mardina admitted.

'I think I do,' Clodia said. 'I heard of this. When the Sapa
Inca dies—'

'The Sapa Inca does not die,' Cura said firmly. 'He lives on in
his palace, he has a household of servants, and he is reunited
with his ancestors and descendants on feast days.'

Clodia stared at the figure in the throne. 'How many palaces
like this are there?'

Ruminavi knew the answer to that. 'Thirty-eight.'

'Thirty-nine Incas, then. Thirty-nine emperors since Yupanqui.'

Mardina stared into the mummy's painted face. Here was a
tough warrior who had built an empire with tools of stone and
bronze, and long after his death had been lifted into a realm he
could never have imagined.

'This is my future,' Clodia said. 'To become like this.'

Ruminavi smiled. 'A *malqui*, stuffed and preserved? Not if the
plan works out.'

Once again Clodia slid her hand into Mardina's.

CHAPTER 53

The Roman century came to the ocean coast at a beach, not far from the delta of a great river.

Quintus Fabius ordered his men to stay in the cover of the forest, rather than move out into the open. Grumbling, they complied, and began the daily process of establishing camp – for the twenty-first time on this march, they had fallen just a day behind the schedule the centurion had set for them.

Quintus himself, ordering Chu Yuen with Collius to accompany him, walked out into the light, onto the sandy beach. They were close to the marshy plain of the delta, where tremendous salt-loving trees plunged deep roots into the mud. The river was a mighty one, draining a swathe of this half-cylinder continent, the *antisuyu*, and when Quintus looked ahead he could see the discolouration of the fresh water pushing far out into the ocean brine.

And when he looked up to left and right, in wonder, he saw how the ocean rose *up* beyond what ought to have been the horizon, splashed with swirls of cloud, tinged here and there by the outflow of more huge rivers – and merging at last in the mists of the air with the other half of this world sea, which hung like a steel rainbow above his head.

Inguill, with a couple of Inca soldiers, was waiting for him here, as Quintus knew she would be. 'You're late.'

He shrugged. 'Within our contingency—'

'Before time runs out for Clodia Valeria?'

Tall, thin, pale, intent, she looked out of place on the beach, in this raw natural environment. She belonged in an office,

Quintus thought, her fingers wrapped in those bundles of string she read. But she was in command.

She turned now, and pointed. 'Down there are your transports over the ocean.'

Quintus saw a series of craft drawn up on the sand, flat wooden frames with sails furled up on masts. 'Rafts?'

'They are adequate. They are built by the Chincha, who are a people who once lived on the western coast of the continent you call Valhalla Inferior. Now they live here. Their rafts are of balsa and cotton. They were the best sailors in our world, until the Xin came calling on our shores in their mighty treasure ships. The Chincha craft will suffice to carry you over to the *cuntisuyu* if the weather over the ocean stays fine – as it is programmed to do.' She glanced up at a sky empty of Condors. 'And of course you will be less conspicuous than in any other form of transport. On the far side you will be escorted to a *capac nan* station. There are freight wagons sufficiently roomy to hide your men, all the way to the hub. It won't be comfortable, but you will be safe enough and will not be betrayed.'

'Well, we've trusted you this far.'

'And I you,' she said drily. 'Some would say I have already betrayed the Sapa Inca, my only lord, simply by keeping secrets from him.'

'Speaking of secrets,' the ColU said now, 'I have studied your records, *quipucamayoc*. I believe I know the nature of the jonbar hinge that separates your reality from ours.'

They both turned to the slave who bore the ColU. He dropped his gaze as always.

'Tell me,' Inguill snapped.

'Yes,' Fabius said with a grin. 'Tell me where we Romans went wrong! Perhaps I can put it right beyond the *next* hinge.'

'There was nothing you could have done. Nothing anybody could have done. There was a volcano, Quintus. A devastating explosion on the other side of the world. This was some hundred and eighty years before the career of Cusi Yupanqui, Inguill, your empire builder.'

379

'The Romans and the Brikanti were already in the Valhallas, the Romans for more than a century. Inguill, your own culture had yet to rise up, but already there were civilisations here – cities, farms. The Romans planted colonies in the *antisuyu* forest, but had only minimal contact with the continent's more advanced cultures.

'Then the volcano erupted, on this world. A great belch. The site of immediate devastation was far away, but the ash and dust and gas must have wrapped around the planet.'

Inguill's eyes widened. 'I know something of this. The Tiwanaku, later a people of our empire, who lived by a great high lake, suffered a "dry fog" obscuring the sky, crops failing, swathes of deaths. All this they wrote down in their histories, which our scholars retrieved in turn when the conquest came.'

The ColU said, 'These western continents suffered, then. But because of vagaries of wind directions and seasonal changes, the eastern continents suffered far more – Africa, Asia, Europa. I have found little evidence for what happened to the Xin. But, Quintus, Rome was grievously damaged. There was mass famine within the Empire, and invasions by peoples from the dying heart of Asia, who brought plague. The Empire never recovered its former strength, and certainly abandoned its holds in the Valhallas, giving up its wars there with the Brikanti.

'And meanwhile, in Valhalla Inferior, under Cusi Yupanqui and others, the Intip Churi rose up—'

'And when we began to push into the jungles of the *antisuyu*, we found Roman colonies.'

'Yes. Though much degenerated, they preserved some of the skills and traditions of the old world. The Incas took what they wanted from these Roman relics – notably the secrets of the fire-of-life and of iron-making. The Incas' strongest metal before this contact was bronze. I doubt that a trace of the blood of those Romans survives today, Quintus. But their legacy transformed the Incas.'

'All because of a volcano,' Quintus said heavily. 'And I wonder if those devils who require us to build their Hatches had something to do with *that*. For all these changes in the fabric of the world seem to be accompanied by huge violence, vast destruction.'

Inguill smiled coldly. 'The intervention of destructive gods. *We* know all about that, Quintus. Well – history is fascinating to me, as you both know. But it is the future that concerns me now. Will you be ready to disembark in the morning?'

They wandered along the beach, discussing details.

Later, Chu Yuen murmured to the ColU, 'You did not tell them all that you had learned, Collius.'

'I told them what was necessary. I considered that a fee to be paid to the *quipucamayoc* for her assistance with this flight.'

'But the evidence Inca philosophers have found of kernel energies at the volcano site – your suggestion that the eruption was made even worse by yet another war inflicted on mankind by the technologies of the Hatch builders – Quintus almost guessed it.'

'They don't need to know that. Not now, not today. Inguill and Quintus must work together; they have much to achieve. I don't want them to feel helpless.'

'Do you feel helpless, Collius?'

'Not I, Chu Yuen. Not I. Come now, we'll go back to camp. You must be hungry after the day's march ...'

CHAPTER 54

The palace of the Sapa Inca was, Mardina learned, not so much a palace at all as a city in itself, a fortified town within a town. Protected on all sides by thick stone walls faced with green tiles and sheets of gold, it was shielded from above by a stout steel grill, and by squads of axis warriors wearing some kind of rocket pack who flew continually in pairs over the compound – Cura said there was even an air shelter to be pulled over the whole compound should Cuzco's main dome fail.

But Mardina and Clodia were led past barriers and guards, straight into this most secure of sanctuaries. They were guided along a kind of ornate tunnel to a central block, and then through corridors and halls whose walls were covered with bewildering displays of coloured tiles, some depicting people or animals, others showing only abstract designs.

They had said goodbye to Ruminavi for now, but his wife Cura rushed them along. 'We must hurry,' said Cura. 'It's a shame not to give you time to take in everything better ... And a shame of course that you're not more appropriately dressed, but that will be forgiven.'

Clodia said, 'These are the best clothes we have, from the *ayllu*.'

'Believe me, *nothing* you brought will be suitable for Hanan Cuzco. And conversely you will be given everything you need here.'

'But our luggage—'

'That will be kept in storage until it's time for Mardina to leave. That's the official plan at least ...'

The girls exchanged glances at that. Mardina would be leaving, then, but not Clodia, if the Incas got their way.

They came to a heavy door, armoured, guarded and evidently airtight, and passed into another chamber of dazzling beauty through which they hurried, dragging themselves along rails and ropes. The deeper in they moved, Mardina noted, the more people they encountered. They all seemed slim and tall – even those not obviously axis-adapted – elegant, dressed in colourful finery, with elaborately prepared hair. Most had huge golden plugs in their earlobes. Many were very beautiful, even the servants, and Mardina remembered how the prettiest children of the provinces were taken away from their families to serve here. In the lack of gravity, they swarmed and swam in the air. To Mardina, rushing after Cura, it was like passing through a flock of exotic birds.

And where the girls from the *ayllu* passed, there were stares and sneers and pretty laughter behind raised hands. Mardina glowered back.

Clodia said, 'There seem to be many soldiers here. I thought everybody loves the Sapa Inca—'

'Who protects and feeds them – of course they do,' Cura said. 'It's his family that's the trouble. On the death of an Inca his successor should be chosen by a council of the *panaqas*, factions within the family. But Incas generally have many sons by many wives – although the children by his full sister should have precedence. So while an Inca is healthy there is squabbling and manoeuvring to gain his favour and that of the *panaqas*; when he starts to fail there is frantic negotiation among the factions; when he dies the succession can often degenerate into a bloody contest; and even when a winner is announced—'

'People hold grudges,' Mardina said. 'I'm told it's often like that for the Roman emperors, or *was*, before.'

Cura smiled. 'Educated people try not to worry about it. The bloodshed generally doesn't extend beyond the court itself. And it is a way of keeping the line strong; only the toughest survive.'

Now they had to work harder, pushing through crowds that were mostly streaming ahead the way they were going.

'I'm getting winded,' Mardina said. 'What is it we're going to see?'

'Why, it's the procession of the Inca himself. You're lucky to have arrived on such a day, to see it in your very first hour here. Once a month he travels around Cuzco – I'm surprised you haven't heard of this even out in the *antisuyu*.'

Mardina glanced at Clodia. 'I think most people out in the country gossip about who stole whose potato, rather than goings-on at court.'

'Well, that's their loss. And this particular month, every year, the Sapa Inca comes to the Hall of the Gaping Mouth.'

'What's that?'

Cura smiled. 'You'll see.'

She led them through one last entrance – huge doors flung open – into a hall containing another three-dimensional crowd, more colourful, gorgeous people flying weightlessly everywhere, and axis warriors aloft, eyeing the populace suspiciously. The hall in some ways was like any other they'd passed through, brilliantly lit by vast fluorescent lanterns, the walls glittering with coloured tiles.

But the floor here was different, for it was panelled with vast windows that showed the blackness of space below – a scattering of stars, a brighter point that might be a planet, the whole panorama slowly rotating as seen from this axis of the habitat.

Mardina was entranced. The vacuum itself was only a pace or two away. 'We must be at the lowest level of the palace – the outer hull. What a sight ...'

'Look, Mardina,' Clodia said.

'Makes me almost nostalgic—'

'*Look.* Above the windows, further down the hall ...'

Mardina looked up, drifting into the air to see over the crowd. Now she saw that to the floor's central window panes were attached upright glass tubes, a dozen of them. And in each of the tubes was a person – young, fourteen or fifteen or

384

sixteen years old maybe, six boys and six girls. Their clothes looked expensive, their faces gleamed with oils, and each wore a dazzling headband studded with precious stones. All drifted weightless in their bottles. And each passively looked out with an empty expression, confused, even baffled, Mardina thought, as if they had no idea what was happening to them.

Clodia's observation was terse. 'They look fat.'

Cura said, 'Well, of course they do. They have enjoyed the Inca's hospitality – oh, for a month or more, since their selection for this procession. And of course only one will be chosen.'

'For what?'

But before Cura could answer there was a blast of horns. The people swarming in the chamber pressed back against the walls and ceiling as best they could.

And through this living archway a procession advanced.

First came a party of men and women dressed in brightly coloured tunics in identical chessboard patterns. They moved in as stately a way as possible, Mardina thought, given they needed to use ropes and guide rails to advance. They glared at anybody in the way; they physically pushed people back or had the warriors remove them. They even swept bits of debris out of the air.

'Every one of them, even performing those menial tasks,' Cura breathed, 'is a noble, a highborn ...'

Next came a troop of noisy musicians, drummers and singers and players of horns and pan pipes, and dancers who wriggled and swam in the air.

Following them came warriors, dressed in armour of heavy plates and with crowns of gold and silver on their heads. The armour, in fact, looked too cumbersome to wear in combat, and it took the soldiers a visible effort to propel their bulk through the air.

And then came a kind of litter, pulled through the hall by dozens of men and women in bright blue uniforms. The man carried in the litter looked almost lost in a heap of cushions to which he was strapped by a loose harness. His clothes were even more dazzling than his attendants'; it looked to Mardina as if his jacket had been woven of the feathers of gaudy rainforest birds. He wore a gold crown, and a necklace of huge emeralds, and a headband from which hung a delicate fringe, over his forehead, of scarlet wool and fine golden tubes. He was younger than Mardina had expected, slim, and not very strong-looking; perhaps the family faction he had behind him was tougher than he was.

Still, he was the Sapa Inca.

Cura pushed Mardina's head down. 'You don't look him in the eye,' she said. 'Nobody looks him in the eye unless he acknowledges them.'

From her peripheral vision, Mardina saw the Sapa Inca throw something out of his carriage. They were birds, she saw, a dozen small songbirds perhaps, but they were unable to fly in the lack of weight, unable to orient; flapping and tweeting, they spun pitifully.

Then one exploded, burst in a shower of feathers.

'One,' said Cura breathless. 'They dose their feed with explosive pellets. It's quite random—'

Another rattling explosion, a gasp from the crowd.

'Two!'

And another. The tiny feathers hailed down close to Mardina's face this time.

'Three!'

And then a pause – a pause that lengthened, and Mardina seemed to sense, under the noise of the music, a vast collective sigh, as the remaining birds struggled in the air.

'That's it! Just three of twelve! The selection is made – number three it is. Look, Mardina, Clodia, the third compartment along...'

Mardina saw the one Cura meant. Standing on the window, above the vacuum, the third bottle contained a girl, slightly younger-looking than the rest, but just as bewildered. Just for a heartbeat she seemed to be aware that everybody in the hall, including the Sapa Inca, was looking at her. Fear creased her soft face.

Then a hatch opened beneath her. The puff of air in her bottle expelled her in a shower of crystals – frost, Mardina realised, condensing from the vapour in the warm air. Already falling into space, the girl looked up, her mouth open. Just for an instant she seemed not to have been harmed. Then she tried to take a breath. She clutched her throat, struggling in the air like a stranded fish, and blood spewed from her mouth.

All this just a few Roman feet from Mardina. People crowded so they could see her through the windows. They laughed and pointed, and some imitated the girl's helpless, hopeless struggle, as she receded from the window.

'You are not of our culture,' Cura whispered in the ears of Mardina and Clodia. 'But can you see why this is done? Yupan-quisuyu seems strong, solid. Yet just an arm's length beyond this window lies death – the Gaping Mouth. The Sapa Inca reminds us all of what will become of us if we fail to maintain the integrity of the habitat, even just for an instant. And it is just as the gods hover, angry, cruel, vengeful, an arm's length in any direction from our world. It is only the Sapa Inca and the order he imposes that excludes them from the human world. Do you see? Do you see?' She stroked Clodia's head. 'And do you begin to see, now, child, why it is that you must die?'

The ejected girl had stopped struggling, to Mardina's relief. She drifted slowly away from the habitat, and then, as she fell out of the structure's huge shadow, she flared with sunlight, briefly beautiful.

CHAPTER 55

Quintus Fabius walked to the crest of the ridge with Inguill the *quipucamayoc,* Michael the *medicus,* and a handful of his men: Titus Valerius, Scorpus, Orgilius the *aquilifer* with his standard, and Rutilius Fuscus, the century's trumpeter.

Once more, in the light of the new day, Quintus inspected his position. They were close to the hub here, having completed, with Inguill's help, their surreptitious journey from the western coast of the ocean by train and other Inca transports. They were in the foothills that characterised this part of the habitat – but just here they were in a relative lowland, a wide valley cut by a river fed by glacial melt. And beyond, the hub mountains rose up, clinging to the steel face of the hub itself.

'Certainly this ridge is the highest ground in the area,' Quintus observed.

'You're right about that, sir,' Titus rumbled. 'The surveyors confirm what you can see for yourself.'

'Perhaps there was once flooding here,' Quintus mused. 'Even a lake. Some of these land forms have a streamlined gracefulness. Is that possible, Inguill?'

The *quipucamayoc* shrugged. 'The history of this landscape is of course a question of engineering, not of nature. I do know the landscape artists allowed the country to evolve through stages of its own, letting it form as naturally as possible. We are always aware of the limits of our knowledge. Give the gods of nature room to do what they do best – that was the guiding principle. So, yes, perhaps it was once a lake, in some early stage of its forced formation.'

'*Engineering.*' Quintus looked to where the mountains rose, one range after another, waves of granite topped by gleaming ice – ranges that curved upwards, very visibly, to left and right, as if he was peering through some distorting glass. 'Yes, one can never forget that this place is an artefact. Now, down to business. War, *quipucamayoc*, is all about the details – about place and time. As for the place: so, Titus – will this do for you?'

'The highest ground for miles around, sir, as you say. Let them come to us.'

'And as for the timing—'

Inguill said, 'Ruminavi has reported to me that the *capacocha* ceremony is to go ahead this afternoon, as previously scheduled. Meanwhile my contact Villac the *colcacamayoc* is ready with the permissions and passes to get your party out through the hub portals to your space yacht.'

Michael said, 'I can confirm that we managed to get messages out to the *Malleus Jesu*. We had men volunteer for the details that wash the Inti windows – the details work all day, every day. As the ColU predicted, the little transmitters and receivers in the ear plugs it uses to speak to us were sufficient to exchange communications with the *Malleus* through the window glass. *Trierarchus* Eilidh knows what we're doing; we made a final check last night and she's ready for the pickup.'

'Good,' said Quintus. 'So all we need to do is get the travellers up to the portal and ready to go. Oh, and fight a battle against the army of the Sapa Inca. So, *medicus*, what of the men?'

Michael shrugged. 'The whole of this continent, the *cuntisuyu*, is at a higher altitude than the *antisuyu* where we've been living – miles higher. The air is that much thinner. However, we've rested here seven days. You've kept the men very fit. I'd judge that they are acclimatised – and they are as ready as they'll ever be to fight.'

Inguill frowned. 'Should I be impressed?'

'You should,' Quintus said. 'You see, *quipucamayoc*, though a battle itself may seem an arena of chaos to you, victory comes

389

through planning and positioning, as well as reacting to circumstances during the combat.'

'Like the *chess* you have taught me.'

'That's the idea. And I'm hoping that your generals, who are used to facing nothing more challenging than rebellions by unarmed, untrained, undisciplined villagers, might prove as poor strategists as *you* are a chess player. We'll make our stand here. This may be no more than a skirmish – but it may also be the last battle a Roman army unit will ever wage. *Aquilifer*, set your eagle standard.'

'Yes, sir,' Orgilius said proudly.

Inguill anxiously scanned the sky, looking for Condors. 'The imperial authorities will see that display.'

'Let them see us now. The die is cast, as Julius Caesar once said.'

Titus Valerius stepped forward. 'There's one detail, sir. If we're to give battle you need an *optio*. Somebody who'll be there to kick the arses of the men in the rear ranks, and hold the formation for you. Now, Gnaeus Junius is of course off on the *Malleus Jesu*. So if I may, I'd like to volunteer for the job. Just for the day, you understand, I'm not angling for a field promotion or a rise in pay—'

Quintus clapped him on the shoulder. 'You're a good man, Titus. But if you were to be taking part in this fight today, I'd turn you down; I'd want you at my side in the front rank, one wing missing or not. You're certainly not getting a pay rise.'

Quintus saw complicated expressions chase across the man's face. 'Thank you for that, sir. But – are you saying I won't be in the century when we give battle?'

'I've a much more important task for you, Titus. Remember – the battle we fight today is only a diversion. The whole purpose of this is to get Collius, and your daughter and her companion Mardina, out of this habitat, and then to Mars, where – well, as I understand it, Collius intends to challenge the strange entities at war over human history. Now, Titus, when everything blows up, I need somebody in place, up in Cuzco at the habitat exit, to make sure the final escape takes place. And indeed to provide protection on the way. Although if it does turn into a battle up *there*, we'll have failed.'

'That's where you want me to go, then, sir? But how?' He glanced down at himself. 'I am an overweight one-armed Roman legionary in uniform. I might be spotted, you know, even by these slow-witted Incas. I remember once on campaign—'

Inguill said smoothly, 'We've worked this out, your centurion and I. I'm going up shortly myself. I'll be on hand, with Villac and our other allies, to make sure Collius's party get to where they need to be. And you'll be at my side, Titus. As my *yanakuna*, my slave. A punishment for some outrageous behaviour or other.' She grinned. 'You're ugly enough, and surly enough, to make that convincing.'

Titus looked doubtfully at Quintus. 'My place is at your side, sir.'

'No, Titus. Your place is at your daughter's side. Take care of Clodia. After all, she is putting her own life at risk in this game we play today, as much as any man of the legion. And remember, I won't be leaving this place.'

'You won't?'

'Of course not,' Inguill said. 'We can get a handful of you out, but there's no way we can break out fifty men.'

Quintus said, 'And their wives and, in one or two cases, young families. It was always a dream that we would *all* be able to leave. No, the men's place is here, now, Titus, where Jesu in His wisdom has delivered us. And my place is leading them.' He peered into Titus's eyes. 'I can see you haven't thought it through this far. Well, I wouldn't have expected you to. Trust me, Titus. Do as I say. Your daughter isn't coming back here, ever – so just be at her side, wherever she goes next, and protect the rest. That's your duty now.'

Titus was visibly struggling with this. But he growled, 'Very well, sir.'

Inguill blew out from puffed cheeks. 'Well, thank Inti that's

resolved. We need to get moving, before it's too late. Look...'
She pointed upwards. 'Your activities have been noticed, at last.'

A Condor craft hung high above the air, a very obvious eye in the sky.

Quintus grinned. 'The moment approaches, then.' He clasped Inguill's hand. 'You must go. Goodbye, then, *quipucamayoc* – I appreciate all you've done for us.'

She pursed her lips. 'I don't see it as a betrayal of the Sapa Inca emperor, you know, as much as a challenge to these history-eating monsters we all face.'

'I understand that. And so we're on the same side. Go now – you too, Titus Valerius, and make sure you tell that daughter of yours what a fine Roman I believe she has grown up to be. Now let's get the century drawn up. Don't want them thinking it's a Saturnalia, do we? Give them a blast of the horn, Rutilius Fuscus...'

CHAPTER 56

There were a dozen, in all, Mardina had slowly learned, as their days had passed in chambers of unimaginable luxury. A dozen victims of the planned sacrifice. Or, depending how you looked at it, a dozen children privileged to have been selected for the *capacocha* ceremony, selected for the glory of living for ever, in the unblinking gaze of Inti.

And today was the first time they had all been brought together. Today the day on which their young lives would be ended – mercifully enough, Cura had assured her, they would never know, never feel anything. 'Why, what with the drugs and drink and rich food, some of them have been barely conscious for days...'

Mardina struggled for self-control.

The ceremony was to take place in the temple called the Qoricancha. This was a pyramid of blood-red stone, topped by layers of green, sky blue, and a chapel of pink stone at the very top.

With Mardina and other companions, Clodia and the rest of the sacrificial victims were led hand in hand through a courtyard filled with sculptures of gold: trees, flowers, hummingbirds frozen in flight, even a llama with a shepherd, as if a garden had in an instant been dipped in the liquid metal. The victims, floating in the air, many already drug-addled, stared at all this as if they could not believe their eyes.

Then they were taken inside the pyramid, and into a grand chamber whose walls were covered with gold and silver plate and crowded with shrines to the gods, and niches where, it

393

appeared, the corpses of more dead Incas resided. Over their head was a roof set with stars and lightning bolts wrought in silver. For a moment they were left alone, staring at the latest wonders.

Then a solemn young woman led them all down through an open door set into the richly carpeted floor – and then down, down through tunnels lined with precious metals and lit by oil lamps. They were brought at last to yet another room set in the basement of Hanan Cuzco, another chamber with vast windows offering a view of space. Beyond the window this time Mardina could see detail, shelves of some kind splashed with bright sunlight and fixed with scraps of faded colour – human figures, like dolls, perhaps, the details were hard to make out.

It was here that the ceremony would be performed, everybody who counted would want to be here, and finely dressed people were already pouring in. The place was soon crowded. But the twelve children with the priests and doctors who attended them were guided to the heart of the ornate mob, along with the personal companions they had been allowed to bring into Cuzco – in Clodia's case, that was Mardina, and Mardina in turn clung to Cura.

And with the children in place, here came the Sapa Inca himself, once more borne on his enormous litter, and his orderly bands of attendants and bearers, all highborn themselves – and wherever the Inca went a mob of courtiers followed, colourful, swooping through the weightless environment of the axis, each of them striving to catch the eye of the Inca or one of his senior wives or sons. As ever, grim blue-faced axis warriors, their long limbs like knotted rope, slid through the crowds, watching, listening.

In all this, however, the twelve children were the focus of attention, as they had been for days.

Attendants now gently led them forward to a row of elaborate seats, almost like thrones themselves, into which they were loosely strapped by embroidered harnesses. The children had been brought here from all over the habitat, Mardina knew, and represented many of the ethnicities controlled by the empire. There was even an *anti* girl, the tattoos on her face still livid, a child who had been even more baffled and disoriented than the rest so alien was the city environment to her, let alone the details of this exotic ritual.

And yet, seeing them side by side, there was a sameness about all the children now, even the *anti* girl – even Clodia Valeria, who had come here from another reality entirely, from beyond the jonbar hinges. For days – if not weeks or months in some cases – the children had been fêted here in Hanan Cuzco, just like those other blessed children in their bottles, and treated with alcohol, maize corn, expensive meats and seafood, even exotic drugs, all of which luxuries, Cura said with some envy, were usually reserved for the most senior of the elite. As a result they had all put on weight, their skin had taken on a kind of glossy sheen, and the drugs had made them passive, dull-witted, hard to scare and easy to manipulate.

Now the shelf Mardina had noticed earlier outside the window began to move, a platform that rose up before the row of slackly gazing children and the excited courtiers behind them. One of the priests began to declaim in the courtly, antiquated version of Quechua that seemed to be reserved for moments like this, a dialect Mardina found impossible to understand, even after months of studying the language in the *ayllu*.

Cura murmured, 'He is describing the terrible glory of Inti, and of the creator gods who give us life, and can take it away. These children are privileged because they will live for ever in the eye of Inti, never ageing as we will, never growing ill or frail – never dying—'

The *anti* girl screamed. It was a shrill, terrible sound that cut through the fog of words, Mardina's own confusion.

And now she saw why the girl had screamed, what she had seen beyond the window. That lifting platform bore, not dolls or dummies as she had imagined – it was a row of children, all around sixteen years old, all richly dressed, with elaborately painted faces and coiffed hair. They lay on their backs, their hands clasped on their bellies. In fact they looked as if they were asleep, their beautiful faces relaxed, at peace.

Mardina, stunned, leaned forward and stared through the window, from side to side. She saw hundreds of children, hundreds of beautiful corpses, stacked on a very long platform. Bodies in vacuum.

Cura whispered, 'The artistry is great, as you can see. The children are put to sleep with the utmost gentleness, and the work of the mummification begins immediately. The greatest skill is in delivering faces to look so natural, so peaceful ... Then the *malquis* are lodged outside the hull, outside the air, so that no corruption can ever taint them. Thus they begin their second life, undying and preserved for ever in the vacuum.'

'You've forgotten why we're here,' Mardina muttered.

Cura glanced at her, and something of the worshipful radiance left her face. 'You're right, of course ...'

The *anti* girl started to struggle against the harness that restrained her. The priests tried to calm her, but some of the other children were stirring now, becoming disturbed. One slightly younger boy started to cry. The disturbance was spreading out through the wider circle of courtiers, Mardina saw.

'Now or never,' she murmured to Cura.

Cura nodded. Stealthily, while the attendants were distracted, she began to loosen Clodia's harness.

And Mardina pulled a headband from Clodia's brow. She had patiently rehearsed this with Quintus and Michael, over and over before they had come here, and rehearsed it in her head daily ever since. The band, a gift from the Romans' *anti* allies, was an array of brilliant blue feathers taken from rainforest birds, the whole contained within a near-transparent cast-off snakeskin. Now she held the band at one end with thumb and forefinger, and carefully slipped off the transparent skin with her other hand, being sure not to touch any of the feathers.

Then, almost casually, she cracked the band in the air, like a miniature whip.

All the feathers came loose and flew away, a linear cloud that quickly dispersed, heading into the crowd of courtiers, in the general direction of the Sapa Inca in his litter. In the weightless conditions the feathers flew in dead-straight lines, but quite slowly, resisted by the air. Even now the priest spoke, his voice like the ringing of a bell, and the attendants tried to calm the children.

It seemed to take an age before the first of the feathers brushed the hand of one of the children's doctors. The instant it touched him he spasmed, his eyes rolled, foam erupted from his mouth – and he drifted, unconscious.

The feathers were coated in a forest toxin that, Mardina had been assured, was potent in the short term, harmless in the long term. And it evidently worked.

Nobody in the wider crowd seemed to notice at first. But when two more courtiers succumbed, and then four, and eight, and people called out, crowded back, yelled in alarm. And still the feathers, almost unseen, drifted among the people with their powerful touch.

In the enclosed space of the windowed hall the panic started quickly. People screamed and pushed for the exits. From nowhere, it seemed, axis warriors flew out of the air and plastered their bodies over the litter of the Sapa Inca, protecting him with their own flesh, and Mardina saw that some kind of armour, like blinds of steel plate, snapped closed around the litter. Meanwhile the bearers positioned themselves to get the litter out of this place of sudden confusion and dread.

And Mardina, with a passive Clodia clasped in her arms, followed Cura out of the chamber, entirely unseen.

Outside Inguill was waiting for them. 'Come. Your father is waiting, child.' She hurried them away.

CHAPTER 57

Quintus Fabius, *gladio* in hand, walked along the front line of his century. He grinned fiercely, and let the men joke with him, nodding their heads in their heavy helmets – those who had helmets at all. Keep them alert during this period of waiting, keep them relaxed, that was the trick.

And check their position and formation.

This ridge, wider than it was long, was deep enough for four ranks. Below the front rank was a respectable slope, up which the Incas were going to have to advance before they even got to the Romans. The legionaries were in an open formation, as they had long drilled, with the ranks offset so the men were standing in an alternating pattern that Quintus thought of as like a chessboard, all the men standing on imaginary black squares and leaving the white clear, so they had room around their bodies to deploy their weapons and support each other.

Some were sitting, and Quintus didn't blame them for that – save your energy, as long as you responded smartly when the trumpet blast came. Others were eating, hunks of meat or forest fruit. And the men grinned and made hushing gestures, fingers to lips, as Quintus approached one man, Marcus Vinius, a tough fighter when the battle got going but known throughout the century for his laziness around the camp. Now Marcus was sitting cross-legged on the ground, his wooden shield resting on one shoulder, his *pilum* spear propped on the other, his big bearded head resting in one hand – fast asleep. His neighbour raised his own *pilum*, as if to clatter it against his shield.

'No,' Quintus murmured. 'Leave him be. If a man can fall

asleep in a situation like this, he's braver than all of us. He has to give up his *pilum*, though. And you, Octavio. You know the rules – no *pila* today. Because the *pila* kill, and we're not here to kill if we can avoid it. Understood?'

'Yes, sir.'

The centurion walked on to the rear of the century to find Scorpus, hastily installed in the role of *optio*, stalking the back line, a bristling example of Roman discipline waiting to pounce on miscreants. Meanwhile the *medicus*, Michael, had set up a kind of open-air hospital further back from the line. He stood ready with blankets and bandages and his surgeon's kit of tools, as well as a rack of vials of potent painkiller drugs, extracted from the flowers of the *anti* forest. He had assistants, a couple of injured legionaries invalided out of the fight, and some of the soldiers' wives. Quintus nodded to him, and the Greek nodded back. Michael was no coward, Quintus knew, and he was no opponent of the military, which he had grown up seeing impose order throughout a sprawling Empire. But no *medicus*, having taken an oath to at minimum do no harm, could relish such a moment as this.

And still the Incas did not come.

Quintus stalked back to the left of his front line, to where Orgilius the *aquilifer* stood with his standard at the appropriate place. Quintus had a small farwatcher tucked in his belt; he lifted the leather tube now to look down on the ranks of Inca warriors, and their commanders at the rear. The soldiers in their units, drawn up in a reasonably orderly way, all looked much the same to him, in their woollen tunics, their helmets of steel with wooden overlays, their armour of quilted cotton with sewn-in metal panels. Their helmets especially glittered with silver and gold decorations. The commanders at the rear were gathered around a table on which rested some kind of model. The senior officers wore red and white tunics with discs of gold glittering on their chests.

'Walk with me,' Quintus snapped to the *aquilifer*. He led Orgilius back to his own command position, at the front rank's right-hand end. 'I know it's not tradition, but I want you to stay close today, Orgilius, and advise me. After all, we are fighting a foe unknown in Roman history – except, presumably, for some long forgotten skirmishes in the mountains of Valhalla Inferior, when we pushed these people out of the way to get at the Xin, our true foe. And you have learned as much about them as any of us.'

'Yes, sir.'

'Well, there's more of them than us,' Quintus said. 'That's the most basic observation.'

'But we have the advantage of position. And probably experience.'

'I know that, Orgilius. And there's no sign of them using their projectile weapons, is there?'

'No, sir. It'll be hand to hand. Sensible in a spacecraft; you don't use projectiles or fire-of-life weapons. Just like the great days of the Empire.'

Quintus grinned. 'Let's hope it stays that way – and that it does turn out to be a great day, for us. What are those generals doing at the back? What kind of toy are they playing with?'

'The model on the table is their version of a map, sir. They mould it in clay, so you can see the nature of the ground.'

'Hmm. Well, that's not an entirely stupid idea.'

'Their field commander is called the *apusquipay*. Supposedly a relative of the Sapa Inca, sir. They have a hierarchy of command—'

'The Incas would.'

'—all the way up to the *aucacunakapu*, the head of the army, who never leaves Hanan Cuzco.'

'What about their forces? They all look the same to me in those uniforms. Except for those lads with the painted faces.'

'*Antis*, sir. Specialist archers. Most of the rest are *awka kamayuq*, taxpayers fulfilling their *mit'a*. Like conscripts, or a reserve. But again they have specialities depending on which nation they're from. The *antis* use bows and arrows, the Wanka carry spears and slings, the Cuzquenos have bolas and clubs and maces.'

400

'Ah. I can see the weapons. Like our specialist auxiliaries. You did tell me much of this before—'

'It always helps to see it for yourself, doesn't it, sir?'

'Indeed it does. The central units seem to have a more standard weapons kit – clubs, axes.'

'They call the axes *chambis*. Some have whips that they call *chacnacs*. Those lads are probably *huamincas*. Veterans, specialist soldiers – not *mitimacs* – based near Hanan Cuzco, or maybe Hurin Cuzco, or at any rate at the feet of the hubs.'

'All right. But still they don't fight – we'll run out of light at this rate.'

'Sir, it might just be that our trick is working. If the girls have managed to create some kind of rumpus up in Cuzco, the top levels of command are going to be distracted, if not paralysed.'

'Yes. I have a feeling that thinking for yourself is even less welcome in the Inca set-up than it is in the Roman.'

'Also they like their rituals. Before a battle they generally have a couple of days of sacrifices, fasting. We haven't given them a chance to do that.'

'I'll send a note of apology on behalf of the Emperor.'

'*I* know how to get them going, sir.' It was Marcus Vinius, stepping tentatively from his second rank through to the front.

'Marcus Vinius! Good of you to wake up and join the party.'

'Sorry about that, sir. But I was having this lovely dream. I had this *anti* woman in my arms, slippery as a snake she was, and then—'

'All right, soldier,' snapped Orgilius. 'Get to the point. What are you doing stepping out of your rank?'

'Told you, sir. I know how to get those Incas mad.' He went to the front of the ridge, set down his sword and shield – and lifted up his tunic, exposing bare legs above the strapping of his boots. 'Hey! Pretty boys! Here's what I think of you!' He pranced up and down, flashing his legs and pulling his tongue, and the men behind him hooted and jeered.

Orgilius grinned. 'Actually he's right, sir. That's a grievous insult to any Inca.'

And, indeed, Quintus saw that Marcus's antics were evoking a response from the Incas. Some of the soldiers, and one or two of the command team, were staring, pointing at the Romans. He rubbed his chin. 'Well, Achilles had his heel... All right, Marcus Vinius, back to your rank. Now then, front rank, shields and weapons down on the ground, you saw the man...' He grabbed his own tunic. 'Follow my lead. Now!'

The entire front rank bared their legs and capered, while their comrades in the rear ranks rattled their swords on their shields, and yelled abuse in whatever Quechua words they knew. Only Orgilius, with his eagle standard on its staff beside him, stood back, laughing with the rest.

It seemed no time at all before the Incas' clay trumpets began to be blown, their sound like the voices of monsters drifting across the broad valley.

Quintus picked up his shield and sword. 'That's it, lads. Come at us in a rush, with your blood up, and your commanders already uncertain of themselves and now itching at the humiliation... Well done, Marcus Vinius, well done—'

'Sir!' snapped Orgilius. 'Missiles on the way!'

Without waiting to see for himself, Quintus stepped back into the front rank. 'Close ranks! Shields up! Come on, you slugs, move, move!'

He heard the hoarse voice of Scorpus, his field *optio*, yelling for the back rows to get into formation. Soon it was done, there was a roof of interlocked shields over the Romans' heads, and a wall before them.

Quintus crouched to see out. The missiles were arrows coming from the right, and stones from the left, for now falling short. He called over to Orgilius, 'So they're sending in their auxiliaries first. Archers and slingshots—'

'The *antis* and the Wanka, sir.'

'Just what I'd have done, if I had any.'

The mood had changed in heartbeats. Nobody was laughing now, nobody posturing. The men huddled determinedly under their wooden shields, each looking to his companions for mutual aid. Quintus heard one man noisily vomiting, and that was a good sign, that was normal too. He glanced out again. 'They're closing...'

Now the projectiles fell on the shields, clattering, battering. The stones from the slings were a harmless hail, though they made you keep your shield up, but the arrows were heavier, and came from a greater height. To Quintus, holding up his own shield, it felt like each landed with a blow like a punch to his shield-bearing arm. The shields had been the best he could get made at the *ayllu*, but they were only wood, and some of the arrows in the storm that fell found weak spots, or gaps in the wall. He heard the ghastly, meaty sound of arrows hitting flesh, and men screamed and fell – but the ranks closed up immediately to close the gap. Flowing like oil, he saw with approval, glancing back, just like oil. Seamless.

'The auxiliaries have stopped advancing, sir,' Orgilius called through the noise. 'Here come the infantry, the veterans, right up the slope towards us. But the auxiliaries are keeping up the fire.'

'Then we'll have to fight with shields raised,' Quintus yelled back. 'Hear that, you men? We've trained for this, you all know what to do.'

'Just as well old Titus Valerius isn't here, though, sir,' called Marcus Vinius. 'With that one arm of his. You couldn't even strap a shield to his stump. Why, he'd be better off fixing it to his—'

'All right, Marcus,' Quintus snapped, huddling under his own shield, his arm rapidly tiring as the pelting of arrows continued. 'Save the jokes for the Incas when we have them on the run.'

'Right you are, sir—'

'The *huamincas* are closing,' Orgilius yelled. 'Almost in range.'

Quintus shouted, 'Front rank, ready. Make every blow count, men, there's more of them than us – for now! But remember, aim to injure, not to kill. *Injure, don't kill...*'

That was a hard command for any experienced legionary to absorb – and that was why the men's precious *pila*, which

403

killed from a distance, had been banned for this encounter –
but Quintus, even as he had prepared for this clash, had been
thinking of the longer term, of a time when he would need to
argue for mercy for his legionaries, who, after all, were never
going to leave this place, whatever the outcome of the battle. If
they could show restraint now, they might be shown tolerance
in the future.

And here came the Incas, at last.

'Advance!' yelled Orgilius. 'Front rank advance, advance!'

With the rest of the front line Quintus raised his shield so he
could see, and he ran down the slope with the rest of the front
rank of the Romans, twenty or thirty paces, shields lowered.
They slammed into the lead Inca warriors. Their sheer momentum and the advantage of height helped the Romans halt the
Inca charge, and even push their foe backwards down the hill,
back into their own ranks, which turned into a confused crowd
of struggling men.

The fight closed up in a static line, a bloody friction.

Trying to keep his shield in the air against the arrows and
slingshot stones that still flew, Quintus hacked with his *gladio*
at the man in front of him, aiming for the bare legs under the
armoured tunic. He struck flesh and the man fell – but another
took his place, standing on the torso of his still-alive comrade,
and Quintus found himself parrying blows from a long-handled
axe with his sword. The Incas had whips, too, and the crack of
one such weapon caught him across the back. But the trick was
to step inside the arc of the whip so it became useless, and to
close with the man himself.

There were men at his back now, the second rank of Romans,
not pushing hard but yelling support, and prodding with their
swords. When a Roman did fall, a man from the rank behind
stepped up to take his place, and the third rank filled in behind
him, just as they had been trained. Even as he fought, hacking
at what felt like a solid mass of Inca flesh in front of him,
Quintus was aware of the wider formation of his men, how they
kept their shape, the chessboard pattern, designed to give each

other room to swing the *gladio*, or thrust with the *pugio*. Quintus could even hear, over the screaming cacophony all around him, the raucous voice of Scorpus still yelling at the rear rank to keep its formation, not to press, to keep the shape, to plug the gaps.

This battle was worth the fighting – he'd understood that as soon as he'd grasped the nature of the strange history-switching conspiracy web in which humanity seemed to be enmeshed. All they *could* do was fight, in the end, he and his men. But if in fighting this miniature campaign – even if none of them survived, in the end – if the last of the Legio XC Victrix did something to loosen the grip of that terrible empire-toppling abstract force of which the ColU had spoken, he knew in his heart, in his guts, it was worth it.

Quintus Fabius the commander had done all he could. He'd prepared and equipped his men, found the best position to give battle, led the line to the best of his ability. Now there was only the fight. Around him there was a roar, a confluence of war cries and the screams of the wounded and dying, and still the air was full of arrows and stones any one of which could kill him in a second, and still the terrible erosion of the clashing front ranks continued. In battle it was always the same. It felt like a training exercise right up until the moment the lines closed. Even then you felt invulnerable – the other man would be hit, but not *you* – and you feared fouling up more than the weapons of the enemy. But there were moments when you faced a foe, and you looked in his eyes, and it was as if only the two of you existed, the war was yours and his alone. So Quintus slashed and stabbed and swung, and held up his shield, and tried to ignore the tiring of his arms, and the pain of the small wounds he'd already taken, a scrape to the belly, a niggling stab in the shin; he would fight on with his men until he could fight no more.

The clay trumpets of the Incas sounded, a ghastly sound.

The fighting continued at the front, but Quintus could see that the rear Inca lines were pulling back – in good order, but retreating back down the steep slope of the ridge.

405

Quintus yelled to his trumpeter, 'Give the order! Fall back!'

There were three short blasts in response, and then the Romans stepped back warily from the last of the Incas. Warily, and wearily too; one man stumbled over a still-warm corpse behind him.

Quintus, breathing heavily, his *gladio* clasped in his bloody palm as if glued there, sought out Orgilius. The man was sitting on the ground, he seemed to have been hamstrung, but he had not abandoned the eagle. Quintus crouched beside him. '*Aquilifer*? Do you know what's happened?'

For answer Orgilius pointed to the sky.

Quintus looked up, and saw a Condor, a great black bird, dipping into the atmosphere above him, the leading edges of its wings still glowing from the air friction. It fired a shell that trailed white smoke. At the peak of its trajectory the shell exploded with a crack that reached Quintus's ears a heartbeat after the flash of light. He winced; he couldn't help it.

Orgilius, obviously in pain from his wounded leg, forced a grin. 'I think that was more noise than destruction. But still—'

'But still it's a projectile weapon of the sort that's supposed to be banned in here. These Incas – just like the Romans! You never use a fire-of-life weapon inside a spacecraft, until you do. So the adults have shown up, and we children must put away our toys.'

'Yes, sir.'

'Trumpeter! Signal that we're standing down.'

Orgilius looked over the field. 'I think there's a party of their leaders coming over, sir.'

'I'm not surprised. Come on, *aquilifer*, let's get you to the *medicus*.' He got an arm under Orgilius' shoulders and helped him to stand, on one leg. 'You, Marcus Vinius – carry the eagle for us. We've got a lot of talking to do, I suspect, and I need you to help me do it, Orgilius. But now we have to make our peace. After all we've nowhere else to go, have we?'

'No, sir,' Orgilius said, 'that we haven't.'

'Maybe if we fought well enough they'll let us join the *hua-mincas*.'

'It was all worth it, wasn't it, sir?'

'If they got away, Titus and the rest. If the *Malleus* was able to pick them up. I don't suppose we'll ever know if they succeeded in what they're trying. Not unless we're scrubbed from history altogether.'

'But we wouldn't know about that either, sir, would we?'

'I certainly hope not, *aquilifer*.'

'And as for Titus and the others—'

'On their way to Mars by now, I hope. But for us it's blood and broken heads, as ever. Let's find that Greek doctor for you, I'm sure he's having a relaxing afternoon ... Now all I've got to do is find one of their generals to put his foot on my neck. Have I got that right, Orgilius? That's how they can tell you've surrendered ...'

A few days later Quintus, languishing in an Inca cell, received a message, sent via farspeaker by Titus Valerius, picked up by a legionary working on an Inti window, and then smuggled to the centurion in the Inca *pukara* where he was being interrogated, or negotiating, depending on your point of view.

The plan had worked. And after escaping from the confusion of the Hanan Cuzco hub, it took the *Malleus Jesu* only days to reach Mars.

CHAPTER 58

Stef Kalinski had to be helped out of the *testudo* rover, and through the improvised airlock into the dome that long-gone Inca explorers had set up over the Hatch they had discovered. Even once she was safely inside the dome she stumbled, and had to be caught by Mardina, and led to the rest of the party.

'Damn Martian gravity,' Stef growled. 'Neither one thing nor the other.'

Mardina laughed. 'But, Stef, if you can't even get out of the *testudo* without a struggle, how will you manage the great leap between the worlds through – *that?*'

Stef glanced around to get her bearings, here on the Mars of the Incas, a heavily mined but intact Mars – very unlike the Mars that had been wrecked by Earthshine at the terminus of the lost Roman-Brikanti history. The *Malleus* had been landed close by, and over they had come in the *testudo*. Aside from the rover tracks back to the ship, *this* Mars, in this area anyhow – a copy of the ancient landscape of the Terra Cimmeria – looked pristine, to Stef's eyes. Pristine and untouched, save for this damn Hatch that shouldn't be here, and the unmanned emplacement around it. Now, holding Mardina's arm, Stef walked over to the Hatch itself.

It was just another emplacement, a rectangular plate marked with the circular seam of the Hatch itself, the surface blank and featureless, in another kernel field. Just like the one she'd first been brought to on Mercury long ago, and in a different history entirely. Just another mundane impossibility.

Already the *Malleus* crew had loaded into the dome a pile of equipment and supplies, anonymous boxes and trunks under woollen blankets, which Stef briefly inspected. Most obviously, there were none of the Romans' clumsy, brass-laden, Jules Verne-type pressure suits. The feeling among the Romans was that the Hatch builders wouldn't send you somewhere you couldn't survive. And besides, none of their supplies would last long in a non-habitable environment. It was all or nothing. There was a stove, however, a compact steel box that would serve as a heater or an oven, a technology the Roman army had developed for campaigns in wintry climes. It was without an obvious fuel source – and Stef was surprised, and somehow appalled, to learn that it was powered by a single kernel, an interstellar miracle of deadly potency stuffed inside a gadget you could dry your socks on.

Stef looked around, at the party gathered here in the dome. The ColU was in its pack on the back of Chu Yuen, of course. The other would-be travellers included herself, Clodia, Titus, Mardina – and Ari Guthfrithson, the *druidh* from Brikanti – and, to everybody's surprise, Inguill the *quipucamayoc* from Yupanquisuyu who had insisted on travelling with them from Hanan Cuzco. Of those who weren't intending to travel onwards through the Hatch, Gnaeus Junius, acting commander of the *Malleus*, stood by, with his *trierarchus* Eilidh, others of his crew – and Jiang Youwei.

They all looked at her expectantly.

Stef said, 'You all seem to be waiting for me to speak. What, because I'm the oldest? If Quintus Fabius was here, he'd be taking charge, you know, *optio*.'

Gnaeus Junius shrugged. 'I am not Quintus. I wish I was. I only wish to complete this mission.'

'Yes. It still seems impossible that we can have got those girls out of the clutches of the Incas as we did.'

'But into whose clutches,' Eilidh said, 'as you put it, some of us will have to return. After all we have nowhere to go in this system save Yupanquisuyu.'

'You will be made welcome,' Inguill said now. 'You know

about the messages I sent to Cuzco, trying to explain all this ... The Inca's advisers won't understand it all now, but with time, and your help, and the evidence I've left behind, it will make sense. I am sure Quintus Fabius and your companions will be pardoned.'

Eilidh said, 'And we can all become good citizens of the Inca empire.'

'There are probably worse fates,' Mardina said. 'Look on the bright side. At least you're too old to become a mummy and stuck on a ledge in the vacuum for ever.'

'Nor am I pretty enough,' said Eilidh drily.

'But you, Inguill,' Stef said. 'You're *sure* you want to come? The rest of us have a personal investment. I have studied Hatches all my adult life. The ColU is – well, it's on a mission. Besides, we are all already displaced. *This* history, this Inca Culture, is your home.'

She arched an eyebrow. 'Perhaps. But you know nothing of the court of Cuzco. The Sapa Inca is a weak boy, and the faction behind him is crumbling. His life expectancy is not long – and nor, as a consequence, is that of his key appointees, such as myself. That's one reason to try something new.

'And besides, I have been talking to Ari Guthfrithson. Like him I have become fascinated by the mystery of the Hatches, and whoever it is we build them for. I am seduced, perhaps, by the idea of the power being wielded here. Once I never imagined any entity could be more powerful than the Sapa Inca. Now ...'

Stef studied her, and Ari. 'Mardina goes in search of her mother. Beth was only trying to go home, as she saw it. Whereas you, Ari, have abandoned your home, abandoned everything you know, for the sake of this ambition. And you too, Inguill. I'm not sure these are the healthiest reasons for progressing with this. I think I'll keep an eye on you two.'

'But I go in search of Beth too,' Ari said. 'Look – I don't care what you think of me, Mardina. Yes, I'm just as fascinated by the enigma of the jonbar hinges as Inguill here. I was a *druidh*, a scholar too, remember. Why, if not for me none of you might have had the chance to be here at all. You might all have vanished into nonexistence when Earthshine triggered the hinge—'

'Very well,' Mardina said. 'You're forgiven, Father. Just shut up, all right?'

'And you, Jiang,' Stef said. 'You're sure you want to stay?'

He shrugged. 'There is more for me here, Stef. Though I feel a loyalty to you, as to your departed sister. Just as these people are the last free Romans in an Inca reality, so I am the last free Xin. I want to find my people. I believe there are colonies in the Yupanquisuyu. I would seek them out.'

'There are worse missions in life,' the ColU said gently.

Gnaeus glanced around. 'There's no reason to delay further.'

Clodia was staring at the Hatch. 'And I think it's ready for us.'

Stef turned to see. The Hatch surface, which had been blank and featureless, was now marked at its rim by a string of indentations: the imprints of human hands.

FOUR

CHAPTER 59

After leaving Earthshine, Beth took her time to get back to the substellar.

She made a number of detours, exploring the scenery along the route. It wasn't as if there was anybody waiting for her. Or so she thought. And it wasn't as if she could get lost; the substellar was the easiest place to find in the entire hemisphere.

She searched water courses and lakes, looking for traces of builders. She found plenty of stem beds, of the kind that had sustained builder communities *before*. The little creatures had been modular, and assembled themselves, literally, from the reed-like stems, which were themselves complicated pieces of biological machinery. But here she found no trace of the builders, or their works: the shelters they built for their young, the middens they constructed from the remains of their dead, the elaborate dams and dykes they built to control the water flowing through their landscapes.

She thought she would have all the time in the world to pursue such interests. She was, after all, home – even if home had changed while she'd been away.

She was almost disappointed when she got back to the substellar and found the Hatch wide open.

She unpacked her stuff, and boiled water for tea, and waited for the new arrivals.

Practical matters came first, as ever.

It was immediately obvious, when Stef and the rest of the group came through the Hatch, that Beth's two-person bubble tent was much too small for the eight of them – or nine, if you counted the ColU. So, just an hour after Titus Valerius had led the way through the Hatch, and as the rain began to fall, Beth organised Clodia and Chu Yuen to take down her tent and fix it up as a kind of improvised roof, stretched across a stand of close-growing stem trees. This arrangement wouldn't be much use in a storm, Stef could see, of the kind she remembered lashing the substellar of Per Ardua even on a good day. And still less would it offer any shelter if Per Ardua fell into another of its starspot winters. But today, as if in welcome of the new arrivals, the rain fell in gentle verticals from a cloudy sky, and the improvised canopy was enough to keep them dry.

Beth even lit a small fire and began brewing tea: tea she had gathered herself, she said, from a plant she'd found growing wild here, brewing in a clay pot she'd cast herself.

'Always takes a while to boil in an open bowl,' she said apologetically.

Nobody objected. The group was very quiet, in fact, gathered by the unnecessary warmth of the fire, as they waited for the tea.

Stef glanced around at her unlikely companions, relics of multiple collapsed histories, participating in what she supposed was a kind of welcoming ceremony. Titus Valerius sat with his daughter, who leaned against his muscular bare legs. Titus himself looked restless, baffled, oddly resentful, like a bull in a cage, Stef thought. Maybe he was still sulking from missing out on the battle at the habitat hub.

And Clodia was staring with obvious hostility at Mardina, who was rubbing some kind of ointment into the bare shoulders of Chu Yuen. The former slave had taken his shirt off, and Stef could see how his shoulders and chest had been chafed by friction from the heavy pack that bore the ColU. Stef, already thinking ahead to how they would survive here in the days and weeks to come, made a mental note that the ointment, whatever it was, wouldn't last for ever. But they had the ColU, she reminded herself, which for now sat on a rock of its own,

416

liberated from its customary backpack, interior lights gleaming. The ColU was a machine specifically designed to survive in the conditions of Per Ardua, and would no doubt be full of recipes for such things as skin ointments...

But Stef's old-lady maundering at this moment was missing the point, she realised, the central theme of the little scene. After their adventure at Hanan Cuzco both the girls had been glad to be reunited with Chu Yuen – but of course there was more to it than that. Chu was the only young man here – perhaps in all this world – and Mardina and Clodia were the only young women, though Clodia was a few years younger. Mardina seemed close to Chu, but Stef had no idea if there was a genuine relationship there. Anyhow, what you had here was a Chinese Adam – and two Eves.

Oddly, Stef recalled, it was not unlike the scheme the ISF and its controlling UN agencies had drawn up for the original colonisation of Per Ardua, in a different reality: to seed the planet with apparently impossibly small groups, a dozen people each or so, screened for genetic diversity, and let them work it out. Beth herself was a survivor of all that. In the end the colonists had found their own way, basically by abandoning the ISF plan and congregating at the substellar. But they had left behind a trail of blood and lust and jealousy. Trouble ahead, Stef thought, just from the difficult triangle of these youngsters alone.

And then there were Inguill and Ari Guthfrithson, sitting side by side on the far side of the fire, not speaking, looking around at the group, at Beth's improvised homestead – at the forest, the tall shafts of Per Arduan stem trees, presumably the most alien life form either of them had seen before. Beth, who had never visited the Inca Culture, was astonished by the sight of this woman in her cloak of hummingbird feathers. Inguill, looking around greedily at this new world, would say only through the ColU's translation interface that she was here to extend the glory of the Sapa Inca.

What did the future hold for those two, Inguill and Ari? They were both scholars, both highly intelligent and manipulative people. They had both, in their separate histories, more or less deduced the existence of alternate realities from the accounts of jonbar-hinge survivors, if not from scraps of evidence they'd turned up themselves. Stef wondered how they felt now that their questing had brought them to this strange, sparse, distant, unexpected place. Watching them, she realised she really had no clear idea what they were thinking – what they were scheming. Penny seemed to have been suspicious too; she had restrained Ari from following Earthshine through the Hatch on that other Mars. It was a strange thought that Stef probably had less in common with them, two fellow humans, than with the ColU: a mind calm, analytical – and loyal.

Loyal, yes. And that reflection made her realise that once again she was missing a central point. Ari, Beth, Mardina were father, mother and daughter. And yet they had barely acknowledged each other, after the initial moments of shock as the group had emerged from the Hatch and the family was reunited. Even now, sitting in this little circle around the fire, they could scarcely be further apart. Not to mention Earthshine, who was Beth's grandfather in some sense, off on the other side of the planet.

'Families,' she muttered. She caught Beth looking at her with a grin. 'Sorry. Did I say that out loud?'

'At least you broke the silence,' Beth said.

'Perhaps we're all in some kind of state of shock. This has been a peculiar … journey. It's difficult to know what to say.'

Beth nodded. 'Well, then, just say what you feel. You, at least, have been here before, Stef. As I have. And indeed the ColU.'

The colonisation unit sat silently, inner lights winking.

Beth pressed, *'You know I'm right*, don't you? Earthshine wouldn't accept it. But you know this is Per Ardua. You knew it from the minute you walked through that Hatch – as I did, months back. I could see it in your face.'

Stef looked out at the world, the mix of muddy Arduan green-brown with the more brilliant splashes of Earth life – the vertical shadows that were appearing now that the rain was stopping, and the clouds above were clearing from the face of the over-head star. 'Yes,' she admitted. 'I spent enough of my own life here. I think I could even sense it in the gravity, that slight, peculiar lightness you feel, like nowhere else I ever walked. Of course it's Per Ardua. But it's different, right? No traces of the human structures that used to be here – this was the UN's administrative centre, after all, and a pretty well-developed city grew up here. But then we don't know what timeline we're in now, what became of Earth and Per Ardua—'

'People got here,' Beth pointed out. 'From whatever version of Earth. They must have. Otherwise no tea.'

'Or, strictly speaking,' the ColU said now, 'no heavily evolved wild descendant of a tea plant.'

Stef said carefully, 'So the evidence of my senses tells me – yes, this is Per Ardua. But the differences are significant.' She glanced up, at the pale image of Proxima that, as the clouds cleared, was beginning to shine through the fabric of the shelter-canopy. 'Even the star seems different, somehow, subtly. My senses, my perception of the world, say one thing. But my head tells me that this isn't the Per Ardua I know. Not quite.'

Titus Valerius grunted, and took an angry, impatient swig of water from a flask dangling from his heavy belt. 'You talk of abstractions. This world is one thing or another, it is what you remember from before, it is not. What does it matter? We are here, now, in this place.' He glanced around at the group, at their pitifully small pile of equipment, Beth's and the Romans'. 'Our hands and hearts and muscles, and the resources we find around us. That is all we have. That is all that matters. And,' he said pointedly, looking at Beth, 'those we share this world with.'

Beth sighed. 'And we are all there is. Look, I can't *prove* that we're alone here. I haven't explored every square kilometre of the planet. But while Earthshine was here we did do some exploring, and I walked a good way off to the south-east when he began his trek to the antistellar. I didn't see anybody else, or any traces of their works. Nothing but the bedrock structures we found buried under the dirt here.' She'd shown them the sonar images on her slate. 'I'm ready to be proved wrong. But I don't believe there's another human soul on this world – nobody save Earthshine, wherever he is now.'

'And he,' Stef said drily, 'is neither human nor has a soul.'

'I didn't even find any evidence of the complex life we saw here *before*. When I was a kid. The builders, the structures they made, the other life forms like the kites in the air, the fish-analogues in the water courses.'

'No animals?' Titus snorted. 'It doesn't sound like much fun. You can't hunt a tree.'

Clodia patted his knee. 'Come, Father. Look on the bright side. We're Romans, the only Romans in all this world. You could be the Caesar of Per Ardua.' She wrinkled her nose. 'The world already has a Latin name. I never thought of that before. How strange.'

'That's a long story,' Beth said. 'I think my own mother was responsible.'

Titus growled and shook a leonine head. 'There's no value in conquering a wilderness. No farmers to tax!'

Beth said, 'But there's plenty of work to do here. I've made a start, with shelter, tools.' She grinned. 'I've dug a latrine ditch. With eight of us using it, we'd better get that extended, fast.'

'We must save the compost,' the ColU said gravely. 'For the farm we will some day build.'

Beth went on, 'The good news is there's air to breathe, water to drink – I don't know if we had a right to expect that on the far side of a Hatch on Mars. There's even food to eat. Not just tea. I've found root vegetables, things like peas, beans, squashes, even something like maize I think but gone wild.'

All this was slowly sinking in for Stef. 'Wild variants, of crop plants presumably brought from Earth. From *an* Earth.'

The ColU said, 'They could be domesticated once more, given time and patience.'

'Time, yes. ColU, how much time must it have taken for the various strains to drift so much?'

'Not long,' the ColU said. 'Not nearly as long as, for example,

420

it must have taken for the installation here at the substellar, whatever it was, to erode away to its foundations and then be covered over by metres of earth. *That* is a better indication of duration. There has evidently been plenty of time here for all this to happen – time behind us – even if, as I fear, there may be little time ahead of us.'

They all stared at the complex little unit, its glistening lights.

'Textbook enigmatic,' Stef said, annoyed.

Titus growled, 'You know, that twisted piece of junk always seems so much less *human* when it isn't in the bag on the boy's back. When you can see what it really is. Do you have something you want to tell us, you glass demon?'

But the ColU was silent.

Beth broke in, 'I'll talk to it … I grew up with it, remember. We'll figure out what's on its mind, and what to do about it.'

'All of which,' Titus said, 'is less of a priority than digging that latrine you talked about. We've got spades and other tools in the bundles of gear from the *Malleus*. At least in the army I was used to *that*.' He rubbed his daughter's shoulder. 'As is my Clodia, who grew up in army camps.'

'I can dig a ditch,' Clodia said defensively. 'I wanted to be in the army, before all *this* made a mess of everything.'

Stef studied Titus. 'This won't be the life you're used to, Titus Valerius – or you, Clodia.'

'We came here in pursuit of Earthshine,' the ColU said simply.

'Well, that's true, but—'

'The glass demon is right,' Titus growled. 'That was the mission we set ourselves. That was what *I* expected, and all I expected. That remains so.' He glanced around, at the stem trees, the face of Proxima dimly visible through the canopy. 'And this is where we have been brought – where Earthshine was brought. We must remember we are not the only agents in this matter. The beings who control the Hatches—'

'The Dreamers,' Beth said. 'As Earthshine calls them. Among other more insulting names.'

'We build these Hatches – we Romans, and you Incas,' and

he nodded at Inguill. 'But we have no control over how they *work*, do we? Over what points they connect, how they take a traveller from this place to that, one world to the next. Any more than a trained ape shovelling coal into the maw of a steam engine has control over the layout of the track. Even Earthshine does not control this.'

And Stef knew he was right. In her own root reality the Hatch at the substellar of Per Ardua had been linked to a Hatch on Mercury, not Mars. Maybe it still was, in some higher-order dimensionality. But for this trip it was as if the points had been changed, the travellers rerouted ...

Titus Valerius said, 'The Dreamers *sent* Earthshine to this world, this place – if it is your Per Ardua or not – they could, presumably, have sent him anywhere. And they allowed us to follow. Yes – allowed! The Dreamers are like our old gods, before the light of Jesu filled the Empire – jealous gods who meddle endlessly in the affairs of humans. We have been brought here for a reason, even if we don't yet see it ourselves, fully.' Titus shook his huge head. 'What we Romans do have is a sense of mission. Of purpose. As far as I'm concerned that mission remains to be fulfilled – and if the first step in doing that is to dig a latrine ditch, well, that was the first step in the winning of most of our provinces, I dare say, so let's get on with it. Just as soon as that tea brews. Well, I remember once on campaign—'

Everybody stopped listening. Beth passed around cups and began to ladle out her tea, which was boiling at last.

And Stef looked over at Inguill and Ari, who had barely said a word since arriving in this new reality.

In the heart of this world, as in a hundred billion others –

In the chthonic silence of an aged planet –

There was satisfaction.

The Dreamers understood little of the beings whose destinies they manipulated, little enough of the primary constructs of organic chemistry, let alone the second-order creature of silicon and metals that had been born in their industries, the creature that had done so much damage to the dreaming. United in wider coherences themselves, they comprehended little of individuality, of identity.

It wasn't clear to the Dreamers if any of these creatures were truly intelligent at all.

So, to minimise the risk of a mistake, they had allowed the organic-chemistry creatures who had clustered around their silicon-metal leader to follow it to this place, this ultimate destination. Perhaps they were necessary to supplement its existence. Perhaps they even formed part of its intelligence, in some collective form. Perhaps this composite group could yet achieve an understanding beyond any individual, just as it was for the Dreamers.

In a sense, Titus Valerius was right. The group had been given a mission, of sorts, by the Dreamers. It had not been compassion that had led the Dreamers to reunite this group on this world at this time: to bring Beth Eden Jones back into contact with her daughter, and the father of the child. It had not been manipulation on a human level. It had been more a question of imposing order. Of tidying up loose ends.

But time was short, and ever shorter.

And the Dream of the End Time was blossoming into actuality.

CHAPTER 60

The new arrivals agreed to live to a clock and calendar based on what Beth had already set up – her twenty-four-hour cycle was some hours adrift of theirs, which they had brought from Yupanquisuyu. But that meant that they had to stay awake a few extra hours, that first night, and then they slept uncomfortably on improvised beds, mostly under the canopy.

Beth, more used to the conditions of Per Ardua, was happy to lie out in the open. And, Stef wondered, maybe that helped her to adjust to this company, to get over the resentment she must feel at this sudden intrusion into the little world she had been constructing for herself – even if her own daughter had been among the intruders.

In the morning Beth served a breakfast of more tea and food from her stock: mostly potato, boiled and dried. The new arrivals ate hungrily but without relish, and Stef could see Beth was faintly embarrassed at not being able to offer them anything better, a totally illogical feeling but understandable.

Titus organised a party – himself, Clodia, Ari and Inguill – to extend that latrine ditch. 'It has to be done!'

And Beth led Stef, Mardina and Chu, bearing his pack with the ColU, on a short tour of her little homestead.

It was a well-chosen spot, Stef could see immediately. Beth had made her camp on top of a low rise, away from any obvious water courses; she'd have lived through all but the most monumental flooding events. But there was a stream for drinking water on the lower ground only a short distance away, and a forest clump on top of the rise that could provide fuel

425

for burning and other materials. And Beth had put in a lot of work. In addition to her bubble shelter she had already started to construct lean-tos and tepees, supported by the sapling-like stems of young native trees, and with dead stems woven to create a kind of thatch. Under the lean-tos, and in holes in the ground, she'd built up a food store: the remains of the rations she'd brought through the Hatch, as well as wild food she'd gathered from the countryside. She was even building a kind of cart.

As they looked around the little compound, Stef was reminded that Beth Eden Jones was after all a pioneer, a daughter of pioneers, who had survived in this unearthly wilderness for decades. And Beth, apparently instinctively, had gone to work applying all the wisdom she'd acquired in those days – wisdom, Stef supposed, that had been entirely useless back on Earth, after she and her parents had returned through the Hatch to Mercury. It must have felt good to use those skills, to find purpose again.

Beth showed them her clocks.

She'd set up a whole array of them, using sand and water dribbling through funnels woven from dead stems: improvised hourglasses, all running independently. And on a tree trunk nearby she was notching off the days. 'I have two chrono-meters,' she said. 'My wristwatch, and a timekeeper in the pack Earthshine gave me from his support unit. This homemade stuff is for backups for when the power eventually fails—'

'Timing will no longer be a problem,' the ColU said blandly. 'I have internal chronometers, which—'

'Which will work until *you* run out of power,' Beth said firmly. 'I did learn some basic disciplines from my ISF-lieutenant mother, ColU. You should know that. You always have backups.'

The ColU seemed to chuckle, to Stef's hearing. Since when had a farm robot learned to chuckle? It said now, 'Just like old times, Beth Eden Jones.'

'Sure it is. I'm aiming for bigger barrels, smaller nozzles, that won't require refilling – oh, for several days, enough time for

426

me to make decent excursions from this site without losing track of time.'

'Of course,' Mardina said, 'you won't need all that now, Mother. Not now that we're all here. As long as there's one person to stay behind and tend the fire and change over the clocks and whatever—'

She was casually holding the hand of the silent Chu Yuen, Stef noticed. She risked a glance at Beth, who raised her eyebrows in response. *She's not letting that boy out of her sight, and to hell with doe-eyed Clodia.*

Beth said breezily, 'If I'd known a whole gang of you were going to turn up I'd not have gone to all this trouble, would I? In the meantime, come and see what else I've built.'

She seemed proud of the plots she'd cleared, and started to seed with crops of her own. 'I may never get to see these potatoes and peas and whatnot become fully domesticated. But it's a start.'

'Of course,' the ColU said, 'now that I am here to advise we can make much faster progress.'

Beth fumed. 'Advise? I was doing pretty well before you ever showed up, you clanking heap of—'

'The work's doing you good, Mother,' Mardina said quickly. 'I haven't seen you look so fit in years. Or as slim.'

'Thanks,' Beth said drily.

'The crops are also going to be a useful winter larder,' Stef said, 'in case Prox ever decides to let us down again.'

'A future winter is very unlikely,' the ColU murmured, peering from the slate on Chu's chest, its voice muffled by the fabric of the pack. 'The Proxima Centauri in the sky above is rather different from the beast we knew, Colonel Kalinski. Much less irregular. And the incidence of flares must be a lot lower too.'

'I figured that,' Beth said. 'But I took precautions even so.' She pointed to a stromatolite garden, a huddle of table-like forms glistening brown in the watery Prox light, only a hundred paces away. 'I picked out a storm shelter to hide in – hacked away the carapace in advance. Of course we need to extend that so there's shelter for all of us. But...' She raised her face to the sky, the heavy bulk of Proxima directly overhead. 'I don't know what's going on here. This *is* Per Ardua. But *why* is it so different from what I remember? Even the jonbar hinges didn't change Earth itself that much, aside from what humanity was able to do to it.'

'We are here to seek answers to such questions,' the ColU said. 'That is true even of Earthshine. Especially true of him, even if his method of enquiry is somewhat destructive. Chu Yuen, would you please turn around? Pan the slate – let me see the sky, the landscape from this vantage ... And, Beth Eden Jones, would you show me a handful of the soil you are so assiduously cultivating?'

'Why do you want to see that? Oh, very well.'

Stef watched the former slave swivel on the spot, slowly, even gracefully. And Mardina was watching him too. He was nineteen, twenty years old now. Having spent a few days with him Stef knew that Chu Yuen was working to get his body in better physical condition, and he studied, too, reading from slates, generally alone. All this was in order better to serve the ColU, he said. Stef felt a kind of faint echo of lust of her own. If she could only shave off a few decades, the Mardina-Clodia-Chu triangle could well become a quadrilateral...

Beth, her cupped hands holding a mass of soil, was grinning at Stef knowingly.

'Beth Eden Jones, please hold the soil up before the slate. That's it – ah! See that?'

Stef and Mardina closed in to see. Something was wriggling in the dark brown soil, pale and pink. It was an earthworm, Stef saw with a jolt of wonder. There could be nothing more mundane than such a thing, and yet here it was burrowing through the ground on a world of another star.

'This is no surprise,' the ColU said. 'A potato from Earth needs soil from Earth, which is more than just dirt; soil is a complex and nutrient-rich structure in its own right. Do you remember, Beth Eden Jones, how my primary duty in the days of pioneering with your parents was to manufacture soil, using Per Arduan dirt as the basis?'

Beth laughed. 'I remember we had to haul tonnes of it with us when we moved.'

'I even had a miniature womb in my lost body, within which earthworms and other necessary creatures could be grown from stored cells. Of course I used these facilities to buy us acceptance by the Romans, on the planet of Romulus.

'But I was designed for Per Ardua, as it was. *Now* look at what we find. A soil that is evidently neither Arduan nor terrestrial, a soil that is evidently capable, still, of supporting Arduan life, like the stems, and yet an earthworm that might have been airlifted from a Kansas farm wriggles through it without hindrance.'

Beth was wide-eyed, looking down at the worm with new understanding. 'You know, when I was digging my fields I forked over these things without even thinking about it. Yet here they are.'

'Colonel Kalinski, how long do you think it would take for earthworms to permeate the continents of Per Ardua? How long for the two ecologies to mesh in this way?'

'I'm a physicist,' Stef said, faintly baffled. 'Not a biologist. A hell of a long time, I'm guessing.'

Beth said, 'A lot more than the few decades since humans first got here – the few decades I remember anyhow.'

Stef said slowly, 'In previous jumps through the Hatches – previous jonbar hinges – we jumped from location to location, maybe reality to reality, but without a jump in *time*. Correct? That's aside from lightspeed delays. If you took the Hatch from Mercury to Per Ardua it was like a teleport from world to world, with a signal taking four light years to get to its destination – so you'd emerge four years later.'

'And when we passed through the jonbar hinges,' the ColU said, 'save for lightspeed delays as you say, as near as I could determine the calendars always synchronised. Given some

429

common starting event like the founding of Rome we could always match our chronologies—'

'*Have we crossed through time, then?*' Mardina asked, a little wildly. 'Is that what you're saying? Are we off in some future? *How far?* What would happen if we tried to go back through the Hatch? And – why should it be this way?'

'I have only tentative answers to those questions,' the ColU said gently. 'We must wait to learn more.'

'OK,' Beth said. 'Then come and learn about this…'

She led them further away from her camp, down a slope towards the narrow, fast-flowing stream that provided her fresh water. Here, by the stream bank and in the water, stems grew more thickly.

Beth paddled out into water that lapped over her boots, and knelt to touch a broken stem, almost tenderly. 'One reason I came back to the substellar to live is because Earth life seems to prosper best here. Well, the stuff I could see – I wasn't searching for earthworms. And I needed that, of course, to survive, the food crops. But if you go further out there are stretches that could be the Ardua we used to know, Stef, ColU. Stem banks and Arduan forests and stromatolites. *But there are no builders.* Not a trace of them. No middens and dams… No kites. None of the complex forms we saw when I was growing up – hell, that helped us survive.'

'No more Mister Sticks,' said the ColU gently.

'What happened to it all, ColU?'

Stef asked, 'Could it have been another jonbar hinge? I was there when you were debriefed, remember, Beth. When you first came through the Hatch to Mercury. You'd seen evidence of a much higher civilisation constructed by the builders.'

'Yes. We found a map, a parchment in a Hatch. A global canal network—'

'None of which you saw evidence of on the ground, or which subsequent human exploration turned up. Wiped out by a hinge, maybe. Is it possible that's happened again, ColU?'

'Unlikely. We've seen that the jonbar hinges tend to redirect the destiny of an intelligent species, rather than eliminate it altogether.'

'You mean,' Beth said sourly, 'they're made into better Hatch builders. Just as happened with humans, whatever the cultural cost.'

'Precisely. Of course it's not a neat process. The builders *we* saw seemed to have fallen away from that capability, somewhere in their own past. But I think what we're seeing here is not the product of a jonbar hinge but—'

'The result of time,' Stef said, looking around, beginning to understand. 'And worlds too, the framework for life, change with time. I'm being slow here, slow to pick up your hints, ColU. I am, or was, a physicist – not an astrophysicist, but I ought to be able to think about huge spans in time, as they did.

'With time – a *lot* of time – as dwarf stars like Proxima age, they settle down. Become more quiescent. Planets too lose their inner heat. Volcanism, tectonic shifts tend to seize up. Per Ardua was a pretty active place when we knew it, Beth, and Prox helped too by serving up star winters, flares. But now, it's evidently much more peaceful. A quieter world under a quieter sky. And on a quiet world—'

'You can live a quiet life,' the ColU said. 'Beth Eden Jones, a big brain is expensive, energetically. On a more static Per Ardua, such luxuries have long since been evolved out. They just weren't needed any more, you see? Instead all you need to do is find a sunny rock, spread out your photosynthesising leaves, and bask for ever more.'

Beth stared around. 'So that's what became of the builders? If they devolved – broke back down to the stems they were made of – how long would that take?'

'So,' Stef said, 'we come back to time again, ColU. And a hell of a lot of it, it seems.'

'A clock is ticking,' the ColU said now. 'I saw this when I was able to study the universe, aboard the *Malleus Jesu*, in the gulf between the stars. Echoes in the sky, of past events and future.'

'What clock?' asked Stef, growing exasperated. 'What events?'

'Beth Eden Jones, you have done a fine job of survival here. But our mission is to do more than survive. We must find Earthshine – while we still have time to do so. And I can't see the sky from here. Not in this permanent day. I must see the sky, I must...'

'Why?' Stef snapped.

'Because *that* is my ticking clock.'

'We'll have to leave here, then,' Beth said.

'Yes. We need to follow Earthshine, we must make for the antistellar... We must cross the darkened face of the world. We'll need to prepare – warm clothes, food. It will take some time – but we must do this as soon as we can. I will tell you more when I know for sure myself,' the ColU said patiently. 'But for now, let's begin to plan. We have a long journey ahead... Come, Chu Yuen, if you please.'

As Chu turned to begin the walk back to Beth's camp, Stef saw Mardina's hand slip into his, and squeeze tightly.

CHAPTER 61

When Stef and the others returned to the camp, and began the discussion about leaving for the antistellar, Ari drew Inguill aside.

They walked away from the others, on the pretence of inspecting the latrine ditch they had been working on. When they were out of earshot, Ari plucked out his earpiece. 'I can speak Latin,' he said in that tongue. 'Can you?'

'A little.' Inguill removed her own earpiece. 'I studied it in the course of my historical surveys. And my grasp has been refreshed by my contact with your group.'

Ari took the earpieces and set them down some distance away. 'Then let us communicate in that way. I would prefer not to have our conversation passed through Collius.'

She smiled. 'I think I know why.'

He eyed her. 'You and I are not like these others—'

'"These others",' she said drily, 'include your daughter and her mother.'

He smiled back. 'That's a long story. Nevertheless. You and I *see* further than the rest. We would not have come on this astonishing journey across the reality sheaves otherwise. Indeed I was blocked, once, from progressing even faster, from following this Earthshine into mystery, through a Hatch on a different Mars. And now we are here, in this place, wherever it is—'

'Wherever and *when*ever.'

'We are not here to dig ditches.'

'I agree with that,' she said.

'Or to grow potatoes, or build lean-tos. Or to wait around

433

until my daughter and Clodia Valeria rip each other to pieces over the Xin boy.'

She laughed. 'You noticed that too. Then why are we here, Ari Guthfrithson?'

'Isn't it obvious? We are fascinated by the jonbar hinges. Whole histories are being wiped away, as if by the wave of a hand. To have such power—'

'You think that is what this Earthshine has gone to seek.'

'Isn't that obvious too?' His eyes glittered. 'Now my wife and the rest, goaded by the ColU, are considering an expedition. We will all march off into the dark and the cold. But first we will grow more root vegetables, so that we won't be hungry. Even then we will move at the pace of the slowest of the group. And all the time we will be in the control of the ColU—'

'What are you suggesting, Ari?'

He stepped closer to her, close enough to whisper. His face was hard, determined. She could smell boiled potatoes on his breath.

'I'm suggesting that you and I should leave, now.'

She'd known this proposal was coming, yet her heart beat faster in response. 'You're talking about walking around the world. How—'

'There may be ways to move more quickly. We can follow the trail Earthshine left.' He pointed to the south-east. 'It's clearly visible. As for food, the store my wife has built up should be enough to sustain two.'

She grinned. 'If stolen from her.'

'If stolen, yes. The pressure suit she has preserved since she came through the Hatch from Mars would provide enough warmth for us, I believe – it is a thing of multiple layers, a thing designed for the harshness of Mars, which, even if separated out, could protect the two of us from the chill of this place, Per Ardua. There are tools, even weapons we could take.'

'You would betray your wife?'

He shrugged. 'I don't think of it that way. Perhaps I am saving her from her own foolishness.'

'Why should we do this?'

'Because of the power this Earthshine pursues. Huge power, for those brave enough to grasp it. And worthy of it.'

She took a breath. 'I feel – intoxicated. As I have ever since I started to uncover the strange mystery of this weaving of history. As if I was a child, plummeting down a hub-mountain glacier, out of control … We have both already walked away from our worlds, the very reality we knew, the history, the culture. Now here we are speaking of walking off into the dark. To our deaths – or unknowable glory.' She looked at him. 'Do you believe that when your history died, your gods died with it?'

He shrugged. 'In the Christian tradition Jesu died and lived again. And in the tradition of my ancestors all the gods die, in a final war at the end of time, but another cycle begins.'

She nodded. 'Our priests also talk of cycles of calamities that punctuate time. Perhaps on some deep level we, our ancestors, already knew this is true, this meddling by the Dreamers – whoever and whatever they are.'

'So,' he said, 'will you come with me? Will you dare outlive your gods?'

Again, a breath. 'When do we leave?'

CHAPTER 62

Titus Valerius, like Ari and Mardina and some of the others, had trouble adapting to the unending day of Proxima, Stef saw. The legionary found it difficult to structure his day, to sleep at night.

But he was in his element when it came to planning the trek to the antistellar. Even the betrayal of Ari and Inguill, who had taken so much of their stock and supplies with them, seemed to make no difference. He had a way of defeating problems just by waving them away.

'So we must walk around this empty world. Pah! In my time I have participated in marches the length and breadth of Europa, Africa, Valhallas Inferior and Superior, and deep into Asia. Marches across hostile territories, into the frozen tundra where wild horsemen still lurk at the fringes of continent-spanning forests – and through Valhallan jungles where every leaf conceals a scorpion, where every shadow is likely to turn out to be a skinny little warrior with a blowpipe. What dangers do we face here? That we will trip over an earthworm? We will do this. I will lead you. We will march – and that is what the Roman army is for, above all else: marching. And if we have the spare energy I might have you all build a road while we're at it, to ease the journey back. Why, I remember once on campaign—'

'I'm enjoying this performance, Titus Valerius,' Stef said with a grin, 'but I don't believe a word of it. For one thing, you're not a surveyor, or a map-maker. There's going to be nothing to wage war against on this trip. This will be an exercise in planning, Titus Valerius. In logistics. In survival.'

'Survival? In a country where potatoes and beets grow wild?

Why, it will be like a stroll through the estates of the Emperor Hadrian.'

She eyed him. 'ColU, do you think he really understands what he's taking on?'

The ColU sat on the ground beside the two of them, on a blanket spread out over the rusty dirt outside the shelter. Nearby, a low fire flickered, slowly boiling up another pot of water. 'Titus Valerius is a brave man and we are lucky to have him at our side.'

Stef grinned. 'Tactfully put.'

Titus Valerius scowled. 'You tell me, then, star lady. Describe what it is about this journey that I don't understand.'

'I *have* done this before, Titus. To begin with, we are going to have to travel all the way around half a circumference of the world.' With a broken stem she sketched a circle in the dirt, alongside a bold asterisk to which she pointed. 'Here's Proxima, the star. The circle is Per Ardua, the planet. Per Ardua keeps one face to the star at all times. So—' She cut Per Ardua in half with a bold stroke, and scribbled over the hemisphere turned away from the star. 'One half is always in daylight, one side is always in shadow – in endless night. The substellar, the point right under the star in the sky, is here.' A thumbmark, on the world's surface right beneath the asterisk. 'Which is where we are. And that's why the star is always directly over our heads. The antistellar is on the other side of the world.' Another thumbmark. 'It couldn't be further away from this spot. And to travel there ...' She sketched a broken line stretching around half a circumference of her planet, from substellar to antistellar. 'You see? The shortest possible distance we have to travel is half of a great circle – I mean, if we just head straight for the antistellar. That's without detours, for such details as mountain ranges and oceans and impenetrable forests and ice caps. And the distance – ColU?'

'Per Ardua is a little smaller than Earth. Around twelve thousand Roman miles.'

'And, can you see, Titus? Half of that will be in daylight, and half in the dark. Six thousand miles across icebound lands and frozen oceans.'

'In the dark?' Titus was frowning now. 'Where nothing will grow?'

'Nothing but icicles on your beard. Exactly. Now do you see the challenge? *We* had a vehicle, motorised. It was still gruelling. Beth has been building a cart.'

Titus nodded. 'Even if we completed it we would have to *pull* it. We have no engines, no draught animals. On the march, without vehicular transport, we expect to cover around twenty miles a day. So the journey would take us ...'

Stef smiled. 'Leave the mental arithmetic to me. Six hundred days. The best part of two years!'

'And one of those years in the dark and cold, where nothing grows.'

She nodded. 'It's easy for us to express an ambition to reach the antistellar, Titus. But it may not be physically possible.'

He grinned. 'You should be a centurion, Colonel Kalinski.'

'Really?'

'You never tell a Roman something isn't possible. Romans know no limits.'

'We have one advantage,' the ColU said. 'Ari and Inguill went ahead of us, as you say – and Earthshine went ahead of them. There ought to be a trail we can follow, easily visible on the surface of this static world. For, even if Ari and Inguill can have had little idea what they were walking into, Earthshine *will* have known what he was doing. I have no doubt he would have carried a full information store on Per Ardua, as explored by our people, Stef, in our home reality.'

Titus frowned. 'You mean, he had maps of this world?'

'More like a memory of maps.'

Titus pointed at the ColU. 'And you, demon. Do you have a memory of such maps too?'

'In my humble way, I was one of the pioneers of Per Ardua myself. And after humanity's large-scale emigration to Per Ardua I made sure I kept track of the latest survey data, the exploration results. Yes, I "remember" the maps – at least of Per Ardua as it was.'

'Very well.' Titus lifted the ColU bodily, and set it at the edge of the blanket, facing an unmarked stretch of dirt. 'Together, you and I will draw a map of this world – the parts I need to know about – so that I understand. Then I will take my daughter Clodia, with light packs, and we will follow the tracks of Earthshine, and Ari and Inguill, to scout out a route. Meanwhile you, Stef, will organise the preparations here. Get that cart ready to travel. Gather potatoes and beets. Grow *more* potatoes! It may be some weeks before we are ready to leave. And as for the dark side – let us get there first, and then we will plan anew.'

She saluted him Roman style, fist to chest and then arm raised. 'Yes, Centurion! You're right, you know.'

'I am?'

'If anybody can get us to that damn antistellar, you can. I have faith in you, Titus. Maybe not as much as you have in yourself... Tell me one thing, though. Why are you taking Clodia on this scouting trip?'

He grunted. 'Isn't it obvious? To keep her away from Mardina and the Xin slave boy. We've enough troubles already. Now then, ColU, tell me where to begin with this well-remembered map of yours...'

CHAPTER 63

In the end it was more like two months before Titus Valerius, having returned from his scouting expedition with Clodia, declared that they were ready to depart.

They broke camp. Everything useful and lightweight was loaded onto Beth's cart, or was stored in improvised packs on the walkers' backs. They loaded as much as they could of the food store Beth had begun, cooked and dried and packaged up. Titus had decreed that they would forage as they moved, saving as much of their store as possible. The ColU itself was placed on the cart to relieve Chu of his burden, bundled up in a blanket and lashed in place.

The camp had been Beth's home since she had first come here through the substellar Hatch with Earthshine. Stef watched her regretfully closing down her array of homemade clocks.

At last Stef found herself helped up onto the cart, with Beth at her side. Titus handed Stef the lightweight ropes that constituted the cart's rudimentary steering system.

'Thanks,' Stef said sourly. 'So the old lady is just baggage.'

Titus scowled at that. 'You're the oldest. You'll walk the least. Your job is to control the cart. But you *will* get off that cart and walk when I tell you, because I need you to stay fit and healthy.' He had a sheaf of bits of parchment and paper on which he'd worked out his schedule for the trip, tucked under his damaged arm. 'It's all in the plan.'

Stef sighed. 'I hate to be a burden.'

'Just do as you're told.'

'Yes, Centurion!'

Beth held Stef's hand. 'I wouldn't worry about it. He thinks of you as a soldier, if maybe a wounded one, or he wouldn't be so tough on you.'

Stef grunted. 'Well, I was military myself. I guess you're right. With men like Titus, it's when they're nice to you that you have to worry.'

'And as for walking...' Beth patted the frame of the cart. 'Be careful what you wish for. This is my design, remember, and we're not exactly overstocked with tools and raw materials, especially since Ari and Inguill took so much of the good stuff. If this gets us halfway to the terminator I'll be impressed.'

'Oh, I think we'll do better than that,' Stef said, though she spoke more in hope than expectation as she looked back at the cart.

The basis of it was the frame of 'wood' – actually split-open trunks of stem trees from the substellar forest – lashed together with rope and vines that Beth had begun to build. It rode on wheels of wood rimmed with tough nylon rope. Rims of steel or iron would have been better, but they didn't want to take the time to build a forge to achieve that, and they'd brought spare wheels.

In addition, the ColU had ordered that sled-like rails should be fixed to the cart's underside, an obvious preparation for the icy dark-side journey to come. And, under the direction of the ColU and Titus, the cart had even been made ready to serve as a shallow-draught boat. The sides had been built up and the whole had been made waterproof, with a coating of the marrow that you could extract from any stem or the trunks of the forest trees. The 'marrow' wasn't marrow but a complex organic product in itself, capable of a kind of internal photosynthesis based on the abundant heat energy available from Proxima. The travellers disregarded this biological miracle, and were only interested in using it as sticky gunk to seal cracks in their cart.

Stef thought it was all a marvel of improvisation and ingenuity, but they could only hope their preparations were adequate to meet the challenges ahead.

At last they were ready to go. Under Titus's rough direction, they formed up into a kind of column. The cart, of course, needed pushing and pulling, and Titus himself, Clodia, Mardina and Chu were assigned to that duty, two ahead, two behind. They'd have some help from Beth, but she was spared the worst of the work. In her late fifties she was being treated as another honorary old lady, to her irritation and Stef's amusement.

'This is it, then,' Titus cried. 'A journey around this strange world – a journey that begins with a single step.' He drew his *pugio*, his dagger, and held it aloft. 'Are you ready for war?'

'Yes!'

'I said – are you ready?'

'Yes!'

'Then we advance!' He settled into his own padded harness, positioned his damaged arm, and leaned into the traces.

The cart jolted into motion, nearly throwing Stef off in the very first moment.

So it began.

Titus and Clodia had scouted out their route well. It roughly tracked the trail created by Earthshine and then followed by Ari and Inguill, but from the beginning it was almost all downhill – or at least on a gentle declining slope – and led them through reasonably open country, following the water courses that threaded away from the high ground of the substellar plateau. The 'draught animals' seemed pleasantly surprised to find that the exercise wasn't as hard as they might have feared, although Stef kept her mouth shut about that, given that she didn't have to share in the labour.

Titus called a halt after about a quarter of an hour, so that people could make minor adjustments to boots and harnesses and other bits of clothing. Then they pressed on for another half-hour, until Titus called another stop for water, and then another half-hour when he rotated the crew, with Beth slipping into the traces vacated by Mardina.

After just three hours – Stef guessed they'd gone only five or six miles – Titus decreed that they were done for the first day.

The rest were anxious to keep moving now they'd started, with the *thousands* of miles that lay ahead of them weighing heavily on their minds. But Titus was nothing if not an experienced marcher, and he knew what he was doing. He had them all strip off their boots, bathe their feet in a stream, and then slip into the loose, open camp sandals he'd had them make. This first day, unpractised, it would take them longer than usual to make camp, to get into the routine of digging a latrine ditch and gathering food and collecting water, and Titus wanted to be sure they did all this properly. Also Titus wanted to check over the cart, to see if it was passing this ultimate test of roadworthiness. They had spare parts and pots of marrow to fix up obvious flaws.

'Come on, come on!' Titus chivvied them as they got to work. 'When Roman legionaries are on the march they set up camp every night—'

'Sure they do.'

'And you don't hear a word of complaint—'

'Sure you don't!'

'Why, I remember once on campaign—'

'Save it, Titus Valerius!'

Once the labour of the camp-building was done, and they were gathered around the fire they'd built for the night, Stef could see the wisdom of Titus's management. They'd all encountered unexpected difficulties, even if Stef's had only been the lack of a cushion under her bony behind. And they were all more tired than they'd expected to be. But they'd got through the day, they'd done everything Titus had demanded of them, and they knew now they only had to repeat this routine in the days to come.

Before they bundled up under their blankets and clothing heaps to sleep, huddling together under Beth's stretched-out tent, Titus came around one more time, accompanied by Clodia with a simple medical pack. The legionary insisted on checking everybody's feet, for bruises, chafing, incipient blisters. 'Now that you're all soldiers on the march you'll learn that your most important items of equipment are your feet. Look after them and the rest follows. And the sooner you're all capable of doing this for yourselves, the better.'

'Goodnight, Titus Valerius.'

'Goodnight, auxiliaries …'

And, after Titus had done his round, Stef heard rustling, saw shadows slip through the dim light under the canopy. They were unmistakable: Chu Yuen and Mardina Eden Jones Guthfrithson, clutching blankets, hand in hand, making their way out from under the canopy and into the shade of the forest.

The next day they made better progress. And the day after that, better still.

Stef made a deliberate effort not to count the days, not even to try to estimate the distance travelled. She knew she could leave that kind of management to Titus and the ColU. And besides, she slept better if she tried not to think about the monumental journey ahead. She thought of this as a new way of life, a long tunnel of routine that was going to fill her days for the foreseeable future. Sleep, break camp, march, make camp, sleep … Without beginning, and without end.

But, gradually, the country began to change.

They descended from the substellar high ground, and the haulers began to lose the benefit of the downward slopes Titus had cunningly scouted for them. On the other hand the weather on the lower ground, away from the permanent low-pressure system over the substellar point, became milder, less turbulent. Day by day there was less wind and rain. And the vegetation around them responded. Now the broken forest that characterised the relatively unsettled substellar gave way to more open country, with forest clumps separated by broad swathes of ground-hugging, light-trapping vegetation.

During the long hours between the days' marches, the ColU had Chu carry it out into the country away from the camp to inspect the changing terrain. Out of curiosity, and when she had the strength, Stef followed them – often with Beth, who was curious to see more of what had become of this world that she still thought of as home.

At the end of one unremarkable day, they walked side by side over a plain almost covered in sprawling green leaves, like tremendous lilies, Stef thought. Systems of three leaves united at a central stem, covering the ground, and basking in Proxima light. When she knelt down to look closer she saw that the leaves were firmly anchored to the ground by fine tendrils, covering every square centimetre. No competitor was going to swipe *this* plant's growing space, this share of the starlight. It was a very Arduan scene. But when she dug her hand into the ground beneath one leaf, she came up with what looked like an authentic sample of terrestrial soil, complete with an earthworm, a thing like a woodlouse, and other creeping terrestrial creatures.

As they walked back to camp, Stef gradually got a broader sense of the wider landscape. With the star static overhead, and every square centimetre of ground colonised thickly by the green of life, this part of the world was like a huge, collective, cooperative system, optimised over time to extract every scrap of energy from the light falling from the sky. Stef felt as if she was in some vast greenhouse, old and decayed, the glass choked by lichen, moss and weeds – with here and there a vivid splash of Earth life embedded in the rest.

In the middle of the next day they came to the bank of a river, wide, placid.

Stef clambered off her bench and hobbled over to Titus. He was standing with his one good hand on his hip, staring out at the water, grinning. 'This is as far as I came with Clodia, during our scouting trip. Well, I judged we need come no further. This river clearly flows out of the substellar point—' and he waved his hand back in the direction of Proxima '—and, no doubt fed by many tributaries, continues to flow in a roughly

445

south-easterly direction. Well, you can see that. Now, Stef, tell me I'm no surveyor. Madam, I present a highway as straight and true as any Roman road. And now, for a time at least, we can all ride in comfort, as *you* have been all the way from our first camp.'

'Aye aye, cap'n.'

'I beg your pardon?'

'I imagine that didn't translate ...'

They made camp in the usual manner. Then they got to work reassembling their cart into a small boat – detaching the wheels and axles, going over the seals with their marrow caulking, and digging out paddles they'd crudely made from dead stems lashed up with rope.

In the breaks they took advantage of the river, washing their feet and clothes, dunking their whole bodies luxuriously in water that ran refreshingly cool. But Titus banned any swimming. Though the river ran with a strong current, it was obvious that the bed was choked with life, and he didn't want anybody getting caught up in that.

It took them forty-eight hours before they were ready to embark. After so long on the road, many days already, they had all learned not to rush.

As with their first day's walk, Titus decreed that their first jaunt in the boat would be a short one, to ensure they ironed out any flaws. He made sure that those to whom he entrusted the paddles had fabric wrapped around their palms for protection, and ponchos improvised from lightweight survival blankets to keep off the spray. They even had to wear their light camp sandals, so that their boots, precious items of equipment, could be bundled in waterproofs. It was all detail with Titus, Stef observed.

It visibly infuriated Titus that, lacking an arm, he couldn't manage a paddle himself. But he insisted on riding at the stern, where a crude rudder had been attached.

Once they were all loaded aboard, their stuff lashed down, Chu shoved them off from the bank with a mighty jab of his

446

paddle against a rock, and they drifted out towards the centre of the river. Titus was at the stern with his rudder, Stef at the prow with her back to the river. Of the four rowers, Chu and Clodia sat together to Stef's right, and Beth and Mardina, mother and daughter, to her left. For the first couple of miles they were all silent, save for Titus's curt commands: 'That's it, we'll keep to the centre where it's deepest ... Paddle a bit less vigorously, Chu and Clodia, you're too strong and you're shoving us to the bank, we'll balance you up better when we stop ... That's it ... If we can let the current take the boat away without us having to do any work at all, I'll be happy ...'

Stef found herself anxiously watching the deck under her feet, looking for leaks. She had crossed interstellar space in kernel-drive starships, and had even walked between realities through a technology that was entirely alien. And yet a ride in this ramshackle craft, with just a few metres of water beneath her, was somehow more terrifying than all of that.

But they hadn't gone far before she was distracted by the atmosphere in the boat itself. Mardina glared at Chu and Clodia, and Clodia glared back.

'Ouch,' Stef said at length. 'I never heard a silence so loud. What the hell's the matter?' But of course she anticipated the reply.

'Her,' Mardina burst out, pointing a finger at Clodia.

Clodia looked ready to leap across the boat and take her rival on.

'Sit still,' Titus commanded his daughter. 'Wield your oar. You too, Mardina. Snarl at each other if you must but you will not imperil this vessel ... What's this about?'

Clodia glared. 'Do you really not understand, Father?'

Titus sighed. 'Being not entirely without senses – yes, Mardina, Chu, I've seen you two sneaking off in the night.'

Chu hung his head, Stef observed, as if he was still a slave who had been caught doing wrong.

'But,' Titus said heavily, 'that doesn't mean you're *lovers*.

Just because you sleep together. I mean, I remember once on campaign—'

Clodia growled, 'Oh, *Father.*'

'Well – whether or not, Mardina, I don't see what your problem is with Clodia.'

Mardina flared. 'You see us sleep together but you don't see what she's *doing*? The way she's sitting beside him now. The way she looks at him. Leans against him. Holds onto his arm when the boat rocks—'

'Don't be absurd.'

'Actually, Titus,' Beth said with a rueful smile, 'I noticed the same thing. I don't think there's any malice, though, Mardina. I don't think she can help it. Look, girls, the problem isn't with the two of you, or with Chu. It's just that there's only the three of you, three youngsters – in this boat, on this whole wretched planet. This problem was always going to come up.'

Mardina glared at her. 'Oh, how helpful that is, Mother. So what do you suggest we do? Kill each other over Chu, the way those colonists did on Per Ardua like you're always telling me?'

'Ideally we will avoid that,' Titus said with a dangerous calm. 'But while you three work it out, here are the military rules. We're on a mission here. And we also face a challenge to survive, as simple as that. You three can bed-hop as much as you like,' and he kept his eyes averted from his daughter as he said it. 'But if you come to blows, if I get a hint of a sniff of suspicion that you're putting us all in danger – why, then, I'll put a stop to the whole business. I'll cut your pecker off, slave boy, and skin it and use it as a wind sock. Let's see these young women fight over you then.'

Chu seemed to think that over. 'It would be a big wind sock, sir—'

'Shut up.'

For a time they progressed down the river in silence.

Then, from inside its waterproof wrapping, the ColU spoke up. 'Well, this is awkward. Shall we sing a song? There's one you may remember, Beth, from your childhood, with Yuri Eden

and Mardina Jones – not that *we* had a boat in those days. *Row,
row, row your boat*... Come, please join in...'

As they drifted on down the river its voice echoed from the
life-choked water.

CHAPTER 64

With time the great waterway broadened and deepened, with many tributaries flowing into it from the surrounding land, just as Titus had predicted.

Then there came a day when 'their' river passed through a confluence and became a tributary of a much wider river still. Soon the flow was so wide that it was difficult to make out the far bank. 'We're in luck,' Stef said. 'We found the local Mississippi.' But of her companions, only the ColU and Beth knew which river she meant, and even Beth, Arduan-born, wasn't sure.

Titus insisted that they should stay close to the bank, fearing stronger currents in the middle of the channel – and, just possibly, more aggressive life forms than they'd yet encountered. Even so, they swept on with what felt like ever increasing speed.

Without the physical effort of the march – the hardest work was the daily labour of hauling the craft up the bank for the night – and with Proxima sinking almost imperceptibly slowly in the sky behind them, the days passed in ever more of a blur to Stef. Even so it was a surprise when the ColU announced, that they had already been travelling for sixty days.

The character of the landscape around the riverbanks was changing once more. Much of the vegetation was waist high, and Stef was reminded of the prairies of middle America – or rather, of museum reconstructions she'd seen of such ecologies as they'd been before the climate Jolts. With the air cooler and Proxima lower still, the ground-blanketing 'lilies' were no longer so successful, and plants that stood up and bore leaves tilted towards the star did better. There were even trees here, or tree-like structures, with big leaves competing for the life-giving light, some stubby and fern-like, some quite tall and rising above the 'prairie flowers'. But in this more open country some terrestrial plants fared better too, and the travellers gratefully scooped up handfuls of wild potatoes, yams – even grapes from vines that grew laced over Arduan trees, a cooperation across the two spheres of life that the ColU said it found pleasing.

The ColU never asked for stops. It seemed too aware of the pressure on them all to make good progress, and to push on with the journey. But sometimes, during their 'night' stops, it would ask Chu, or perhaps Beth or Stef, to take it to sites of particular interest. Such as exposed rock formations – which were rare; this Arduan continent was worn as flat as the interior of Australia. And the ColU would ask for samples to be taken, for fossils to be sought.

'You'll remember, Beth Eden Jones, how frustrated I used to get! This planet was once so active, chunks of its surface forever churning up, that any fossils were destroyed, the very layers they had formed in disrupted – the whole fossil record was a mess. Now that the world is so much more quiescent there's at least a chance of finding some kind of decent record, at least of comparatively recent life forms ...'

But all it ever found were what looked to Stef like matted banks of reeds, compressed into the sandstone and petrified. If there was no significant change, no extinction or evolution, she supposed, you were going to get a featureless fossil record, no matter how well preserved. Nothing but stems for – how long? Millions of years?

What Stef did notice herself, and she discussed it with the ColU, was an utter lack of evidence of the works of humanity.

'We know people were here, once, on *this* Per Ardua. Right? The potatoes and the grapevines wouldn't be here otherwise. But where are their towns? Oh, the buildings would burn down and crumble away, but where are their foundations, and the waste dumps, and the outlines of farmers' fields? Where are the remains of their roads and rail tracks? We were on the way to setting up farms and mines all the way to the terminator. But it's all just as it was at the substellar – gone. How long would it take to erode all that to dust, ColU?'

But as always the ColU refused to speculate about time. 'We will know soon enough,' it said. 'As soon as I see the dark-side sky. We will know how long then.'

Once the ColU asked to be taken into a stromatolite garden, where those complicated mounds of bacterial layers, each about chest high, were growing together in a close crowd.

'Of all the Arduan life forms I have observed – save only the builders themselves – the stromatolite is perhaps the most characteristic,' the ColU said happily from its pack on Chu's back. 'And the most enduring. Here before all the rest, probably, and still growing strong, even now in the end days.'

And Stef wondered, *End days?*

'Yet,' the ColU said now, 'there seems to be something subtly different about these particular specimens. Beth, Chu, do you have knives?'

It had Beth slice open one of the stromatolites, through its carapace and thick trunk. Within was a greenish mush, vaguely stratified. Beth dug in with her hands, but yelped, 'Ow!', and pulled back quickly. 'Something *bit* me ...'

She called Chu and Stef over, and, more cautiously, they dismantled the slimy interior of the stromatolite, chunk by chunk.

Then they found the ants' nest. Black bodies, big, each maybe a thumb-joint long, came swarming out in protest at the intrusion of daylight.

The ColU seemed thrilled. 'How wonderful! More ecological integration, more cooperation. Perhaps the terrestrial insects feed off detritus trapped in the layers of the growing stromatolite. And the structure as a whole must benefit from the internal mixing-up by the insects. Two life forms originating on worlds light years apart, evolving ways to live and work together, for the benefit of all.'

'I expect there's a moral lesson in all this,' Beth said drily.

Again Stef was left with more questions than answers. Yes, she could understand the evolution of a cooperative community like this. But how *long* had that evolution taken? Time – the great mystery of this new Per Ardua.

They cleaned off their knives, packed the mushy organic material back into the wounds they'd created, and – with one last silent apology from Stef to the mutilated stromatolite – they returned to their riverside camp.

Ninety days out from the substellar, their faithful river at last flowed into a broader body of water, a lake perhaps, maybe even a sea. It was wide, stretching beyond their horizon, and choked with green life.

They decided not to try to cross it in the boat. So they camped on shore for a couple of days while reassembling their boat into a cart, and began the process of hauling their way around the lake, hoping to find a way to continue south-east, following their great circle. The haulers grumbled, and Titus chided them for their lack of fitness after so many days on the river.

After a couple of days they came to what appeared to be a broad isthmus, a neck of land separating their own lake and a neighbour that looked even more extensive. The isthmus led to what appeared to be higher ground to the south-east, densely carpeted with forest.

With relief that they were able to resume their course, they continued across this natural bridge. Titus strode boldly at their head, hauling on his harness with the vigour of a man half his age, Stef thought. He was magnificent in this setting, with the light of the slowly descending Proxima glimmering on the water around him, and casting an ever lengthening shadow ahead: he was the last of the Romans, pursuing one last impossible mission. Not that she was about to tell him so.

They reached the bank of forest at the far side of the isthmus. Compared to the substellar forest this was sparse, patchy – but, in the long shadows, quite gloomy. Titus and Clodia spent a day scouting out a likely route, and settled on another water course, heading south from the isthmus and cutting a track through the forest.

On they marched. As Proxima lost ever more height in the sky, so the nature of the vegetation around them changed again. The trees grew taller now, with big flaring leaves that strained to the north-west towards the lowering star, and at their feet the gathering shadows were broken by a greenish glow, reflections from the huge sprawling triple leaves. In some of these pools of illumination they found termite mounds, familiar from Earth, feeding off the reflected light of another star: another cute example of the cooperation of interstellar life in this strange environment.

They reached yet another milestone: a hundred and twenty days since leaving the substellar camp. When Stef looked back she saw that the disc of Proxima, dimmed and bloated by refraction in the thickening air, now touched the horizon. And when she looked ahead she could see splashes of light, islands in the sky. She remembered this from her last jaunt across the terminator, with Yuri Eden and Liu Tao, long ago. She was seeing the light of Proxima catching the peaks of mountains, while their bases were in permanent night, the shadow of the planet.

That was when Mardina announced she was pregnant.

CHAPTER 65

They built a camp in a valley of twilight.

They had walked into the shadow of the world, Stef realised. The sky, laden with thick cloud, was pitch-black. The only light they had, save for their own torches, came from the mountain that loomed over this valley, worn by time but still so tall that its summit and higher flanks were splashed by sunlight, and some of that daylight reflected into the valley below. Stef suspected they had stalled in this last scrap of light, before penetrating the interminable dark ahead, for reasons of instinct as much as logic; they couldn't bear to leave the unending Proxima day behind.

Titus Valerius, as always, took charge. First he had them build a camp on a rocky outcrop rising from the generally muddy ground – and it always would be muddy here at the terminator, the ColU had warned, when it wasn't snowing or icebound. It always rained at the terminator. As warm air from the day side spilled over into the chill of endless night, it dumped its moisture, and the ground everywhere would be waterlogged. But at least on this rock they could build a fire, and sleep out of the damp, and keep any rain off with their tent canopy supported by a frame of stem-tree trunks.

Then, once they were established, Titus gathered them in the glow of the fire. In the deepening cold they were already wearing extra layers of clothing, stuffed with padding; they all looked fat and clumsy.

'We've done well so far,' Titus said. As he spoke he ladled out a stew of potatoes and cabbage. 'Mostly thanks to the rivers. A

455

hundred and twenty days to these shadow lands, faster than I anticipated. But we've still got the same distance to cross again, and in the dark and the cold all the way, as I understand it. Yes?' He looked around at them sombrely. 'Some of you know this world; I was never here before. Sitting here I find myself uncertain about whether this mission will even be possible, the six of us dragging a cart through the dark for thousands of miles. Well, we must do the best we can. Just as we planned, we will now consider our situation, and prepare for the adventure ahead.'

Stef smiled at his choice of words. *Adventure*, not ordeal. The man was a natural leader. Looking around the group, she saw that he held everyone's attention – everyone save Mardina, perhaps, who seemed unable to eat the cabbage, and was folded over on herself, her knees drawn up to her chest.

'There are six of us, plus the ColU,' Titus said now. 'Four of you, all save myself and Clodia, will make one last effort to gather supplies. Clearly nothing will grow on the ice of the dark side, I understand that, so you must gather what you can from the nearside vegetation that grows in the sunlit areas a little way back, or even on the illuminated peak above us. By the time we leave our cart must be full, our packs bulging. Perhaps we can find a way to reduce more of the food, to boil it, compress it. If the challenge is too much we can do this more gradually, setting up a series of caches, pushing deeper into the cold step by step.'

Stef put in, 'At least we'll have no trouble with warmth, thanks to the Romans' kernel oven. There will be no trees growing on the farside ice, no fuel for fires.'

'True,' Titus said.

Beth said, 'So while we're foraging and boiling potatoes, you and Clodia—'

'We will be scouting,' Titus said with a grin. 'We'll go exploring into the dark, a little way at least. Looking for a route forward. And looking for a way to shorten this trip.'

Beth frowned. 'How would that be possible?'

'I've no idea. But then I've never been here before.' He

glanced at the ColU, which sat on a folded-up blanket. 'And, in a sense, neither have any of you, since – if I understand your hints correctly – somehow a great span of time separates *this* world from the one you knew before. Who knows what might have happened in all that time? Perhaps Per Ardua had its own Romans who left behind a road, straight and true as an arrow, leading us straight to the antistellar.'

Stef smiled. 'I suppose it's worth a look.'

Now Titus turned to Clodia. 'And I will have you at my side, child, because you will be a valuable companion on such a mission. I've seen enough on this journey already to know that.'

'Thanks,' Clodia said flatly.

Titus looked at Mardina. 'The alternative is for you to stay here and assist Mardina. You may imagine how much I know about pregnancies. Perhaps it would help Mardina to have another young woman at her side.'

Mardina looked back at him bleakly. 'Forget it. My mother's here. And Stef.'

'And me,' the ColU said. 'Remember my programming. I was designed to fulfil the medical needs of a growing colony. Indeed I administered the birth of Beth Eden Jones herself, many years ago. While I am no longer capable of practical intervention, I can—'

'You can shut up,' Mardina snapped at it. 'That's what you can do. I don't need anything. Not yet.'

Titus glared at her and at Clodia. 'At any rate, your rivalry over the boy, Chu Yuen, is over, at least for now. Yes? When the baby comes, you can work out for yourselves how you want to organise your lives, and your loves.'

Stef smiled at him. 'Titus Valerius! I'm shocked. I thought you upright Romans were monogamous.'

'Different moralities apply on the battlefield.'

'I wasn't aware we were on a battlefield.'

'Tell that to the ice. Why, I remember once on campaign—'

'Not now, Father,' Clodia said, and she turned her back.

*

457

After a night's sleep Titus and Clodia bundled themselves up in layers of clothing, packed bags, and slipped away, off to the south-east, deeper into the dark.

The rest got on with collecting foodstuffs and fuel for the fire. Chu, Mardina and Beth explored the diffusely lit valley, and made longer treks back into the lands of daylight. Chu and Mardina also made some climbs up the flank of their mountain, into the island of life and light up there. Beth found the steeper climb all but impossible herself, and she was unhappy about leaving it to her pregnant daughter. But the ColU pointed out the pregnancy was barely begun, its own tests showed that Mardina was as healthy as could be expected, and there was really no reason to hold her back.

Stef assuaged her own guilt by doing what she could at the camp: refurbishing the cart, preparing the food they gathered, fixing meals.

And she worked with the ColU at its studies, biological, geological, astronomical.

The species of vegetation the youngsters brought down from the illuminated summit turned out to be complex. Some of it was familiar, descendants of either Arduan life or terrestrial. But some was stranger, what appeared to be essentially terrestrial root crops but with leaves with a peculiarly Arduan tinge to the green. The ColU grew excited at this, and insisted that Stef dice up samples to be fed into its own small internal laboratory for analysis.

'Do you remember our own trek to the far side with Yuri Eden and Liu Tao, long ago? We passed these terminator islands of light, which I longed to explore. I could see even then that such islands really were isolated from each other, especially as we pressed deeper into the dark, just like islands in an ocean. And just as on Earth, islands are natural laboratories for evolution ...'

It took it a full day of analysis before it was prepared to announce its conclusions.

The remnant ColU unit had only a tiny display screen, meant for showing internal diagnostics of the AI store itself.

Stef squinted to see with tired, rheumy eyes. 'That's a genetic analysis,' she said at last. 'But there's a mixture there. Of terrestrial DNA, and the Arduan equivalent ...'

'*All from the one plant*,' the ColU said. 'An unprepossessing tuber that you might trip over in the dark. I'm not even sure if it would be edible, for humans—'

'Just tell me what you found, damn it!'

'Integration. A product of a deep integration of the two biospheres. Colonel, this plant is like a terrestrial vegetable, but with Earthlike photosynthesis replaced by the Per Arduan kind – the version tuned to Proxima light, which exploits the dense infra-red energy that Proxima gives off. Do you see? In the very long run, it is as if there have been *two* origins of life on this world, Stef Kalinski. The first origin was when Arduan life emerged – and we know even that was related to the emergence of life on Earth, there was a deep biochemical linkage enabled by panspermia. And the second origin was when humans arrived at this world – Yuri Eden and Mardina Jones and all the rest – and brought with them a suite of life forms from Earth.'

'Ah,' Stef said. 'The ISF thought they were exploring the stars. In fact they were seeding life.'

'Ever since Lex McGregor walked here and made his speeches, the dual biosphere has been evolving. At first there must have been extinctions on both sides, as forms unable to adapt to the new conditions went to the wall. After that, over a hundred thousand years, a million years, there must have been speciation as new forms emerged and adapted to the new conditions. New kinds of potato, adapted to the thinner Proxima light. And in ten or a hundred million years there would be time for integrated ecologies to emerge, as the surviving life forms evolved together.'

'Like the ants in the stromatolite. Like bees and flowers, back on Earth. But this is more, deeper, this mutated metamorphosis. A symbiogenesis,' Stef breathed.

'Exactly. The deepest symbiosis possible, the most intimate life cooperation of all. It is just as the mitochondria in your own body's cells, Stef, were once independent organisms. They

459

became integrated into your cells to serve as sources of energy, yet they retained their own genetic heredity, a kind of memory of their free-swimming days. Terrestrial life, from amoebas and complex cells upwards, is a product of a deep integration of many forms of life. Genesis through symbiosis, indeed.'

'And now, here on Per Ardua, we're seeing the same thing over again. *How long* would it take? How much time has elapsed here since humans arrived? How far into the future have we been projected, ColU? More than millions of years, more than hundreds of millions...'

The ColU simulated a sigh. 'I apologise for my reticence. You have asked these questions many times before. I can make only rough guesses based on the data I have so far, the evidence from the geology here, the biology – even from the evolution of the star itself. I will be able to make much more accurate estimates of the date when I see the dark-side sky, and I can gather astro-nomical data. But of course there is an upper bound.'

Stef frowned. 'An upper bound? How can there be an upper bound on the future – *what* upper bound?'

'The End Time,' the ColU said simply.

That was when Mardina and Chu burst into the camp, scuffed and dusty and breathing hard.

Mardina said, 'You keep saying you want to see the sky, ColU.'

'Yes—'

'Well, your luck is in. You can see it from the slope, not much of a climb from here. Chu, get him into his pack.'

'See what?' Stef demanded. 'The stars?'

Mardina gave her only a quizzical look. 'Sort of. See for yourself. Come *on*! And where's my mother?'

The four of them, Stef, Chu, Mardina and Beth, stood on a hillside, looking out over the night lands of Per Ardua, over an ocean of dark. Only the faintest reflected glow from the summit above reached them here.

And above them, in a terminator sky marred for once only by scattered cloud...

Not stars, no, Stef saw. Not *just* stars. It was a band of light, an oval, an ellipse – no, surely it was a disc tipped away from her, all but edge on. The overall impression was of a reddish colour, but bright white sparks were scattered over the pink, like shards of glass on a velvet cushion. There was a brighter blob at the centre, and lanes of light sweeping around that core. As eyes adapted to the low light she saw finer detail, what looked like turbulent clouds in those outer lanes, and here and there a brighter spark, almost dazzling. When she looked away from this tremendous celestial sculpture, she could see stars – ordinary stars, isolated sparks scattered thin, though many of them seemed reddish too. But the sky was dominated by the great ellipse.

And, oddly, the thing she noticed next was Mardina's hand slipping into Chu's, and squeezing tight.

Stef said sharply. 'You know, ColU, you should have warned us about all this.'

'But I was never *sure*. I can never lead; I can only advise.'

'It's a galaxy,' Beth said, a little wildly. 'Even I know that much. Like our galaxy, the Milky Way ... But what the hell's it doing up there? *Is* it our galaxy?' She shook her head. 'I grew up on Per Ardua, remember, on the day side. I never even saw the stars until I got to Mercury. Has Proxima been – I don't know – flung out of the galaxy somehow, so we see it from the outside?'

'Nothing like that,' the ColU said gently.

'That's not our galaxy at all,' Stef snapped. 'That's Andromeda, isn't it? Bigger than ours, I think. The two galaxies were the biggest of the local group. Now, when I was a kid playing at astronomy with my father, on the rare nights we had clear skies in Seattle' – and, in some realities, with her impossible sister Penny by her side – 'we used to look for Andromeda. Fabulous in a telescope, but you could just see it even with the naked eye. A smudge of light. Now *that*, I would say—' and she started taking rough sightings of the width of the object with her thumb '—is, what, thirty times the apparent diameter of Earth's sun?'

'More like forty,' the ColU said.

Mardina was staring at her. 'So how did that thing get so big?'

'It didn't. It got closer.' Stef closed her eyes, remembering her own basic astronomy classes from long ago. 'In my time Andromeda was two and a half-million light years away. Right, ColU? But even then we could see it was approaching our galaxy. The two star systems were heading for a collision, which – well, which would be spectacular. Now, as I recall the best predictions for the timing of that collision were way off in the future. Four billion years or more?'

'More like four and a half,' the ColU said.

Stef squinted. 'So if that beast, which is around two hundred thousand light years across, is *that* apparent size in the sky, I could estimate its current distance—'

'Done,' the ColU said. 'Colonel Kalinski, I now know we have travelled – or rather the Hatches have taken us – some three and a half billion years into the future. That is, after the epoch from which we set out.'

Beth, Mardina, Chu just stared at each other, and then into the slate hanging from Chu's neck, as if the ColU's mind resided there, as if behind a human eye.

But Stef understood immediately. 'Yes, yes. So the collision is still a billion years away—'

'If it were to happen at all,' the ColU said enigmatically.

'I wonder what it must have done to cultures who emerged after our own, to have *that* hanging in the sky. Growing larger century by century. How many religions rose and fell in its light, awed and terrified?'

'We'll never know, Stef Kalinski,' the ColU murmured.

'And, over three billion years – that's presumably more than enough time for all the processes we've seen here on Per Ardua to have come about. For almost every trace of humanity to have eroded away. Even for species from two different star systems to find a way to evolve into one ecology.'

Mardina looked around the strange sky. 'I don't understand. Three and a half billion years ... It's meaningless. Where is Terra? Where's the sun?'

'I'm afraid I'm not sure,' the ColU said. 'The sun and the Alpha Centauri system, the Centaur's Hoof, were once near neighbours. But by now they will have wandered far from each other, as the galaxy has turned on its axis. Earth, Terra, and the other planets will still orbit the sun. But Earth is probably lifeless; the sun, slowly heating, will have sterilised the inner planets – oh, as much as two or three billion years ago. But the ageing sun has not yet entered its terminal cycle, the red giant phase when the sun will swell and swallow the inner worlds.'

Earth lifeless. Suddenly Stef shivered, despite the comparative warmth of her clothing. To be alone on this world was one thing. To be taken out of one reality stream and dumped in another was extraordinary. But to be stranded in a future so remote that Earth was dead, that presumably nothing like the humanity she had known could still survive …

'This is terrifying,' she murmured.

'Indeed, Colonel Kalinski,' the ColU said.

Chu was looking around the sky. 'I rode on starships,' he said slowly. 'I was held in slave pens. But when I passed windows, I glimpsed the skies of many worlds. And this is quite different. I mean, even aside from the approaching star storm, Andromeda. The stars seem more dim, more sparse.'

'That's a good observation,' the ColU said. 'Even in our time the great ages of star making were ending. Now there are fewer young stars, more ageing ones.'

Chu asked, 'And where are the other stars of the Centaur's Hoof? They should be two brilliant lanterns in the sky.'

'Even Alpha Centauri has evolved with time,' the ColU said sadly. 'Its stars were older than the sun. The brightest of the main pair will have lapsed into its red giant stage perhaps half a billion years ago, sterilising any worlds in its own system, and its partner's, before collapsing to a white dwarf – and Proxima will have become decoupled from its weakening gravity field. The lesser of the main pair would have had many billions of years left before it, too, entered its terminal phase. Smaller stars last longer. Proxima, the runt of the litter, would likely have lasted for six *trillion* years before running out of its carefully processed hydrogen fuel. But Proxima, now, is alone.'

'You say *would*,' Stef said. '*Would* have lasted trillions of years. And you seemed remarkably precise in your estimate of the date, given only a cursory look at this sky above us—'

'As I told you, I do have more information,' the ColU said. 'About the future of the universe, gathered during the long years of my journey home to Earth in the *Malleus Jesu*. Subtle signs of times to come: evidence of titanic future events, smeared across the sky of the present. Events whose date I was able to estimate. Once I saw that Andromeda was so close, once I realised roughly what epoch this is, it was easy to deduce that they would have brought us, not to some arbitrary earlier point, but to *this* point in time. This most special time of all. With more observation, especially of the cosmic background radiation, I will be able to be more precise still—'

'*They*,' Stef snapped. '*They* brought us here. You mean the Hatch builders. Who Earthshine called the Dreamers.'

'The Dreamers – yes.'

Chu asked now, 'And what is so special about this time, this future, this age?'

'Nothing.' The ColU sighed. 'Nothing, save that it is the last age of all.'

'The End Time,' Stef said.

She saw Mardina place her hand on her belly, over her unborn child.

That was when Titus and Clodia came clambering up the slope. '*Here* you are. Camp discipline: leave a note before you all clear off next time.'

Beth said, 'We're stargazing. Looking at *that*.' She pointed up at Andromeda.

Titus snorted. 'Who cares about lights in the sky? I've got something much more important to show you. Come and see what we found!'

CHAPTER 66

It was a walk of around three kilometres – two of Titus's Roman miles.

They came down off the flank of the mountain and made their way along a dry, shadowed valley. The going was easy, even for Stef, who had walked little save around one campsite after another since the expedition set off. Titus and Clodia both carried torches, of dry stems bundled up and dipped in pots of marrow; they burned, if fitfully. But the glow from Andromeda was surprisingly bright, especially from that brilliant central core. Billions of suns in lieu of moonlight, Stef thought idly.

And, as Titus had predicted, when she came to the structure Titus and Clodia had found, Stef too forgot the wonders of the sky. She even forgot, for a while, the ColU's dark and still obscure mutterings about the End Time.

It was another ellipse, tilted like Andromeda in the sky – but this one, much longer than it was wide, was cut into the ground. And as Stef approached the cut she saw that in fact she was looking into a circular tube, a cylinder – no, a tunnel, it was big enough to be called that, several metres in diameter, that slid into the ground at a shallow angle, making this elliptical cross-section where it met the flat ground surface.

The ColU had his bearer, Chu, walk around this formation, studying it closely.

But Titus warned them all sternly not to step into the tunnel, onto the smooth curved interior. 'We were wandering around at random, hoping to find a convenient river or some such to carry us further on our way ... Then we found a kind of way marker. Solid granite, and barely eroded.'

'We are all but beyond the terminator weather here,' the ColU said. 'Weathering, erosion, will be slow. The marker, like this structure, could be extremely old.'

'Well, the marker had a distinctive arrow, you couldn't mistake its meaning. Which led us straight to this.'

'Remarkable,' the ColU said. 'Remarkable. And for us to have happened on such a structure so close to where we crossed the terminator – it cannot be chance; the cold side of this world must be laced with such constructs.'

'I don't understand,' said Stef. She walked closer to the ellipse lip. 'I see a tunnel.' She glanced back at their mountain for reference. 'Pointing pretty much south-east – that is, away from the substellar—'

'And directly towards the antistellar,' the ColU said.

'A tunnel sloping down at a pretty shallow angle.' She took Clodia's torch and held it up. The tunnel continued dead straight, into the ground, beyond the glow cast by the flickering torch. 'Some kind of transport system?'

Titus grinned. 'You philosophers haven't spotted the most interesting thing about it. I told you to stay off the surface. Why? Because it is perfectly slippery – less friction than the smoothest ice, I would say. Though I can tell you it is no colder than the rest of the world – I touched it with my hand, I dared that. But if you were to step on it ...' He took a pebble and set it carefully on the sloping surface of the cylinder. It seemed to rest still, just for a moment, and then began to slide into the mouth of the cylinder, picking up speed gradually until it disappeared into the shadows. 'See?' Titus grinned. 'You would fall on your backside and you would slither off out of sight, for ever.'

'Not for ever,' the ColU said. 'Titus, I dare say you've tried this experiment a few times. When exactly did you drop your first rock down this shaft?'

'Actually it was a spare torch, I wanted to see how far it extended ...'

466

They compared times. Titus always kept a careful check on times when marching or scouting. He had dropped the torch about an hour and fifteen minutes earlier.

'Good,' said the ColU. 'We won't have long to wait.'

Stef frowned. 'Wait for what? This enigmatic manner of yours is irritating, ColU.'

'I'm sorry. When I was a mere farm machine, you know, people rarely listened to my speculations—'

'Spill it, tin man.'

'Colonel Kalinski, I think this is a gravity tunnel. It's an old idea, dating back to contemporaries of Newton.'

'Never mind the history lesson. Just *tell* us.'

'Imagine a tunnel dug *through the ground*, in a dead straight line between two points on a planet's curving surface. The tunnel is straight, but you can see that it will *seem* to dive down into the ground at one point, and then climb up again at the destination.'

Stef nodded. 'I get it. So if you line the tunnel with a friction-less surface, and climbed on a sled—'

'You would slide down into the ground, reaching some maximum speed at the midpoint of the tunnel, until slowing to the other end. It would feel as if you had descended a slope and climbed another, but in fact you would have followed the tunnel's straight line all the way. Do you see, Stef Kalinski? The passage is energy free, once the tunnel is cut. Powered by gravity alone. And if you built a network of tunnels, and made them durable enough—'

'You've built a transport system that could last a billion years.' Stef grinned at the audacity of it. 'All but indestructible, and free. I love it. So the people who built this, whether they were our descendants or not, must have been pretty smart.'

The ColU said, 'They may not have been people at all. This is Per Ardua. Remember we had evidence that there was a builder culture that achieved planetary engineering. Maybe this is somehow a legacy of that.'

Titus was frowning. 'I am trying to work this out. So my

torch will have slid along this tunnel to the terminus. And then, with nobody to collect it – or so I presume – it will have started to slide straight back again. You say we must wait only a few minutes, ColU. Do you mean until my torch returns? But how can you know that? You don't know how *long* this tunnel is ...'

'It doesn't matter,' the ColU said. 'It's an odd quirk of physics. The time the journey takes only depends on the density of the planet, the gravitational constant ... Even if you could cut a tunnel right through the centre of the planet—'

'Which would have been handy getting from substellar to antistellar,' Stef said drily.

'Even then, though you'd have reached much higher speeds at the midpoint, the journey time there and back would be the same.'

Titus said, 'All this sounds like philosophical trickery to me. And how long is this magic transport time you predict, o glass demon?'

The ColU said, 'Just wait ... About *this* long.'

And, right on cue, a bundle of reeds came sliding up out of the mouth of the tunnel. As it slowed to a halt, Titus carefully reached down and swept it up with his one good hand. 'Ha! A fine trick, demon. But now we have some planning to do. Come! Let us return to camp.'

The first trip through the gravity tunnel, Titus decreed, was to be made by sled, Beth's cart, with the runners they had made to replace the axles and wheels on the undersurface. Of course they had anticipated having to drag the cart over farside ice, but Stef could see that this arrangement ought to work even better in the frictionless tunnel.

So they wheeled the cart the couple of miles to the tunnel mouth, established a temporary camp, spent a day fixing up the cart with its sled rails. They ate and slept, according to Titus's stern orders.

Titus decreed that the first to take a trial trip through the tunnel would be himself with his daughter Clodia – and the

468

ColU and Stef, who might be able to interpret the experience, and what they found on the far side. The pregnant Mardina, the baby's father Chu, and prospective grandmother Beth, would not be split up come what may; they would be staying behind.

They were evidently going to have to do some fancy work getting the crew loaded on at one end of the tunnel, and successfully off at the other before the sled started to fall back, without any outside help. Before they hauled the cart over to the tunnel Titus had them practise the art. They had most success with Titus and Clodia leaping out at the destination, carrying rope to tie up the cart, while Stef stayed in the cart cradling the ColU.

Then the cart crew bundled up in their warmest gear – they were after all going an unknown distance deeper into the chill of farside – and loaded food, water, blankets, material for a fire and a few of their precious tools onto the cart itself. Beth, Mardina and Chu had an easy enough time pushing the cart over the lip of the sloping tunnel, and held it steady while the passengers climbed aboard.

Then Titus ceremoniously lit a torch and held it aloft. 'Onwards, and into the unknown!'

The support crew let go of the cart. Slowly, almost imperceptibly, it began to slip down the slope.

Stef glanced back at the grinning, somewhat anxious faces of the three left behind. 'It's taking an embarrassingly long time to get going,' she said. 'I feel like the King of Angleterre in his coronation carriage.'

'We will be in the dark soon enough,' the ColU said. 'But remember, even if the torch were to fail, it is only forty minutes to complete the one-way trip to the far end.'

Now the mouth of the tunnel was all around them, swallowing them up, their speed gradually increasing. The dark was deepening. The movement was utterly smooth, and entirely silent.

Stef felt a frisson of fear. 'It's like a roller-coaster ride. Magic Mountain at Disneyland. None of you have the faintest idea what I'm talking about, do you?'

Titus, cradling his torch with his burly body, was suspicious. 'I don't understand. We are moving quite rapidly already. And yet there is not a breath of wind.'

'As I anticipated,' the ColU said smoothly.

Stef snarled, 'What now, ColU? I wish you'd be open with us.'

'I apologise, Colonel Kalinski. There could be no air resistance in here. Otherwise, you see, the friction would slow us; we might pass the midpoint but would not reach the tunnel end, and would slip back, eventually settling at the centre, the lowest point. Human engineering designs based on this idea always imagined a vacuum tunnel.'

Titus took a deep breath. 'We're in no vacuum.'

'I think there is an invisible subtlety to the design. The air we breathe is carried with us – perhaps the tunnel air is held aside. Given time, Stef Kalinski, you and I could no doubt investigate the engineering. Whatever the detail, it must be robust to have survived a billion years ...'

The dark was deep now. They didn't seem to be moving at all, and Stef soon lost track of time. In the light of the torch, Clodia cuddled closer to her father.

Stef, unable to resist it, moved closer to the big Roman too.

Titus said, 'I am sorry I do not have a hand for you to hold, Stef.'

She clutched his stump of an arm and rested her head on his shoulder. 'This will do.'

'It won't be long,' the ColU murmured, from the dark. 'Just forty minutes. Not long.'

They emerged on an icebound plain.

Stef walked a few steps, away from the tunnel mouth and the disgorged cart. She swung her arms, breathing in deeply; the cold stung her mouth, and her breath steamed. 'This is the far side, all right. Just the way I remember it.'

She looked around. Andromeda still hung huge and looming in a crystal-clear sky; there wasn't a shred of terminator-weather cloud here. In the crimson galaxy light, the land seemed featureless, flat. But there was a peculiarly symmetrical hillock in the ice a few hundred metres away, like a flattened cone, or a pyramid with multiple flat sides – or like a tremendous jewel, she thought. Could it be artificial? There was no other feature in the landscape to draw her eye.

She walked that way, trying to place her booted feet on ridges in the ice to avoid slipping.

Inevitably Titus called after her. 'Don't go too far!'

She snorted. 'I'm hardly likely to have marauding barbarians leap out at me, legionary.'

'You might slip and break your brittle old-lady bones. And with my single arm it would be a chore for me to have to carry you back to the cart and haul you home.'

'I'll try to be considerate.'

The ColU called, 'In fact, Colonel Kalinski, would you mind carrying my slate for a closer inspection? And if you could find a way to bring back a sample of that formation …' With surprising grace on the ice, Clodia jogged out to hand Stef the slate, and a small hammer from their rudimentary tool kit.

As Stef approached the pyramidal structure, she listened to the ColU's analysis.

'I can deduce our change in position quite clearly from the shift in the visible stars' position. Andromeda has shifted too, of course, but that is too large and messy an object to yield a precise reading …'

The closer she got, the less like a geological formation the pyramid seemed. It was too precise, too sharply defined for that. She supposed there might be a comparison with something like a quartz crystal. But she had an instinct that there was biology at work here, something more than mere physics and chemistry. She took panoramic and close-up images. The pyramid looked spectacular and utterly alien, sitting as it was beneath a sky full of galaxy. Then she bent to chip off a sample from one gleaming, perfect edge.

Titus called, 'How far have we travelled then, glass demon?'

'Not very far at all, Titus Valerius. Only a hundred kilometres

471

– just a little more. That's perhaps sixty Roman miles. Not very far – but that means we were never very deep under the surface. Two hundred metres at the lowest point, perhaps.'

With her sample of what felt like water ice tucked into an outer pocket, Stef headed carefully back to the group.

'Not very far, as you say, demon. But we know this tunnel is not the only one of its kind in the planet.'

'Quite so, legionary. There will be many such links, perhaps a whole network, perhaps of varying lengths.'

'Yes. And a way for us to go on, deeper into the dark. There must be another entrance close by – all we need do is find it. And then—'

'And then we can proceed in comparative comfort, if we're lucky, all the way to the antistellar,' said the ColU. 'For that central locus must be a key node of any transport network.'

Stef had got back to the cart, within which the ColU sat, bundled against the cold. 'You want me to put some of this sample in your little analysis lab?'

'Yes, please, Stef Kalinski. Titus Valerius, let us consider. If this length of tunnel is typical, at sixty miles or so, and if we have a journey of less than six thousand Roman miles to complete to the antistellar—'

'We'll need a hundred hops. And if each hop takes us two-thirds of an hour, as you said, that will take, umm ...'

'Sixty, seventy hours,' Stef said. 'I always was good at mental arithmetic. Even allowing for stops, and for hauling the cart between terminals, that's only a few days.'

'It may be hard work,' Titus said. 'But we will not freeze to death, or starve, or die of thirst on the way.' He nodded. 'Excellent! But you know, Stef, I, Titus Valerius, anticipated that we would find some such fast road as this.'

'You did? How?'

'Because if not, we would have encountered Ari Guthfrithson and the Inca woman walking back the other way. Would we not? For if we could never have mastered this world of ice on foot, and I suspect that is true, *they* could surely not. Clever fellow, aren't I, for a one-winged legionary? Now then – Clodia, come with me. We will do a little scouting before we return. Let's see if we can find the terminal of the next link, somewhere in the direction of the antistellar ...' He glanced up at the sky, taking a bearing from Andromeda. '*That* way. Come now! And you, Stef Kalinski, you and your old-lady bones stay put in this cart.'

'With pleasure, legionary.'

As they walked away, she heard father and daughter laughing.

'It's good to hear them happy,' Stef said. 'Suddenly a journey that did look impossible has become achievable.'

'You too should be happy,' the ColU whispered.

'I should?'

'For the discovery you have just made.'

'What discovery? The pyramid?'

'It's no pyramid, Stef Kalinski. It's nothing artificial, and nor is it a merely physical phenomenon, as I'm sure you guessed. It is life, Stef Kalinski. Life. An ambassador, perhaps, from a colder world than this ...'

As they sat huddled together in the cart, the ColU spoke of Titan, moon of Saturn.

Titan was a mere moon, a small world subsidiary to a giant, but a world nevertheless – and a very cold one. Its rocky core was overlaid by a thick shell of water, a super-cold ocean contained by a crust of ice as hard as basalt was on Earth. And over *that* was a thick atmosphere, mostly of nitrogen, but with traces of organics, methane, ethane ...

'But it is those organic traces that made Titan so interesting,' the ColU said. 'On a land of ice rock, where volcanoes belch ammonia-rich water, a rain of methane falls, carving river valleys and filling seas. And in those seas—'

'The probes found life. I remember the reports. Some kind of slow-moving bugs in the methane lakes.'

'Yes, life based – not on carbon, as ours is – but on silicon. Just as carbon-carbon bonds, the backbone of your chemistry,

Stef Kalinski, can be made and broken in room-temperature water, so silicon-silicon bonds can be made in the cold methane of Titan's lakes. A form of life not so very unlike ours superficially, but with a different biochemistry entirely – and very slow-moving, low in energy, slow to reproduce and evolve. We found nothing but simple bugs on Titan, simpler than most bacteria – not much more complicated than viruses.

'But Titan is not the only cold world. Here at Proxima, while the Earth-like Per Ardua was the planet that caught all the attention—'

'Ah. Proxima d.'

'Yes. That was a Mars-sized world just outside the zone that would have made it habitable for humans, like Per Ardua.'

'So far as I know it was never even given a decent name. Nobody cared about it – or the other Proxima worlds.'

'They did not. But it was very like Titan – another common template for a world, it seems. And room for another kind of life.

'Stef Kalinski, Earthshine has spoken of a panspermia bubble, of worlds like Earth and Per Ardua linked by a common chemistry carried by rocks between the stars, worlds with cousin life forms. But there could be *other* bubbles, worlds with different kinds of climate, different kinds of biochemistries, yet linked in the same way. Maybe one bubble could even overlap another, you see – for clearly a stellar system may contain more than one kind of world.'

Stef was starting to understand. 'You always speak in riddles, ColU, whether you intend to or not. But I think I see. The sample I brought you—'

'The pyramid-beast over there has a silicon-based biochemistry very similar to that recorded on Titan, but not identical. Maybe it is a visitor from Proxima d, do you think? Somehow hardened to withstand what must be for it a ferocious heat, even here on Per Ardua's dark side. As if a human had landed on Venus. But it is here, and surviving. And with more time still...'

'Yes, ColU?'

'Stef Kalinski, we have seen that, given billions of years, life forms from across the same panspermia bubble can integrate, grow together.'

'The Earth ants in the Arduan stromatolite.'

'Exactly. Now, is it possible that given *tens* of billions, *hundreds* of billions of years, even different kinds of life could mix and merge? Your fast, quick kind, and the slow-moving Titanian over there? Could that be the next stage in the evolution of the cosmos itself? You already share a world, you see.'

'It's a fantastic thought,' she said slowly. 'But it's never going to happen. Is it, ColU? Because this is the End Time, according to you. There will be no tens or hundreds of billions of years—'

'I'm afraid not, Colonel Kalinski. Here on the dark side I have been able to make quite precise assays of the sky: the state of the stars, the proximity of Andromeda – even the background glow of the universe as a whole, which contains warp-bubble clues to its future.'

'Hmm.' She looked up into the dark. 'Well, it is marvellous to see, for an astronomer. And you've come to a conclusion, have you?'

'I have. And a precise estimate of the time remaining.'

Stef felt chilled, as if she'd been given bad news by a doctor. 'You're going to have to explain all this to the others, you know. In language they can understand.'

'Yes, Colonel Kalinski. Of course. And the importance of finding Earthshine soon, by the way, is only increased.'

Stef could hear the others returning, father and daughter laughing, full of life and energy. And she looked across at the silicon-life explorer from Proxima d, the ice giant. 'I wonder if that thing can *see* us … Just tell me,' she said. 'How long have we got?'

'A year,' the ColU said flatly. 'No more. The data's still chancy.'

And Stef immediately thought of Mardina, and the baby.

She pursed her lips and nodded. 'A year, then. For now, not a word. Come on, let's get ready to go on.'

CHAPTER 67

The party gradually penetrated deeper into the cold of the Per Ardua farside.

The forty-minute tunnel hops all felt much the same to Beth, but in the short intervals during which they trekked from one tunnel exit to the entrance of the next, always following trails carefully scouted out by Titus with Clodia or Chu, Beth did get glimpses of parts of her world she had never seen before. After all, during the years she'd spent growing to a young adult on Per Ardua, she had never gone further than the tall forests that screened the terminator zone.

Stef and the ColU had made such a journey as this once before, with Beth's father and Liu Tao, in a purloined ISF rover. That party had followed a more or less direct course to the antistellar, cutting over the ice surface of a frozen ocean. The gravity tunnels, however, naturally enough, stuck to continental land, detouring around the shores of frozen oceans. As a result the journey was longer than a direct route, and was taking longer than the handful of days that Titus and the ColU had first estimated – but still it would be brief enough.

And while Stef in that earlier party had spent mind-numbing days crossing geometrically perfect ice plains, now Beth saw more interesting features. Eroded mountain ranges from which glaciers spilled like huge, dirty tongues. Places where earthquakes or other geological upheavals had raised and cracked the ice cover, creating frozen cliffs that gleamed a deep blue in the light of their torches.

Yet even these features were probably impressively old, the

ColU said. There would always be a lot of weather activity at the terminator, where the warm air and water from the day side spilled into the cold of the night. But here in the dark, weather would always be desperately rare: no clouds, no fresh falls of snow or hail. Even meteor impacts would be infrequent in such an elderly system as this, with much of the primordial debris left over from the planets' formation long since swept up. So they drove across a sculpted but static landscape – and a landscape bathed in the complex, red-tinged light of an ageing Andromeda.

Sometimes they saw more 'Titanians', enigmatic, sharp-edged pyramids standing like mute monuments. But the ColU assured them that the Titanians, in their way, on their own timescale, could be exploring just as vigorously as the humans.

Beth noticed, however, that Stef barely glanced at the sky, or the icebound landscape, or even the 'Titanians'. As they travelled, and in the 'evenings' as they rested, Stef sat huddled with the ColU at the back of their sled-cart, or in a corner of their shelter, talking softly, Stef making occasional notes on the glowing face of her slate. Everybody knew what they were discussing: the ColU's ideas about the fate of the world. Beth tried to read Stef's expression. There was nothing to be discerned from the ColU's neutral tone.

At last, one evening, after they had cleared away their meal, with them all bundled in their warmest clothes, their feet swathed in layers of socks, gathered around the warmth of the kernel stove, Stef announced that they needed to talk about the End Time.

'In a way,' Stef began cautiously, 'the idea that the world will have an end – that the universe *itself* will end, and relatively soon – ought to feel natural to us.

'We have no direct experience of infinity, of eternity. Our own lives are short. And the scientists in my culture proved quite definitively that eternity doesn't lie *behind* us, that our universe had a beginning, a birth in a cataclysmic outpouring of energy.

Why, then, should we imagine that eternity lies ahead of us, an unending arena for life and mind?'

Beth was sitting beside her pregnant daughter. Now, under a blanket, she took her daughter's hand, and Mardina squeezed back. Mardina's eyes were wide in the firelight, her expression blank. This was *not* a conversation either of them wanted to be part of, Beth was sure.

The ColU was on Chu's lap, next to Stef. Titus Valerius sat beside the slave boy, listening intently.

And Titus was sceptical. 'Well, we Romans had no trouble imagining eternity. Or at least, we failed to anticipate an end. Because we never anticipated the *Empire* to end – do you see? Unbounded and eternal ...'

That sounded magnificent in the legionary's guttural soldier's Latin, Stef thought. *Imperium sine fine.*

The ColU said, 'Our own culture, mine and Stef's and Beth's, had its own account of an undying empire – but an empire of scientific logic. We thought we could know the future by looking out at the universe, working out the physical laws that govern it – and then projecting forward the consequences of those laws.

'The universe only has so much hydrogen – the stuff that stars are made out of. The hydrogen will, or *would have*, run out when the universe is ten thousand times as old as it is now. No more stars. After the stars there would be an age of black holes and degenerate matter – the compressed, cooling remnants of stars – and the galaxies, huge and dim, would begin to break up. There would be a major transition when protons began to decay – that is, the very stuff of which matter is made ... In the end everything would dissolve, and there would be nothing left but a kind of sparse mist, of particles called electrons and positrons – a stuff called positronium – filling an expanding, empty universe. Even so it was possible that minds could survive. Minds more like mine than yours, perhaps. Thoughts carried on the slow wash of electrons – thoughts that might take a million years to complete.'

'That sounds horrible,' Mardina said, and Beth could feel the grip of her hand tighten. 'It doesn't even make any sense. How could a single thought last a million years? I can't imagine it.'

'But experiences of time can differ,' the ColU said. 'In my culture there was a Christian scholar called Thomas Aquinas – I wasn't able to trace him in your history, Titus. He distinguished three kinds of time, or perhaps perceptions of time. *Tempus* was human time, which we measure by changes in the world around us – the swing of a pendulum, the passage of a season. A Titanian ice giant would experience a slower *tempus* than a human. *Aevus* was angel time, measured by internal changes – by the development of thoughts, understanding, moods. For the angels, you see, stood outside the human world. And then there was *aeternitas*, God's time, for God and only God could apprehend all of eternity at once. The electron-positron minds would not be God, but in the timeless twilight of the universe they might have been like angels ...'

'Might have been,' Mardina said, almost bitterly. '*Might have been.*'

The ColU said, 'The positronium angels *will never exist*. Our universe won't last long enough for that. And the reason our universe is not eternal is because of the existence of *other* universes. And we know they exist because we, all of us, have visited several of them.'

'Aye, and fought in them,' Titus said, stirring from his space and pushing back blankets. 'But in *this* universe my bladder's full. Anybody want more tea? Chu, maybe you could put another pot of ice on the fire ...'

It took an hour before they were settled again.

When they took their places Beth thought they seemed calmer, more attentive – more ready to take in this strange news from the sky. The break had been a smart bit of people management by Titus Valerius, she thought. Who in the end hadn't really needed a piss at all.

'So,' Titus said now, slurping the last of his tea, 'as if the fate

479

of this universe wasn't bad enough, you have to talk about all the other ones.'

Stef smiled. 'All right, Titus, I know we are leading you on a march you'd rather not be following … It's all about logic, though. When all else fails, ask a philosopher. Sorry. Old physicist's joke.

'Look, *we* all know from personal experience that other universes exist, with histories more or less similar to this one – or to the one into which each of us was born. And in my culture our philosophers had predicted the existence of those universes. Our laws of nature were well founded, you see, but they did not prescribe how the universe had to be. Many universes were possible – an infinite number. It is just as our science would have predicted the six-fold symmetry of a snowflake, which comes from the underlying geometry of ice crystals, but within that six-fold rule set many individual snowflakes are possible, all different from each other.'

'Universes as numerous as snowflakes,' Beth said. 'That's wonderful. Scary.'

Stef said, 'But what are these universes? *Where* are they? You know that the science of my culture was more advanced than in any other we've yet encountered—'

The ColU said, 'And Earthshine would say that was because we had been the least deflected into efforts to build Hatches for his Dreamers.'

'We did have some models of the *multiverse* – I mean, of a super-universe that is a collection of universes. After centuries of study we never came to a definitive answer. We probably never got far out enough into our *own* universe to be able to map the truth.

'Still, we believed our universe had expanded from a single point, out of a Big Bang. Expanded, cooled, awash with light at first, atoms and stars and planets and people condensing out later. But our universe was like a single bubble in a bowl of boiling water, like a pot we put on the fire.' She gestured at the clay pot, within which water was languidly bubbling. 'You see?

There is a substrate, something like the water in the pot. And out of that heated-up substrate emerges, not just one bubble, but a whole swarm of them, expanding, popping ... *They* are the other universes we've been visiting.

'And what's inside those universes is going to be different, one universe to the next – a little or a lot. Some could differ wildly from the others, not just in historical details. Suppose gravity were stronger – I mean, the force that gives us weight. Then stars would be smaller, and would burn out more quickly. *Everything* would be different. And if gravity were weaker there might be no stars at all. Of course some universes are going to be more similar than others.'

It seemed to be Chu who understood most readily. Not for the first time Beth wondered what kind of scholar he might have become, given the chance. 'All the universes we have seen *are* similar. They all have planets, suns, people. They even have the *same* people, up to a point.'

'Yes,' Stef said eagerly. 'You've got it. When you think about it the differences are pretty small. I mean, whether Rome falls or not would be a big deal for us—' and she smiled as Titus scowled ferociously '—but from Per Ardua, say, you wouldn't even notice it.'

The ColU said, 'We believe that the Dreamers can somehow reach out to other universes that are – *nearby*. There is no good term for it. What is nearness in a multiverse? Beginning in one universe, they reach out into another that is similar, yet which contains a human culture that is more – conducive – to Hatch-building. And we, our small lives, are swept along in the process.'

Beth found herself frowning. 'But why? Why would they do that?'

Stef said, 'We need to find that out. In fact I suspect Earthshine may already be learning that secret. What's important now is that we know the multiverse exists. OK? We've *been* there. Now, the multiverse is big. Surely that's true. But it can't be infinite.'

Titus scratched his head. 'Here we go again ... Dare I ask, why not?'

'The trouble is, Titus,' the ColU said, 'some scholars have always believed that nature does not contain infinities. Infinities are just a useful mathematical toy invented by humans, with no correspondence to reality. Unlike the number *three*, say, which maps on to collections of three objects: three people, three potatoes ...'

Stef said, 'Infinities can make sensible questions meaningless. Titus, start with the number one.'

'I think I can grasp that.'

'Add another one.'

'I have two.'

'Subtract one.'

'I have one again.'

'Add one.'

'Two.'

'Subtract one.'

'One!'

'Add one!'

'Two!'

'Subtract one!'

'One!'

She held up her hands. 'OK, that's enough. You get the idea. Now if I asked you to stop doing that after some finite number of steps – twelve or twenty-three or five hundred and seventy-eight – what answer would you get?'

'That's easy. Either two or one.'

'Definitely one or the other?'

'Of course.'

'But if I asked you to go on *for ever*, what answer would you end up with?'

'I – ah ... Oh.'

'You see?' Stef said. 'The answer can't be determined. The question becomes absurd, once you bring infinity into it.'

Titus said, 'I can feel my brain boiling like the water in that pot.'

'Physics – my philosophy – is about asking sensible questions and expecting sensible answers. About being able to predict the future from the past. When you bring in infinities, sensible questions have dumb answers. The whole system breaks down.'

The ColU said, 'So the point is, the multiverse – the collection of the universes we visit – *must* be finite. Because nature won't allow infinities.'

Mardina scowled. 'Well, so what? What do I care if there is one reality, or ten or twenty or a million?'

Stef said, gently but persistently, 'It matters because a finite multiverse *has an edge*. And if one of the member universes should encounter that edge ...' She looked into the pot of water, and pointed out one largish bubble slowly migrating from the boiling centre towards the side of the clay pot. 'Watch.' When the bubble reached the edge, it popped, vanishing as if it had never existed.

The ColU said, 'Given that one simple fact – that the multiverse must be finite – and knowing how old the universe is, or was in the age we came from – it has always been possible to make an estimate of how long the universe was going to last. How long it was likely to be before we hit the multiverse wall. Probabilistic only, but ...'

Titus snapped, 'How long, then?'

The ColU said, 'My latest estimate, based on my inspections of the sky as far back as our time on the *Malleus Jesu*, is three and a half billion years after the age of mankind.'

Titus shook his head, growling under his breath. 'An absurd number.'

'Not to an astrophysicist,' Stef said with a smile. 'That is, a philosopher who knows the stars, Titus. In my culture we were pretty sure that the universe was a bit less than fourteen billion years old. So why should the universe last *longer* than a few billions more? You see? Not trillions or hundreds of trillions of years, or beyond the age of proton decay ... In my culture we used to call this the Doomsday Argument. Why should the future be so dissimilar to the past? Shouldn't we expect to find ourselves somewhere in the middle of the life span of the universe, not in its first few instants?'

Mardina was touching her belly again, as if trying to shield her baby from all this. 'Three point five billion years. You're saying the universe will die, three point five billion years after the year I was born. If I understand these numbers at all – that's still an immense stretch of time.'

'Of course,' Stef said. 'But here's the catch, Mardina. We have been brought to the *end* of that stretch. That's what we've determined – what the ColU has established definitively from his study of the sky.'

'It isn't just the ageing of the stars, the position of the galaxies,' the ColU said. 'That would be enough for a rough estimate. There are also distortions in the background glow of the sky, the fading relic of the Big Bang explosion. Distortions caused by events from the future.'

Titus tapped the pot with a fingernail. 'Because of the proximity of this wall of yours.'

'Which is a tremendously energetic horizon that sends back signals, back through time. Signals that show up as distortions in the background radiation. That is why I am able to be so precise. *This*, the age in which we find ourselves, is the End Time—'

'I don't want to hear it.' Mardina stood, suddenly, pulling away from Beth, the weight of her blankets almost making her stumble into the fire. 'I don't want to hear any more.' She clamped her hands over her ears, and stomped out.

Beth half-rose. 'She needs her boots, her cloak if she's going out there—'

'No.' Chu was already on his feet, and grabbing his own boots. 'Let me. It is our problem.'

Titus nodded. 'Let him go. It will be harder for them, to be so young, to have to face this. We must let them find their way.'

Beth longed to go after her daughter, but she made herself sit still. 'You're a wise man, Titus Valerius.'

He smiled, looking tired. 'No. Just an old one, and a survivor. So, Collius. Here we are in the far future, as I understand it. How long until we encounter this – edge?'

The ColU said simply, 'A year. No more.'

Titus nodded. 'And what then? What will happen?'

Stef said, 'A wall of light.'

Titus heaved a huge sigh. 'Very well. From the ethereal to the practical. Shall we consider our route for tomorrow? And then we all need sleep, if Morpheus grants it tonight.'

CHAPTER 68

The antistellar was the place where all the gravity-train tunnel mouths converged.

At the final destination, as the rest of the party went through the by-now practised routine of grappling their sled-cart out of the frictionless tube, Stef walked forward, away from the tunnel. The ice under her booted feet was concrete-hard but ridged, crumpled, wind-scoured – evidently old – and was not slick, maybe it was too cold for that; the footing was good. Once, back in her original timeline, she'd skimmed in space over the polar caps of Mars, which were very old accretions of water ice, the deepest layers perhaps a couple of million years old. The ice under her feet now might be a thousand times older than that. She really had been brought to an antique time, an old universe.

And the dark side cold itself – she seemed to remember that too, from her first experience here. This point furthest from the warmth of the star was the centre of a hemisphere of endless night, of ice and dark. Yet there was a limit to the cold, even here; some warmth at least washed around the world from the day side. It was evidently a survivable cold. Still, her breath steamed, and the frigid air plucked at her lungs and nose and eyes.

As she walked she could clearly see, by the light of an Andromeda reduced to a bloated sunset sitting on the horizon, more tunnels, dark gashes in the ground: a network of tunnels lacing this chill hemisphere of the planet, and all converging here, at the antistellar, at this point of geographic symmetry.

And at the precise antistellar point itself, the place all the tunnels seemed to be pointing to – *something was there*, a kind of flattened dome from which came a glow of pale light, with structures dimly visible within.

Earthshine. It had to be him.

Stef walked back to her companions. By now they had the cart set up on its runners, ready for the final haul over the ice to the dome. The ColU was in its pack on Chu's back. Mardina, more visibly pregnant every day despite her layers of cold-weather clothing, stood at Chu's side, their gloved hands locked together, breath wreathed around their faces.

Titus grunted, pointing to the dome. 'So our long journey is over – and *there* is the obvious destination. We should be ready to defend ourselves.'

The ColU said now, 'You may be right, legionary. But consider this. Earthshine needs no such shelter as that dome, whereas you do need shelter. Perhaps the dome itself should be seen as a gesture of welcome.'

Titus nodded cautiously. 'I see your reasoning. But consider this, in turn. If we would be welcome, so would Ari and Inguill have been, if they got this far. We should be prepared for whatever *they* are up to in there. Also, if Earthshine, or his image, could walk around on this ice butt-naked—'

Beth laughed. 'Titus, he could fly through the air if he wanted to.'

'Then why isn't he here now? I'm quite sure he's as aware of us as we are of him. Why not come out and see us?' Titus glanced around at the group. 'It's clear that there's much about this situation that we don't yet understand. We go to the dome. It's the obvious destination. The only destination. But we go in with our hands open in gestures of peace and friendship, and our weapons sheathed at our backs. Agreed?'

Stef shook her head. 'You're a terrible cynic, Titus Valerius. And I'd like to see you in a knife fight, you're like an overweight panda in that cold weather gear … But you and your instincts have kept us all alive this long. Agreed.'

They formed into a loose party, with Titus, Chu, Clodia and Beth hauling the cart towards the dome, and Mardina walking with Stef at the rear. Titus and Chu were in the front rank, and Stef could see their *pugio* daggers tucked in the back of their belts, glittering in Andromeda light.

Mardina linked her arm through Stef's, and they walked cautiously together. Stef peered up. 'That sky isn't what it was when I came this way before, with your grandfather Yuri, in that other timeline. It's been so long, the stars have swum around the sky, or aged and changed, the constellations have all melted away. I thought I would still be able to see *her*, though, up at the zenith. Brilliant she was, and as we walked to the antistellar we saw her steadily rise in the sky unlike any star.'

'"Her"? Who are you talking about, Stef?'

'A creature called Angelia. A creation of my father.'

'Another artificial person, then. Like the ColU, like Earth-shine.'

'Yes. Actually she was also a kind of ship. She and her lost sisters ... I got to know her. I don't suppose she could have survived this long. Why, in a billion years or two her very substance would have sublimed away, probably.'

Mardina squeezed her arm. 'We're in another history. She was probably never *here* at all.'

'Maybe not,' Stef said with a bitterness that surprised her. 'Just another story, erased by the Dreamers' meddling.'

'No, not erased. Not as long as you remember her.'

Stef felt unreasonably touched. She patted Mardina's hand. 'You're a good person, Mardina.'

Mardina laughed. 'Despite my great-grandfather being a criminal mastermind downloaded into a box of metal and glass?'

'Yes. That's quite a legacy, isn't it? But Yuri at least was a good man, your grandfather, I can tell you that much. And you're going to make a fine young mother.'

But that was the wrong thing to say. Stef could feel Mardina stiffen.

'Well, there's not going to be the time to find out, is there?

Not if the ColU is right that all *this*—' and she gestured at the starry sky '—is about to roll up like a closing scroll.'

Stef could think of nothing to say.

She was relieved when Titus, in the van of the party, reached the translucent wall of the dome.

CHAPTER 69

The dome was perhaps fifty metres across, Stef estimated as they walked around it, maybe ten metres tall at its midpoint, the highest point. Its skin was reasonably clear, translucent, and she saw no signs of support, no framework, no ribbing.

Titus glared in through the wall, as if he was scouting out the war camp of a bunch of unruly barbarians. Well, perhaps that wasn't so far from the truth. He pointed out structures within the dome, piles of materiel. '*That* looks like what might have brought Ari and Inguill here.' A sled, much smaller and cruder than theirs, with heaps of garments and blankets roughly dumped around it – heavy coats, thick boots. 'And that object in the centre, a kind of pillar in the middle of a mesh framework—'

'I believe that is Earthshine,' the ColU murmured. 'His support unit anyhow. But evidently heavily modified, for some purpose. And, over there ...'

They could all see what it meant. At one side of the dome was a Hatch emplacement, set into the rocky floor.

Stef cupped her hands around her eyes and peered in through the wall, trying to see better, cursing the vapour that rose up from her breath. A Hatch like any other Hatch. Just like the one she'd been brought to on Mercury, the first she'd seen – like the one Dexter Cole had found here on Per Ardua, right here at the antistellar – just like the Hatches she'd seen on worlds of other stars. All of them were alike, just a rectangular panel a few metres across set in the ground, the fine circular seam that marked the position of the lid. Crude functional simplicity.

Yet these simple gadgets were responsible for altering history itself, for adjusting the destinies of billions of souls. Stef was a physicist, and she'd been studying Hatches most of her adult life. Still they made her shudder.

And on this particular Hatch that lid gaped open.

'So,' the legionary snapped. 'Now what? Do we cut our way in?'

Clodia pointed. 'Either that, Father, or follow the arrow on the wall.'

They came to a doorway, a blister that protruded from the smooth dome wall.

Titus said, 'This door has a handle; that's simple enough.' He squinted through the wall. 'And a second door within.'

'I think it's a kind of airlock,' Stef said, surveying the dome again. 'This structure has no internal skeleton. Has to be air pressure holding it up. So we need to go through these double doors to avoid letting out all the inner air, and the warmth.'

Titus said sourly, 'I have served on starships, you know; I do know what an airlock is. Not that I was expecting to find one here. The practicalities concern me more. Such as, I doubt if this lock could take more than three of us at a time. Two, if laden with baggage. We'll have to be separated to enter.'

'I sincerely doubt there will be any threat,' Stef said briskly. 'Legionary, you can *see* through the wall. There is only Earth-shine … Even Ari and Inguill are nowhere in sight. I think we can take the risk, don't you?'

'And I for one,' said Beth, 'am keen to get out of this cold, for the first time in *weeks*.'

'Lead us, Titus Valerius,' Stef said.

It proved simple enough for Titus and Clodia to cycle through the airlock. Experimenting, Titus found there was a failsafe. 'The inner door won't open unless the outer one is firmly shut,' he boomed, his voice muffled by the thick dome wall. 'The air within is warm and moist.' Still inside the airlock, he pressed his hand against the material of the dome. 'This is pliant, yielding a little, but evidently thick and strong. It will be interesting to see how it withstands the blade of my *pugio*—'

'Not now, Father,' Clodia said. 'Come *on*.' She led the way through the airlock's inner door and into the interior of the dome, pulling open her heavy clothing as she walked.

Stef took Mardina's hand, and they both stepped into the airlock together, leaving Chu and Beth unloading stuff from the sled. Mardina closed the outer door, and Titus opened the inner for them – and, just as Titus had described, warm, moist air gushed over them. Stef took deep, shuddering breaths, already feeling warmer than she'd been since crossing the terminator.

She walked out of the lock and stood by Titus. Mardina followed, more uncertainly. The dome itself, lit by small, hanging lamps, was a silvery, translucent roof that excluded the sky. Even Andromeda was reduced to a washed-out crimson glow. The ground was bare rock, blackish like some kind of basalt, scraped and grooved – presumably by the action of ice across millions of years. Stef looked over at the central clutter of gear. There was Earthshine's support unit, clearly identifiable, embedded in a nest of other equipment. There was no sign of Earthshine's avatar projection.

Titus said, 'The air smells – funny. Like a ship. Or a factory.'

Stef's senses were dulled by age, but she agreed. 'I smell ozone. No scent of people, or not much—'

Mardina wrinkled her nose. 'Maybe my nose is sharper. *I* can smell a hint of sewage. Yuck. Not unlike what *we* smell like in the mornings, after a night under the canopy. They are here, then. My father and Inguill.'

Titus snapped, 'Well, we can't hover by the door all day. Clodia! With me. We will organise the work of moving our equipment in. Beth and Chu have made a start.'

'Bring in the ColU first,' Stef suggested. 'It will help us make sense of all this ...'

Soon the ColU was set on a heap of grubby blankets just inside the lock, and Mardina had hung its sensor unit around her own neck.

Then, as the pile of their belongings gradually accumulated inside the lock, a puddle forming at its base as residual ice melted in the warmth, Stef and Mardina approached the Earthshine unit.

The processor pillar stood at the centre of what looked like a sculpture of a spider, itself a few metres tall, with angled rods hingeing from the central unit and plunging into the rocky ground. The rods seemed to Stef to be made of some kind of ceramic, milky and smooth. The pillar itself had long lost the wheels Beth had described, on which it had rolled around the planet. Stef could see that the casing of the support unit had been broken open, much of its innards removed or redeployed.

Because of the framework of rods they could get no closer than a few metres from the central unit. Beyond the support unit Stef made out what looked like a manufacturing area of some kind, with various devices littering the ground – devices of an uncertain function, but an oddly smoothed-out appearance. The materials used seemed to be similar to the ceramic-like substance of the spider legs.

And beyond that, set in the ground, that open Hatch.

Stef faced the support unit. 'Earthshine. Are you in there?'

'You took your time.'

The voice sounded as authentic as ever, but there was still no sign of a virtual human body, any of his 'suits' as he'd once called them, Stef recalled.

Mardina said, 'Hello, Great-grandfather. We did come as fast as we could. Given that you abandoned us in the first place ...'

'Mardina, I can see *you*, even if I'm not much to look at. Come closer, child ... My word. You're pregnant!'

Mardina blushed.

'The dynasty continues,' Stef said drily.

'If only for now. Who is the father?'

'Chu Yuen,' said the ColU, speaking from the slate at Mardina's neck – and, perhaps, directly to Earthshine by other means, Stef thought. 'You recall, the slave from the Rome-Xin

Culture who is my bearer. An intelligent boy, evidently of good stock, even if he did fall on hard times.'

'A good father, then. I look forward to getting to know him better. And I already know you too well, ColU.'

'I told you on Mars – on that other Mars – that I would hunt you down, wherever you fled.'

'And so you have. Well done. Perhaps you will do me the courtesy of hearing about what I have discovered here ...'

Stef was starting to feel dizzy. 'I'm too hot, damn it, after months of being too cold.' She began to pull ineffectually at her outer coat.

At a call from Mardina, Beth and Chu hurried over with blankets from the cart, and heaped them up on the rocky ground. Beth helped Stef remove a few layers of clothing, and Chu handed her a canteen of water, brought in from outside – icy, but refreshing – and they sat her down on the blankets. Beth and Mardina sat with her, and soon Stef felt a lot more human. She refused food, however. 'If I never eat another mouthful of freeze-dried potato I won't be sorry.'

Earthshine said, 'I, of course, need no food of that sort. But since the arrival of the others one of my fabricators has been devoted to manufacturing human-suitable food from the raw materials of the environment – broken-up rock, organics filtered from the ice.'

The others. It was the first time he had mentioned Ari and Inguill, even tangentially.

'A fabricator.' Mardina frowned. 'What's that?'

'Advanced technology from our own timeline,' the ColU said. 'A device that can take apart matter at the molecular level, or even below, and assemble it into – well, whatever you desire. It's slow but effective. My own physical frame once contained such machines. Once Earthshine and his two brothers, artificial intellects as powerful as him, lurked in holes in the ground, on Earth. And they were surrounded by fabricators and other gadgets, like miniature factories, that used the raw materials of the planet to supply them with all they needed – materials for maintenance, energy.'

Earthshine said, 'I carried such gadgets with me in this support module. Now, here, I have broken them out and have put them to work. Everything you see here, the dome, this framework around me, has been manufactured from local materials, the rocks, the ice. Over on the far side of the dome I have created a pond, a body of standing water, to refresh the air. As for energy, though I have an internal store of my own, I have plumbed the planet itself for its inner heat. Manufactured drills to penetrate the surface rock layers ...'

Stef asked, 'Why did you build all this?'

'I came here because of the Hatch, Stef. To study it, and its makers. That's why we were brought to this planet in the first place, to this epoch – what other reason could there be? That's what I've been doing since I got here, primarily. But I always expected you, some of you at least, to follow. So I prepared this habitat.'

'Generous of you—'

'Although I did not expect those others to be the first of the group to come here.'

Mardina pushed herself to her feet. '"Those others." You mean my father and the Inca woman, don't you? You keep hinting they're here, but I don't see them. Well, there's only one place they can be.' She set off towards the open Hatch.

Beth called, 'Be careful, Mardina.'

But Mardina didn't slow her pace.

Stef said now, 'This frame you've put up around yourself, Earthshine. You've rooted yourself into the ground. Is this part of your thermal energy mine?'

'Oh, no,' he said now. 'You'll see *that* outside – a few panels flush to the ground, deep bores beneath. All *this* is to achieve a more intimate kind of contact.'

Beth asked, 'Contact with who?'

'The Dreamers,' the ColU said suddenly. 'You're trying to talk to the Dreamers, aren't you?'

'This ancient world is infested with them,' Earthshine said. 'Well, I imagine it always was. ColU, it is as if I have dropped an antenna into a brain. And I think—'

'Yes?' The ColU sounded breathless, eager.

'I think I hear their thoughts ...'

And Stef Kalinski heard a gunshot.

CHAPTER 70

Mardina, who had been approaching the open Hatch, threw herself down on the ground.

Chu and Titus were with her faster than Stef would have believed possible. Sprawling, they grabbed Mardina by the arms, slithered back along the ground, and delivered her to Stef and Beth. Beth took her pregnant daughter in her arms.

To Stef, Mardina looked shocked, furious.

'I'm not hurt, Mother. Really, I'm not. I heard the shot – I thought I saw something fly past me – I dropped to the ground – I guess it was a warning shot. I can't believe he did it. My *father.*'

Beth stroked her head. 'Frankly, love, you and I always meant less to Ari than his ambition.'

'I'll give them a warning shot,' Titus yelled. With *gladio* in his good hand, he approached the pit. Chu, too, followed the legionary, a dagger in his hand, looking coldly furious. It was after all his lover and the mother of his baby who had been shot at. That quiet intensity seemed to have burned away the last of his slavish deference, Stef thought.

Titus called, 'You, Inguill, *quipucamayoc*! Ari the *druidh*!'

'Come no closer, legionary!' It was undoubtedly Ari's voice, Stef could hear, though it sounded strained, weak. 'We are protecting our property ... We have rights of priority which ...' He broke up in coughing.

'Wait, legionary,' Stef called. 'Let's see if we can talk our way out of this.'

'Talk? Ha! And who in Hades gave them a *ballista*?'

'It was manufactured here,' Earthshine said. 'Using a fabricator. I was naive – I showed them how to operate the fabricator with voice commands. It uses an electrical charge to drive a projectile of—'

'And who fires a *ballista* in a dome like this?'

'The dome material is self-sealing,' Earthshine said, still more softly. 'In that regard at least we are secure. Besides, the outside air is breathable, if cold. We are in no danger.'

Stef got stiffly to her feet. 'I don't understand any of this. What property do they think they own? What do they mean by priority?' She draped a blanket over her shoulders and began to shuffle towards the pit.

'Stef Kalinski,' Titus said, 'stay back!'

'Oh, nonsense, legionary. Somebody's got to deal with this. At least *I* won't be missed if I get shot. And when it comes to Hatches I'm the expert, remember.'

'Take me,' the ColU said urgently. 'The slate, an earphone ...'

Beth ran up to hand her the slate, which Stef hung around her neck. It felt inordinately heavy. 'Now, then ...'

Feeling neither brave nor scared, maybe she was just too old to be bothered any more, Stef neared the pit. The material of the emplacement panel felt very eerie under her feet, smooth, alien, neither hot nor cold.

'Ari Guthfrithson! Inguill! It's me – Stef Kalinski. I'm coming to talk to you. Shoot me if you must, but try not to hit your pregnant daughter at least, Ari ...'

She came to the lip of the open pit. Ari and Inguill were sitting together at the base, huddled against a wall – near a rounded doorway, she noticed. If this was a typical Hatch, that door would lead to a transitional chamber, with another door beyond leading to – somewhere else. But for now the door was sealed shut, featureless save for a seam in the wall.

Ari and Inguill, their knees up against their chests, wore filthy remnants of the clothes of their cultures, Ari his *druidh*'s gown, Inguill in her formal attire as a *quipucamayoc*. Stef was particularly shocked by the state of Ari, who like most Briganti had always been finely groomed. They were surrounded by the basics of living, a heap of grimy blankets, piles of food – tired-looking vegetables, what might be dried meat – and simple buckets in which slopped piss and watery shit. The source of Mardina's sewage smell, then. They looked impossibly skinny, even skeletal, in their loose clothing. Stef saw glossy, dead-looking patches of skin on Ari's cheeks, his forehead. Frostbitten?

But in two bony hands Ari held a convincing-looking gun, pointing it out of the pit at her. 'No closer, Stef Kalinski.'

Stef held her empty hands in the air. 'I'm no threat to you, Ari. I never was … Can I lower my hands? I'm kind of tired, and only just got over a dizzy spell.'

He nodded curtly.

'Thank you. Mind you, I'm a picture of health compared to you. You should have waited for us, you two. Travelled with us.'

'You are all fools,' Inguill snapped. 'And *we* got here *first*. Which was the whole point.'

Stef leaned down, cautiously. 'So why in heaven's name are you sitting in that hole?'

'We're waiting for Earthshine to let us in,' Inguill said. 'Through that door. We know he can open it; we've seen it … We want to go through the Hatch. We want to be *first*.'

'And now you're mounting a sit-down strike? But *why*? After plodding all that way across the ice muttering to each other, do you even remember any more?'

Ari raised his gun; it wavered uncertainly. 'You won't trick us out of here.'

'I've no intention to. Believe me, I've been through enough Hatches, you're welcome to this one. But, look – will you let me bring you some fresh food, at least? Or one of the others. And how about I get the legionary to take out those slop buckets for you?'

'Not Titus,' Inguill snapped.

'Chu, then.' Stef looked directly at Ari. 'Who is the father of your grandchild.'

The gun lowered at last. 'I heard you speak of this … It's true, then?'

'I'm afraid so. Look, I'll go and get help. Don't go away, now.'

As she walked away she heard Inguill's ranting voice. 'We won't be tricked, Stef Kalinski! We won't be tricked!'

With Ari and Inguill fed, and their slop buckets emptied out of the airlock, Titus's group gathered, sitting on heaped blankets and bits of Earthshine's equipment, before Earthshine in his spidery cage. They had hot drinks and portions of food manufactured by Earthshine's fabricators, bland but nutritious.

Beth had spoken to Ari. But Mardina had refused even to look at her father, who had taken a shot at her.

'I fear they are no longer sane,' Earthshine whispered.

'Oh, you don't say,' Stef said drily.

'They have developed an obsession with the power they perceive to lie beyond the Hatch. That was why they abandoned the rest of you, stole your equipment … Why they abandoned the history they had been born into. Even abandoned you, Mardina, Beth. Why, the trek here itself nearly killed them, but they would not be stopped.'

Beth grunted. 'I'm not surprised at *that*. Whatever other qualities he's got, Mardina, your father is not a practical man.'

'And Inguill was a bureaucrat,' Stef said. 'In her culture. A wily one, a very clever individual, but not prepared for such a journey. Whereas *we* had a Roman legionary to lead us. Perhaps neither of them truly imagined what it would be like. But once they had set off—'

Earthshine said, 'They were driven on by pride and greed. Their obsession with the antistellar, with the Hatch they expected to find here. They clung to that dream, even though they left behind their health, even their sanity.'

Titus snapped, 'What is this dream?'

'I think they believe,' the ColU said, 'that the Hatch will give them the power of gods. The power to remake worlds. After all, they've seen it happen – we all have, more than once.'

500

Stef nodded. 'And maybe the deep shock of those experiences has taken a toll on them, more than we realised.' She closed her eyes, looking inward. 'A toll on the rest of us too.'

'In a way, I admit,' said Earthshine now, 'we aren't so dissimilar. I was outraged by what I saw as the meddling of the Dreamers in our histories, as it gradually unfolded. I struck at Mars, *a* Mars, to attract their attention. Well, it worked. I was brought here. I intended to challenge them again. And above all to try to *understand* ...'

Stef prompted, 'Earthshine, Ari said you had control of the Hatch in some way.'

'In a sense, I do. The Hatches have always chosen who they will respond to.'

'That's true,' Beth said. 'I remember the first Hatch I ever saw, at the substellar. It – developed – grooves in its upper surfaces, for builders to lie in, like keys in locks.'

Earthshine said, 'With humans, handprints are commonly used. Here, the builders evidently sensed something of my presence. In my case the interface is electromagnetic, not physical contact. Not visible. But when I sent it a certain message – echoing a signal I received – the Hatch opened, the great lid.'

Stef pressed, 'And then the second door, to the next chamber?'

'I have explored the second chamber,' Earthshine said. 'Or at least I have sent secondary units in there. I believe I know what lies beyond the *next* door – and on the far side of this Hatch itself. But I have yet to open that final door. I have constructed a probe. You might be interested in the details, Stef. A sphere, of material of very high heat capacity. I hope it will last a measurable time, even as much as a nanosecond.'

Stef tried to imagine this. 'What are you saying, Earthshine? *What lies beyond that door?*'

Earthshine whispered, 'The ColU knows – or suspects.'

'The boundary,' said ColU. 'The edge of the multiverse. The death of the future. Yes. *That* is what they would bring you here to show you. So that you could understand ...'

'There need be no spatial deviation, you see,' said Earthshine.

'You need not travel across space to reach it. And you need journey only a short distance into the future. After all, the event will occur everywhere, simultaneously. On every world.'

The ColU said, 'We must compare our estimates of the time remaining.'

The humans absorbed this terrible conversation in silence.

Stef said at last, 'And that's what you've told Ari and Inguill they will walk into, if—'

'If they are in the second chamber when the Hatch opens, yes. But they won't listen, Stef. They don't believe me. They believe that the Hatch will fulfil their dreams of power and wealth.'

Titus shook his head. 'Then what are we to do?'

Stef sighed. 'I suggest we try to get Ari and Inguill out of there. After all you are family, Beth, Mardina. You might get through where Earthshine couldn't. And then—'

'And then,' the ColU said, 'we must consider how best to use the time remaining to us.'

Mardina rested her hand on her belly, dropped her head, and reached blindly for Chu.

CHAPTER 71

The group spent two full days trying to coax Ari and Inguill out of the pit. Beth tried the hardest, tried to get through to the man she'd almost married. Even Mardina reluctantly consented to speak to Ari, about the baby she was carrying, his grandchild.

Neither basic human appeals, nor Earthshine's cold logic about what must lie beyond the Hatch door, made any difference. Ari did seem anguished about the fate of the baby. But nothing would change his mind, nor Inguill's, who babbled about the power of Inti, the Inca sun god. They were both convinced of only one thing: that Earthshine was trying to keep them from – well, from glory, Stef supposed.

Titus remarked, 'No mortal should seek the power of a god. It would burn him in a flash.'

The ColU seemed to agree. 'But who are we to stop them, Titus Valerius?'

At last, they gave up. Earthshine agreed to open up the Hatch for them.

The group gathered at the lip of the pit to see the outcome.

In response to Earthshine's invisible signal, the door to the Hatch's middle chamber swung back at last. In that chamber Stef could see the 'probe' Earthshine had mentioned, a fat ceramic sphere sitting on the chamber floor.

Ari and Inguill stepped through, moving gingerly, helping each other. At each step of the way Earthshine paused to allow them to reconsider, to pull back.

But at last they pulled the door closed behind them, without a backward glance, and they were gone.

'I gave them a control,' Earthshine said. 'To emulate the signals I use to communicate with the Hatch. A simple hand-held thing ... And I found a way to send signals through the emplacement substrate, so I will know, from my probe, when the final lid is opened.'

Stef was intrigued. 'You sent signals through Hatch substrate material? That's more than we ever managed, in the years I spent studying Hatches and kernels on Luna and Mars—'

'They are gone,' Earthshine said simply.

When it was safe, Earthshine opened the second door once more. The central chamber, with its door firmly closed once more, seemed entirely undamaged to Stef, and was completely empty.

Earthshine said that his probe had after all lasted a healthy fraction of a nanosecond, and it had learned a good deal about the nature of the 'multiverse boundary'. It and the ColU immediately locked into a silent, high-speed electronic communication about the new data.

And Clodia and Chu, exploring the Hatch, found something new: grooves to take human hands, on the inner side of the Hatch's second door. Three pairs of them.

'That,' the ColU said enigmatically, when it was told, 'deserves further consideration.'

CHAPTER 72

Earthshine said, 'I believe that the Dreamers have spoken to me as they have spoken to none other of our kind. And by "our kind" I mean complex life forms, equivalent to your own multicellular nature, although the details differ from world to world, biosphere to biosphere ... That sounds arrogant, I know. Even grandiose.'

Stef said sceptically, 'I'll say. Of all that vast cosmic host—'

'Yet I am unusual, for them. I am a product of human technology, of course. And yet I think that *humanity itself*, all of our biosphere above the level of the single-celled creatures, is a kind of technology to them. Created for a purpose, you see, or at least modified. But I am a secondary creation – as if one of my fabricators produced, not a copy of itself, but an entirely new design of its own. As such I am perhaps of – interest – to them. And I am not entirely under their control.'

'As we are?' Stef asked sourly.

'Well, aren't you?'

Titus grunted. 'This all sounds too philosophical to me. What am I, a Greek?' He, Stef, Beth, the ColU, the elders of this tiny antistellar colony, sat in a loose circle, beside the comfort of an open fire burning on a hearth of stone slabs, in the shadow of the strange spider-like structure that encompassed Earthshine's support unit. Now Titus dipped his clay mug into the slowly boiling bowl of tea on the fire. 'Face it, Earthshine. You got the Dreamers' attention because you smashed Mars to pieces, and murdered a whole world of these clever animalcules in the process. That would get most people's attention.'

'Well, that's true. And that, of course, was the intention.'

'And so they brought you here,' said the ColU, a glittering mass of technology set on a blanket away from the fire. 'They guided you through their Hatch network to this place. And—'

'And they spoke to me,' Earthshine said, cutting in. 'They told me their story. If that term is adequate for such a biography ... In a way, you see, it is the story of life, in this universe.'

'Tell us, then,' Stef said, leaning forward, swathed in a blanket. 'Tell us, Earthshine.'

'From the beginning, even when the universe was still very young, there was life.

'Life self-organised, from collections of more or less simple chemicals, blindly following the laws of chemistry and physics, guided by mathematical rules evidently inherent in reality. Microbial life, single-cell life, viral life ... Some scientists used to think life could have emerged even when the Big Bang glow was still bright, and the whole universe was warm enough to be one big habitable zone.

'On worlds with similar surface conditions, similar kinds of life emerged. Earth and Per Ardua, for example. But life spread, too, as rogue comets and asteroids blasted the surfaces of the young worlds, and handfuls of bugs buried deep in rock fragments survived chance journeys between the planets, and, more rarely, between the stars. Panspermia bubbles formed, worlds with similar conditions hosting related forms of life, sharing common origins. Across the galaxy such bubbles jostled, and even permeated; worlds of warm-Earth life could share stellar systems with worlds of cold-Titan life, as you've seen for yourselves.

'And life spread inward too, down into the guts of the worlds, following deep water flows, mineral seeps, leaks of heat energy, radioactivity ... The interiors of worlds, too deep even for the immense bombardments of the young cosmos to do any damage, were warm, safe cradles in those early days, and life got down there pretty quickly – on Earth we found deep bugs all over the world, all of similar species. The deep rock is a static shelter, though, and relatively starved of energy. Life was slow to spread, even slow to procreate. To survive on such thin resources, living things learned to *repair* rather than to reproduce. But gradually a kind of complexity grew and spread, as the microbes gathered themselves into mutually supportive colonies, and the colonies combined into supercolonies.

'A threshold was passed. Consciousness emerged.

'On Earth, and on Per Ardua, most of the biomass of the planet – most of its weight of living stuff – dwells in the deep subsurface rocks. For most of their history humans never even suspected it existed. And it is aware, a constellation of huge, slow minds. These are the Dreamers. They remember their birth, when the universe was young.

'And world after world woke up ...'

The story was told in fragments, day by day, amid intense inter-rogation by Stef and the others.

As the weeks and months passed since their arrival at the antistellar point of Per Ardua – as the deaths of Ari and Inguill faded in the memory – the audience around Earthshine came and went. They all needed to sleep and eat; they all had chores to do with the maintenance of the colony that kept them all alive – and they were all determined to support Mardina through her pregnancy. That drew even the ColU away from Earthshine, and its slow, sometimes rambling monologue.

But they listened, and they questioned Earthshine on confus-ing details from their different viewpoints. Gradually a kind of summary of the story was emerging, one which they could all grasp, one way or another.

And in the midst of cosmic strangeness, human life went on.

As Mardina's pregnancy approached its full term, she became ever heavier, ever more slow-moving. At least she felt she had good support, isolated as she was here. The ColU had been specifically instructed in childbirth procedure to support the growth of the original ISF colonies, and Earthshine's fabricators were capable of synthesising any medicinal support she needed. She had at her side wise women in her own mother and Stef Kalinski. And Chu was turning out to be a doting parent-to-be. Only Clodia remained a problem for now, her residual jealousy over Chu getting in the way – and, perhaps, Mardina thought, Clodia's resentment at having her own ambitions to be a soldier thwarted. It was a shame that the comradeship they'd built up on Yupanquisuyu was gone now – or maybe they'd just grown out of it, she thought.

No, Mardina couldn't complain about the support she had, even if she would have preferred to have Michael the *medicus* on hand, or better yet a fully equipped Brikanti hospital.

Still, as time passed, she felt less and less enthusiastic about work. Even about moving around too much.

And, in a dome where there wasn't a lot of entertainment, she found the slow processes of the fabricators' labour an increasing distraction. One morning Mardina found one little gadget, no larger than a loaf of bread, sitting in a pool of ground-up Arduan rock dust, which in turn it was processing into machine parts that it gathered in neat heaps. She knelt to watch it, rapt.

Chu said, 'It is proceeding faster than I imagined.'

'This one's actually making a copy of itself.'

'I suppose it is giving birth, in a way. Bit by bit.'

Mardina, sitting on a heap of blankets, rubbed her belly. 'I wish I could do it that way. Take out this little monster one limb at a time and then assemble it on the floor.'

'You don't mean that.'

'No, I don't suppose I do. But if these machines keep this up, we'll start to become a real colony. Titus wants to call it "Nova Roma".'

But Chu did not smile. 'It is a shame that we will have so little time to enjoy what we build.'

Mardina flinched; it wasn't the kind of thing Chu usually said. She looked down at the solidity of the rocky floor, and up at the star-strewn sky beyond the dome, and she reached for Chu's hand. 'We can't think like that.'

'No. I am sorry. For even if what the mechanical sage says is true, it is up to us to behave as if it is not so.'

She tried to absorb that. Then she stirred. 'Come on. Help me up, I'm getting stiff. Time for my exercise, a couple of tours of the dome ...'

'From the beginning the great communities of Dreamers apprehended something of the universe around them.

'They sensed the early battering of their worlds by the debris of planetary formation. They were tugged by the subtle tides exerted by their worlds' parent stars and sister planets. They could *feel* the slow geological evolution of their host worlds – an evolution shaped from the beginning by life itself; there's evidence that the presence of life on a planet like Earth, for instance, even helps stabilise the formation of continents.

'Even multicellular life, when it evolved – infrequently, sporadically – served as a kind of sensory mechanism for the living worlds.

'For some worlds, given the right conditions, with an atmosphere reasonably transparent to the parent star's radiation, energy could pour down from the sky onto the land and into the upper layers of the oceans, and the familiar miracles of complex life could come about. Photosynthesis, a chemical means to exploit the energy of stellar radiation. Grand rebuildings of oceans and atmospheres through the injections of such gases as oxygen or methane. The evolution of secondary forms of life – like Earth's animals – to feed off those products. But the outer layers of complex planetary life, so important to creatures like humans, were all but an irrelevance to the Dreamers. They only ever amounted to a trivial fraction of any world's total biomass. And the complex creatures were usually not even aware of the noostrata that permeated the rocks beneath their feet.

'Yet, through the frantic reactions of the complex forms, "animals" and "plants", to external events like asteroid strikes or stellar flares or supernova explosions, the Dreamers came to know the universe in more detail.

509

'I think even then, far back in cosmic time, the Dreamers began to get the first hints of the approach of the End Time.

'And then there was communication, between Dreamer worlds.

'The complex forms, in their haphazard way, built spacecraft, or infested comets and other wandering bodies, and began a new kind of contact, supplementing natural panspermia, the slow drift of impact-loosened rocks. Panspermia had always been a way for the worlds to be linked to each other. A package of living things and genetic data is a kind of communication, a message from one minded world to another. With the coming of complex life and interstellar travel that process remained random, without central direction, but did become more frequent.

'From the beginning the living worlds had been aware of each other's existence. Now, slowly, sporadically, imperfectly, they began to talk.

'Imagine a community of minded worlds, then. All different in detail, yet all with fundamental similarities, engaged in a slow, chance conversation. They shared ideas, perceptions. Some grew in stature, while others became more inward-looking. They were all effectively immortal, of course – and they were stuck with each other. I imagine them as like a college of bickering professors, locked in decades-long rivalries. But in the case of the Dreamer worlds, aeons-long. Not *quite* immortal, though; in a dangerous universe, whole worlds can be lost, sometimes, and all their freight of life and mind with them.

'But this slowly developing community was disrupted by the freak emergence of one mutant world.

'The human categorisation of complex creatures into "animal" or "vegetable" is too simple. Anthropocentric. Even on Per Ardua, the builders were animals that photosynthesised.

'Well, then. Consider a world in which *every* complex organism, every plant and tree, every creature motile or not, is, if not sentient itself, then a sense organ for a larger mind. Every flower is like an eye or an ear on the world. Sensory impressions chatter down tendrils like nerves, and feed into root masses of huge complexity: aged vegetable brains. And these in turn, on this world, speak directly to the true minds of the planet, the Dreamers in their deep rocks. This world was called Alvega in some human cultures.'

Stef wondered how Earthshine could possibly know that.

'All this came about because of a peculiar origin of life on this one particular world. On many worlds there can be several origin events; but on most worlds, like Earth or Per Ardua, a single design, a single DNA-like coding system controlling a single protein set – or the equivalent in different biospheres, like the Titans – emerges as dominant, and usually quite quickly, with small advantages rapidly becoming overwhelming. But not on Alvega. Here, two quite different and inimical biospheres battled down long ages for control, even after the emergence of complex life. When the war was won, the winner had become by necessity much more closely integrated than most worlds, with the complex surface florescence feeding directly into the Dreamer communities below.

'On this world, then, the Dreamers were much more engaged with the external universe – and they had the means to achieve direct contact with others like themselves, for their complex partners on the planetary surface were, uniquely, entirely under the Dreamers' control.

'From Alvega a new wave of emissaries were sent out, in interstellar craft not unlike huge trees, their mission to link one world with another.

'It took many hundreds of millions of years for the new living technology to spread across the galaxy. But, gradually, on one world after another, isolated Platonic Dreamers woke to the possibility of community, of deep and rapid communication with others of their kind.

'There was a new urgency now – if you can ever call a billion-year-programme "urgent". The value of complex life was seen for the first time, and panspermia of a new kind became intentional. Across the panspermia bubbles waves of modification were sent

511

out, so that worlds that had not known photosynthesis were raised to that level, and then living complexity became possible on worlds suddenly rich with the energy provided by oxygen or methane, or other reactive chemicals. Creatures like plants, creatures like animals, new kingdoms of life blossomed on world after world—'

'I knew it,' the ColU breathed. 'I found this, even on Per Ardua – the first world beyond the solar system reached by humans. The coincidences of timing. Photosynthesis appeared on Per Ardua two billion years before humans showed up, just as on Earth. And the first complex creatures appeared on both worlds with quite precise coincidences of timing: five hundred and forty-two million years before humanity on Earth, the same on Per Ardua. I *measured* this. I knew it! I remember speaking of this to your mother and father, Beth Eden Jones. Not that they understood the implications, not then. Well – nor did I. Not then.'

'The coincidences were real,' Earthshine said. 'I have no detail on how this was done, what kind of agency they used to trigger a complexity explosion on Earth, say. I imagine farmers striding across the stars ... But these events are indeed evidence of a deep, galaxy-wide bioengineering on multiple worlds, by communities of Dreamers who were becoming more knowledgeable, more communicative – and more willing to intervene in the destiny of life.

'And as they grew in power and understanding, and as they learned more of the universe around them, so they developed a new urgency. Because—'

'Because they became aware of the imminence of the End Time,' Stef whispered.

'Yes. Even the Dreamers, who, huddled in the deep rock, might survive even the supernova detonation of a parent sun, could not survive that.

'And so they laid their plans.'

*

They might be a short-lived colony, but they were a busy colony.

They all had projects of one kind or another – well, Stef thought, there were so few of them there were always plenty of chores to do, ranging from stitching ripped clothing or fixing a leaking boot to supervising the synthesis of some new component by the clattering fabricators.

Meal times were the only occasions when they all gathered together, breakfast, lunch, supper. That included Earthshine, for they always sat around his spidery framework. The ColU too. Titus had mandated that from the beginning, once they had got over the loss of Ari and Inguill. They were too small a group to be able to afford to break up into cliques or factions. Stef supposed this was another relic of Titus's field experience, presumably dating from when he had had to lead small isolated parties on long expeditions. She applauded his leadership.

It was unfortunate, though, that he always used language like 'lancing boils' or 'spilling the pus' to describe the process of talking out their problems. Especially when she was trying to force down the freeze-dried potato or fabricated slop that passed for food here.

And she tried not to let her dissatisfaction with the food distract her from listening to Earthshine's long, complex account.

'So. After the complexity waves. That was when they started to build the Hatches,' Stef prompted.

'That was when,' Earthshine agreed. 'I don't know where, how, when the technology emerged. But a Hatch link is essentially a communications technology optimised to fit within the limits of the universe in which we find ourselves.'

'Limits? What limits?'

'To begin with, lightspeed. That seems to be a fundamental physical barrier – just as Einstein predicted all those years ago. And the other—'

'The end of the universe,' the ColU said.

'A wall across the future. And very close in time, to such long-lived beings. There was never a sense that the minded

513

worlds, or that any of the Dreamers – or any of *us* – could survive that final limit. But they felt the urgency to talk, to communicate – to share as much as they could, to make the most of the time available.

'But here were these vast minds, dependent for their communication on the slow trajectories of crude starships, or on the still slower drift of rocks from star to star. It is as if Einstein and Newton, two tremendous intellects, both under sentence of imminent death, were able to communicate only by means of Morse code tapped out on a cell wall ... They had to do better.'

'And the Hatches were the way,' Stef said.

'Yes. The Hatches are something like wormholes, flaws in spacetime connecting one event to another. As you know, Stef, theoretically wormholes can even link different universes – different cosmoses drifting in the great hulk of the multiverse. Any transition would be limited by lightspeed—'

'But with a Hatch one can step from Mercury to Per Ardua, say, four light years apart, in no more than four years.'

'Exactly. It is the best one can do. But to build such engines, rips and twists in spacetime, requires huge amounts of energy, as you can imagine. Where is such energy to come from?'

'The kernels,' Stef said immediately. 'Which are also like wormholes, through which energy pours. That was basically a *lure* – right? The cheese that baited the trap, into which we clever tool-making apes thrust our greedy paws. And all the time the true purpose was to get us to build those damn Hatches.'

'True, although *you* never got that far, did you? You saw that kernels were associated with Hatch emplacements, of course. But, Stef, you never understood how the presence of kernels facilitates the setting up of a Hatch in the first place. You never even discovered the process by trial and error, as did the Romans, the Incas.

'Stef, there is actually only one kind of technology here. *Kernels are Hatches*; a Hatch is a specialised form of kernel. The Hatches emerge when a kernel field is perturbed by an energetic

514

event – I imagine it is almost an organic process, a self-selection, as a single dominant tree will emerge from a grove of saplings.'

'Maybe. But what about the energy? For all the decades I spent studying those beasts we never came close to understanding where that energy came from.'

'True,' said Earthshine. 'And *I* was never allowed access to kernels and Hatches to study them for myself. I had to rely on your work, at second hand. How much time was wasted!'

'We guessed stellar cores, supernovas, gamma ray bursters, quasars—'

'Wrong, wrong and wrong again. Remember, Stef, both kernels and Hatches are forms of wormholes. As we have experienced ourselves, a wormhole can link events separated by space *and by time*. We walked through a Hatch from the Mars of Inguill's Inca era, the human age, to – this, a world light years distant and well over three billion years separated in time.'

'Yes,' said Stef. 'But these wormholes aren't as they were predicted by our own science, by relativity. *They* were rips in space and time held open by impossible kinds of antigravity … You could have travelled faster that light through Einstein's wormholes. And you could have dragged such a wormhole around with a sublight ship to make a functioning time machine. But this is different. Kernel/Hatch wormholes are sublight. But they can link different universes. And so you could connect the present of one universe to the past or the future of another …' The pieces of the puzzle moved around inside her head. 'That's it. If you're right about the nature of the multiverse, then all the universes in our local ensemble share the same future, if you look ahead far enough …'

'They all must face the End Time,' the ColU said.

Earthshine said, 'And *that*, Stef, is the answer to where a kernel's energy comes from. Not from some quasar, from some point distant in space. It comes from a point distant *in time*—'

'The future.' Stef saw it now. 'The End Time itself.'

'Yes. You have it. The End Time will be a hugely energetic event. The Dreamers *have tapped into that very energy*, using the

515

kernels, in order to build their Hatch network. Now, we multi-cellular toy-creatures are allowed to play with the technologies, to build our kernel-driven starships and to wage our wars, but—'

'But it's all secondary to the true purpose,' Stef said. 'Which is for the Dreamer worlds to be linked to each other. You know, my father saw this, right at the beginning. He sensed that whoever was giving us kernels – he never lived to learn about Hatches – had some agenda of their own. He was wary about that.'

'He was right to be. Humans, however,' Earthshine said softly, 'could never resist such deadly toys. Even if they were powered by the energies of Ragnarok itself.

'So the Hatch network spread. So the worlds were linked, as never before; so they learned and grew.

'But that's not the end of the story. For even this was not enough. The time left, mere billions of years, seemed horribly short to such minds as the Dreamers. And so, having intervened several times before in the destiny of life in the galaxy, now they intervened again. Seeking to find a way to have us serve their needs even more completely ...'

As the final months passed Titus Valerius led many expeditions back to the nearside of Per Ardua. Given the gravity-tunnel network, the terminator was only days away; they always needed supplies, so why not travel back?

Titus didn't retrace the journey that they had made to get here every time. He and his companions took the chance to explore the rest of the branching gravity-train system that fanned out across the dark face of Per Ardua, and to study different regions of the terminator and the edge of the star-facing side. This amounted to a kind of inspection of the tunnel system itself, of course, and Titus did report a few breakages, even collapses, times they had had to come back the way they'd travelled and find another route. The tunnel system was tremendously ancient and wonderfully robust – Stef joked in the silence of her head that it had kept working almost to the end of the universe itself – but nothing was perfect, it seemed.

Titus never forgot his primary purpose. Each time he returned he would faithfully deliver a sled full of root vegetables and fruit, plus anything exotic he found, such as, once, what looked and tasted like peaches.

But he also brought home specimens he thought might be of interest to the ColU or Earthshine. The ColU had specifically asked for samples of stems of any kind, the rod-like forms that had once been the fundamental unit of complex life on Per Ardua. And once Titus brought back a miniature stromatolite, a cylinder maybe a metre and a half tall, half a metre wide. He and Chu dragged this thing home strapped to the bed of the sled with ropes.

They had already given over part of the dome to a 'Per Ardua garden', where the ground-up rock floor had been laced with native soil, and the ColU was growing his stem samples and other native forms. Here they planted the stromatolite, bedding it deep in the worked ground. Not even the ColU had any experience of transplanting stromatolites before, and the little community spent some days fretting over the health of its new arrival before the stromatolite seemed to flourish, with its bronze-coloured carapace acquiring a new sheen. It was another example of the integration of life, Stef supposed, of living beings from different stars working together: humans from Earth tending a stromatolite from Per Ardua.

And it was the lack of time in this doomed universe for integration, of biospheres and cultures and minds, that had driven the Dreamers to attempt their most radical rebuilding.

'Even humans had such fantasies,' Earthshine said. 'Of cultures crossing the stars and coming together. Perhaps there would be conflict at first, but in the end there would be integration. A galaxy united under a common civilisation – imagine it.'

'I remember some of the scientists' dreams,' Stef said. 'Perhaps if mind could encompass the universe it could change its destiny.

Save it from a Big Crunch, or a Big Rip. Make the universe *better* than nature intended.'

'Or at least,' the ColU said, 'mind, by filling the universe, could *observe* it. And thereby make its existence worthwhile.'

'But there is no time for any of this,' Earthshine said now. 'No time! Not in a universe with such a short lifespan, and constrained by lightspeed. Even a single galaxy is too large, the Dreamers concluded, to be united in such a time. The Dreamers grew restless – though that's an odd word to apply to billion-year-old minds. *They wanted more time.* But there was no more to be had, not in the future.'

'Ah.' Stef nodded. 'I think I see where this is going. To gain more time, they started to reach, not into the future – but *into the past.*'

'You have it. Remember, the Dreamers were becoming masters of wormhole technology; they had kernels and Hatches. By tapping the End Time event itself they had an effectively infinite energy supply. Now they began to reach out, not across time and space in this universe, but to other universes entirely. Universes with different histories.'

Stef laughed. 'Of course. I see it now. Suppose you're dissatisfied that humans in my reality sheaf, the UN-China culture, didn't even start to work with Hatches until the twenty-second century. You wish it had been earlier. Well, then, you simply pluck another copy of the universe from the tree of possible realities, one where we *did* get to the Hatches earlier.'

Mardina nodded. 'I see – I think. Which happened to be a history in which Rome survived, as it did not in your history.'

'That's it,' Earthshine said. 'So the destiny of the human race is altered fundamentally. Billions who might have lived were never born at all. Billions more rise up to take their place. And those billions strive to extend the Hatch network, long before it would have happened in the earlier reality – for that, you see, was the point.'

Titus frowned. 'But if this is true, what of the other histories, other realities? Are they simply discarded, like – like early drafts of a note of command?'

'Not discarded,' said Earthshine. 'They all continue to exist, out there, somewhere in the multiverse. And all, incidentally, will be terminated at the End Time; they are too closely related to be spared. But there is only ever one universe that is *primal*. As if it is more real than the rest. And before the Dreamers' meddling, the primal universe would have been the most logical, the most neat, the most self-consistent in terms of causality. Self-consistent as the others were not.

'Magnificent it may be, but this project of the Dreamers is – untidy. Only the original primal universe was clean in a causal way, where for every effect there was a cause, neatly lined up in an orderly history. No anomalies, no miracles. But the fresh universes these creatures have selected are less optimal. They have rough edges. Effects preceding causes. Effects with *no* cause. Trailing threads. Threads to be picked out by the likes of me ... You might even find gross violations, I suppose. Absurdities. For example, a universe where Julius Caesar never lived – but where a mass of evidence, documents and monuments, happened to be found that described his non-existent career. Effects without cause.'

'And we found some of those threads,' Stef said. 'So did Ari, with his remains of the Drowned Culture. And Inguill with her mission patch from a flight to Mars that never happened.'

'But all of this is an irrelevance, to the Dreamers. All *they* care about are the Hatches we build for them. And in each new reality we follow a cultural and historic logic that, yes, enables us to reach the stage of building Hatches ever earlier.

'And so in each successive draft of cosmic history the Dreamers' network of interconnectivity and communication reaches back, deeper into time, deeper into the past. The number of thoughts they are able to share grows, and their apprehension of the universe grows deeper. The Dreamers are essentially contemplative. If the universe is to be brief in duration – well, it is beautiful nonetheless, and deserves to be apprehended to

519

the full. To be appreciated, to be studied and cherished, from beginning to end.'

'It is monstrous,' the ColU said. 'It is magnificent. As if the universe itself, a finite block in space and time, is a kind of garden. A garden of which every square centimetre is to be tended, made as beautiful as possible, all the way to the back wall, so to speak. I am a gardener, or was; I can see the appeal of a cultivated cosmos. And all of it contained by the walls of birth and death.'

'But the price of all this is raggedness,' Stef said, dissatisfied on a profound level. 'A universe of holes and patches, where scientific enquiry doesn't necessarily make sense. And how far would they go to get to build their empire of the Hatches? Maybe in some realities mankind was eliminated altogether, and replaced by some other clever creature. Rats, maybe. Smart rodents burrowing through the multiverse like it was some roomy loft ...'

Earthshine said, 'And all of it, tidy or otherwise, doomed to incineration when the End Time comes. You see it now. *We* never mattered. *We* really are just a kind of technology to the Dreamers – created by their uplift programmes and then modified for a purpose. In fact I suspect the Dreamers don't really believe we are intelligent at all. We are too small; there were always too many of us, getting in each other's way. To them we are more like social creatures, industrious animals who blindly build things. Like ants or beavers.'

'Or builders,' Beth said.

'Or road-laying legionaries,' Titus said. 'And given some of the lads I've worked with in my time, they might have a point.'

One morning Beth came to find Stef. She was grinning widely. 'There's something you need to see. As one veteran Per Arduan to another.'

She led Stef over to the ColU's small Arduan garden. The ColU itself sat on a chair by the garden, roughly made by Chu from Arduan tree stems. 'Colonel Kalinski,' it said. 'Look what I did.'

Beth took Stef to the edge of the worked soil. Reed-like stems grew in the earth in the shadow of the dwarf stromatolite, and in a shallow, marshy puddle.

Beth said, 'Remember scenery like this? The ColU says it believes that the stems we see today are descendants of those of our time, of the first colonies. And it was those stems that bundled up to make builders. The ColU thinks the genetic potential to create builders is still in there somewhere; all he needs to do is cross-breed enough samples to restore the native stock.'

Stef thought that over. 'You won't have time, ColU. There are only months left—'

'I know, Stef Kalinski. But you'll forgive me for trying even so ...'

'*I* asked the ColU to do this,' Beth said. 'The builders saved my life, and my parents', when we migrated with their lake – even if they didn't know it. I always felt guilty about how the builders kind of got shoved aside when humans came pouring through the Hatch to Per Ardua. I wanted us to at least try.'

'The ColU hasn't succeeded, though, has it?'

'No, but it's made some progress. Come and see. Take a closer look. Just don't get freaked out the way my father always said he was, when he first discovered these things ...'

Curiosity pricking, Stef stepped forward to the edge of the pond and bent to see. The artificial pond was shallow, and its base was covered with mud, thick with lichen, from which the stems were growing. The stems themselves came up to her waist. They were an unusual kind, darker, flatter, more like blades than the usual tube-like structures, yet still substantial, still no doubt filled with marrow.

She crept closer, right to the water's edge.

And on every stem, facing her, growing from the muddy pond scum, a single eye opened.

*

Earthshine said, 'It was you, Stef, who first brought the Dreamers to my attention, in a sense. At least, their history-meddling. For *your* personal history was tinkered with in a minor way when you first opened that Hatch we found on Mercury—'

'And suddenly I had a sister I didn't remember. Suddenly my memory didn't fit the facts of the universe as it existed.'

'In retrospect, that was a classic loose end. An effect with no cause, in a universe that was now non-perfect, its causality become ragged. Or rather, *more* ragged.'

'And later you found another loose end. The grave of my mother—'

'Which still recorded she'd only had one daughter. Even as the second daughter stood there looking at the stone. And later, as you know – now I knew what to look for – I found more evidence of meddling. More evidence of lost timelines.'

'The Drowned Culture.'

'From these traces I deduced the existence of the Dreamers. Oh, not their nature, the fact that they were ensconced in the hearts of the rocky worlds. *That* came later. But I knew they were *there*, meddling, tinkering... In my fancy, I identified them with Loki, the trickster god of the Norse. Well, in the myth, Loki's actions brought on Ragnarok, the final war – and in the course of that war another god, Heimdall, finally killed Loki himself. Was that to be my role? That was what I began to believe.'

'And you did try to kill them,' Stef said. 'Or at least you made a start. You used Ceres to hammer Mars. Even much of the subsurface life, the Dreamers, must have been destroyed in that action. But what were you thinking? Would you have roamed the galaxy smashing one world after the next, trying to eradicate bugs hidden kilometres deep?'

'I would probably have come up with a better strategy,' Earthshine said evenly. 'Consider this. Each infested world is isolated, biologically, in its deepest layers. Isolated and therefore vulnerable, to an engineered virus, perhaps, a bacteriophage... It might take a thousand years or a million, but such an agent could rip through the noostrata of such a world, and – behead it. Yes, there are many such worlds, but they are connected by the Hatch network – and again that's a weakness. Perhaps some agent could be delivered *through the Hatches themselves*, targeting the destination world, before moving on...

'This is a sketchy scheme. The point is that every life form has vulnerabilities, and every community is made vulnerable by interconnectedness. Given time and motivation, I believe that I, or another, could find a way.' He said softly, 'It may not have taken much effort. In Norse myth, Loki killed Baldr, favourite child of the gods, with an arrow made of mistletoe. A single arrow. Perhaps I wasn't even the first to try.

'But that initial assault on Mars – call it a spasm of rage – was enough for me to attract the Dreamers' attention. Enough for them to send me here, with the rest of you as a presumably unintended consequence. I think they wanted me to see this, you see. The End Time. I think they wanted me to understand what they were trying to do – and to make sure I gave up my efforts to hinder them.

'And I did understand. In any event I would not try to harm them now – that ambition is gone. I feel – honoured – to have had my strength recognised, at least. And to have been brought to this place. To Ultima.'

Titus frowned. 'Ultima?'

'You know, every starfaring culture we found had a legend of Ultima, the furthest star. Even the Incas you met spoke of *Kaylla*, nearest star, and *Karu*, furthest. Perhaps alien minds frame such ideas too. We were all surprised to be delivered to Proxima, the *nearest* star to the sun. But in the end, you see—'

'Every star is Ultima,' Stef said. 'Even Proxima. Every star is the last star. For all the stars will encounter the End Time.'

Titus looked around the group. 'So,' he said. 'That's the story told. All we need to do now in the time left is sit around and wait for the end. Is that it?'

Beth, impulsively, embraced Stef. 'If so, there are worse places to be. And worse people to be with.'

523

And then the ColU coughed, making them all stare.

'A polite interruption,' said Stef. 'What do you have to say, ColU?'

'Just that the situation may not be quite so simple. Perhaps we have – an option. If not hope.'

'An option? What do you mean?'

'Do you recall that when Ari Guthfrithson and Inguill foolishly lost their lives in the Hatch—'

Mardina's scream filled the dome.

Chu called, 'It is time! The first contraction!'

The conversation broke up. Falling into a much-practised routine, the group hurried to Mardina's side.

CHAPTER 73

After the birth, the baby grew healthy and happy, a little girl who absorbed all their attention, soon repaying in smiles.

But the time they had left dwindled, from months, to weeks, and at last to days.

Earthshine said he was calling a group conference, by the Hatch. He had matters to discuss.

Titus just grunted at this news. 'In any other circumstances that might sound ominous.'

Of course they would all come, they would do as Earthshine asked. They were nothing if not a team by now.

But first, this morning, as every camp morning, Mardina, Beth and baby Gwen took a walk around the growing colony. They gravely inspected the rows of terrestrial plants, sprouting from carefully manufactured and tilled soil, under ever-extending banks of sunlight lamps constructed in turn by an army of fabricators. And as they walked past the banks of Arduan green there was a soft rustle: the sound of eye-leaves turning to watch them go by. At the wall of the dome they peered out to see the further extensions of the colony beyond, scars in the ground where more fabricators were toiling to turn more Arduan rock into soil, to complete the manufacture of a second dome yet to be inflated – and it probably never would be, Mardina thought. The vision of an hourglass coalesced in her head, to be firmly pushed away.

Cradled in Mardina's arms, bundled in a blanket, little Gwen gazed around at whatever she could see. She was three months old now. Her hair looked as if it would be crisp black, a legacy of her grandmother, Mardina Jones, and she had dark eyes, like her father's. And those eyes were wide and seemed full of wonder, gazing at this world of marvels into which she had been thrust. Even if, and Mardina couldn't help the thought, it was a world that would betray her long before she could hope to understand why. Just months old. Just *days* left to live ...

'We're doing well,' she said aloud, to distract herself from her own thoughts. 'The colony, I mean. Given we started from nothing but the gadgets in Earthshine's support kit.'

Beth said, 'I grew up a pioneer, with my parents, alone on this world. It's pleasing to build stuff, isn't it, to bring life and order to a world – to make it right? Just as the builders always did. Maybe we've got more in common with them than people ever understood.'

'Even if we're running out of time,' Stef said.

'But that was always true, I suppose,' Beth said. 'Time for people, for worlds, for the stars. You just have to do the best you can in the here and now.'

Mardina hugged her baby. 'But it all seems so solid. So real, so detailed. That big old galaxy sprawling across the sky. The way Gwen's hair feels when I brush it. It's hard to believe ...'

Beth waited for her to finish.

'If I don't speak the name of this thing, it still feels like it isn't real. Does that make any sense?'

The ColU spoke to them now, whispering in their earphones. 'It makes plenty of sense, Mardina Eden Jones Guthfrithson. The power of names: probably one of the oldest human superstitions, going back to the birth of language itself. To deny a name is to deny a thing reality. And yet now it is time to name names. I am sorry to disturb you. Earthshine is ready for us ...'

Once more they gathered around Earthshine's support unit, under its spidery tree of extensors, his connection with the dirt and rock of Per Ardua and the legions of dreaming bugs that infested it. They sat on heaps of blankets, and low benches made from the remains of the ramshackle sled Ari and Inguill had towed here.

In the crib Titus had made, Gwen wriggled and gurgled, half asleep and content for now.

'Only three,' Earthshine said.

Titus frowned. 'What's that?'

'Call it a headline. A key point. A summary, perhaps. For all that I myself have human origins, for all I infested the human world for decades, I still find myself clumsy when delivering ambiguous news. But if you remember this in what follows it may help. *Only three.*'

Titus growled, 'No doubt you've brought us here to speak of what's to become of us.'

'And how we must respond, yes. You know that we have only a few days left, now. And there are preparations we must make.'

Only a few days. A few days, before Mardina would have to lose Gwen. She felt as if a *pugio* were twisting up her guts at the thought of it.

And Titus laughed sourly. 'What preparations? Myself, I plan to get blind drunk, and sleep through the twilight of the gods—'

'You will not,' snapped Clodia. Sitting behind him, she grabbed his hand. 'You'll be right here with me, Father, that's where you'll be.'

Titus seemed to calm quickly, as if suddenly remembering he wasn't trying to motivate a bunch of recalcitrant legionaries. 'Of course I will, child.' He wrapped his stump of an arm around her shoulders. 'Of course I will.'

Stef said now, 'But Titus asked a good question, Earthshine. What meaningful preparations *can* we make? I think it's time to stop being enigmatic. Tell us straight what's on your mind.' She scowled. 'Or is this some cruel trick?'

'No,' he said earnestly. 'Not a trick. It is a sliver of hope. Listen, please. We have discussed this many times. You do understand what is to happen? This universe – and all those near it in the multiverse, near in probability space – this universe will intersect

527

a boundary, the edge of the multiverse itself. In essence, time will cease. The End Time – that is a literal description.'

The ColU unit was sitting on a blanket, an honorary human among humans. It said, 'Imagine that the whole of this world is a simulation, supported in the memory banks of some vast computer – the way Earthshine can project a simulation of a human body. When the boundary comes it will be as if that simulation is frozen. Paused. You would not *feel* anything. But your stories would be ended, as cleanly as if you had paused some projected virtual show, and never restarted it, leaving the characters in limbo.'

'Except,' Earthshine said, 'we know it won't be as simple as that. It won't be a perfectly sharp cut-off. Everything in nature is uncertain – everything is smeared. And so will be the multiverse boundary.'

Stef said, 'Which is why the kernels work. They are worm-holes connecting us to the boundary, and what we find there is a huge outpouring of energy.'

'That's it,' Earthshine said. 'Every particle in the universe follows a world line, a kind of graph threaded through spacetime. And every world line, every particle, *must* end at the multiverse boundary. In that way it's like an event horizon – like the edge of a black hole, but a black hole absorbs. *This* is like a tremendous mirror, or a furnace, if you like, where every last grain of creation will be thermalised – burned up as heat energy. And as the energies of all the terminating particles pile up there, indeed are reflected back, there will be a last infernal carnival of creation, as that energy nucleates into new particles, which will immediately be swept over by the advancing boundary... '

The ColU said now, 'These huge energies have already had an influence on our universe, observable effects. These were distortions I detected in the cosmic background radiation, as if our universe is recoiling from what is to become of it. That was how I was able to calculate the timing of this event, roughly, long before we got here.'

Earthshine said, 'The important point now is that the boundary *is* smeared, just a little. Quantum uncertainty mandates it. The destruction it brings will not be *quite* instantaneous. And that gives us a sliver of an opportunity—'

'No,' Beth said, suddenly understanding. 'The Dreamers. It's given the Dreamers an opportunity, to help us.'

'You understand, Beth Eden Jones,' the ColU said. 'You always did have a good intuition about Hatches.'

Mardina frowned. 'What are you talking about?'

'The Hatch,' Beth said, and she took Mardina's hands. 'Remember? After Ari and Inguill went through, and Earthshine's probe. After we opened it again, *the Hatch had changed.* It's just like the first Hatch I ever saw, with my father, at the substellar. Buried in the jungle. Grooves appeared in its surface. I was the first to understand – they were grooves to hold the bodies of builders. And when the builders climbed into the grooves, it was like putting a key in a lock. You see?'

'Ah,' Titus said. 'And now in the doorway, when *our* Hatch was opened up for Ari and Inguill – recesses for hands. Human hands.'

'I think the Dreamers are telling us something,' Earthshine said. 'On some level they know we're here. I always have the impression that they can't *see* us clearly – they don't understand us, or our nature, or not sufficiently. But they know we're here.'

Beth said eagerly, 'Yes, that's it. They're saying we can go through the Hatch. We humans. Through to—'

'*The past,*' Earthshine said gravely. 'It must be someplace *else* in space, some other world, another history. But it has to be the past, from this point, for there's no future. And there is plenty of past to choose from. Seventeen billion years of it ...'

Chu frowned. 'How could you even know where you were? In space or time.'

'Good question,' Earthshine said. 'If the travellers remain on Per Ardua, perhaps we could prepare maps of the stars, at different epochs. Even of the position and size of Andromeda. But if you translate through space as well as time ... Well, these are details. The journey is the thing.'

Mardina clutched her baby, who stirred and gurgled. 'Then there's hope.'

But Stef said gravely, 'Only three. Remember? That was how he opened this conversation. *Only three.* Only three of us can do this, pass through the Hatch. Is that what you mean, Earthshine?'

And suddenly the group seemed an enormous crowd: Mardina and her baby, sitting between Chu and her mother Beth; Titus with his daughter clutching his one good hand; Stef sitting alone – and the ColU and Earthshine, two artificial people. Seven of them, or nine, depending on your definition. Of whom only three could survive.

'Why?' Mardina found her voice came out as a snarl. 'Why only three?'

Earthshine sighed. 'I suspect it is simply because of the world we sit in. Per Ardua. The records show that the builders, using Hatches—'

'Ah. I remember,' Beth said. 'The builders did everything in threes. Their bodies had triple symmetries – three legs. They moved in groups of three, or threes of threes – nine, or twenty-seven.' She laughed, bitterly. 'These Dreamers of yours can't tell how many we are, Earthshine! They can't tell the difference between us and builders!'

'Which only shows how remote they are from us,' Earthshine said. 'Yet they are trying to be – kind.'

Titus growled, 'And so we have the game before us – the board set out, and we can't change the rules. Three to go through, six to remain. And we must decide which three, right now.'

Mardina saw people pull back, as if more shocked by that pronouncement than by Earthshine's revelations. As for herself, she clutched her baby harder. The sting of hope in her chest was more painful than the despair.

Stef looked small and frail, a blanket over her shoulders. But she said firmly, 'Titus, it's too soon. We have a little time left, time to think.'

'No. In war I have seen similar situations. Some must die

so the others can live. We decide this now, and we stick to the decision. Otherwise we will tear ourselves apart. Perhaps literally; we might destroy each other, fighting for a place. Why, I remember once on campaign—'

'*We* would not do that,' Clodia said.

'We might,' Stef said ruefully. She turned to Mardina. 'You, Mardina, and the baby. If nobody else – you. You two are the future of this peculiar little extended family of ours. Of course you must live.'

Mardina felt tears well. 'But—'

'No.' Titus held up his hand. 'No arguments. Of course she is right; we would not be human if we chose otherwise.'

The ColU said, 'I am not human at all, and I concur. And as for myself and Earthshine, we should be ruled out. We are created beings, created to serve humanity. And how better can we serve humans now than by saving as many of you as we can? But I speak for myself. Earthshine, your origin is more complicated than mine—'

'Oh, I'm staying right here,' Earthshine said. 'I want to see the End Time firework display. Seventeen billion years in the making – I wouldn't miss it for the world.' He seemed to think that over. 'Ha! I made a joke.'

'And I will stay,' Stef said. 'I've done my Hatch-hopping, and I'm too old for babies. Too old even to babysit. And, yes, I admit I'm curious too about the End Time. An entirely novel physical phenomenon. We should work up an observation suite, Earthshine. Do some decent science. Perhaps there will be time to debunk a few theories before the lights go out.'

'I look forward to it, Stef Kalinski.'

Titus said sternly, 'I, of course, will stay. After all, you would probably all be dead before the End Time anyhow if not for my organisation and leadership.'

Stef smiled. 'I won't deny that, Titus Valerius.'

Clodia clutched her father, burying her head against his chest.

'So,' Stef said now. 'That leaves three candidates for one place.'

Again there was a dismal silence as they shared looks. The remaining candidates were Beth, mother of Mardina. Chu Yuen, father of the baby. Clodia, who was younger than Mardina herself.

Clodia spoke first. 'It must be Chu,' she whispered. 'The baby needs her father. And Mardina will need Chu's strength and wisdom. Take Chu, not me.'

Her father embraced her. 'Good girl. *Romanitas* to the end.'

'She's right,' Beth said impulsively to Chu Yuen. 'Of course it must be you. You're the father. You're a good man, Chu. And you're much stronger than I ever could be—'

Mardina broke down completely now. With her baby in her arms she stumbled over to Beth. 'No! Mother, I can't be without you.'

'Yes, you can.' Beth took her by the shoulders, and held her, looking into her daughter's face. 'You can do this. You must – you will. My father, Yuri, used to speak of doors he passed through in his life. He fell asleep on Earth, woke up on Mars, and wound up on Per Ardua, light years from home and a century out of his time. Just another door opening, he would say. You go through it and deal with what you find.'

'When he died,' the ColU said, 'he said the same thing, even at the end. I was with him, in deep space ... Just another door, he said.'

Mardina gasped, 'But what about you? Mother, what about you?'

'I'll be fine. Don't worry about me. I won't be alone.'

'You will not,' the ColU said. 'Just as I attended your father's death, Beth Eden Jones, so I was there at your birth. I will be honoured to have your company now.'

Stef let out a deep breath. 'I admit right now I could use a hug. But I'll wait my turn. So, Earthshine, you got your news out, and the decision is made.'

'And we have a lot of work to do,' Earthshine said gravely.

CHAPTER 74

Time ran down quickly after that.

Stef Kalinski found herself counting down landmarks. Things she'd never see again, or do again. A last shower, in the crude lash-up they'd set up at one end of the dome. A last dinner with the group. The last time she flossed what was left of her teeth...

Suddenly it was the final time there would ever be a *tomorrow*.

They had taken to sleeping in separate little huddles around the dome, Chu with Mardina and the baby, Titus close to his daughter. That last night, by unspoken consent, they pulled their sleeping gear together in a rough circle close to Earthshine's static installation. The last nine, including Earthshine and the ColU, alone on this world – perhaps the last humans in the universe – gathered together in a dome illuminated by low-level lights, and the sunset glow of Andromeda.

Stef surprised herself by sleeping pretty well, for an old buzzard, she told herself. It was almost a comfort to be woken a couple of times by the baby's demands to be fed, and the murmuring of Beth as she helped her daughter. Stef smiled in the dark. Poor Mardina still had her duties to perform, end of the world or not. Who would be a mother?

Actually Stef would, right now.

When she woke, there were only hours left.

In the dome morning, after a subdued breakfast, the first order of the day was to get Chu, Mardina and the baby installed in the Hatch.

Earthshine had created a protective sphere, like the one in

which he'd encased his probe to the End Time: a thick heat-absorbent shell that, he believed, had kept the probe functioning for fractions of a nanosecond, while Ari Guthfrithson and Inguill had been immediately destroyed. Maybe it could help now, in this new transition – and the ColU had agreed that it could do no harm.

The shell, scaled up to take humans, was like a big smooth egg, the cross-section of its shell thick – it had taken a squad of fabricators some time to construct. It looked scary, the threat it embodied was scary, and Mardina and Chu looked suitably anxious as they wriggled their way into the tight interior, with their packs of tools and clothes and food and water and baby stuff – even pressure suits, improvised from the Mars gear Beth had brought with her. With all that stuff crammed in, there was barely room to move. But the young family would just sit out the remaining time in the shell. Earthshine said it was confident the Dreamers would take care of their destiny from that point on; no more need for palm prints in indentations in doors.

Then it was time to seal the shell, and close up the Hatch. Time for Beth to say goodbye to her daughter, the others to lose their friends.

Stef had always had a feeling she was going to have trouble getting through this part of the day without making a fool of herself, and so she said her farewell with a quick hug of Chu and Mardina, a last stroke of the baby's smooth and untroubled forehead. Then she took herself away from the sundered family.

She set off around the dome, on a last round of chores. She checked the lights and heating that excluded the Per Arduan farside cold and dark, preserving the banks of green growing things they cultivated here.

And she found Clodia.

The Roman girl was carrying cans of water, and packets of plant food synthesised by Earthshine, some for the potatoes and beets and other terrestrial imports, some for the Arduan plants. As she worked her way along the rows of young eye-leaves, Stef saw that Clodia was smiling.

Stef joined her. 'This place is pretty neat and tidy.'

'That's my father for you. He's been preparing for the end of the world like it was an inspection by Centurion Quintus Fabius.'

Stef laughed.

'Meanwhile,' Clodia said, 'I don't see why these should go hungry. Even today.'

'No indeed. Look, the eye-leaves are turning to follow you.'

'They always do. Every day. I make sure I don't walk too fast, so they can track me.'

'Considerate. And you always smile at them?'

Clodia shrugged, as if embarrassed. 'Why not? I never saw a builder, only pictures of them. But I see those eyes looking at me, and I don't know what kind of mind lies behind them. I never knew anybody who didn't feel better for being smiled at, did you?'

'I suppose not ...'

Stef was aware of time passing. They had all said resolutely that they didn't want a countdown, but on this last day at least Stef couldn't help have at least a rudimentary sense of the hour. And she knew –

A horn sounded, a signal Earthshine had insisted on.

'Come on. Let's get back to your father.'

Once again the group gathered beside Earthshine's spidery enclosure. A fire had been lit, though it wasn't cold in the dome; its crackling was comforting, and a bowl of water was bubbling to the boil.

Titus was squatting on a bench, with a mug of what looked like beer in his one hand. Stef knew he had been experimenting with home brewing; he said that all legionaries learned such skills on long marches away from home. Stef herself had assiduously avoided any contact with the stuff.

Clodia helped herself to a mug of tea and went to sit by her father, on blankets at his feet, and cuddled up against his legs. Now Stef could see Clodia's eyes were puffy, her cheeks streaked, as if she'd been crying. Stef cursed herself for not noticing before. Crying over what, the coming end for her father, the loss of her own military dreams? If so, at least she seemed calm now. That was the gardening, Stef thought. Nothing calmed you quite so much as cultivating your garden. Even when it didn't have eyes to look back at you.

Beth was sitting alone, wrapped in a blanket – no, not alone, Stef realised; she was close to the winking unit of the ColU, her friend from childhood. Beth had seemed unable to move far from the Hatch since it had been closed over Mardina and Chu and Gwen. Stef found it hard to blame her, and nobody was minded to force her away. But now Beth was clutching a kind of crude doll to her chest: Mister Sticks, a toy from her own childhood, made for her by the ColU when it still had a body and manipulator arms to do it. This copy had been made from dry Arduan stems by Clodia, under the ColU's strict instructions.

Stef poured out two mugs of tea, and carried them over to Beth. 'May I join you?'

'Why not?' Beth's voice was bleak, empty. But she responded reflexively when Stef handed her the tea, moved along her bench a little, and let Stef sit down. Stef pulled a blanket over her own shoulders, and reached under layers of cloth until she found Beth's hand.

'So we are all here,' Earthshine said. 'I take it you still don't want a countdown—'

Titus snapped, 'No, we do not!'

'Very well. But, Stef, you may wish to have your slate to hand.'

'Damn.' She'd forgotten about that. Just as they'd decided, she and the ColU and Earthshine were going to keep monitoring the science of this event, as long as they could. She had to rummage under her blanket in her capacious pockets until she found the slate, dug it out and wiped its surface clean of bits of lint with a corner of her blanket. Here was another survivor, she thought, another relic of a different universe. She wondered where she'd first picked it up. Mars? The moon? Never imagining that it would still be here with her now, in such a place, at such a time.

The screen lit up with displays: simple counts, graphics. She scanned the material quickly, immediately understanding the most basic implication. 'There's a radiation surge. It's already started, then.' She felt dismay at the first physical proof of the end: it was real after all, just as Earthshine had predicted, despite all their efforts to believe otherwise.

'In a sense, yes,' said the ColU. 'Already we're seeing high-energy radiation, heavy nuclei – rather like cosmic rays. A flood of it coming backwards in time. And pretty bad for your health, by the way.'

She had to laugh. 'What, we'd all be dead of radiation poisoning in a year? Remind me not to renew my life insurance.'

'It's going to ramp up from here. Soon we'll be seeing new heavy nuclei, elements nobody ever saw before – or named. Stef Kalinski, you'll be the greatest explorer of exotic physics that ever lived.'

'Yeah ... So how are you feeling, ColU? Do you understand what is about to happen to you?'

'Yes, Stef Kalinski. I am to be turned off at zero.'

'Well, that's close enough.'

'It may be easier for artificial intelligences to understand than humans, organic creatures, in fact. The possibility that consciousness may terminate, suddenly: anybody fitted with an off-switch knows all about that.'

Beth stroked its shell. 'Good luck, ColU. And thank you.'

'Thank you for loving me,' the ColU said, to Stef's surprise.

The dome lights flickered once, twice, and failed.

Even Stef's slate went down. She patted its surface, and set it aside. The end of science.

The ColU said, 'That's probably the radiation. Earthshine and I have hardened power units. We should keep functioning a little longer.'

Now the only glow came from the sky, from the sprawl of

537

Andromeda – a tremendous galaxy doomed to destruction just as was her own feeble frame, Stef thought. Her friends were shapes in the dark around her. And as her eyes adjusted Stef began to see the stars above.

Earthshine whispered, 'The wolves that have always chased day and night through the sky are catching them at last ...'

Under the blanket, Beth's fingers tightened on Stef's.

Stef heard Titus take a long, satisfying draught of his beer. Then he said, 'You know, this reminds me of a time on campaign when

FIVE

CHAPTER 75

Earthshine's protective egg broke open around them, just as it was supposed to, dumping Mardina, Chu and the baby on the floor of the Hatch pit, with all their bits of gear.

But the Hatch lid was open above them. Looking up, Mardina saw a slice of what looked like the roof of a dome – higher, more solid-looking than the one Earthshine had built.

Mardina clutched her baby and stared at Chu. 'Alive,' she whispered.

'Alive. But where?'

'Or rather, when?'

Gwen, half asleep, yawned hugely.

'Come on,' Mardina said softly. 'Let's get out of here.'

They had a lightweight, fold-up ladder fabricated by Earthshine for just this instance. They dug it out of the baggage and the shell shards littering the pit, quickly set it up against the wall, and Chu scrambled up. He didn't look around, Mardina saw; he had eyes only for his family, still in the pit. He reached down. 'Pass her up.'

Mardina took a couple of steps up the ladder, and then, clumsily, lifted up the bundle that was Gwen. They fumbled the handover, making Gwen squirm and grumble, and they laughed.

'Look at us,' said Mardina. 'Two idiots, travelling in time.'

'But we're here.'

'That we are.'

Once Chu had Gwen safely in his arms, Mardina scrambled quickly out of the pit herself, and took back the baby.

Then they stood together and faced a new world.

They stood on a smoothly finished floor, of neatly interlocking tiles. Over their heads soared that dome, and now she could see it fully Mardina could make out its scale; it was indeed much wider, taller than Earthshine's improvised tent. There were smaller buildings, structures under the dome, banks of machinery, some kind of towering monument at the very centre of the dome – there was a smell of industry, of electricity, and all of it brilliantly lit by suspended fluorescent lamps.

In this first moment, clutching the baby, Mardina could take in none of the detail. She looked up at the sky, which was easily visible through the dome.

'No Andromeda,' said Chu. 'A starry sky. And look ...'

There was one very brilliant pair of stars, close to the zenith.

Mardina raised herself on the balls of her feet, rocked up and down. 'How does the gravity seem to you?'

'The same as before. And you?'

'Yes ... I think we're still on Per Ardua. But a younger Per Ardua. Before the double-star system they all spoke of from the olden times broke up and drifted away. Maybe that's it up there, the Hoof of the Centaur. We have our star charts. Maybe with those we could figure out where we are – or rather, when.'

'Or,' Chu said, 'we could just ask.' He pointed to the centre of the dome.

Where a woman stood with her back to them, making some kind of note on a scroll. She stood beneath that central monument – which, Mardina saw now, was a pillar of stone, finely worked, engraved with what looked like Latin letters to Mardina though she didn't recognise the words, and with a kind of lightning-bolt sculpture of steel at the very top.

And an animal came bounding around the corner of the monument, heading straight at them.

A dog? No. It ran on two legs. It was feathered green and crimson, as gaudy as any Inca priest she'd ever seen, like a running bird, perhaps. But its head was huge, and nothing like a dog's, nothing like a bird's, a big blocky head dominated by a huge jaw – a jaw that opened now, and the animal *roared*.

They'd both been frozen with shock. Now Chu reacted. With one hand he pulled Mardina and the baby behind his body, and with the other drew his *pugio* dagger and took a stance. 'Stay back!'

The woman by the monument turned at the noise. '*Halt, Hermann!*'

To Mardina's huge relief the beast slowed immediately, skidding to a stop on the smooth floor. She saw now that its feet were clawed, each talon longer than Chu's *pugio*. For a heartbeat it stared at its prey with evident anguish.

'*Komm! Hermann, komm!*'

The feathered beast hung its head and loped away.

The woman approached the new arrivals, her hand resting on a weapon at her belt. She wore a uniform of jet black, with lightning flashes at the collar and sleeves. She wore no hat, and her grey hair was pulled back tightly from her forehead. She was *old*, Mardina saw immediately, though she walked confidently enough. And she looked hauntingly familiar.

'*Wie heißen Sie?*'

Mardina, clutching Gwen, murmured to Chu, 'Put your dagger away ...'

'*Was machen Sie hier?*'

Mardina stared at the woman. It was Stef Kalinski. Or Penny. Or, Mardina thought wildly, another Kalinski twin. 'You!'

But the woman had eyes only for Chu. Just as Mardina had recognised her, now she, evidently, recognised Chu.

The woman dropped to one knee and hung her head. '*Verzeihung, Eure Exzellenz!*'

Chu just stared back, astonished.

Always another door, Mardina thought. Just as grandfather Yuri had said. 'Let me handle this.' She handed the baby to Chu, spread her hands, and walked forward, towards the kneeling stranger.

543

In the hearts of a hundred billion worlds
  Across a trillion dying realities in a lethal multiverse –
  In the chthonic silence –
  All that could have been done had been done.
  In peace and satisfaction, minds diffuse and antique submitted
to the End Time.

AFTERWORD

Since the publication of *Proxima* the scientific study of the potential habitability of tidally locked planets of red dwarf stars has continued. For example, the first three-dimensional atmospheric model of a world like Per Ardua was published in 2013 (D. Abbot et al, *Astrophysical Journal Letters*, vol. 771, L45).

A recent reference on the Roman Empire and its provinces is *Roman Britain* by Patricia Southern (Amberley, 2011). Roman dates given here are based on the system used from the later republic, when scholars counted the years from the founding of the city of Rome. The founding date used here is that given by Varro, but other scholars differed. 'AUC' is an abbreviation for *ab urbe condita*, 'from the founding of the city'.

A recent if speculative reference on Celtic culture is Graham Robb's *The Ancient Paths* (Picador, 2013). A useful recent reference on the Incas is Kim MacQuarrie's *The Last Days of the Incas* (Simon & Schuster, 2007). Recent evidence on the Incas' use of child sacrifice is given in *Current World Archaeology* no. 61, 2013. Anglicised spellings of Quechua terms vary; I have aimed primarily for clarity.

There was a devastating volcanic eruption in the year 1258, the eruption of the millennium and with global effects (see, for example, *Current Archaeology*, September 2012). Its location has quite recently been identified as Indonesia.

The 'gravity train' was devised in the seventeenth century by British scientist Robert Hooke, who presented the idea in a letter to Isaac Newton. The idea has been seriously presented a few times, such as to the Paris Academy of Sciences in the nineteenth century.

There is a large literature on the feasibility of space colonies. The Inca design depicted here is extrapolated from the work of O'Neill in the 1970s (G. K. O'Neill, *The High Frontier*, William Morrow, 1976). The use of modern materials and techniques to build very large structures has been explored, for example, by T. McKendree ('Implications of Molecular Nanotechnology Technical Performance Parameters on Previously Defined Space System Architectures', *Turning Goals into Reality*, NASA, 2000, http://www.zyvex.com/nanotech/nano4/mckendreePaper. html#RTFToC17).

The far future of the Alpha Centauri system has been described by Martin Beech ('The Far Distant Future of Alpha Centauri', *Journal of the British Interplanetary Society*, vol. 64, pp.387–95, 2011). A recent reference on natural panspermia is 'Dynamics of Escaping Earth Ejecta and their Collision Probability with Different Solar System Bodies' by M. Reyes-Ruiz et al (2011, arXiv:1108.3375v1).

Recent references on the collective behaviour of bacteria are relevant essays in *Chimeras and Consciousness* by Lynn Margolis et al (MIT Press, 2011). New extensive surveys of the 'dark energy biosphere', life deep underground, were reported in June 2014 at a conference at the University of California, Berkeley (*New Scientist*, 21 June 2014).

The 'Doomsday Argument', developed by Brandon Carter and others and referred to by Stef Kalinski in Chapter 67 – one version of which suggests that our future may not be infinite but of the same order of magnitude of our past – is explored in John Leslie's *The End of the World* (Routledge, 1996). The alarming suggestion that our universe may have only a relatively short future because of our existence within a 'multiverse', an ensemble of universes, was set out in 2010 in a paper called 'Eternal Inflation Predicts that Time Will End', by Raphael Bousso of the University of California, Berkeley, and others (arXiv:1009.4698v1). A recent background work on the subject is *Universe or Multiverse?* ed. Bernard Carr (Cambridge University Press, 2007). The physical consequences of the end-time event as depicted here were suggested by Igor Smolyaninov of the University of Maryland and others ('Hyperbolic Meta-material Interfaces: Hawking Radiation from Rindler Horizons and the "end of time"', 2011, arXiv:1107.4053v1). The science of ripples-in-spacetime faster-than-light warps derives from a seminal paper by Miguel Alcubierre (*Classical and Quantum Gravity* vol. 11, L73–L77, 1994). The detection of primordial gravitation waves, by the BICEP2 telescope in Antarctica, was first announced in March 2014 (*New Scientist*, 22 March 2014). For an exploration of how to turn an Einsteinian wormhole into a time machine, see my own novel *Timelike Infinity*, in *Xeelee: An Omnibus* (Gollancz, 2010).

Once again I'm deeply grateful to Prof. Adam Roberts for help with my Latin homework.

Any errors or inaccuracies are of course my sole responsibility.

Stephen Baxter
Northumberland
July 2014